THE CAMPBELLS FROM CAMDEN TOWN

FOR THE TENANTS OF
ARLINGTON HOUSE WITH WHOM
I WORKED FOR ALMOST 7 YEARS

Doug

SEPT. 2009

THE CAMPBELLS FROM CAMDEN TOWN

Doug Dovey

JANUS PUBLISHING COMPANY
London, England

First published in Great Britain 2009
by Janus Publishing Company Ltd,
105-107 Gloucester Place,
London W1U 6BY

www.januspublishing.co.uk

British Library Cataloguing-in-Publication Data
A catalogue record for this book is available from the British Library

ISBN 978-1-85756-730-4

Cover Design: Edwin Page

Printed and bound in Great Britain

This book is dedicated to the memory of Jean, my lovely wife of 46 years and the much loved mother of our four children, Mark, Karen, Michael and Glenn.

Chapter One

'Dagenham!' exclaimed one of the men standing at the bar of the Spread Eagle public house in London's Camden Town. 'Why the bleeding hell do you want to go and live in a poxy hole like Dagenham?'

'We don't have any choice, Alf,' said Dickie Campbell, sipping his beer. 'Freda and the kids have been staying with her mum since our place was bombed out, but now I've been demobbed, there's not enough room for all of us. It'll take years before they can rebuild around here, so it's Dagenham or nothing. Last Sunday, me and Freda took her mum Gertie to have a look at the house the council have offered us.'

Alf signalled to the barman for two more pints of beer. 'So what did Gertie make of it?'

Dickie waited until the barman had refilled their glasses before continuing. 'Gertie reckons it's not natural to have a bog inside the house,' he laughed. 'She said I'd stink the whole place out, bloody cheek. My Freda can't wait though; she said it will be heaven to have a proper bath all on her own, instead of traipsing down to the public baths in Mornington Crescent.' He sighed sadly. 'Born and bred in Camden Town I was and so were the two boys, but that's the way it goes and we're off on Saturday.'

Alf almost dropped his beer. 'Saturday! This Saturday?'

Dickie nodded. 'There's no point in putting it off, Alf, and as I said, Freda's as keen as mustard to get going.'

1

Alf's face fell. 'All the same, I thought you'd be around for at least a few more weeks yet.' Suddenly, Alf had an idea. 'I'll tell you what, how about you and Freda coming round to our place on Friday and we'll give you a bloody good send-off. Bring Gertie and the kids as well, if you like. My old woman thinks the world of those two boys.'

'Yeah, you're on, mate,' Dickie sounded pleased. 'By the way, how is Bella these days?'

Alf screwed his face up. 'Don't fucking ask, Dickie, she's driving me round the bloody twist. Ever since her sister told her that her old man was taking her down to Clacton for a week's holiday it's been "Why can't we have a holiday" and "You never take me anywhere".

'Nothing but moan, moan, fucking moan. I have to come down the pub to give my poor old bleeding ears a rest.'

'I've never known you to need an excuse to get down the pub, Alf,' laughed Dickie.

The two friends stood silently for a while, each reflecting on the friendship that had lasted for over twenty years but now seemed likely to be severely restricted, if not severed completely.

Dickie and Alf had first met in 1924, when they had been 14 years of age. They began work as van boys with the well-known haulage firm Carter Patterson, and then both became drivers as soon as they reached twenty-one and they had remained with the company ever since.

Each had been the best man at the other's wedding and Alf's wife, unable to have children of her own, was godmother to Freda and Dickie's two sons. This had been on Dickie's insistence, for Freda and Bella did not actually get on very well with each other and neither of them would be very pleased to hear of the leaving party being planned by their husbands. Before the war, although Alf and Dickie saw each other at work every day, they usually met up again two or three times a week at the Spread Eagle pub on Parkway, not far from Camden Town tube station. Every Saturday, they went off to watch Arsenal football team play at Highbury, or if their team was playing away from home, Tottenham Hotspur would be their second choice.

As Freda and Bella were not the best of friends, they seldom went out together as a foursome, so on Saturday evenings, Dickie and Freda would usually go to the cinema or for a quiet drink on their own, leaving Gertie to keep an eye on the boys. Sunday had always been a special day for Dickie and if the weather was fine, he would take the boys to Regent's Park to play football or to sail their model boats on the lake, and when the weather was poor Dickie and the boys would spend many pleasant hours in London Zoo. The outings that Freda also enjoyed had been when they had taken the train from Liverpool Street station for a day out at Southend-on-Sea. This was one trip that Gertie had refused to share with them; a long walk along the often windswept pier was not for her, for she preferred to put her feet up and listen to the radio at home. The boys – Joe, who was the elder by four years, and Jimmy – loved the funfair called the Kursaal and Freda, as soon as Jimmy had reached the age of 3 years, always insisted they walked the entire length of the world's longest pier, at a distance of one and a quarter miles. After a pub lunch at the end of the pier, they would take the miniature train back to the seafront to paddle in the sea or to build sandcastles.

That peaceful and pleasant way of life came to an abrupt end in 1939, when war was declared. As Dickie had been under thirty, he was one of the first to be conscripted into the army and he spent most of the war in North Africa, fighting with Field Marshal Mongomery's Eighth Army against the German Army led by General Erwin Rommel. Alf had also been conscripted, but he had been captured at Dunkirk and spent the rest of the war as a prisoner. Alf was no Douglas Bader or Airey Neave and made no attempt to escape from the prisoner-of-war camp where he had been held captive, but he had felt no shame that he had been content to sit out the war in relative comfort.

'Bollocks to being a bloody hero,' he often said. 'Leave all that shit to the officers, that's what us squaddies used to say.'

With the end of the war barely three weeks away, the lorry Dickie had been driving ran over a land mine, the explosion leaving Dickie unconscious for three days, and when he awoke, he found that his vision was impaired. Little could be done for him in Africa and even the surgeons at London's Moorfields Eye Hospital back in England had only been able to partially restore his sight, meaning that Dickie would never be able to drive a lorry again.

After the war, Alf returned to Carter Patterson and resumed his job as a driver, while Dickie was employed as a yardman, making sure the lorries were clean and sparkling before leaving the depot. Dickie was aware that perhaps he should be grateful for having any job at all, but he sorely missed the freedom of the open road, for it had felt almost as though he had been his own boss when he had been behind the wheel of his lorry.

Now, six months after their demobilisation from the army, Dickie and Alf still went for their pints of beer and their Saturday jaunts to the football matches and Dickie still kept his Sundays free for the family outings.

'Got time for another, Dickie?' Alf said, reaching into his pocket.

'Yeah, alright, but it's my shout.' Dickie held the two empty glasses out towards the barman, who quickly refilled them. 'Alf, there's something I haven't told you yet. I've got an interview next week for a job in that big car firm in Dagenham. It's called Ford's, but I suppose you must have heard of it.'

Alf shook his head. 'Jesus Christ, Dickie, you won't last five fucking minutes in a bloody factory, 'cos you'll go stark-staring bonkers cooped up like a battery hen all day. Fuck me; you must need your head examined to even consider it. Can't you find a job out in the open air? Even emptying dustbins must be better than being a fucking robot on a production line.'

'The trouble is, Alf, what with the extra rent to pay and those boys of mine getting bigger and bigger every day, I can't afford to turn down the money. Did you know, with a few hours overtime, some of the blokes there are taking home fifteen quid a week and those on the night shift earn even more.'

Alf was about to take a gulp of his beer, when he stopped himself and put his glass back on the table. 'Night shift,' he said it quietly at first, nodding his head. Then, almost shouting, he repeated, 'Fucking night shift! Only burglars and bleeding bats fucking well go out to work at night. The next thing you're going to tell me is that Freda is going to get a job as well.'

Dickie did not reply. Alf looked as though he was in shock. 'She's going to get a job, ain't she? You're going to let your old woman go off and find herself a fucking job.' Alf shook his head in bewilderment. 'It's not right, Dickie, a woman's place is in the home taking care of the old man and the kids.'

'It's not my idea, Alf. Now that we're getting this new place, Freda wants new carpets, new furniture, the lot. Gertie will keep an eye on Jimmy and Joe will be starting work soon anyway.'

4

Dickie sipped at his beer. 'Things have changed, Alf, and don't forget, during the war, women took on lots of men's jobs. They drove trucks and buses, they worked in the factories and some of them even worked down the coal mines. This is 1946, mate, and they won't be kept chained to the kitchen sink any more.'

'They bloody well would if I had my way,' Alf retorted.

Dickie did not respond, for in many ways, his friend was as stubborn as a mule and rarely listened to anyone else's point of view once he had set his mind to something.

The two men finished their pints and left the pub, Dickie going back to his mother-in-law's small apartment in Bayham Street and Alf to his flat above one of the shops in Parkway. Today was Monday and Dickie had given his notice to Carter Patterson's that afternoon and would be leaving on Friday. His heart felt heavy as he walked slowly home, knowing that his whole way of life would be changing in just a few short days and he admitted to himself that he was quite scared about what lay ahead of him. Would Alf be right about working in a factory? How would the boys fit in with their new surroundings?

Would the two women get on with their new neighbours? And Freda, how would her new job affect their marriage?

Freda had already been interviewed and accepted for a job with a large chemical company in Dagenham called May and Baker, her first paid work for over fifteen years. Freda would no longer be dependent on her husband and Dickie was not sure that he liked that idea very much.

Freda was in the front room, her face flushed as she confronted her eldest son.

'If you have any sense at all, Joe, you'll not say anything to your father when he comes in. He has enough on his plate as it is, without you making things worse.'

Joe glared at his mother, his jaw set in a thin determination. 'I'm serious, Mum, I'm not leaving Camden Town. All my mates are here and Bobby Boyce said he will take me on to run one of his stalls in the market.' Then his voice softened as he almost pleaded, 'Come on, Mum, I've been working the market every Saturday almost as soon as I learned to walk and that's all I've ever wanted to do. One day, I'll have my own stall in Camden Market, but anyone will tell you that this Dagenham place is full of carrot snitchers and turnip heads.'

Freda raised her eyes to the ceiling and clicked her tongue.

'Christ Almighty, anyone would think Camden has the only market in England the way you go on about it and anyway, most of the people moving to the new estate come from the East End.'

Before Joe could protest further, they heard Dickie's key being turned in the front door.

'Hello, you two.' Dickie could feel the tension between his wife and his eldest son as soon as he entered the room, but tried to ignore it. 'Where's Gertie and Jimmy?'

Joe did not answer, but Freda told him that Gertie had taken Jimmy to Kentish Town to visit his uncle Fred. The atmosphere in the room was intense and Joe's body language told Dickie that he could no longer postpone the inevitable. He went into the kitchen and returned with a quart bottle of brown ale and two pint glasses. He poured both to the brim and handed one to his son.

'Sit down, Joe, and let's talk this through.'

It was hard to tell who was more surprised, Joe or his mother, for Dickie had never given his son alcohol before and even though Joe felt very grown up and proud, he was determined he would not change his mind about not moving to Dagenham. He explained his feelings to his father and Dickie listened carefully, until Joe had finished speaking his mind.

'I've listened to what you have to say, Joe, and now I want you to hear me out.' Dickie could sympathise with his son, but like it or not, Joe would be coming with them to their new home. 'Given the chance, do you really think your mum, your granny or me would want to leave Camden Town? You know we wouldn't, but right now, we have no choice. I've had to kip on the sofa in this room for months, while your mum sleeps in one room with your granny and you and Jimmy in the other. It's not natural and it's not right, Joe, and it doesn't mean that we have to live in Dagenham forever, because once the council rebuild some of the houses that the Jerries bombed, we should be able to move back to Camden again.'

Joe stared at the floor, sipping his beer. He was pretending to enjoy it but in fact, he did not much care for it at all. 'Come off it, Dad,' he said scornfully, 'it will take years to clear away the bomb sites, let alone get on with the rebuilding, and where is the money going to come from? Answer me that, if you can.'

'I read in The Daily Mirror that the Yanks are going to help us out, but I make you right on that one, it's not going to happen overnight.'

Dickie paused while he rolled himself a cigarette. Joe was dying for one himself, although he thought it better not to push his luck.

His dad giving him a glass of brown ale was a minor miracle, but he was sure neither of his parents knew he had been smoking for the past six months. Joe, like most teenagers, greatly underestimated the awareness of their parents, because Freda and Dickie remembered well the day their son had smoked his first cigarette by his green pallor, the perspiration running down his face and the desperate dash to the outside toilet, which could only mean one thing. His parents had hoped that the experience would put Joe off cigarettes forever, but the occasional whiff of tobacco and the brown stains on his fingers told them that Joe had overcome the initial unpleasantness and that he was now a confirmed smoker.

Before they could resume their discussion there was a knock at the front door. Freda went to open it and a few seconds later, she ushered in a small, smartly dressed man holding a trilby. The man was perhaps in his early thirties, his hair was plastered down with hair cream, his Salvador Dali moustache was heavily waxed and to Dickie, he looked the epitome of a typical wartime "spiv".

'Bobby,' cried Joe excitedly. 'Dad, Mum, this is Bobby Boyce. Bobby owns half the stalls in the market.'

'Yeah, I know who he is and I have a feeling I know why he's here as well.' Dickie also had a feeling that he was not going to like the reason for the visit.

Bobby Boyce moved forwards, with his hand outstretched, which Dickie reluctantly shook. Bobby Boyce then shook Freda's hand.

'Mrs Campbell, Mr Campbell, please forgive my intrusion, but it's just that Joe has explained the situation and I think I may have just the solution that will benefit all of us. Everything Joe has told me about the pair of you tells me that you are loving and caring parents that would never wish to see their son unhappy.' Boyce smiled patronisingly. 'Coming to the point, I believe Joe has a real future as a true costermonger and believe me, there are not many of them around these days. He could earn a small fortune in a few years time, when he can save enough to buy a stall of his own, but until he does, I have my own selfish reasons for wanting him to stay in Camden.'

Without waiting to be asked, Boyce sat down in one of the armchairs. 'I have a sister who owns her own house in Mornington Crescent and she is looking for a lodger. Her husband was killed during the Normandy landings, leaving her with a kid to bring up on her own, so she could do with an extra few bob coming in to help with the bills. I do my bit, you understand, but she's a stubborn little cow and says she can stand on her own two feet.'

'So what's in it for you then?' Freda asked bluntly.

'I won't beat about the bush, Mrs Campbell. I want Joe to run one of my stalls until he gets one of his own, but I also want my sister to have a lodger, who I can be sure won't try to take any liberties. Joe would be perfect for her.' Bobby Boyce stood and beamed at them, as though expecting a round of applause. 'So, what do you think, Mr Campbell?'

Ignoring the pleading look on Joe's face, Dickie also rose to his feet and confronted Boyce. 'I'll tell you what I think,' he said, staring coldly into the other man's eyes. 'I think bugger the lot of you, for a start. You know where I work and you know where I go for a pint, so you could have had a quiet word with me about this anywhere and at any time, but instead, you come to my house and poke your nose in where it's not wanted.'

Dickie was trembling with anger, but Freda eased him gently back into his chair. 'Sit down, Dickie, love, I think we need a bit of time to think this through carefully.'

Dickie sank back into his chair, too stunned to make any further comment as he watched Freda show Bobby Boyce to the door. He said nothing for several minutes after Freda had returned, although she was expecting an onslaught at any moment and she did not have long to wait. Joe sat on the sofa, hardly daring to breathe.

'I can't believe you two have been taken in by that slimy git.'

Dickie's voice was close to being a shout. 'He's the biggest bloody crook in north London. Look what he got up to during the war. By all accounts, he made a fortune from the black market and other dodgy dealings and it didn't stop there, either. I hear all sorts of things down at my depot. For instance, that van load of frocks that was hijacked a couple of weeks ago was down to him and what's the betting he's flogging them on some of his stalls right now. I don't want our Joe getting mixed up with the likes of that crook when we're not around to keep an eye on him.'

Joe said nothing but sat quietly as he waited for his mother to reply.

'Bobby Boyce wasn't the only one to line his pockets during the war,' she reminded Dickie. 'As a matter of fact, you were glad enough to buy your tobacco from him before you went away and I was more than happy to get a tin of salmon from one of his stalls every now and then. I don't know anything about frocks, but he's not been nicked by the law, has he? And another thing, Dickie, our Joe has never given us a moment's worry, not even bunking off school. He's got more sense than to get mixed up in anything like that.'

'Too right I wouldn't,' said Joe sincerely. 'I promise both of you on my life that I will never do anything to make you ashamed of me, but you've got to at least give me this chance. Look, how would it be if I came down to Dagenham every Saturday after work and stayed till Sunday evening, or I could even get the first train back on Monday morning.'

Dickie was not convinced. 'You say that now, but how long would it be before you pack away your stall one Saturday and say to yourself, "sod it, I can't be bothered this week". That would leave me and your mum worrying our guts out all week, unless, of course, I came back here to check on you for myself.'

The discussion came to an end as they heard Gertie and Jimmy coming through the front door. Jimmy, although only 10 years old, took in the atmosphere as soon as he walked into the front room and it worried him considerably. He could sense the tension between his father, whom he adored, and his brother, who was his hero. These two men – for in his eyes, Joe was, indeed, a real man – meant everything to Jimmy and it was unthinkable that they should be glaring at each other in this way. Jimmy was only 4 years old when his dad had gone off to war and it was Joe who became the man of the house, often taking him to Regent's Park, but never bullying him the way some of his friends' older brothers did. It was Joe who cuddled him when he was frightened by the noise of the bombs during the air raids, even though they were deep below the surface of the underground platforms of Camden Town tube station. It was Joe who had comforted not only his little brother, but also their mother, when they emerged from the shelter one morning after a heavy raid to find their block of flats completely demolished; twenty-five families had been made homeless in just that one block alone.

Jimmy could not remember his father leaving to go to war, although he could vaguely recall the kind man who used to take him to the park, or the zoo, and who would give him his weekly bath. Jimmy had been a little nervous when he had been told that his dad was coming home, but it was as though his father had never been away. His dad never shouted at him or hit him with a belt, like some other dads did. Indeed, only a couple of weeks ago, Jimmy's friend Johnny Briggs had pulled his trousers down to show Jimmy his crimson backside, inflicted upon him by the leather belt of Mr Briggs.

His granny took him by the hand. 'Come into the kitchen, Jimmy,' she said. 'I'll make you a nice cup of Ovaltine before I tuck you up in bed.'

They left the front room and as Gertie put a saucepan of milk on the stove, she, too, was worrying about the tension in the house, although was not at all surprised by it. She knew Joe would resist all attempts to persuade him to leave Camden Town and in her heart of hearts, she did not blame him one little bit. Like her son-in-law, Gertie had been born and bred in north London, although she had lived in Kings Cross until she married her husband Bert, moving into the flat in Bayham Street, where she had lived ever since. Her daughter Freda had been born in this flat and, in fact, she had been born in the very same bed they now shared. Gertie often wondered why it was that her daughter did not hold the same love of north London that she, Dickie and Joe shared, although Jimmy was perhaps too young to be very much bothered about where he lived, so long as he had a roof over his head and a full stomach. Gertie did not really have to move at all, she could remain in Camden Town by herself, but she could not bear the thought of not being able to see her lovely Freda and the boys every day of the week. Her relationship with Dickie was that of a son rather than a son-in-law, for the old mother-in-law jokes did not apply to them. Dickie and Gertie genuinely liked and respected each other and they rarely disagreed on anything, but Gertie could not help but wonder if this current situation may cause a rift between them.

After Jimmy had finished his bedtime drink and said goodnight to Joe and his parents, Gertie tucked him into his bed and read him a bedtime story. After five minutes, Jimmy pretended to be asleep, for he felt far too old to listen to fairy tales, but he loved his granny dearly and would not hurt her feelings for the world. He was snoring gently as Gertie tiptoed from the bedroom and gently closed the door behind her. Jimmy then crept out of his bed a few minutes later, turned the light back on again and took his copy of *The Dandy* from under his bed.

Chapter Two

G ertie came down the stairs slowly, knowing that she would be asked to take sides in this family dispute and she was dreading the outcome if she was forced to choose. She opened the door to the front room to see Joe standing with his back to the fire, his hands clasped resolutely behind his back, rocking to and fro, while Dickie, hunched in his armchair, suddenly looked frail and vulnerable, almost as if he believed his position as head of the household was under threat.

Gertie looked towards Freda, whose face was ashen.

'I'll go and put the kettle on,' said Gertie, 'you look as though you could all do with a nice cup of tea.' Gertie secretly thought it would take more than a cup of tea to solve the problems in this house, but she made the pot nonetheless. After handing round the tea, Gertie said, 'I saw Bobby Boyce standing outside talking to one of his cronies, has he been in here yet?' Freda nodded. 'So what did that bugger want?' demanded Gertie.

Freda repeated almost word for word the conversation of a short time ago.

Gertie nodded. 'I thought it might be something like that and I think I can hazard a guess as to your reaction, Dickie.'

Dickie looked up at his mother-in-law. 'You said it all, Ma, when you asked what the bugger wanted, 'cos he doesn't do anything for nothing, does he?'

Joe was on tenterhooks as he waited to hear what his grandmother would say next. He felt as though his whole future could depend on this woman, for he knew his father greatly valued her opinion and if his granny was on his side, the battle would be as good as won. But his hopes were dashed when she stated, 'I wouldn't trust Bobby Boyce while he's got a hole in his arse.' She paused for a few seconds and then added, 'But maybe we don't have to.'

Joe looked expectantly at his grandmother. She had something up her sleeve, he was sure of it.

Freda licked her lips that had suddenly become very dry. 'What are you on about, Mum?'

'It's quite simple when you think about it. Joe doesn't go and I don't go, either; I stay here and Joe can stay here with me. He can work the market and we can both come down to Dagenham at the weekends, or you can come back here now and again to see your old mates. It's the best of both worlds, if you ask me.' Gertie could see the shocked look on their faces. She turned to Dickie. 'I wouldn't have the family split up for anything, Dickie, but if it means Joe staying here with me rather than some stranger, what would you prefer?

'Even if you tie him up and drag him to bleeding Dagenham, he'll be back here the first chance he gets and then he'll go into hiding. I know it, you know it and Freda knows it. Joe doesn't want to live in Dagenham and I might as well be honest, I bloody well don't, either.'

Joe held his breath, waiting for his father's reaction to his grandmother's suggestion. Freda also waited for her husband to speak, a great sadness descending upon her at the thought of her family being separated.

Dickie cleared his throat. 'It isn't that simple at all, Gertie,' he said. 'Firstly, we've already given notice on this place and a two-bedroom flat is like gold dust around here. I reckon there would have been a stampede down at the letting office when word got out that this was available and I know for a fact that two Carter Patterson blokes were after it, but they were too late. The other thing that you might have forgotten about is that we've been given a three-bedroom house, with a front and back garden, because with you coming with us, Gertie, we need the three rooms. Without you and Joe, they'll never allow us to stay there and we'll probably end up in one of those bloody great tower blocks they're starting to build.' Dickie poured himself another glass of beer, but this time did not offer to refill Joe's glass. He looked at Freda, who seemed as though she was about to say something. 'It's no good saying nobody needs to know, because you can bet your life that the first time the rent man comes round, some bugger will grass us up.'

Both Freda and Gertie knew Dickie was right and Gertie felt dreadful that she had raised Joe's hopes only to have them dashed.

'I'm sorry, Joe,' she whispered. 'I meant it for the best, but your dad's right, it won't work.'

Joe did not answer, but his eyes looked suddenly very bright and he was afraid that he was very close to embarrassing himself. He grabbed his jacket, rushed from the room and out of the house.

Freda had not spoken, although her head was whirling with mixed emotions. She had been horrified at the possibility of living so far away from her mother, but she was also extremely worried about leaving Joe to fend for himself in Camden Town.

Gertie broke the silence that had lasted for several minutes after Joe had left. 'I've made things worse, Dickie, and I'm sorry for that,' she said. 'You do know what I mean about not wanting to leave Camden, don't you? I mean, none of us want to go, but as you told Joe, we haven't got a lot of choice.'

'No, it's alright, Gertie, you ain't made things worse,' Dickie replied. 'We're just back to square one, that's all. Freda, you haven't said a word since Gertie and Jimmy came in. What are your thoughts now?'

Freda looked first at Gertie and then at her husband. 'I'll tell you what I'm thinking,' she told them both, 'I'm thinking that one way or the other, Joe is not going to come with us to live in Dagenham. I think that what Mum said about not being able to keep Joe tied down is right and God knows what could happen if he doesn't have a proper roof over his head. I think we should find out a bit more about Bobby Boyce's sister and ask if we could meet her. Just because Bobby Boyce is a toerag, doesn't mean his sister will be as well, does it?'

Gertie looked at Dickie, believing that Freda was right, although she had no intention of voicing her opinion before Dickie had given his. Gertie felt she had already spoken out of turn and was determined not to make the same mistake again. Dickie felt the sudden urge to have a drink, and not just a beer. He walked over to the sideboard, took out a bottle and poured himself a very large whisky. With his back towards the two women, he swallowed almost half in one gulp. He then refilled the glass and without turning round, said, 'I'll go and see Bobby Boyce tomorrow.'

He then turned round, raised his glass and said, 'I'm taking this up to bed with me, 'cos I think I'm going to need a bit of help getting off to sleep tonight. Joe can sleep on the sofa or on the floor tonight when he comes in. Help yourselves if you fancy a drop.'

After Dickie had gone to bed, Freda also got up, walked over to the sideboard and poured two measures of whisky into a couple of glasses, adding equal measures of ginger ale.

'What's sauce for the goose is sauce for the gander,' she said as she handed one of the glasses to her mother.

'And if ever I needed a drop of sauce, it's right now,' said Gertie, taking the glass from her daughter.

The two women sat together for the next few hours, sipping at their whisky, all the while looking anxiously at the clock. Midnight came and went and still Joe had not returned.

'Do you reckon he's trying to give us all a hard time by staying out this late?' said Freda.

'Well, if he is, he's bloody well succeeding. I've a good mind to give him a clip round the ear'ole when he gets in.'

At last, they heard the key being put into the lock, or perhaps, more accurately, the sound of fumbling around by somebody trying to locate the keyhole.

Then they heard a voice neither of them recognised. 'Come on, we've got him home, let's scarper,' followed by the sound of running feet as Joe's companions made off.

Freda and Gertie opened the front door to find Joe holding on to the door frame, hardly able to stand and with an idiotic expression fixed on his face. When Joe opened his mouth to speak, his tongue refused to obey him and the sounds that did emerge could have been made by a man from Mars for all the sense they made.

'Bloody Nora, he's as pissed as a newt,' cried Gertie. 'For Gawd's sake, let's get him inside.'

Together, they managed to heave Joe onto the sofa, covered him with a blanket and then left him to sleep it off. Gertie and Freda then went into the kitchen to make a pot of tea, before they went to bed.

'He's going to have some head on him come morning,' said Freda. 'What's bothering me though, is where he got the booze from, because no pub around here would serve him. I reckon he must have gone up to the West End, where they'd serve King Kong as long as he had the money.'

Gertie pursed her lips thoughtfully. 'Unless he went round to Bobby Boyce's place.'

'Shit, I didn't think of that. One thing's for sure though, we're not going to find out tonight.' Freda put her empty cup in the sink.

'Come on, Mum, let's get some kip.'

Dickie, who had to be at work at six thirty, was the first up the following morning. He went straight from the bathroom and into the kitchen, where he made himself a mug of strong tea and prepared a flask and a huge cheese sandwich for his midday break. He had no need to go into the front room, although he popped his head round the door before he left, just to make sure Joe had got home safely.

Gertie was the next to rise. She made a mug of black coffee and took it in to Joe. Joe sat up when she gently shook his shoulder, but he quickly lay down again, clutching his head in agony as a violent spasm of pain threatened to squeeze his head like a vice. He had never felt as bad as this before and prayed he never would again.

'Never again, I swear it, never again,' he promised himself out loud.

Joe little knew how many countless others before him had made the same pledge and how many countless others would swear the same oath in years to come. Gradually, he managed to focus his eyes on Gertie, although it seemed as though she was speaking to him from a great distance, when he heard her say, 'I'm not going to have a go at you, Joe, I think you're suffering enough right now, but you could have picked a better time to go on a bender. Thank Christ your dad had gone to bed before you staggered in, so he hasn't a clue about the state you were in, but you still have your mum to face.

'She'll not be as tolerant as me, you can bet your life on that.'

Gertie looked down at her grandson, struggling to control the lump in her throat that was threatening to choke her. 'Where did you get the booze from, Joe, was it Bobby Boyce?'

'I might have known someone would try and blame him,' Joe protested. 'I haven't seen him since he left here last night. The truth is, I went round to see my mate Jerry Procter and he took me to his cousin's house in Muswell Hill. This cousin of Jerry's is about seventeen and his parents trusted him to stay at home, while they went on holiday, but when we got there it was open house, with at least two dozen other kids raiding the biggest bar I've ever seen outside of the Spread Eagle. One thing led to another and I haven't a clue how I got home.

'Bobby Boyce had nothing to do with it though, so don't push the blame onto him, Gran.' The effort of explaining himself to his grandmother was almost too much for Joe. 'Do we have any aspirin, Gran, my head feels as though it's about to explode?'

It was Freda who answered, having just walked into the front room. 'Aspirin's no good for a hangover. What you need to do is to drink a pint of water, put your head under the cold tap and go for a brisk walk. That's the best cure for a hangover.'

'What's the second best thing then?' Joe was not at all keen on his mother's recommendation.

'You're in no position to get sarky with me, my lad,' replied Freda angrily. 'You should be bloody well ashamed of yourself, coming home in that state. And you really think we can trust you to look after yourself on your own? In fact, you proved last night just how much you can't be trusted.'

Joe was mortified. 'I know I've been a right prat, Mum, but I was gutted last night when Dad had a go at Bobby. I was in the wrong and I'm sorry, but I swear it will never happen again, 'cos I can't say I even like the stuff much anyway and I certainly don't like the end result.'

Freda relented and told Joe that his father was going to talk to Bobby Boyce sometime later that day, but she warned him, 'Don't think it's all cut and dried, Joe, me and your dad have to make sure you're going to be alright before we agree to anything. Anyway, as far as I know, you've not even met the woman yourself yet and you might hate each other on sight, for all you know.'

Joe shrugged, but at least he felt a little better, for he now had a little hope to cling to. He took his mother's advice, or some of it, anyway, and drank a pint of cold water and then went for a long walk along Regent's Canal, but he baulked at putting his head under the cold tap.

After Joe had left, Gertie and Freda began the laborious task of packing some of their belongings into the tea chests Alf Spinks had delivered in preparation for the move to Dagenham on Saturday.

Dickie was called into the manager's office that morning and was told that in appreciation of his long and loyal service to Carter Patterson, there would be an extra four weeks' wages in his pay packet on Friday. Not only that, but there would also be a Carter Patterson van at his disposal, free of charge, for the whole of Saturday, as Alf Spinks had volunteered his services without claiming any overtime. It was a great boost for Dickie, for although he had enough money to get by for a couple of weeks and Gertie had said she would help out until they got settled, this unexpected windfall was nonetheless very welcome. As for the use of the van, Dickie had planned to use the open-backed lorry owned by Ben Jacobs, even though Ben used it for just about anything, including carting away the odd horse that had dropped dead in the street, so Dickie knew that Freda would be highly delighted that they would now arrive at their new home in style. I bet Dagenham don't see Carter Patterson vans very often, Dickie chuckled to himself.

During his lunch break, Dickie went to the Spread Eagle, knowing Bobby Boyce often popped in for an afternoon pint, but not today.

Dickie decided not to leave a message, but resolved to call in again after work.

Just after five o'clock that evening, Alf Spinks drove his lorry into the yard, where Dickie greeted him and then thanked him for giving up his Saturday to help them move.

'Think nothing of it, Dickie, you can buy me a pint though. My fucking throat's as dry as a witch's tit.'

On the way to the Spread Eagle, Dickie explained to Alf about last night's events and his desire to meet Bobby Boyce that evening, so that they could arrange to meet his sister.

'My younger brother George went out with Mary Boyce for a while,' Alf told Dickie. 'Bobby knew about it, but he insisted that George never brought her to any of the pubs around here, especially the Spread Eagle, so he used to take her across the river to Southwark or Brixton. I don't know her married name, but I can tell you this, Dickie, she's a real diamond. Alright, so she gave George the elbow, but that just goes to show she's got her head screwed on the right way, don't it? She never took him for a ride and she was straight with him all the way. Your Joe won't go far wrong with Mary, take it from me.'

Dicky was feeling considerably better as he walked into the pub ten minutes later. The promised bonus, the use of the van plus Alf's glowing tribute to Bobby Boyce's sister had put him in a much more positive frame of mind, although he was still not totally convinced about the wisdom of leaving Joe behind in Camden Town.

Bobby Boyce was not in the bar, so Dickie ordered a pint for himself and Alf, who had promised to make himself scarce the moment Bobby appeared. They did not have to wait very long, for a few minutes later, Boyce walked in with a strikingly good-looking woman at his side and Alf duly moved away as Boyce and the woman came over to their table.

'Dickie, I thought I might find you here. I would like you to meet my sister Mary. Mary, this is Dickie Campbell, the father of the lad I was telling you about.'

Boyce and his sister sat down without going to the bar to order a drink first. Bobby Boyce had no need to take his turn in the queue, because, assured of a generous tip, the barman hurried over to take his order.

'A large scotch with ice, a large port and lemon and a pint of brown ale.' Boyce handed the man a one-pound note. 'Keep the change,' he said, loudly enough for almost the whole of the bar to hear.

It would be all the same if I fancied a large scotch myself, Dickie thought to himself resentfully, but he accepted the pint all the same.

It was Mary who spoke first after the drinks had been served.

'I would like you to know straight away that this is not my idea, Mr Campbell.' Her accent was not from London, but Dickie was unable to pinpoint it. He tried to remember if anyone had ever mentioned where Boyce had originated from, but it eluded him.

'When I told Bobby that I was thinking of taking in a lodger, a 15-year-old was certainly not what I had in mind. I already have a 10-year-old son and I am not looking to be a childminder.' Her tone was friendly but firm.

Bobby Boyce interrupted. 'I keep telling you, Mary, Joe Campbell is no child. He may only be fifteen, but you'd never believe it if you could see the way he works the market. Is that not right, Dickie?'

'I make you right on that one, except that Joe is still only fourteen and me and the wife are not very keen on the idea of leaving him on his own in Camden, no matter who he is staying with.'

'And I would feel exactly the same way myself, if he was my son,' said Mary. 'Mr Campbell, why don't you come to my house later with your wife and Joe? He could meet my son David and we'll see how we get along with each other from there. If any of us, including David, of course, feels unhappy about it in any way, we can simply forget about the idea, with no hard feelings on either side.'

Dickie was beginning to warm towards this woman, tinged, perhaps, with just a hint of sexual attraction. Dirty old sod, he laughed inwardly as he and Mary arranged to meet together with Freda and Joe later, while Bobby Boyce wrote down the address.

'There will be no need for you to be there, Bobby,' Mary told her brother. 'As a matter of fact, I think it would be better if you kept out of the way altogether.'

Boyce shrugged his shoulders. 'If that's the way you want it, it's fine by me. I'll pop over about ten o'clock.'

Bobby Boyce left the pub with his sister, leaving half of his large whisky on the table. Alf returned to the table and pointed to Boyce's glass. 'You're not going to leave that there, are you?'

'I don't want it, but help yourself, if you fancy it.'

'Waste not, want not,' said Alf as he drained the glass.

The family were waiting expectantly as Dickie walked through the door, although young Jimmy was more interested in hearing the latest adventure of Special Agent Dick Barton on the wireless. Dickie told them about the conversation with Boyce and his sister and concluded, 'So you, me and Joe are going round to meet Mary and her lad this evening. She lives in Crowndale Road, about a twenty-minute walk away, or we could take the tram.'

Freda indicated to Dickie to come into the kitchen, a sure sign that she wanted to speak to her husband alone. 'Dickie,' she said, after closing the door, 'I can feel something's changed. Are you coming round to the idea of Joe staying in Camden now?'

'I'm not sure, love. Let's wait and see how things go tonight, but, in the end, it may even be her that puts the kibosh on the plan and not us.'

After they had finished their tea, Freda, Dickie and Joe strolled along Camden High Street towards Crowndale Road, where Mary lived. They could have taken the tram or even the tube to Mornington Crescent, but it was a fine evening and they decided to walk.

'Do you know what Bobby Boyce's sister's married name is, Joe?' asked Dickie.

'Er, yeah, it's Davis. Her husband's name was Dickie as well. He was a boxer before the war.'

'Blimey! I remember him,' exclaimed Dickie. 'Me and Alf went to see one of his fights at the Blackfriars Ring, it must have been 1937 or 38. He was up against a Scots geezer and he knocked ten bales of you know what out of him. Who knows, he could have been the business if it wasn't for the war.'

They arrived at Mary's house and she opened the door at Dickie's first knock, almost as though she had been waiting behind the door, and she greeted them warmly, before inviting them in. Dickie introduced Freda and Joe and they all shook hands.

'Come into the front room; I've got the kettle on or I have some beer if you would prefer it?' She addressed the last remark to Dickie, unsure whether or not to include his son.

'No, lass, tea will be fine, thanks,' answered Dickie, at which Mary left the room to make tea.

Freda looked around the room and was quite impressed. It was smart, without being ostentatious, a balance not always easy to achieve. The large carpet almost covered the whole of the floor and, although a little faded, the high quality was still evident. None of the furniture was of the latest design, but Freda's practised eye told her that everything in this room had been looked after with loving care.

Dickie inspected two framed photographs of a young man whom he recognised immediately. One was of Dickie Davis the boxer, posing in his boxing shorts and gloves, and the other was of Dickie Davis the proud soldier, wearing the uniform of the same regiment that Dickie Campbell himself had served with – The Royal Fusiliers!

Mary returned carrying a tray of tea and biscuits and after handing them around, she said quietly, 'David is in his room playing with his toys, but before I bring him down to meet you, I have to warn you that he is a Down's syndrome child.' Dickie and Freda looked blankly at each other, not understanding in the slightest, but Joe nodded, for he was aware of the term. 'Down's syndrome is the correct name for what most people refer to as mongolism,' Mary explained. 'Many would call David a mongol, but he is a Down's syndrome child.' She turned to Joe. 'You knew what Down's syndrome meant, Joe. Did someone tell you about David?'

Joe shook his head. 'No, I never even knew you had a son until my dad told me a couple of hours ago. I read about Down's syndrome in the Reader's Digest, while I was waiting to have my hair cut a couple of weeks ago.'

'Good for you, Joe, at least you read the article. Most people would just turn over and read something else.' She looked at Freda and Dickie. 'David is a lovely boy, who thinks that everybody he meets will be his friend. He can become very upset when other children poke fun at him when we go out together, or when some ill-mannered adults stare at him. David would never do anything to upset anyone and he finds it difficult to understand why people can be so cruel to him.'

Mary left the room to fetch David, leaving Freda and Dickie feeling a little ashamed at their ignorance, although they had no need to be, for the term "Down's syndrome" was not yet familiar to most of the population. Just as "mongol" had been seen to be a vast improvement on the terms "cretin" or "imbecile", it was hoped that "Down's syndrome", named after Doctor Down, would lessen the stigma associated with the condition.

Mary returned with David, who wore a beaming smile that seemed to light up the whole of his face and after introducing him to the Campbell family, Mary suggested to her son that he might like to show Joe around the rest of the house and the spacious back garden.

David eagerly took Joe by the hand and almost dragged him from the room.

'Did you notice how Joe accepted David straight away?' said Mary.

'Not many people can do that, most people need a little time to get used to Down's syndrome children.' She poured the tea. 'Up until just a few minutes ago, I was not at all sure about taking in such a young lodger, but after seeing the way the two boys reacted to one another, I think it could work out very well. What do you think?'

Mary addressed both of them, but felt sure that it would be Joe's mother who would make the final decision. Mary felt that she would now feel more than a little disappointed if the answer was negative, for Joe had won her over completely by the way he had greeted David, without a trace of awkwardness. Freda and Dickie had done their best to greet David naturally, but they had not quite succeeded and even Freda had been touched at the way Joe had been able to ignore David's strange appearance to embrace the person underneath.

Freda believed that this could work out well, although she knew that her husband still had reservations about the connection with Bobby Boyce.

'I think Joe could be very happy here,' Freda told Mary, 'but I have to tell you, we keep hoping he'll change his mind and want to come with us. His little brother Jimmy will be lost without him.'

'It's not just that,' interrupted Dickie. 'I have to be honest with you, Mary, it's your brother that bothers me and I know you shouldn't believe half of what you hear, but some of the stories that go round about Bobby make my hair stand on end. I'm worried that without me and his mum to keep an eye on him, Joe could get way out of his depth.'

Mary nodded in agreement.

'I understand completely, Dickie, but let me tell you a few things about Bobby. Everyone knows he's a wide boy or a spiv, as some people call him, but he does nothing from this house; he thinks too much of me and David to bring any trouble round here.' She took a packet of Senior Service from her apron pocket and offered one to Freda and Dickie. Freda did not smoke, but Dickie eagerly took one, for it was not often that he enjoyed the luxury of a tailor-made cigarette. Mary continued after they had lit up. 'This house is where me and Bobby were brought up and he stayed here until the day I got married. Both of our parents died young and Bobby more or less took over their role. I met Dickie Davis at a wedding, when I was just fourteen, but I told him I was seventeen. I fell head over heels in love with him and one thing led to another, as they do, and I found myself pregnant at fifteen. Bobby was all for killing Dickie and I really believe he would have done, except for the fact that I had lied to Dickie about my age.' Mary took a long draw of her cigarette. 'I know this is all very personal, but I think you have a right to know if you are to leave your son with me and David. Anyway, as I was saying, Bobby was with me all the way when Dickie swore we would be married on my sixteenth birthday and married we were, even though David had been born by then and we knew he was what everybody referred to as a mongol.' Mary took another cigarette from the pack and offered one to Dickie who shook his head.

'Mongol!' Mary almost spat the word out. 'How I hate that word, but it's one me and David have to live with every day. When David was born, I thought my Dickie would lose his mind, because he has a Down's syndrome niece, but he merely assumed it must run in the family. It was then that he took up boxing and I've always believed it was because he wanted to hit out at something or somebody for the condition his son had been born with. I also believe it was the same reason he enlisted as soon as the war started. As a married man with a retarded child, he did not need to go straight away, but he couldn't wait to have a go at those Germans. It was Bobby who paid the mortgage after Dickie was killed and then, as soon as I turned twenty-one, he paid off the mortgage and signed the house over to me and David.

Bobby comes to see us every week and he never comes empty-handed, either, but none of his business is conducted from this house. You would have no need to worry about Joe while he is under my roof.'

Freda knew that this young woman was sincere and would look after Joe as though he was her own son. The thought brought a stab of pain to Freda's heart. But he's my son, not hers, she told herself.

Dickie was not so easily convinced. This was the first time he and Freda had ever been inside a home that was not owned by the council or a housing association, for people like themselves didn't own property – they rented from those who did. Dickie was forced to admit that a part of him was worried that if Joe lived in this house for very long, he would learn to speak the way Mary did and look down his nose at his working-class family. For the second time that evening, Dickie felt ashamed of himself, because he knew Joe was not that sort of person and then, almost triumphantly, Dickie remembered the Senior Service cigarettes. Clearly printed on the packet were the words "Not for Resale", and only cigarettes sold cheaply in the forces NAFI were marked in this way. Bobby Boyce must have supplied his sister with them. Oh, fuck it, Dickie said to himself. I'm only jealous, 'cos I can't get any.

David ran into the room, closely followed by a breathless Joe. 'I've shown Joe all round the garden and taken him up to see his room,' David said excitedly. Then he stopped, suddenly remembering that his mother had told him that this first meeting was only to decide whether or not Joe would be coming to stay with them. David crossed his fingers behind his back, for he longed to have Joe as his big brother.

Dickie looked at Freda, who smiled and nodded her head. He then turned to David and said, 'How about showing Joe's mum and me where Joe will be kipping down then, David.'

Chapter Three

It was moving day. The last few days had simply flown by, with Freda and Gertie taking charge of the final packing, leaving Dickie to work out his notice with Carter Patterson. On their final evening in Camden Town, Freda, Gertie and Dickie had met up with Alf and Bella in the Spread Eagle for a farewell drink with a few old friends and workmates. Joe had volunteered to stay at home with Jimmy, who was feeling quite dispirited, for not only was he facing a huge upheaval in his young life, but he would have to face it without the support of his elder brother and he knew he would miss Joe terribly.

Alf's wife Bella had vetoed Alf's proposal that they should play host for the Campbells' leaving party. 'I'm not having that lot round here,' she had told her husband firmly. 'It wouldn't just be Dickie and his lot. Before we knew it, half the bloody street would be in as well, spilling beer all over my best carpet and stubbing their fags out on the sideboard. Sod that; let them do it down the pub.'

In fact, Bella was quite pleased that the Campbells were going, because she had never really liked Freda and she felt that Alf spent far too much time in the pub with Dickie, not to mention every Saturday afternoon at the football matches. Well, not any more, she had told herself smugly as she watched her husband doing his best to make the Campbells' final evening in Camden a merry affair, although none of the others had appeared to be feeling very cheerful from what she could see.

Freda, Gertie and Dickie were preparing to leave a lifetime behind them in north London and they were also leaving one member of their family behind and even though Joe had promised to come to Dagenham every weekend, it was not the same.

Joe borrowed a handcart and with help from one of his friends, he moved his belongings into Mary's house early on the morning of the departure. Then, just as he was about to leave to see his family off, he noticed David looking wistfully at him. 'Do you want to come with me to see them off, David?' Joe asked him.

David's eyes lit up and he rushed to put his jacket on.

'Thanks, Joe,' said Mary. 'I can't remember the last time he went out with anyone else but me, even Bobby never takes him out, unless I come, too.'

Mary had no worries about David being with Joe, for she knew her son would be perfectly safe with the young man.

It was a fine day, so Dickie and some of the neighbours had cleared the house, putting the furniture and the tea chests out onto the pavement to save time for when Alf arrived. It was thirsty work, but Dickie had anticipated this and there was a good supply of brown ale for the men, stout for the women and lemonade to make shandy for those who preferred something lighter, with cups of tea for those that wanted, supplied by the woman in the flat below.

'Here he comes,' shouted one of the men as Alf's Carter Patterson van turned the corner into Bayham Street.

There were plenty of willing hands, so it was not long before the van was loaded. The rent collector had told Gertie to put the keys through the letter box when they had finished, so that he could collect them later, as the new occupants would be moving in that very same day.

Gertie could not resist saying a final goodbye to the home she had lived in all of her married life – thirty-six years. She wiped the tears from her eyes as she walked from room to room and then she closed the front door behind her and put the keys through the letter box, as instructed. That done, Gertie wanted to be away as quickly as possible.

The Carter Patterson van was one often used for removals and had a tailgate, which closed in such a way as to leave the top half open, ideal for carrying any passengers. Dickie left the settee till last, allowing a comfortable seat for Freda and Gertie, who would also have a good view of the passing scenery, while he and Jimmy would sit in the driver's cab with Alf.

Joe and David stood together, watching the van disappearing down Bayham Street, with Joe's mother and grandmother waving goodbye from the back. Once out of sight, Joe and David then walked slowly back to Mary's house, the ever-sensitive David knowing that his new friend was feeling sad. But he did not intrude, even though he would have done anything to make Joe feel better again.

In the van, Alf was explaining the route he had planned. 'I'm heading through the city to Aldgate,' he told Dickie. 'Then we go past the Blackwall Tunnel to Canning Town and from there, we take the Barking Road all the way to Dagenham. I know we have to turn off at a place called the Chequers onto a long road they call the Heathway, but you'll have to direct me after that.'

'Yeah, sure,' said Dickie. 'The Heathway is about 2 miles long and our place is not far from Heathway station. It shows you how big Dagenham is though, Alf – it has two stations, Dagenham Heathway and Dagenham East.'

'It could have a fucking airport, for all I care; I still wouldn't want to live there.'

Fortunately, Jimmy was too busy looking from the passenger window to listen to the conversation, but Dickie gave Alf a warning nudge and Alf grinned in response. Alf was well used to driving around the ports and docks of London and had driven to Dagenham Dock several times beforehand to collect a consignment. He was used to seeing the bomb-damaged ruins throughout London and the Home Counties and hardly noticed them any longer. Not so the Campbells. They were utterly shocked and dismayed by the devastation that was unfolding before them, as mile after mile of flattened houses and factories, most of which had still to be cleared, brought it home to the Campbells that it was not just the centre of London that had suffered during the Blitz.

When Dickie had been brought home after the war, he had been taken straight to Moorfields Eye Hospital, with his eyes covered in bandages, and the only time he had left Camden since then was when he, Freda and the boys had taken the main-line train to Liverpool Street station and the tube to view the house in Dagenham. All the bomb damage had been cleared within 100 yards or so from the tracks above ground, so they had no idea of the extent of the devastation that was all too evident from the main roads.

The traffic was light and it was a little more than an hour after leaving Camden, that Alf turned his van into Heathway. Quite a few of the bombed-out houses had already been cleared and were now in the process of being rebuilt, but Dickie could still see a few actual bomb sites along the Heathway. Mostly though, there were just empty spaces, where once a house had stood, and those empty spaces would have to be filled long before any work could begin on the bombed-out houses of London.

'I can't believe they've got this lot sorted, before they've even made a start round our way,' Dickie said bitterly. 'Who the bloody hell decided Dagenham was more important than Camden?'

Alf stopped at the traffic lights of Church Elm Lane and noticed a pub on the corner called, as one would expect, The Church Elm.

Alf wondered if this would be Dickie's local from now on.

'They started to build this estate in the thirties,' he told Dickie. 'The idea being that they would clear the slums all over London, but mostly from the East End and north London. They say this will be the biggest housing estate in Europe when it's finished, but even before the war, no bugger wanted to come and live here. But now, like yourselves, people have no choice, so that's why they've pulled out all the stops to rebuild as fast as they can.'

The lights changed to green and Alf drove them up the hill, passing a row of shops, including Woolworths, Boots the Chemist, the Fifty Shilling Tailors, Burtons and many more smaller establishments.

At the top of the hill stood Heathway station, with a cinema on the opposite side of the road. Then there were some more shops as they drove down the other side of the hill, before arriving at the Campbells' new abode. At Dickie's signal, Alf pulled up outside a very smart-looking row of terraced houses, many of which had an outside close to the front door.

'We were lucky to get one with an outside entrance,' he told Alf, 'it will be handy to get in and out without having to traipse through the passage every time.'

'Bloody handy for burglars, as well,' remarked Alf, but he was quite impressed, nevertheless.

Unloading the furniture and installing it in the new house would take much longer than it had before, as there would be only Alf and Dickie to do the heavy work. They all felt the need for a little light refreshment before rolling up their sleeves, so Dickie brought out the beer and lemonade. Dickie gave Alf a conducted tour of the house, including the bathroom, for Alf had never seen an indoor toilet before, apart from the ones at the cinema. Even the toilets of the Spread Eagle were outside.

'I bet you can't even fart in here without everyone hearing it,' Alf said to Dickie.

Overhearing his remark, Gertie retorted, 'The whole of bleeding Bayham Street could hear him when he got going.'

There was a knock at the front door. They all stood still for several seconds, surprised that they would have their first visitor so soon and wonder who it could be. Freda opened the door to a rather plump, elderly woman, who was carrying a tray of tea and biscuits.

'Hello there,' she smiled at Freda, 'I thought you might need a cuppa. My name's Mrs Peake and I live next door.'

Freda showed her new neighbour into the front room and introduced her to the family and to Alf. Ignoring the beer and lemonade for the time being, they gratefully drank their tea as Gertie chatted merrily away to Mrs Peake. Ada Peake was about the same age as Gertie and although Mrs Peake did not hold with being on first-name terms with all and sundry, within a very short time of meeting Gertie, she had invited her to call her Ada. She did not extend this invitation to the rest of the family, however, and she would remain Mrs Peake to the rest of the Campbells for as long as they could remember.

Ada Peake was originally from Bethnal Green in the East End of London and, with her husband and daughter, theirs was one of the first families to move to Dagenham in the early thirties. When they moved here, the town was still in its infancy and the long road called the Heathway was the first of many thousands of houses that would make up the estate that was far from being completed, even after the rebuilding of the bomb-damaged properties. At the far end of Heathway was a green common known as Nanny Goat Common that even had a blacksmith's forge for shoeing the farmers' horses or making wrought-iron gates and suchlike. The common would soon become part of the Becontree Estate, for the foundations were being laid to erect tower blocks and maisonettes covering the whole area.

Ada's husband had died of a heart attack just before the war, but Ada missed him not one iota. As she was fond of telling her friends at the over sixties club, 'Bloody good riddance, all he ever thought about was his beer, his belly and the other. The tight git never even bothered to get himself insured and all he left me was a bloody great bill for his funeral.'

After Mrs Peake had left, with a promise to Gertie that she would take her to the next over-sixties club meeting, the Campbells set about the task of unloading the van. Dickie had spotted a fish-and-chip shop at the bottom of Heathway Hill, no more than 50 yards from the house, so at midday, Jimmy was sent out to buy some lunch.

'At least that's one job we don't have to worry about,' Freda said thankfully.

At last, everything was installed in the appropriate rooms. Freda and Dickie were to have the large master bedroom and Gertie said she would have the smaller room, so that Jimmy could share the middle-sized bedroom when Joe came to stay at weekends. They were exhausted by the time they had finished, but Alf declined the offer to stay the night. 'Nah, I'd better be off, mate,' he said, 'the old woman's got the hump as it is. No point in making it worse.'

Dickie walked to the van with Alf, when they shook hands and then, impulsively, they hugged each other tightly.

Feeling a little embarrassed, Dickie released his friend. 'Fuck off, you soppy old git, you'll be giving me a kiss next.'

It was said in an attempt to lighten the moment, but both felt the strong emotion of the parting.

'Camden Town's not that far away,' Alf reminded Dickie. 'Come back and see us soon, me old mucker.'

Dickie knew that he would be greeted with open arms by Alf, but Bella was a different kettle of fish altogether. She had hardly been able to conceal her glee last night in the Spread Eagle and had not even bothered to see them off that morning.

Dickie watched Alf's van disappear over Heathway Hill and then went back into the house. Freda and Gertie looked pale and drawn, while Jimmy was curled up into a ball and was fast asleep in one of the armchairs. Dickie also felt exhausted and suggested they all take themselves to their beds. 'Tomorrow's another day, let's leave it off for now,' he said.

Gertie went over to one of the packing cases and produced a bottle of Johnny Walkers. The glasses were in one of the tea chests, but cups would do for now. 'Come on, you two,' said Gertie, 'we have to christen our new house before we do anything else.'

Freda hugged her mother. The strain of the past week was beginning to tell and Freda felt near to breaking point, but the simple gesture from Gertie eased at least some of the tension she was feeling. Dickie also silently blessed his mother-in-law as he sipped neat Scotch from a cup and he hoped that the whisky would help them to unwind before they went to bed, for they could all do with a good night's sleep.

'Here's to us and our new home,' he said, raising his cup to the others.

'To us and our new home,' replied Gertie and Freda.

The Campbells were woken early the next morning by the raucous crowing of Mrs Peake's cockerel.

'Fucking Nora,' cried Dickie as he leapt out of bed. 'Don't tell me we have to put up with that bleeding row every morning.' He looked at the bedside clock. 'Sod me; it's not even six o'clock yet.' He put his slippers on, muttering, 'Might as well make us a cuppa, I suppose; there's no point in trying to get back to sleep with that racket going on.'

By six thirty, the family had finished breakfast and were ready to tackle the many tasks that lay before them. Dickie had linoleum to lay on the floors, with shelves and cupboards to be to be put up, plus numerous other jobs. Gertie and Freda would be kept busy fitting curtains in every room, ensuring that their hand-operated Singer sewing machine would in full use that day. But Jimmy was left free to explore his new surroundings. He wandered into the back garden and peered over Mrs Peake's fence. He was amazed. 'It's just a city farm in Hackney,' he said out loud.

'That's right, love,' came a voice from behind the fence. 'Just like a city farm.' Mrs Peake had been bending down picking side shoots from her tomato plants. She stood up straight. 'Hello, young 'un; you're up early.'

Jimmy refrained from informing her that it was her cockerel that was responsible for the whole family being up and about at such an unearthly hour as this. Mrs Peake's backyard, if not quite a city farm, was certainly something of a menagerie. As well as the cockerel, there were six hens, two ducks, a pigeon loft containing half a dozen birds, one cat with her four kittens, two dogs, half a dozen rabbits and even a tortoise tethered by a long length of string tied through a hole that had been drilled into its shell. Somehow, Mrs Peake had also managed to find room to grow tomatoes and runner beans in various locations around the garden and Jimmy had never seen anything like it before.

After a while, he went to the front of the house and stood by the gate, although he did not expect very much to be happening at this time on a Sunday morning. But, to his surprise, a lad of around his own age rode up to him on his scooter.

'I see old mother Peake's cockerel's got you up then,' the boy grinned. 'My name's Reggie Godber and I live the other side of you.'

Jimmy discovered a great deal about Reggie Godber during the next fifteen minutes or so and his family, like Jimmy's, had moved from north London and had only been in Dagenham for three months. Reggie told Jimmy the name of the school he attended and it happened to be the same one Jimmy had been signed up to.

'I have to report to Mr Dradge at half eight,' said Jimmy.

'Drippy Dradge,' Reggie chortled. 'He's my teacher as well, so we'll be in the same class.'

'What's it like here, Reggie?' Jimmy asked anxiously.

'In Dagenham?' Reggie said. 'It's not bad, really, but you have to get used to the bloody racket old mother Peake's lot make and don't forget, we have another lot on the other side of us. It seems that everyone in Dagenham keeps geese or chickens, or anything else they can put in the pot, for that matter. Whoever talked about the peace and quiet of the countryside surely never spent a night away from the city. Apart from that, I like it here. There's a big park just up the road and Hainault Forest is only a bus ride away. I make Saturday the best day of the week myself, 'cos I go to the Saturday-morning pictures and then jump on a bus to Romford Market. In the school holidays, I go there on Wednesdays as well, because that's the day when they auction all the cattle. You can come with me next Saturday, if you like.'

It was a generous offer that Jimmy very much appreciated and his spirits had been lifted far higher than he could have dared to hope in such a short space of time. Reggie scooted off to fetch the Sunday paper for his father, with a promise to call for Jimmy when he returned and take him to the park. He also promised to go with him in the morning, to show him the way to his new school.

Their first full day in Dagenham passed quickly. Dickie had completed a great many tasks, although he knew it would take many more hours of toil before he was through. Gertie and Freda had cleaned every window in the house and had fitted all the curtains, achieving all this while still managing to prepare a traditional Sunday roast. Jimmy had spent virtually all day with his new friend, only dashing in to wolf down his dinner, before dashing back out again with Reggie.

Now, at last, it was evening and they could all sit and relax as they listened to the radio with a glass or two of brown ale for Dickie and

31

shandies for Gertie and Freda, but all three of them ached in muscles they never knew existed. Tomorrow, Freda and Dickie would accompany Jimmy to school, much to Jimmy's dismay, for he dreaded to think that the other kids would think he was a baby, who needed his mummy and daddy to hold his hand. Freda would not be swayed though, for she felt it was her duty to meet his teacher and at least have the opportunity to see where her son was to be educated.

Dickie's appointment at the Ford factory was not until three o'clock in the afternoon, so he and Freda planned to take the bus to Ilford after visiting Jimmy's school, because Freda wanted to look at some furniture and carpets. Gertie would stay behind and prepare something to eat for Jimmy, when he came home at lunchtime.

Dickie did not expect any difficulty in being taken on at Ford's, because the company were always advertising for assembly line workers and he was confident that his work record would stand him in good stead, having worked for Carter Patterson ever since leaving school. Dickie had not mentioned his eye problem on his written application form, hoping that he would not need to have a medical examination just to work on a production line.

Freda, who had already had a successful interview a week previously, was due to start work at the pharmaceutical company, May and Baker, on Wednesday.

So soundly did most of the Campbell family sleep that night that it was only Gertie who was woken by the cockerel the next morning.

She got dressed and then went downstairs to make some tea, but it was still not quite six o'clock and there was no need for the others to get up yet. Dickie joined his mother-in-law for a cup of tea half an hour later.

'I've just been looking at Mrs Peake's back garden from Jimmy's bedroom window,' Dickie told her. 'Even from up there it smells like a farmyard and I'm surprised the council allows her to get away with it.'

'Ada told me that they won't say anything, unless one of her neighbours makes a complaint.' She looked long and hard at Dickie. 'And there will be no complaint from us, will there, Dickie?' It was not a request, but more of an order.

'Not from me, Gertie,' Dickie replied. 'Live and let live, that's my motto.'

Dickie walked around his own backyard, the first he had ever owned, or perhaps rented was the more accurate term. He had no gardening tools or lawnmower and realised that this meant more expense, as the grass was already at least 2 feet high. Dickie had seen the runner beans and tomatoes that were growing in Mrs Peake's garden and he was determined that his own back garden would yield a crop for the next season. The only trouble was that Dickie did not have a clue how to set about planting produce, which Gertie was quick to point out.

'I can learn,' he told Gertie. 'I can always ask Mrs Peake or get a book from the library.'

'I never expected to see you turn out to be a "Capability Brown",' said Gertie.

'Capability who?' said a puzzled Dickie.

'Never mind,' replied Gertie.

After breakfast, Freda, Dickie and Jimmy were shown the way to school by a proud Reggie Godber, who also introduced them to Jimmy's teacher Mr Dradge, known to the boys as "Drippy" Dradge.

After completing a form, they said their goodbyes to Jimmy and waited at the bus stop outside the school for the bus that would take them to Ilford. There were no trams or trolley buses in Dagenham, although trolley buses were still in use running from the nearby town of Barking into Ilford itself.

'That Reggie didn't tell us why they call that teacher "Drippy" Dradge, did he?' observed Dickie.

'No, the little sod didn't,' laughed Freda. 'I thought it was because he was a bit dopey, until he kept getting his hanky out every two minutes to wipe his nose.'

Freda insisted on sitting on the top deck of the bus when it arrived, for she wanted to have a good view of the neighbourhood. All of the houses in Dagenham looked more or less the same and it was not until they reached places called Goodmayes and Seven Kings just before Ilford that these privately owned properties took on their individual characteristics. Freda was greatly impressed with these fine houses and wondered what sort of people could afford to actually buy their own home and she said as much to Dickie.

'Not Ford workers or lorry drivers, that's for sure,' he replied. 'City gents, doctors, lawyers, people like that, I suppose.'

'And bloody crooked market traders like Bobby Boyce,' Freda interjected bitterly.

They left the bus when it reached Ilford High Street and headed for the huge furniture store that dominated the whole area. Freda had seen this store advertised in the Evening Standard many times beforehand and she and Dickie had compared prices with some of the smaller stores. As well as having by far the largest selection of all kinds of furniture displayed over seven floors, their prices were also competitive. Freda had wanted to purchase a three-piece suite, a sideboard, a large carpet for the front room, a dining-room suite and a chest of drawers for each of the bedrooms. Dickie adamantly refused to agree, for it was he who would be required to sign the hire-purchase agreement and he insisted they must wait until they could be sure that they would be able to meet the repayments. For the time being, Freda would have to make do with a new three-piece suite and a large carpet for the front room. Deep down, Freda knew her husband was right, but she so badly wanted to be surrounded by nice new things.

Dickie would later swear to Gertie and Jimmy that he been made to sit on every three-piece suite in the entire store and tread on mile after mile of carpet, before she eventually made her choice. Freda was very happy with her selections and with the assurance that the store would deliver that same afternoon, Dickie paid the deposit, signed the contract and then he and Freda went to the pie-and-mash shop for lunch. Dickie would have preferred a pie and a pint, but thought it best not to arrive at his interview smelling of beer.

It was a very contented Freda who took the bus back to Dagenham, leaving Dickie to catch another that would take him right inside the factory premises and into a whole new world.

Chapter Four

Dickie was directed by a security guard to the personnel office, where he was given a form to complete. There were three other men sitting in the waiting room filling in the same forms and one of them looked up as Dickie came in and gave him a friendly nod. As Dickie nodded back to him, a stern-looking woman, whom Dickie assumed to be the personnel officer, collected their completed forms and inspected them.

'Yes, these appear to be in order,' she told the men, 'follow me please.' She led them from the office and along a wide road for half a mile or so, until they came to a building that was so colossal that Dickie was not sure where it ended or where it began. But he guessed that the door that they eventually stopped at was probably about half way. 'Before we go in, I'd better warn you that the noise inside is deafening,' said the personnel officer. 'Try not to let it put you off, you'll soon get used to it and we do supply earmuffs for those who want them. This is where the four of you will be working.'

Even through the thick door they could hear the sound of heavy machinery, but when she opened the door, Dickie had to force himself not to cover his ears with his hands.

'Jeeeesus Christ Almighty!' he exclaimed, earning himself a disapproving glare from the officer.

This one won't last five minutes, she thought.

Dickie had been totally unprepared for this and he was horrified at the thought that he would be working in this nightmare of a place day after day. The four men were taken to a conveyor belt, where dozens of men were crawling in and out of the partially assembled cars. It was some time before Dickie realised that the line was inching forwards slowly but unrelentingly and as it passed through each section, another team of men sprang into action. After watching with fascination, or with horror in Dickie's case, ten minutes later they were taken to the foreman's office, which at least was soundproof.

'My name is Mr Walsh,' he told them as he shook their hands.

The four men introduced themselves and he found out that the friendly chap who had nodded to Dickie was Tommy Smith. Dickie was pleased when Mr Walsh told them that he and Tommy would be working on the same shift as each other and the other two men would be starting on the opposite shift.

'By the way,' said Mr Walsh, 'everyone is supplied with a pair of earmuffs, although most of the men don't use them. But my advice to you is to wear them, at least until you get used to the noise.'

He handed each of them a pair of the clumsy-looking earmuffs that looked to Dickie as though they were army issue. He did not care what they looked like, for surely anything would be better than having to put up with the infernal noise of the assembly line. Dickie put them on before leaving the foreman's office and the noise, whilst still loud, was greatly reduced, which made Dickie wonder why on earth so many of the men were choosing not to wear them.

Back in the personnel office, they were asked when they could begin work. Dickie and Tommy said they could start on Wednesday, the other two agreeing to begin work the next day.

Dickie and Tommy chatted together as they waited for the bus.

Tommy was a couple of years younger than Dickie and lived with his wife and his mother in a road just around the corner from Dickie.

Like Dickie, he, too, had been wounded during the war and he had spent several months in a French hospital, having been wounded just a week before the hostilities had ended, but it took six months of treatment until he was well enough to be sent home. The injuries to Tommy's legs had been so severe that it seemed the surgeon would have to amputate one, if not both of them, and it was only because teams of specialists had been flown in to France as soon as the war was over that Tommy's legs had been saved, although he would walk with a limp for the rest of his days. Back in England, Tommy had undergone several more painful skin grafts and would still only be able to bathe in lukewarm water for many more months to come. He had only recently been declared fit enough for work and this would be his first civilian job since joining the army back in 1940.

The Smith family had moved to Dagenham from Poplar, in the east of London, in 1938. He told Dickie that he loved Dagenham and would never move back to the East End, even if he was given the choice, and Tommy said his wife and mother both felt the same way.

The bus eventually came along and the two men continued chatting as the bus left the Ford complex and made its way to Heathway. Neither of them wanted to discuss the prospect of starting work the day after tomorrow, for even Tommy had been shocked and dismayed at the conditions they were expected to work under.

Tommy had often heard the Ford factory being referred to as "The Hole" and it was only now that he knew why.

Tommy was glad that he and Dickie would be working together, for he was certain that they would get along just fine. As they lived close to each other, he hoped they might go for the occasional pint together or perhaps Upton Park Football Ground on a Saturday to watch West Ham play, forgetting that Dickie was a north Londoner and would probably support Arsenal or Tottenham Hotspur. They got off the bus at Heathway station and walked the short distance to where they would go their separate ways, agreeing to meet each other on Wednesday at five thirty in the morning, as they would have to start work at six o'clock. For the rest of the week, they would be on the early shift from 6.00 a.m. till 2.00 p.m. and then the following week from 2.00 p.m. until 10.00p.m. and the third week they would be on the night shift, working from 10.00 p.m. until six the next morning.

That was to be the pattern of Dickie's working life for perhaps the next thirty years, if he was to remain at Ford's. The thought of thirty years cooped up inside that dreadful place filled Dickie with dread and a blind panic suddenly overwhelmed him. He turned and almost ran back to the bus stop and caught the next bus to Dagenham Town Hall in the hope that as it was still only four o'clock, it might still be open. Dickie was trembling as though in shock, which he very nearly was, and even though the money would be considerably less, he resolved to apply for a job on the dustcarts. The man on the door told Dickie that the depot was in Fritzlands Lane, a couple of hundred yards down the road, but warned Dickie that it would be closing soon. Dickie ran all the way and was directed to the depot manager's office by a man who was on his way out. Dickie knocked on the door, his fists clenched tightly with tension. A voice called from within and Dickie stood face-to-face with a slim, slightly bald man of around his own age.

'Sir,' Dickie said desperately, 'is there any chance of me getting a job on the bins?'

Jack Doyle the manager had been about to lock up and go home, but there was something about this man that held his attention. He reminds me of a drowning man trying to clutch at a straw, he thought to himself. I've never seen anybody so anxious to become a binman before.

'I'm very sorry, mate,' he told Dickie, 'but we have no vacancies at the moment.' He watched the colour drain from Dickie's face and quickly offered him a chair. 'Here, sit down for a minute, mate, you look as though you need to.' He offered Dickie a Woodbine, which Dickie accepted gratefully, taking deep draws to calm his nerves, and then they introduced themselves. 'Oh, incidentally,' said Jack Doyle with a grin, 'nobody in this depot even calls me Mr Doyle, let alone sir.'

Dickie told Jack about the interview with Ford's and all about how he had spent his entire working life in the open air. He then went on to tell the sympathetic man of the dread he had of working in that factory.

Jack Doyle nodded understandingly. 'I've never been inside the place myself, but half the men in Dagenham work there. Most of them said they were only going to be there for a few months to earn a few bob, but then they became trapped, because they couldn't afford to leave.' Jack stubbed out his cigarette. 'Binmen aren't exactly overpaid, you know, although if they work flat out, they get finished by midday and some of them do a bit on the side. All the same though, none of them can earn the sort of money the Ford workers make.'

Dickie could not hide his disappointment. 'I've never earned the sort of money those lads get in my whole life and when I couldn't drive any more, I was earning even less. What you've never had you never miss and a job on the bins, out in the fresh air, sounds like heaven after spending just half an hour in that place.'

Jack shook his head sadly. 'If there was a job going, I would give it to you like a shot, believe me. The only thing I can do is to take your address and promise to get in touch as soon as anything comes up. I don't think it should be too long though, because we took on two young lads quite recently and from past experience, the younger ones tend to not like getting soaked when they find they still have to go out in the rain.'

Dickie was grateful for the other man's concern and after Jack had noted Dickie's address, they shook hands and then Dickie returned to Heathway, resigned to the fact that he would be starting work on the Ford assembly line the day after tomorrow.

When Freda saw Dickie's face as he walked into the front room, she was certain that he had failed to get the job.

'You've been gone a lot longer than I expected,' she said, hardly daring to ask how the interview had gone.

'Yeah, well, a big concern like Ford's aren't going to worry about keeping blokes like me hanging around now, are they? Anyway, I got the job and I start on Wednesday morning, six o'clock sharp.'

Dickie had no intention of telling his wife that he had gone running to the council depot in a blind panic, begging for a job as a dustbin man.

Freda was surprised and a little annoyed at her husband's reaction. 'Most people celebrate when they get a new job, not act as though they've lost a pound and found a penny.'

'Leave it out, Freda, I'm not in the mood,' Dickie replied gruffly. 'I'm going to check out that pub on the other side of the hill.'

Dickie did not stay long in the Church Elm pub. He was not used to drinking alone, but made no attempt to engage anyone in conversation, for he was in no mood to be sociable. Dickie felt that this was the lowest point of his entire life, for even when he had feared that he had been blinded, he could not remember feeling as desperate as he did at this moment. Alf was right, he told himself, I'm not going to last five minutes in that place.

Then, much to his surprise, Dickie sensed a change coming over him. Not of optimism exactly, but he found that his feeling of desperation gradually seemed to be less acute than it had been when he had first walked into the pub. He finished his pint and left, determined he must shake off this awful depression, otherwise he would make everyone else's life a misery and not just his own. He trusted Jack Doyle and was sure that the manager would get in touch with him when there was a vacancy at the depot. He had no idea what Freda would have to say about that, but he would cross that bridge when he came to it. For the time being though, he would just have to put up with the assembly line of the Ford Motor Company, or at least he hoped he would.

Bobby Boyce was holding court in the Spread Eagle and when Boyce had something to say, everyone stopped to listen.

'Young Joe Campbell is now working for me full time and I want the word put around that I don't want him mixed up in anything dodgy. No offering him bent gear to sell on the side and when you see those toerags the Murphy twins, tell them as well. Joe is lodging with my sister and I've given her my word that I'll make sure the boy is kept out of the scams that go on around the market.'

'That's easier said than done, Bobby,' said one of the market traders. 'Most of us can double our wages by knocking out iffy gear.

When Joe finds out what he's missing out on, he's bound to want in himself.'

'No he won't. One whiff of trouble and his old man will be back here like a shot to drag him off to Dagenham. My concern is that although he may work the market like an old-timer, he's still only a gullible kid, so put the word around that anyone who tries to put one over on him will have me to answer to.'

In fact, Joe had already been approached by the Murphy twins.

They had shown him two ladies' coats that carried a well-known manufacturer's label, but at a fraction of the normal retail price.

'No thanks,' Joe had told them. 'At that price, they must be knocked-off and I'm staying well clear of any bent gear.'

'Now, would we try to flog you bent gear, Joe?' Mick Murphy sounded hurt. 'These are not bent, they're just copies. We run a sweatshop in Aldgate and the girls turn these out at the rate of two dozen a week. We have a supplier who provides us with the labels and we just sew them in. The punters are happy at getting one of these at a third of the shop price and all of us make a few quid. Now where's the harm in that?'

Joe shook his head. 'I think I'll pass, thanks all the same.'

The young woman who was working the stall next to Joe's wandered over. 'I couldn't help overhearing what the twins were saying,' she said. 'Some of their stuff is just like the real McCoy.' She brought over a dress from her own stall. 'Here, take a look at this. You'd never be able to tell this from the real thing; seven quid this would cost you up West, but I knock 'em out for three and a half. I get them from the twins for thirty bob. That's two quid clear profit for every one I sell and I can't get enough of them; in fact, I even have a waiting list.' She looked over her shoulder at Joe as she went back to her stall. 'You should get in while the going's good, if you want to earn yourself a few bob.'

Joe was certainly tempted. He was determined to save as much money as quickly as he could, so that he could set up his own stall, but he knew that at the rate he was able to save his money at the moment, it would take years before he had anywhere near enough.

The opportunity of making a handsome profit on the Murphy twins' merchandise was irresistible and he convinced himself that this was not really bent gear. Like so many young men, Joe was impatient and prepared to cut a few corners to achieve his goal, although he would never knowingly sell anything that had been stolen. Joe decided he would accept the twins offer when he saw them next.

It was Duggie Murphy who wandered by his stall that same afternoon, having been advised by the girl on the stall next to Joe's that he may have changed his mind about buying the coats. Joe told Duggie that he would take half a dozen and Duggie told him they would be delivered first thing in the morning. The die was cast.

The Murphy twins were among an up-and-coming breed of young villains, mostly fresh from the armed forces. Many had been on active service during the war and were contemptuous of the men who had avoided being conscripted and who had stayed at home to make a fortune from the black market. Both Mick and Duggie Murphy had served their country well and had war medals to prove it, but they had also served themselves well at the same time. They had served with distinction in North Africa for over two years, being rewarded with promotion to sergeant and then being sent back to England as drill sergeants to train new recruits at an army camp in Wiltshire. A crooked manager in charge of the nearby warehouse that supplied NAFI canteens all around the country supplied the Murphy twins with boxes of cigarettes, bottles of brandy and assorted tinned meats and fish, including the much sought after tins of salmon and tuna.

Some of the goods were sold at a discount to the recruits, although the bulk went to local shops, to be sold at twice the price it would have cost before the war. The deprived population were only too willing to hand over their money for items that were almost impossible to come by through legitimate channels.

The twins had not squandered away their money and after they had been demobilised, when the war was over, they began to challenge the authority of men such as Bobby Boyce. Several stallholders had told them of Boyce's order that Joe Campbell was not to be offered any dodgy goods, but the Murphys had ignored the order, virtually throwing down the gauntlet. The ladies' coats that Joe had agreed to sell were not copies at all, they were the real thing, stolen on a regular basis from the manufacturers.

Early every Monday morning, one of the Murphys was let into the manufacturer's yard by a crooked foreman, whereupon coats and dresses were loaded into the van and driven off to one of the twins' many lock-up garages. Naturally, neither Mick nor Duggie were ever involved in the actual theft, but they would meet up with the foreman later to pay him off. This arrangement had been successful for the past six months and the Murphys believed that if they did not get greedy, there was no reason that the scam should not continue for a long time to come.

It was not the Murphy twins that became too greedy, however; it was the foreman. Not content with the money he was receiving from the

Murphys, he decided he would increase his earnings by selling more of the stock on to other customers. Soon, too many people were involved and word spread, reaching the ears of Detective Sergeant Stone from Kentish Town Police Station. The sergeant had worked long and hard to be promoted to sergeant, but he knew he would be unlikely to attain a higher rank unless he pulled off a high-profile arrest, and very soon at that. He was well over 40 years of age and it rankled that his superior, a detective inspector, was not yet even thirty, but if the sergeant could put the Murphy twins behind bars, it could boost his prospects considerably. Detective Sergeant Stone already had one eye on his pension and a detective inspector's was far more attractive than the meagre pension of a sergeant. Arresting the Murphy twins could be the answer to his prayers and not only the arrest of the twins, but also any other stallholders who were handling the stolen goods.

On Tuesday evening, Dickie set the alarm clock for 5.00 a.m. the following morning. He, Freda and Gertie had worked hard throughout the entire day, but the main tasks had now been completed and Dickie had even bought a second-hand lawn mower, although he had not started on the back garden yet. It had been Jimmy and Reggie Godber who had mown the smaller patch of grass in front of the house that evening and they had made quite a good job of it as well. Freda and Dickie had both gone to bed early, each wondering what the next day would bring. In Dickie's case, it would be almost a totally new experience, for he had not worked for anyone else since joining Carter Patterson, when he was fourteen, and he had only ever worked in the open. Dickie did not consider joining the army as being the same as starting a new job, because, after all, every recruit was as raw and as nervous as he had been. As for Freda, she would have to adjust to working with people she had never met before and learn to cope with the hustle and bustle of a busy production line, but Freda tried not dwell on the fact that she had not held down any paid job for the past fifteen years.

Surprisingly, they both slept soundly and when the alarm clock went off, Dickie quickly silenced it and then re-set it for Freda, who did not need to get up until 7.00 a.m. That's unless the bloody cockerel wakes her up first, Dickie grinned to himself.

Dickie left the house after swallowing a mug of tea and a slice of bread and dripping. He was amazed to see hundreds of men heading towards the Ford factory, some on bicycles, a few in motor vehicles, but the majority were on foot, making their way to the bus stop. The queue seemed to grow longer and longer by the minute, but there was still no sign of Tommy Smith, and then two buses arrived together and were quickly filled. Dickie managed to get a place on the third, but had to stand all the way. He wondered if Tommy had changed his mind about working for Ford's, or even if he had found himself a job elsewhere. The bus conductor made no attempt to collect fares whilst the bus was on the move, he simply stood on the platform and collected the money as the men got off at the various places where they worked in the huge Ford complex. Dickie could not help noticing that for every two men that got off, only one ticket was punched by the conductor, so he could only assume that half of the morning's takings would find its way into the conductor's own pocket.

Dickie reported to the foreman's office, where he was given two pairs of overalls, at which point he was taken down to the restroom, allocated his own personal locker and told that he would have to take his dirty overall home to be washed every few days. He was also informed that the two pairs of overalls must last him for at least a year. There was still no sign of Tommy Smith, even though it was now 6.30 a.m. Mr Walsh told Dickie to wait in the restroom, until the leader of the team to whom he had been allocated came to show him his duties. Then, just as the foreman was about to leave, Tommy Smith came dashing in.

'Sorry I'm late, guv,' he panted, 'it's the bleeding buses, they were all full up.'

Mr Walsh had no sympathy at all. 'Set out earlier in future, because you'll be getting a clocking-in card today and three minutes late means a quarter of an hour's money off your wages. At six thirty every morning, one of the other foremen collects every card from the rack in this section and that's the cut-off point. If you arrive later than that and your card is not there, you might as well turn around and go back home, because you won't be working that day. But three lates in a week means you'll be getting your cards.' He was about to leave, when he turned back to Tommy Smith. 'And another thing, my name is Mr Walsh. Not guv. Do I make myself clear?'

'Yes, g … er, Mr Walsh,' Tommy replied. After Mr Walsh had left the room, Tommy turned to Dickie and said, 'Fucking well overslept, didn't I.' He nodded to the door that the foreman had just walked through.

'Mind you, that miserable sod's not exactly going to be a bundle of laughs, is he?'

Before Dickie could comment, the door opened again and another man entered.

'Hello, you must be the new lads. My name's Wally Thwaites, but everybody calls me One-eyed Wally,' he grinned. 'Doesn't need much to work out why, does it, lads? But it don't bother me.'

They both attempted to ignore the glass eye that was staring eerily at them when Wally closed his good eye. The glass eye was permanently fixed in the open position, for Wally had lost his eyelid as well as his eye in an explosion when he had worked in the foundry.

He had been offered plastic surgery, but had refused, for reasons known only to himself and certainly not to his wife, who had left him shortly after the accident.

He explained to Dickie and Tommy that his team was responsible for securing the seats into the cars. The easiest to fit was the long back seat, the most difficult being the two in the front, especially the one for the driver. The newcomers in every team were always given the most difficult tasks, but would be "promoted" as other workers left. Wally decided that Tommy, who had previous factory experience, would be better suited to working on the driver's side, whilst Dickie took care of the passenger seat.

Dickie and Tommy put on their earmuffs when they left the restroom, although they noticed that the team leader did not bother.

Wally escorted them to the assembly line and introduced them to four men, who were working on the same vehicle. Because of the noise, the only way to do this was to point to the name badges pinned on their overalls. The other men waved a greeting, without stopping, and the two men, using a form of sign language, showed Tommy and Dickie what was to be done. Dickie's instructor showed him a metal box that contained hundreds of nuts, taking out four of them as the next car arrived in their section. The seat had already been put in place, so all that needed to be done was for the four nuts to be screwed onto the bolts that were protruding from the floor and through the seat braces. The instructor had all four nuts tightened very quickly and Dickie believed that the task did not appear to be very difficult; after all, the line was barely moving.

A few minutes later, he discovered how wrong he could be. Dickie had managed to secure just two of the nuts as the vehicle approached the next section. A hand shook his shoulder and the instructor jerked his thumb to order him out, as an inspector would pick up any omissions further down the line. Dickie made another attempt with the same result, and then another and another, but he had still not managed to secure more than two nuts when his instructor indicated that it was time for their break. Another four men took over and they trudged into the restroom for a well-deserved break of thirty minutes.

Wally Thwaites plonked himself down between Dickie and Tommy. 'It won't ever be as bad as that again,' he told Dickie. 'Nobody ever puts all the nuts on for the first few days; you're doing fine and quality control knows that I have two new workers, so they'll be on the lookout.' To Tommy, he said. 'Well, Tommy, it didn't take you long to get rid of your earmuffs, did it?'

'The fucking things just get in the way when you're crawling around under a seat and they're all hot and sweaty, as well.' Tommy munched at his sandwich. 'To tell the truth, I stopped noticing the racket after the first hour.'

'Those two instructors and the ones who relieved us, can they do every job on the line?' Dickie asked Wally.

'Not on the entire assembly line, but they can do any job on this section. As well as the seats, we put on the windscreen wipers, the wheels, the hub caps and all of the front and rear lights.' He lit a cigarette, without offering one to Tommy or Dickie. 'Those lads get more money, of course, but they're worth every penny.' He grinned at the two men. 'Give it a week and the pair of you will finish all four nuts and have time to roll yourself a fag before the next one comes along.'

Dickie knew this was a gross exaggeration, for no Ford worker would have the time to stand around smoking. Except the bosses, of course, Dickie thought cynically. And then it was time to go back to work.

Chapter Five

S ome three miles away at the May and Baker pharmaceutical factory, Freda had just begun her own working day. She had taken the District line train from Dagenham Heathway to Dagenham East, just one stop away, although it would have meant a journey of nearly 2 miles if she had chosen to walk. There was no shift system in operation at May and Baker, as most of the production workers were women, who needed to be able to work flexible hours in order that they could still take care of their children. Some of the women worked for only four hours a day during the school term and none at all during the holidays. This was an arrangement that suited the workers, although this was not altogether altruistic by the management, for the wages they paid were the lowest of any of the other local factories, but the women, some of whom were war widows, were at least able to supplement their pensions. As a goodwill gesture, every worker was presented with a generous hamper at Christmas, with a toy for every child under the age of ten.

Freda had arranged to work full time, from 9.00 a.m. until 4.00 p.m.

She was given a white coat and a white cap and was then taken by the forewoman to a small conveyor belt, where she was placed next to several other women. They were chatting and laughing together as they approached, but they soon stopped what they were doing and waved to Freda in a friendly manner. The forewoman explained that Freda had to take a small pillbox from the tray by her side and fill it with twenty-five of the pills that were travelling towards her on the conveyor belt. It was a simple enough task and Freda quickly got into the rhythm and although she felt shy at first, she was soon put at ease by the friendliness of the other women.

There was very little noise from the conveyor belt and soft, soothing music was being played over the overhead speakers and within a very short time, Freda knew that she would enjoy working at May and

Baker as she swapped life stories with her new friends. The only cloud on her immediate horizon was Dickie, for Freda was extremely worried about him. Whilst it was true that he had bucked up somewhat after coming home from the pub the other night, she knew he had been dreading his first shift at Ford's. She could only hope that his first day had gone as well as her own and that perhaps it would prove to be not quite as dreadful as he had been expecting.

The money that he could earn plus her own wages would mean that they would soon be able to buy lots of lovely things on the never-never, but Dickie was still the main breadwinner and much would depend on whether he could knuckle down to working on the assembly line.

The conveyor belt on a Ford assembly line was relentless and when one broke break down, all hell was let loose, with klaxon horns hooting loudly to summon every available engineer and manager to the scene. In the past, the workforce had been greatly amused at the frenzied activity erupting around them as they enjoyed an unexpected break and the expression "Throwing a spanner in the works" could well have originated from the Ford Motor Company, as it was not unknown for a worker to sabotage the assembly line by doing exactly that. The company had more or less solved the problem by paying the workers a bonus for each vehicle produced in the previous week, which meant for every five minutes of lost production time, there would be less money in their wage packets on pay day. As money was now at stake, there were very few men who would risk incurring the wrath of their workmates for the sake of a few minutes extra break.

Each assembly line worker was allowed three breaks during a shift and at last, Dickie returned to the line having taken his final break.

He had not eaten at all on any of his breaks, just drinking a cup of tea and smoking several of his hand-rolled cigarettes instead. He actually felt quite nauseous when he saw some of the men unwrapping huge bread-and-dripping sandwiches or tucking into pork pies, but some of the men, realising that this was Dickie's first day and remembering their own experience, gave him words of encouragement, for which he was grateful. Nobody seemed to think it necessary to encourage Tommy Smith, for Tommy had taken to the assembly line like a duck to water and by the end of the first shift, he had secured all four nuts on each vehicle that arrived in the section.

Wally was impressed, as Tommy had the more difficult task, but he was making it look almost simple, while poor Dickie was struggling to complete half of the job he'd been allocated. Wally knew that Tommy Smith would be a great asset to his team, although he was not too sure about Dickie Campbell.

An assembly line worker could not leave his position at the end of a shift until he was relieved by the next man, so punctuality was considered as being next to godliness by a Ford worker. Even on the early shift, it was seldom a man was late, but some of them waited in the toilets until the very last minute before taking over. Fortunately, Dickie's relief took over from him three minutes early, but it was a very weary and dispirited man who made his way to the restroom to change out of his overalls. Tommy followed a couple of minutes later, looking almost as tired as Dickie, but with a look of satisfaction on his face, and he told Dickie that the only reason he had managed to move around so quickly was because he had removed his earmuffs.

Dickie was sure he would not be able to work without some protection for his ears, although he also knew he would not keep his job unless he could keep up with the conveyor belt. He decided that tomorrow he would try putting some cotton wool in his ears, a thought that encouraged him slightly, because he knew that he would be coming back again for the next shift and that he had lasted five minutes after all.

Dickie regained his appetite as soon as he entered the house and Gertie willingly made him a mug of tea and a thick spam-and-pickle sandwich. Freda had told her how worried she was about Dickie being cooped up in a factory and she had been on tenterhooks all morning, waiting to see how he had fared. Indeed, Dickie looked very tired, and she would have been amazed if he hadn't been, but the almost panic-stricken look that had been on his face for the past two or three days was no longer there. Gertie went back to the kitchen to fetch her cup of tea, intending to ask her son-in-law all about his first day at the factory. She had barely been gone a minute, but when she returned, Dickie was fast asleep, his untouched mug of tea on the floor by his side and the plate with no more than two bites taken from one half of the sandwich perched upon his knees. Gertie gently took away the plate, removed the mug and crept from the room, closing the door behind her.

Gertie had shared a pot of tea with Ada Peake earlier that morning and the two women had been glad of each other's company.

Tomorrow was the day for the over-sixties club and Ada had promised to take Gertie with her to introduce her to some of her friends, telling Gertie that the women outnumbered the men by almost three to one, adding, 'So don't hold your breath if you're looking for a leg over.'

'Leg over! Get away with you. The only thing that gets over my leg these days is me flannel drawers.'

Ada nearly spilt her tea, she was laughing that much. Although Gertie knew that a part of her would always remain in Camden Town, she was determined to make this new phase of her life as happy as she possibly could. She was thankful that fate had placed the Campbell family next door to Ada Peake and Ada felt exactly the same way, for one over-sixties club meeting each week was not the same as having a next-door neighbour to have a good gossip with every day. Mrs Peake's last neighbour had been a grumpy old widower, who rarely spoke to anybody, but, thankfully, Gertie seemed to be a different kettle of fish altogether

Apart from Dickie, Gertie had the others to worry about as well and she hadn't stopped thinking about her daughter and both of her grandsons since leaving Ada's house. How was Freda getting on in the May and Baker factory? Would Jimmy settle down in his new school? How would Joe cope in Camden all by himself? She told herself she was being like a fussy old mother hen, as Jimmy seemed fine when he brought Reggie Godber home for lunch and he went back afterwards as though he didn't have a care in the world. Joe wasn't exactly all on his own in Camden anyway, because from what Freda and Dickie had told her, Mary Davis seemed to be a responsible young woman, but Gertie was so looking forward to seeing Joe at the weekend nonetheless. As for Freda, they would know soon enough how she had fared on her first day at work.

Jimmy returned from school hungry as usual, so Gertie made him a thick slice of bread and jam to keep him going until their evening meal, which he wolfed down, before rushing out to play with Reggie again. Freda came in at four thirty and Gertie had no need to ask if her day had gone well, because her shining eyes spoke volumes.

Freda just nodded happily to her mother's questioning look and then went into the front room, where she had guessed Dickie must be resting or perhaps having a snooze. Dickie was still asleep, but awoke the moment Freda walked into the room and accepted the mug of tea that Gertie had poured for him. Freda thought he looked pale and tired, but not as bad as she had feared; in fact, he sounded quite proud of himself when telling her of his first shift at Ford's.

Freda was careful not to be too enthusiastic about her own day, merely telling him that it was not too hard and that the other women were nice and friendly enough.

That evening, Gertie brought out the now half-empty bottle of Johnny Walkers, so that they could drink a toast to Dickie and Freda's new jobs. They had all come through a testing time and with luck, things should get better from now on.

As promised, Joe took the train to Dagenham after finishing work on Saturday evening. He was somewhat put out, perhaps even a little jealous, that Jimmy had arranged to meet Reggie Godber for a game of cricket with some other boys in the morning though. Joe had not expected his brother to have settled in so quickly and he was not sure that he liked the idea of this Reggie Godber trying to fill his shoes.

Alf Spinks had dropped by Joe's stall the day before, not only to ask him to give his father his regards but also to warn Joe that even three days of working in a factory could have taken effect on a man who had worked in the open air all of his life. So Joe had been pleasantly surprised to find his father mowing the lawn in the back garden with the second-hand mower, looking pale but actually quite cheerful.

Alf Spinks would have seen through Dickie's act in a second, but Joe believed his father's job on the assembly line could not be as bad as some people said it was. It was also obvious that his mother was enjoying her job and his grandmother enthused about her new-found friend next door and all the others she had met at the over-sixties club. Gertie took Joe into the backyard to introduce him to Ada. Joe, like Jimmy, thought her backyard looked like a city farm, although he refrained from saying it aloud.

After a traditional big fry-up on Sunday, Dickie poured Joe a glass of brown ale, ignoring the frown from Freda and the tuts from Gertie, as it was barely ten o'clock.

'Did you know there's a big market in a town not far from here?' said Dickie. 'It's called Romford and every Wednesday, they sell cattle, sheep, pigs, goats, cows, the lot, but on Fridays and Saturdays, it's back to being a normal market, just like Camden.' Dickie sipped at his beer. 'Apparently, Romford Market's been there for over 500 years.'

Joe was impressed. 'I've heard about these old country town markets, but I can't see me trying to flog a sheep, can you? Mind you, I might be able to flog a dead horse.'

Dickie shook his head and laughed, although he hoped he may have planted a tiny seed in his son's mind.

Joe decided he would like to see this famous market for himself and after the Sunday lunch, it was a willing Jimmy who offered to go with him on the bus. Jimmy did not ask Reggie to come with them as well, for he wanted time alone with his brother; in fact, he was pleased when their father did not suggest that they all go together.

Compared to Camden, Romford Market was quite small, but Joe could sense the atmosphere even though there were no stalls out on a Sunday and he vowed to ask Bobby Boyce for a day off one Wednesday, so that he could see for himself what a cattle market looked like.

It had been a long day and if Joe was to catch the first train in the morning, he would have to be up very early, what with having a full day's work ahead of him. He decided to take the last train instead, which meant that he would arrive back in Camden well before midnight and so there would be no need to get up much before seven o'clock. Both Freda and Dickie agreed that it made sense, even though Freda was a little disappointed that she would not be able to get up early to cook Joe a full breakfast before he left.

Jimmy and Gertie both went to bed before nine o'clock, giving Freda and Dickie the opportunity to talk to their eldest son on their own. There was no mention of Bobby Boyce, although Freda did ask how Mary and David were, a question tactfully answered by Joe, at least it was as far as Mary went, because Joe had a good idea that his mother would not be overly pleased to hear that her son was being spoiled rotten by another woman. Joe mentioned nothing about the Murphy twins and the coats he had bought from them and neither did he mention the fact that he had sold all of them on the same day. Joe had earned more money in a single day than his father could earn working a whole week even at Ford's, and that included the night shift. Joe was looking forward to collecting the next supply, either in the morning or on Tuesday.

He said goodbye to his parents and although it was late when he arrived back at Mary's house, she had not gone to bed yet.

She made him a hot drink and then said, 'Bobby came round this afternoon, Joe. He thinks the Murphy twins are up to something and he's afraid they may try to involve you. He's away on business for the next few days, so he asked me to tell you that if the twins offer you anything at all, not to touch it with a bargepole.'

Of course, Joe had no intention of telling Mary that it was already too late and that he had already ordered his next consignment.

Nobody welshed on a deal with the Murphy twins if they valued unbroken legs or a face free from razor scars. Joe cursed himself for his greed and stupidity, but it was too late to turn back now; he was in this right up to his neck and the thought sent shivers down his spine.

It appeared that every stallholder in the market, except Joe, realised that Boyce's days as the top dog in the market were numbered and it would be just a matter of time before the Murphy twins forced him out. Many of the men and women who now worked for Boyce secretly hoped that their boss would see sense and sell off his stalls, hopefully to themselves, for the twins had no interest in the stalls at all. They only wanted to use the people who owned them to fence their stolen goods and if they could get rid of Boyce, they would be able to bully individual stall owners to take on whatever they had to offer. Joe still had a great deal to learn, but he promised Mary that he would be very careful if offered anything from the Murphy twins, no matter how tempting the offer may be.

Joe went up to bed, but Mary stayed in the front room and poured herself a gin and tonic. She was worried about Joe and she had her suspicions that he had already been approached by the twins. She shook her head sadly, for all she could do was to pass on her brother's warning. The rest was up to Joe.

Chapter Six

E arly the following morning, the Murphy twins met in one of their lock-up garages to inspect the latest consignment of stolen clothes, paying off the foreman and his driver when they were satisfied.

'Shall I put half a dozen to one side for Joe Campbell?' asked Mick Murphy.

'Yeah, but we won't give them to him for a few days,' answered his brother Duggie. 'I want him to think we're doing him a big favour and besides, Boyce is away until Wednesday and he'll think we've lost our bottle when he finds out we haven't let Joe have any. Nobody knows about the first lot we let him have, but when we deliver this batch on Thursday or Friday, we'll make sure the whole bloody market knows about it.'

'And Boyce will be told in two minutes flat. One more nail in his coffin,' said Mick gleefully.

As the firstborn, Duggie was the bigger, the more cunning, the more dominant and the more vicious of the two. He would never allow any insult or slight, real or imaginary, to go unpunished and even Mick had felt the power of his brother's fists on more than one occasion. Mick was sure that if Bobby Boyce did not abdicate soon, Duggie would dethrone him – for good!

Little did the Murphy twins realise that the first part of that morning's operation had been under surveillance by a small team of detectives led by Detective Sergeant Stone. They had seen the foreman open the factory gates to allow a small van to enter and ten minutes later, the gates had opened again to allow the van to drive out, but instead of heading towards north London, it turned towards the East End. The unmarked police vehicle had been facing the wrong way and by sheer bad luck, a plodding horse-drawn milk cart prevented them from turning quickly enough to follow the van. A radio call to control with a description of the van and its registration number produced no results and as soon as the delivery was made to the Murphy twins' lock-up, the number plates were switched back to the original ones.

DS Stone now had the unenviable task of facing his superior to explain what had gone wrong. The young detective inspector, like so many of the high-flying university graduates who were being fast-tracked to early promotion, relied on his sergeant, who possessed a wealth of experience that could never be gained from a piece of paper that merely proved an examination had been passed. It was a practice observed throughout the force, for although a middle-aged sergeant may not be too bright, it would be a foolish superior who did not listen carefully when he ventured an opinion.

'Not to worry, John,' the inspector said genially, 'we got caught on the hop this time, but next week we'll arrange for two vehicles to be standing by, each facing in the opposite direction. I'll sort the overtime out with the chief super.' DS Stone nodded with satisfaction. Next Monday could not come soon enough for him.

Joe set out his stall that morning and waited for his delivery from the Murphy twins. At 10.00 a.m., one of Duggie Murphy's men carried a bundle of dresses to the stall next to him. Joe eagerly waited for his turn, but the man did not return. After half an hour, he walked over to the other stall. 'Was that Murphy's bloke here a little while ago?' he asked.

'Mind your own bloody business,' she snarled at him. 'Go on, piss off. Just because I gave you a bit of advice the other day doesn't mean to say you can poke your nose into my affairs.'

Joe turned a bright shade of red as he returned to his stall. 'Bloody hell, there was no need for that,' he muttered.

No delivery was forthcoming that day and although he made a nice profit for Bobby Boyce, Joe had not made the handsome earner he had anticipated for himself. Well, maybe tomorrow, he told himself as he packed away the stall.

Dickie was working on the middle shift from 2.00 p.m. until 10.00 p.m., known as the "Graveyard Shift" by the workers. For the many men who enjoyed a pint or two in the pub, it meant they could only have a drink before beginning a shift and all of them knew that once in the pub at eleven in the morning, the chances were that they would stay there until throwing-out time at three o'clock and lose a whole shift. The more determined drinker managed to dash to the nearest pub, which was the Church Elm, for last orders, but it was not the same as having a leisurely drink and a game of darts with his mates.

Dickie and Tommy Smith went straight home after their shift, with Dickie still being unable to complete his full task. He now managed three nuts and the cotton wool did help to some extent, but it just seemed to him that as soon as the next vehicle appeared on his section, it was gone again.

On the bus, he asked Tommy, 'Tell me straight, Tommy, is anything being said about me not being up to the job?'

Tommy looked uncomfortable. 'Well, I'm rather glad that you've brought it up yourself, Dickie, because Wally told me to pass the word to you that he can only give you to the end of the week and then he will have to report it to Walsh if you still can't keep up.'

'So then I'll be out on my ear?'

'You've still got the whole week and Wally told me that lots of men take as long as you, but make it in the end. Keep at it, mate, it'll be alright, you'll see.'

Dickie did not share Tommy's optimism. It was easy for him to say, for Tommy had adapted to a way of life that would claim him until the day he retired and he actually looked forward to when he could become a roving worker and, according to Wally, that day would not be far away, either.

Dickie said goodbye to Tommy when they got off the bus at the bottom of Heathway Hill and trudged slowly towards home. It seemed to him that every other member of his family was happy with this situation: Freda loved her job at May and Baker with her new friends, Gertie and Mrs Peake were as thick as thieves and young Jimmy had settled into his new school remarkably well, thanks to Reggie Godber. Even Joe seemed to have fallen on his feet when Bobby Boyce had recommended him as a lodger to his sister, but Dickie himself loathed the Ford factory and now it seemed likely that he may well even be sacked. Losing his job, however much he hated it, would be a calamity for the whole family and Dickie vowed he must try even harder on his next shift.

* * *

Earlier in the evening, Freda had confronted her youngest son.

'The answer is no!' she had told him firmly. 'No son of mine is going to climb into a boxing ring to have the sh… well, whatever, punched out of him.' Freda glared at her son. 'And don't tell me what Reggie bloody Godber says. I know that all the Ford workers' kids can join their boxing club, but you're not going to and that's that.'

Freda had looked across to her mother, expecting her support, but was dismayed when none was forthcoming. In fact, Gertie was in favour of boys being taught how to look after themselves and approved of the discipline that came with the teaching. Gertie felt sure that Dickie would feel the same way and that this was one argument her daughter couldn't win.

Gertie was proved right. After she had poured her husband a glass of brown ale, Freda broached the subject, making sure Dickie was aware of her objections, but Dickie ignored them completely.

'Good idea,' he said enthusiastically, 'it's the best thing for a kid of his age. I used to box when I was a kid and it never did me any harm.'

As far as Dickie was concerned, the matter was closed, but Freda went up to bed with a heavy heart and decided she would seek the advice of her fellow workers in the morning. Deep down, she knew that even though it was 1946, it was the man of the house who still had the final word. Her last thoughts as she drifted off to sleep were, I wonder if it will still be the same fifty years from now. I don't suppose I'll still be around in 1996, but I'd love to see if those buggers are still ruling the roost then.

In Camden Market, Tuesday and Wednesday had passed and Joe had still not received his goods from the Murphy twins. Bobby Boyce had paid him a visit as he was clearing away his stall on Wednesday evening and had been pleased with the profit Joe had made for him.

Boyce was confident that the Murphys had thought it prudent not to involve Joe in any of their shady dealings and his own position in the market was as strong as ever. It was not until Friday morning that the twins made their move. As soon as Joe set out his stall, Duggie Murphy strolled through the market with a bundle of coats in his arms and went straight to Joe's stall.

'Here you are, Joe, six top-of-the-range coats, just as you ordered.'

Joe winced, for he knew that every stallholder within earshot would have heard and seen the transaction, although there was nothing he could do about it now. He paid Duggie the agreed price and waited anxiously for the reaction from Bobby Boyce, for it was a certainty that somebody would be sure to let him know all about it.

Somebody did let Boyce know; in fact, it was more than one who dashed off eagerly to give him the news, but Boyce did not rant and rave as most of the stallholders had expected. Instead, Bobby Boyce was a worried man and felt he needed some time to plan his next move; if, indeed, he planned to make a move at all.

By the end of the day, Joe had sold all six coats and was feeling very pleased with the profit he had made for himself. He was surprised that Bobby had not been to see him and perhaps confront him about his dealings with the Murphy twins, but Joe believed he was only lining his pockets the way many of the other stallholders were doing. He fingered the pound notes in his pocket as he walked back to Mornington Crescent, happily calculating how much his post-office savings book would be swollen with this next deposit. The door to Mary's house was swung open by David, who had been waiting patiently for Joe, as he did every evening. David had grown very fond of Joe and Joe was equally happy to take the boy out for a walk or play games with him before their evening meal.

'Uncle Bobby's here to see us,' David told Joe, taking his hand to lead him inside.

Joe groaned inwardly, for he was convinced Bobby Boyce was only here to have a go at him about the coats, although he had not expected the confrontation to be at Mary's house.

Bobby Boyce greeted Joe quite warmly and did not mention anything about coats or the Murphy twins, and neither did he talk about the market at all. He accepted a large brandy from Mary and after they had eaten, he told them that he was thinking about taking a long holiday in Portugal.

'It's been all work, work and more work for years and it's time I took a long break,' he told them. 'Sammy Barnard is going to look after things while I'm away and he'll supply the gear and collect the takings at the end of the week. He knows the market like the back of his hand, so woe betide any silly bugger who tries to put one over on him.'

Joe felt that perhaps this was a subtle warning directed at himself, but Bobby Boyce had seemed affable enough as he'd made the statement.

After Boyce had left and David had gone to bed, Joe poured himself a glass of brown ale from the quart bottle he had bought on his way home, because, after all, he was a working man now and working men always enjoyed a glass of beer after work. Joe sensed that Mary had something on her mind and he did not have very long to wait before she voiced her concerns.

'What's going on in the market, Joe?' she asked him openly. 'I've never seen Bobby looking so stressed and jumpy and I could be wrong, but I have this feeling that somehow you're involved in whatever's bothering him.'

Joe looked her squarely in the eyes. 'When my mum and dad agreed that I could stay in Camden, I promised them that I would never do anything that would make them ashamed of me and I never will.' Joe did not consider that selling fake clothing was anything to be ashamed of. 'I've kept my word and I'll also give you my word as well. I will never sell stolen goods from my stall. Fair enough?'

Mary nodded. 'Fair enough, Joe, and I'm sorry to have even mentioned it.' Mary poured herself a small brandy. 'You must have noticed that Bobby has been, well, a bit edgy lately, Joe, and I can't help wondering about this holiday as well. He's not had a holiday for years, so why has he decided to take one now, all of a sudden? Something's going on, isn't it?' Mary finished her drink and poured another one.

'What is it, Joe? Have you any idea what's going on?'

Joe answered her as truthfully as he could. 'All I can tell you, Mary, is that the word around the market says the Murphy twins are trying to muscle in on Bobby's patch and it's not only Bobby who has to look out for himself. There's two or three others who are not sleeping too well these days, but I keep well out of it, 'cos it's bugger all to do with me.'

Mary had no alternative but to accept Joe's explanation, although she promised herself that she would pay a visit to Bobby's wife Maureen the next day. Maureen had never visited Mary's house in Mornington Crescent and she and David had only been to Maureen and Bobby's house in Muswell Hill on two occasions. Mary believed it was time her brother took a step back from trying to be the King of Camden Market and take early retirement, before he was retired permanently. She hoped that her sister-in-law would agree with her.

Saturday passed uneventfully, although it had been raining heavily for most of the day, which meant that the takings were well down from what was usually expected on a Saturday. Joe was about to give up for the day, when Duggie Murphy appeared.

'Hello, Joe, how's it going?' he said. Then, without waiting for a response, he continued, 'I've got a dozen more of those coats going spare on Monday. Are you up for them, or shall I put them out to someone else?'

Joe could see the pound note signs before his very eyes and quickly agreed to Duggie Murphy's terms, without so much as a secondthought.

Joe spent Saturday evening and all day Sunday in Dagenham and again took the last train back to Camden on the Sunday, rather than the first one out on Monday morning. Jimmy was a little disappointed, but Freda and Dickie made no comment, for they were just happy to see their eldest son at all. Joe was eager to take delivery of the Murphys' merchandise and could already envisage his post-office savings book swelling even further.

On Monday morning, Duggie said to his brother, 'Mick, sort out Joe's stuff and deliver it to him, I've got a bit of business to attend to.'

Mick Murphy did not question his brother. He had no idea what Duggie was up to and felt perhaps it was better to remain in blissful ignorance.

After leaving his brother, Duggie Murphy took a bus to Muswell Hill and then walked to the house where Bobby Boyce lived. He did not knock on the door or make his presence known in any way, but secreted himself between two large conifers in the driveway and waited for Boyce to emerge. Duggie was a patient man and his patience was rewarded less than half an hour later, when Boyce stepped out of the front door and opened his garage doors. Duggie then slipped into the garage behind him and thrust a gun into Boyce's back.

'You know what this is, Boyce,' he hissed, 'so don't fuck with me, just get in and drive. I'll tell you where.'

Strangely, Boyce felt almost relieved, for he knew that this moment had been inevitable, but now it had arrived, he was confident that he would be able to talk some sense into the younger man. With a little compromise here and there, Camden Market could still be big enough for both of them. Though sadly, he was mistaken, for Duggie Murphy was not prepared to share with anyone, not even his own brother, and certainly not with Bobby Boyce. He ordered Boyce to drive to the Surrey Docks, where he knew there would be no policeman on duty, as not one freighter was waiting to be loaded or unloaded. He instructed Boyce to park the car behind one of the warehouses and ordered him out of the vehicle at gun- point.

'This is it then, Bobby,' said Duggie, pointing his gun at the other man's groin.

Boyce almost doubled up as he held both of his hands over his private parts.

'Oh Christ, no, Duggie, there's no need for this,' he pleaded.

Duggie Murphy felt the adrenalin pumping through his veins as he watched Boyce squirming in front of him. He released the safety catch, knowing that just a gentle squeeze on the trigger would send Bobby Boyce into oblivion, or at least shatter his honeymoon tackle.

Boyce was now convinced that his last moment was upon him and stood shaking with fear, his head bowed almost in resignation, and Duggie savoured the moment. He had the power of life or death over another human being and the feeling was incredible. He had no intention of actually shooting Boyce, but he did intend to make sure that after today, Boyce's reign as King of Camden Market would be well and truly over.

'On your knees, you fucking arsehole,' snarled Duggie.

Boyce obeyed the order, now certain that Duggie intended to shoot him through the head and not his balls. Instead, Murphy undid his fly, took his penis from his trousers and urinated over Boyce's head. Boyce did not make a sound and neither did he make a move as he suffered a humiliation that no man should be made to endure. Murphy adjusted his clothing and then put the gun to Boyce's forehead.

'I could have fucking well blown you away, Boyce, so just remember that if you have any thoughts about coming after me. I could have blown your fucking head off, bunged you back in your car and then pushed it in the docks.' He suddenly lashed out at Boyce and caught him on the side of his face with the barrel of the gun, causing a 3 or 4 inch gash that immediately began to spurt blood.

'You're finished, Boyce. Fuck off back to Muswell Hill and stay there.'

Murphy got into Boyce's car and drove off, leaving the man still on his knees and in a state of shock. Bobby Boyce had truly believed he had been about to be killed and he knew that feeling would remain with him for the rest of his life and he felt a deep sense of shame that he had begged on his knees and allowed another man to piss all over him. He knew that Duggie Murphy would waste no time in telling the market traders how he had brought down Bobby Boyce and the gash to his face would serve as a reminder that the old King had been dethroned.

Boyce remained on his knees for several more minutes, his blood soaking into his jacket and mingling with the urine. His face would need to be stitched at the hospital, but there was no way he could present himself in this condition. Maureen couldn't drive, so he had little option but to try and make his way to the nearest telephone box and get some help from one of his associates. He knew many people would gloat over his downfall, but he also knew that never again would he set foot in Camden Market. The Murphys could have total control now, for Bobby Boyce had retired as from this moment.

Boyce picked himself up and walked unsteadily, until he came to a telephone box, where he called Sammy Barnard. Sammy arrived twenty minutes later, with an overcoat to cover Boyce's soiled suit, and drove him home to Muswell Hill. Sammy Barnard did not gloat, for he was also now out of a job himself.

Chapter Seven

In another part of London, Mick Murphy sat in one of the lock-up garages awaiting the arrival of the next van load of stolen goods. The van driver tooted the horn and Mick quickly opened the garage doors for the vehicle to enter, swiftly closing them behind it, without noticing two unmarked police cars that had cruised by and stopped at the end of the road.

Detective Sergeant Stone leaned from the passenger-seat window and spoke to the other driver. 'Turn around and park down the other end and depending on which direction they take, one of us will follow the van when it comes out and nick the foreman and his driver, but not until they're back over the water. Whichever one of us is left will try to follow the twins and nick them as soon as they make their first drop.'

The second car turned around and parked at the opposite end of the road. The garage was easily big enough to contain two or three cars or vans and DC Stone was positive that the Murphys were inside loading their own van ready for delivery.

Inside the garage, Mick Murphy was giving his driver instructions.

'Take the coats over to Joe Campbell's stall and the dresses to Flo on the stall next to him. Tell them me or Duggie will be around later and they can settle up with us then.'

A few minutes later, the garage doors opened and the van was driven out.

'Shit,' said the detective sergeant, when he saw the Murphy van leave the garage with only the driver inside. He had expected the Murphy twins to deliver the stolen goods themselves, but they must still be inside. He quickly made a decision. As well as the police driver, there were also another two detective constables in the vehicle.

'You and Baker follow Murphy's van and nick him and whoever he delivers to, but radio for a backup here. Tell HQ we need another car ASAP.' He elbowed the constable sitting next to him. 'Meadows, me and you, my son, are going after the Murphy twins.'

John Stone was feeling well pleased with himself, for he was expecting at least five or six arrests from this operation and he and Detective Constable Peter Meadows were left standing on the pavement as the unmarked police car sped after the Murphy van.

Mick had closed the doors behind the van, but less than two minutes later, he heard a knocking on the door. Thinking that his driver may have forgotten something, he opened the doors again, only to be confronted by Detective Sergeant Stone and another man.

'Hello, Micky,' said DS Stone, 'how nice to see you again. I haven't had the pleasure for ages.' He looked anxiously around the garage.

'So where's the bold Duggie then?'

'How the fuck should I know; I'm his brother, not his poxy keeper.' They heard the sound of sirens as a police car screeched to a halt outside the garage. 'I see the cavalry have arrived,' Micky grinned, knowing that he would likely be sent down for quite a while, but accepting his situation quite philosophically.

DS Stone was furious. He had been convinced that he would arrest both of the twins and the pair of them would be put away for three to five years, but there was no way either twin would grass on the other, so this one would have to do, at least for the time being.

He read Micky Murphy his rights, receiving the stock answer, 'I want my brief.'

Leaving the detective constable to stand guard over the garage, he put Micky Murphy into the backup car and drove to Kentish Town Police Station, where Micky would be formally charged with receiving stolen goods.

Joe Campbell was busy serving customers when the Murphy van driver approached him.

'Where do you want them, mate?' said the driver, his head barely visible over the pile of coats he was carrying. Like Joe, he was unaware that these coats were not copies at all and that they were the real thing.

'Can you put them on that rack over there?' said Joe, pointing to an empty rack that he had made ready for the delivery.

The driver neatly placed the coats on Joe's rack and then took another pile of dresses to the stall next to him, when two men appeared and presented warrant cards to Flo, the driver and Joe.

'I am Detective Constable Mussett and this is Detective Constable Lucas. I am arresting you on suspicion of handling stolen goods. You are not obliged to say anything unless you wish to do so but what you say may be taken down in writing and given in evidence.

Joe and the driver were stunned, but Flo had always known that the dresses she'd bought from the Murphys to sell on her stall were no fakes.

A large police van was sent for and then Flo, the driver, Joe, the coats and the dresses were taken to Kentish Town Police Station, where Micky Murphy, the clothing factory foreman and his driver were already sitting in the cells. Joe and the Murphy driver's protestation of their innocence had fallen on deaf ears and even though the main man Duggie Murphy had eluded him, DS Stone was pleased with this haul of "villains" that he had captured that day. His superior was also satisfied that his records would show that six arrests and convictions had been achieved through this operation, but, naturally, the detective inspector's report would indicate that he had been instrumental in bringing about the satisfactory conclusion of the operation.

Word of the arrests spread quickly around the market and later to Duggie Murphy, who was taking a liquid lunch in the Spread Eagle pub.

'Bollocks,' he told the barman, 'I don't fucking well need this right now,' but he did not elaborate.

The fact that his brother was in custody did not concern Duggie very much, for he knew Micky would keep his mouth shut and take the full rap. Unless someone grassed, there would be no actual proof that Duggie was involved and none of the people now in custody would dare to implicate Duggie Murphy, not even Joe Campbell, although Duggie could anticipate a possible problem with that young man. Micky would be advised to plead guilty, as would all the others, even his driver, but if Joe protested his innocence and the jury believed him, a judge would come down very harshly on anyone who had duped a poor, innocent lad into accepting stolen goods. Instead of three to five years, Micky's sentence would almost certainly be increased to five to seven. Duggie knew that Joe would not be interviewed or charged without one of his parents being present, so it was possible that his father could be persuaded that his son's best interests would be served if Joe pleaded guilty as charged; after all, he may just get away with probation and at least he would get away without his legs being broken.

Dickie left the house to begin the middle shift, when he spotted a police car being driven slowly along Heathway, the driver obviously looking for a certain house number. Dickie stood by his front gate, holding his breath as the car stopped in front of his house, and Dickie was aware that the front door had opened, because Gertie had also seen the police car from the window. The constable asked him if he was Richard Campbell and Dickie nodded without speaking. The constable then asked if he had a son called Joe. Dickie nodded again and walked back into the house, dreading the outcome of what was to come next, with the copper following behind.

Joe must have had an accident, was his first thought. Coppers don't come knocking on doors, unless something bad has happened.

His mind went blank when the constable informed him that Joe had been arrested, was in custody and that Dickie must accompany him to Kentish Town Police Station.

'Arrested!' exclaimed Gertie. 'Arrested for what?'

'I don't know, luv, I'm from Dagenham nick and all I've been told to do is to bring an adult relative to the station at Kentish Town, so that Joe Campbell can be questioned. I'm sorry, but that's all I know.'

Dickie had regained his composure and turning to Gertie, he said, 'Don't try and get in touch with Freda just yet, we may be able to get this sorted and get back before she even gets home.'

All the way to Kentish Town, Dickie's mind was in a whirl as he wondered what sort of a mess Joe had got himself into, but he was sure that Bobby Boyce must be involved in some way. The police driver was very much aware of his passenger's distress and wished him luck when they arrived at the police station. Dickie was surprised, but the gesture gave him some small degree of comfort. He was taken to an interview room and told that a Detective Sergeant Stone would be along to see him soon.

DS Stone was not in the best of moods, even though he had six people under arrest, for he wanted both of the twins, not just Micky, who could hardly be described as the brains of the outfit. Unless he could persuade one of the accomplices to give evidence against him, Duggie Murphy would walk away scot-free. Micky was saying nothing, as expected, and was talking to his solicitor at this very moment. The foreman was telling the usual story of meeting a man in a pub, who had offered to sell him top-of-the-range coats and dresses for a third of the cost, but insisted the man had not told him his name and neither had he asked.

'Honestly, Mr Stone,' he had told the sergeant, 'this was a one off. I've never done anything like this before and Christ knows what my old woman's going to say about it.'

He knew perfectly well what his wife would have to say about it. It was her that had egged him on to steal more and more goods, for she had greatly enjoyed spending the proceeds on luxury weekend breaks, where she could be pampered to her heart's content, or by treating herself and her sister to lavish meals in some posh restaurant or other. Now that was all finished and so was his job, for he would surely be sacked and sent to prison. Oh yes, his wife would have plenty to say to him and perhaps prison would not seem so bad after all, because at least it would give him a rest from her nagging tongue.

DS Stone considered the Murphy driver. He was known to the police as a petty criminal, mainly as a shoplifter or acting as a runner for one of the street-corner bookmakers. He had been discharged from the army, classified as having LMF, or "Lack of Moral Fibre". He was very close to being mentally defective and should never have been conscripted in the first place, but would certainly not be a reliable witness, even if he did agree to testify against Duggie Murphy, which was doubtful anyway. The detective sergeant believed his only hope of obtaining a conviction against the second twin was through young Joe Campbell. If Campbell could be persuaded to give evidence against the twins, DS Stone believed the lad would make an excellent witness, for he had an openness and honesty about him that would appeal to most jurors. Even the sergeant himself was convinced that the Murphy brothers, for reasons best known to themselves, had set Joe Campbell up, but that was no concern of his and he was now about to convince the boy's father that it would be in Joe's best possible interests to cooperate fully.

The sergeant ordered one of the constables to make a pot of tea, but when it arrived, he took it into the interview room himself. He placed the tray in front of Dickie and adopted his most sincere voice as he poured out two cups.

'Mr Campbell, your son has been arrested for receiving stolen clothing to sell on the stall he manages for Bobby Boyce.' He noticed the jerk from Dickie at the mention of Boyce's name. 'No, it has nothing to do with Boyce, at least not this time,' he assured Dickie. 'I have not charged Joe yet, because he claims that the Murphy twins offered him what they said were counterfeit copies of well-known brands of coats and he had no idea that they were stolen goods. I believe he is telling the truth, but there are five other people in custody, including one of the twins, who are all telling a different story. They claim that Joe knew all along that the coats he bought had been stolen. We have Micky Murphy in the cells, but his brother is still laughing up his sleeve at us.' The sergeant sipped his tea, but Dickie had not touched his. 'Mr Campbell,' the sergeant continued, 'we have enough evidence to convict every single one of them, but your son is not even fifteen yet and I would like to give him a chance, if he agrees, to testify against both of the twins in court.'

He paused as Dickie rolled himself a cigarette, realising that Joe's father was allowing himself time to consider his proposition. Dickie remembered Joe telling him that the Murphy twins were attempting to oust Bobby Boyce from the market and was well aware of their reputation, especially that of Duggie, and it was the most dangerous twin that had so far eluded this crafty copper. Dickie had no illusions about this Detective Sergeant Stone, for he knew the man would throw Joe to the wolves if it meant the conviction of both of the Murphys.

'Can I talk to Joe on my own for ten minutes? I want to find out for myself what's been going on,' asked Dickie.

DS Stone stood up. 'I'll go and fetch him, but if he was my son, I'd give him some good advice. Tell him to cooperate and agree to stand up in court and testify that both Murphys have sold him stolen goods, not just once, but several times, and you can take him back to Dagenham this very evening.' He looked long and hard at Dickie. 'You do realise that he won't be able to stay around here afterwards?'

Dickie made no reply and the sergeant left the room, returning a few minutes later with a very crestfallen-looking Joe. The sergeant left the room and Dickie rolled a cigarette, handing it to his son, who accepted it gratefully. Joe told his father the whole story and then implored, 'What do I do, Dad? That Stone bloke wants me to grass up the twins and says that if I don't, he's going to make sure I go to borstal.'

Dickie felt helpless. It was virtually carved in stone around the working-class areas of London, in the north, south, east and west, that you did not grass and if Joe did actually agree to be a witness for the prosecution, he would never dare to show his face around these parts ever again, and certainly Dagenham would not be far enough away to keep him safe from the wrath of the vengeful twins. Dickie also had to consider the safety of the rest of the family, who could also be at risk, for it would not be the first time that a petrol bomb had been hurled through the window of a suspected grass. Joe had been cruelly tricked by both Duggie and Micky Murphy, who had used him as part of their plan to oust Bobby Boyce, but Dickie sadly felt that his son would have to pay the price for his naivety and, it must be conceded, his greed. Even selling fake goods was illegal, not to mention taking advantage of unsuspecting customers, who believed they were getting a real bargain, but Dickie hugged his son as he gave him his opinion and Joe agreed without coaxing.

'At least I'll be able to hold my head up when I get out,' he said.

Both Dickie and his son's eyes were moist as they waited for the detective sergeant to return.

When the detective sergeant came back into the room, Dickie told him that Joe was prepared to admit to handling stolen goods, but would not name anyone else, and Dickie also requested that a duty solicitor be appointed, before Joe made any statement. DS Stone stormed from the room, slamming the door loudly behind him, but made sure Dickie and

Joe had to wait almost two hours before the solicitor arrived, a beautiful young woman, who introduced herself as Miss Bromhead.

After hearing Joe's story and the reason why he had been living apart from his parents, she told him, 'I cannot advise you to plead guilty to something you are clearly not guilty of, but, of course, the final decision is yours, although I think you should seriously consider the consequences. Most magistrates take the view that if there were no fences, there would be no thieves, and receiving is the offence you are to be charged with. You know, Joe, that even if you refuse to cooperate with DS Stone, you can still plead not guilty in court.'

'Nobody would believe him unless he dropped Duggie Murphy and the others in it,' said Dickie. 'His mind is made up, so is there anything you can do for him?'

Miss Bromhead looked doubtful. 'I will use his age and his gullibility in mitigation, but I have known DS Stone for a number of years and he can be very vindictive when someone crosses him.' She looked at Joe. 'He will inform the magistrate of your non-cooperation, but, as you intend to plead guilty, it won't really make much difference, for you will certainly be sent to borstal for training.'

'Is that definite, I mean, could he not just be put on probation?' asked Dickie.

'Not a chance, I'm afraid. The others will be sent for trial at Crown Court, because a magistrate can only impose a sentence of six months, but borstal is not considered to be a prison sentence.' She looked at Joe sadly. 'Joe, borstal is where you will be sent if you plead guilty.'

Joe gulped nervously, but met her gaze firmly. 'Then that's how it has to be.'

Dickie nodded his agreement and asked Miss Bromhead, 'What happens next?'

'Joe will be kept in custody overnight and will appear before the magistrates in the morning. If Joe was under fourteen, he would have been placed in care or even released on bail, but DS Stone will never agree to bail, although I will go through the motions of making an application.' She stood up. 'I will be at Seymour Place Magistrates Court by nine thirty in the morning, Mr Campbell, and I would like to spend a little time with you to go over Joe's background before we go in. I intend to stress the fact that your family were forced to leave Joe in Camden through no fault of your own, but I would be giving you false hope if I told you that there may be a chance of anything other than borstal for Joe.'

'Thank you for your honesty, Miss Bromhead,' Joe said, with a dignity far beyond his young years.

Miss Bromhead was greatly impressed with the young man and made one final effort to persuade him to change his mind. 'Joe, it's not only borstal that you are facing, you will also have a criminal record for the rest of your life. If you were to plead not guilty, I could tell the court that if you were to be released, you would leave Camden and go to live in Dagenham with the rest of your family and they may give you the benefit of the doubt altogether.'

Joe shook his head. 'I have to do it this way. I know it and my dad knows it.'

Joe knew that his dream of owning his own stall in Camden Market was over, at least for the foreseeable future, but he had no choice other than to accept the inevitable.

Miss Bromhead conceded, 'Alright, Joe, but it will be a formality, even though the magistrates are obliged to go through the motions of listening to my plea of mitigation. After sentence, you will be taken to the young offenders' wing in Wormwood Scrubs, before being taken to a borstal at least 100 miles from your home.' She glanced at the pale-faced Dickie. 'At least 100 miles, Mr Campbell, but quite often they place the trainees much further away than that to deter them from attempting to run away.' She turned to Joe again. 'It will be a minimum of nine months before you can be released on licence and the licence will last for a total of three years from the time of sentence. Not many get out in less than a year and the average is about fourteen or fifteen months.' Miss Bromhead stood and shook their hands. 'I will make the application for bail, but I don't believe in Santa Claus any more. I'll see you both in the morning.'

Almost as though he had been eavesdropping outside the door, DS Stone burst into the room, just as Dickie was handing his tin of tobacco and a box of matches to Joe.

'Oh no you don't,' snarled the sergeant. 'You get food and water, but bugger all else. No fags, no sweets, no poxy radio and no bloody newspaper to read, either. You made your choice, Campbell, andbelieve you me, I'll make sure you get what's coming to you.'

Dickie was seething, but knew that if he attempted to remonstrate with the bullying detective, it would make things even worse for his son. He managed to give Joe a reassuring pat on the arm as DS Stone led him back to the cells.

Dickie felt sick at heart as he walked towards Camden Town. He knew Freda, Gertie and Jimmy would be waiting anxiously for news and were probably expecting the head of the family to bring Joe back with him. As it was still quite early, Dickie decided to pay Mary Davis a visit, before facing his family. At one point, he had considered seeking out Duggie Murphy, but common sense told him that the villain would be surrounded by his thugs and having his own head kicked in would serve no purpose at all.

Mary Davis had heard the news about Joe's arrest and so had her son David, who had hardly stopped crying since he had returned from his day centre.

'I want my Joe,' he sobbed, and nothing Mary could say to him brought him any comfort.

When Dickie knocked on the door, David rushed to open it, for he was convinced that his best friend in the whole world had come back to be with them again. On seeing Joe's father, he demanded:

'Where's my Joe? I want my Joe.'

His mother calmed him and persuaded him to go to his room while she spoke to Dickie. He explained what had happened and added bitterly, 'I wish I'd never heard of Bobby Boyce, or you, for that matter.'

He was being unfair and knew it, although Mary accepted that Joe's father needed some sort of target to aim for. She made no effort to convince Dickie that her brother was not responsible for what had happened to Joe, but, instead, took a bottle of brandy from the cupboard and poured him a large measure. Earlier that afternoon, her sister-in-law had been to the house to tell her that something had happened to Bobby. She said Bobby had been brought home shaking almost uncontrollably with a deep gash to the side of his face and smelling terrible. Her sister-in-law told Mary that Bobby had spent over an hour in the shower before Sammy Barnard had driven him to the hospital to have his head stitched and then when he got back home, he had taken a whole bottle of brandy to bed and was still there.

Dickie accepted the brandy, for he was in desperate need of a stiff drink. The warmth of the brandy slowly mellowed him. 'I'm sorry, girl,' he told her. 'My Joe's going down for this and now I have to go home and tell the others. I know it's not your fault, but we should never have left him here on his own.'

He finished his drink and did not protest when Mary refilled his glass, pouring herself one at the same time.

'None of us could have expected this,' said Mary, 'but I don't think Bobby is involved; in fact, my sister-in-law told me this afternoon that she thinks he's finished in the market and that Duggie Murphy is now cock of the walk.'

Dickie nodded. From what Joe had told him, it would make sense, but it was Joe that he was concerned about, not who had control of a market he had no wish ever to see again.

'I'll ask Joe to write to you and David once things have settled down,' he promised Mary before he left. He called goodbye up the stairs to David, but the boy was too upset to answer.

Mary watched the forlorn figure trudge wearily down the road and then she went back inside to try to explain to David why Joe was no longer with them. Joe had been with them for such a short space of time, but he had brightened their lives more than she could ever have imagined and he had certainly left his mark.

'Oh Joe,' she whispered. 'You can never know how much we will miss you.'

Chapter Eight

Dickie did not remember very much of the journey back to Dagenham a surprise when he found himself getting off the train at Dagenham Heathway Station.

Freda put her hands to her mouth with horror when Dickie entered the house without Joe.

'Oh, Dickie,' she cried, but could say no more, before falling into his arms.

Gertie had been to the off-licence earlier to buy a bottle of whisky, certain that it would be needed later, hopefully to celebrate Joe's release, although it turned out that now it would be needed to try and ease the pain, for it was obvious that her grandson must be in deep trouble. Gertie poured them a large measure each and a teeny one for Jimmy, his being heavily drowned with lemonade. Gertie knew that Jimmy would be affected just as deeply as the rest of them by whatever was to happen and it was only right that he should not be left out of anything.

After Dickie had told them all that he could recall of the past few hours, Freda announced firmly, 'Right then, I'm coming with you in the morning. If Joe's going down, I'm going to be there to say goodbye.'

Jimmy was trying his best not to cry, but Gertie was sobbing openly.

'The whole family has to be there,' Gertie said. 'We'll all go together, the lot of us.'

Later that evening, Dickie walked round the corner to Tommy Smith's house. He explained the situation and asked Tommy to tell Mr Walsh that he would be back to work on Wednesday. Tommy felt very sorry for his workmate and offered him a glass of beer, but Dickie shook his head.

'No thanks, Tommy. I've already had two hefty measures of brandy from Joe's landlady and another triple scotch from Gertie. I'll need a clear head come tomorrow.'

Tommy shook his hand as Dickie left the house. 'Good luck to all of you, Dickie. I'll be thinking about you tomorrow.'

Dickie returned home and sat talking with Freda and Gertie, but Jimmy was already in his bed.

'I don't know about you two,' said Gertie, 'but I'm going to have a nightcap. I reckon I'll need something to see me off tonight.'

Dickie looked at Freda, who nodded her agreement.

'Go on then, Gertie,' Dickie said for the both of them, 'that last one you poured me has just about worn off by now. One more won't harm.'

They had a final drink and went to their beds, hoping that they would be able to rest, for tomorrow was likely to be a very long day.

In the police station at Kentish Town, Joe was going to have little to help station sergeant Gibbs to make sure that Joe Campbell was made as uncomfortable as possible, although regulations stipulated that all prisoners must be provided with meals at certain times of the day and a mug of cocoa before lights out.

'We have to feed and water the little bastard, but I want you to leave everything until it's stone cold.' The sergeant guffawed at the intended pun on his name. 'Everything, even his cocoa and his bowl of porridge in the morning, should all be as cold as a witch's tit.' He went to walk away and then spun round and jabbed his finger towards sergeant Gibbs. 'And another thing,' he snarled, 'none of your bleeding-heart shit with this one. Keep your fags and your bloody toffees on your desk and that goes for your Evening Standard as well.'

It was well known that sergeant Gibbs, an old-time copper, who was just a year or so away from retirement, was a soft touch as station sergeant and he always brought extra cigarettes to work with him, plus a half-pound bag of toffees, to share with the prisoners in his charge. He also brought two copies of the evening newspaper, one for himself and one for the prisoners to take turns at reading it. The constable disliked DS Stone intensely and was very much aware that the sergeant regarded him with contempt, for sergeant Gibbs had never once been commended during a career that had spanned over thirty years and neither had he ever requested to sit the examination that could have led to his promotion to sergeant.

As DS Stone left the custody area, sergeant Gibbs stuck two fingers up at the closing door and walked over to the cell that Joe was occupying. It was 7.00 p.m. and the ageing constable would be on duty until 9 o'clock the following morning. His shift began at six o'clock, but the fifteen-hour shift was seldom arduous and he could usually manage to nod off from time to time throughout the night. sergeant Gibbs was quite content to see out the remainder of his service as night station sergeant, because after one spell of duty, he then had two nights off.

All the prisoners including Joe Campbell were in their cells awaiting their first appearance at court, although the female stallholder known to the traders as Florence "Nightingale" had been granted bail after giving her real name as Florence Higgings.

Sergeant Gibbs had no intention of making things any more difficult than they were already for the young lad, especially when he opened the cell door to see Joe sitting on his bunk with tears streaming down his face. Joe turned away hurriedly and wiped his eyes, ashamed at being discovered at such a vulnerable moment.

'It's alright, lad,' the kindly constable told him, 'I've just come to tell you that I'll be bringing your dinner in soon. It's pease pudding with faggots tonight and I'll bring you a nice hot cup of tea to go with it.'

Joe had composed himself enough to respond to the constable, who he felt bore him no grudge, unlike the detective sergeant.

'Thanks, but I'm not really hungry,' he answered. 'A cup of tea would be nice though.'

'I'll bring it in anyway, because you never know, the sight and the smell may help to make you change your mind.'

The constable was right. Ignoring his sergeant's instructions, Constable Gibbs provided Joe with a piping-hot meal of pease pudding and faggots, together with a mug of scalding-hot tea. Joe had not eaten since earlier that morning and was suddenly ravenous.

Sergeant Gibbs smiled with satisfaction when he collected the empty plate some time later. Before he left the cell, he lit a cigarette and handed it to Joe.

'Flick the ash and the fag end down the bog,' he told Joe. 'There's no chain in here, but I'll flush it away later.'

All things come to an end and so, too, did the darkest night for Freda, Gertie and Dickie. The late-night drink had not helped very much and the only member of the Campbell family who had slept soundly was Jimmy. Gertie came down to make a pot of tea at five o'clock, with Freda and Dickie following her a few minutes later, for neither of them had been asleep. Dickie turned the radio on, although none of them took any notice of what was being broadcast, for it was as though they were just marking time until the hour they were to leave for the magistrate's court in London. Jimmy finally emerged at seven thirty to announce that he did not want to go with them.

'I didn't tell you yesterday, but me and Reggie Godber have been given permission to take the afternoon off, so that we can go to Ford's boxing club. They will be choosing the team to compete against Tate & Lyle in two weeks' time and our headmaster says we could be a credit to the whole school if we get into the team,' Jimmy appealed to his father. 'I feel really bad about Joe, Dad, but this is about me as well.'

Without consulting Dickie or Freda, Gertie interceded. 'You go off and do your best, Jimmy. Joe will be proud of you.'

Dickie did not hesitate. 'Your gran's right, son. There's no point in you missing out as well. You can tell us all about it when we get home.'

Some two hours later, Freda, Dickie and Gertie were sitting in the juvenile section of the magistrate's court waiting for Joe to be brought in. The three magistrates were already in their positions on the bench and Dickie studied the man in the middle, whom Miss Bromhead had told them was the senior member of the bench. Miss Bromhead said he would be the one who would do all the talking and that he would ultimately make the final decision. The man's face was implacable and gave Dickie no clue as to how he would view Joe's case.

Joe was brought in accompanied by Miss Bromhead, closely followed by Detective Sergeant Stone. Joe confirmed his name and address and then pleaded guilty to the charge presented by the clerk of the court that he had knowingly received stolen property.

DS Stone was called to the witness stand. He had written his report and each magistrate was given a copy, which they took several minutes to study. The senior magistrate finished first, taking off his glasses to polish them, while staring at Joe with obvious distaste. After his two colleagues had finished reading, he addressed the detective sergeant.

'I am sure you must feel extremely frustrated, Sergeant, that because this dishonest boy refuses to cooperate, a dangerous criminal is still at large.' He pointed an accusing finger at Joe and without bothering to consult the other two magistrates, told him, 'If I had my way, I would send you for trial with the rest of your gang of thieves, but the law decrees that I can only impose a sentence of borstal training and borstal training it shall be.' He motioned to the court attendant. 'Take him down.' Miss Bromhead stood to protest, but the magistrate refused to listen. 'I am not interested in any of your airy-fairy excuses and I will not waste any more of this court's time on this here ... scum.'

Both Dickie and Freda needed to restrain Gertie, who was about to rush towards the bench, but they were unable to prevent her from crying out loudly, 'Scum! Scum! How dare you say that about our Joe.'

The magistrate ignored her and left the courtroom, followed by his two colleagues.

Freda and Dickie could hardly take in what had happened; it had all been over so quickly. Dickie turned to Miss Bromhead. 'How can they do that without at least giving somebody a chance to say a few words on

Joe's behalf?' Dickie pleaded with the solicitor. 'Is there anything you can do? Can we appeal?'

'Joe pleaded guilty, so there can be no appeal and because he has not received a prison sentence, a plea of mitigation does not have to be heard, although most magistrates will usually at least go through the motions of hearing it through.'

Miss Bromhead considered that she had done her duty, but Joe and his father had ignored her advice and she had not been at all surprised at the outcome. The magistrates had probably read DS Stone's report before they had come into the court and had made up their minds before even setting eyes on Joe. It was not her fault and now she was eager to get back to her office, where she was working on a nice, juicy divorce case. She left a stunned Freda, Gertie and Dickie in the courtroom, wondering what they should do next. The duty constable of the court approached them. He had been appalled at the way Joe Campbell had been treated, but he did not consider it to be his place to comment on the rights and wrongs of the matter.

'Mr and Mrs Campbell,' he told them gently, 'I will take you down to see your son in a few minutes. You can only stay for ten minutes, but it may help all of you to get through these first few hours.'

Gertie sensed the compassion of the man. 'The solicitor told us that Joe will be taken to Wormwood Scrubs, is that right?'

'For a few days, yes, but he will be put in the young offenders' wing, so he will be kept well away from the hard-core villains.' The officer knew he was breaching confidentiality when he added, 'No magistrate can recommend how long a boy should stay in borstal and the parole board are not allowed to know why he has been sentenced, in case it may prejudice their decision. All they can consider is the reports from the instructors and the principal, so if your son keeps his head down and his nose clean, he could be back with you in next to no time.'

'But not less than a year though,' Freda sad bitterly.

'No, not less than a year,' answered the officer sadly.

He led all three of them to the basement and showed them into a small room that only had two chairs. The officer would be in serious trouble if his superiors discovered that he had allowed three members of the family to see a prisoner, for regulations stipulated that only one was allowed. He was a family man himself, but in this job he was well used to dealing with dysfunctional families, who considered themselves to be a law unto themselves. He had read the report from the detective sergeant and he was convinced that the Campbells had not been treated fairly at all and this was definitely not a dysfunctional family.

'I'll bring Joe in and then I'll wait outside to give you a little privacy,' he told them.

Joe had steeled himself for when he would come face-to-face with his family before being sent to prison, but he was determined to be strong, so that it would not make things worse for his mother and his gran.

'I think that old git of a magistrate would like to have thrown away the key,' were his first words as he entered the room.

His somewhat feeble attempt to sound cheerful fooled nobody.

Gertie was crying quietly, although Freda did manage to keep her composure. There would be time enough for her to let go later and she knew that once she did, she would take some stopping.

Dickie was full of admiration for his son, for Joe had not flinched when the sentence had been passed and even now, he was still holding himself together. Dickie patted his son on the shoulder.

'I'm proud of you, Joe.'

It was almost unbearable for Joe and he knew he must end this painful parting before he broke down completely. He hugged his mother, his gran and his father and then left the room, before they could see the tears that were blinding him. The duty constable pretended not to notice as he led Joe back to the cell to await transport to the London prison called Wormwood Scrubs.

Dickie decided he would go to Mary Davis' house to break the news to her and he desperately felt the need to meet up with Alf Spinks, so he could have a drink with him. Freda and Gertie made their way back to Dagenham, steeling themselves to break the news to Jimmy that he would not be seeing his brother for some considerable time. Miss Bromhead had already told them that children under the age of twelve were not permitted to visit prisoners, unless they were offspring.

David was still at his daycare centre when Dickie arrived at Mornington Crescent, so he was at least spared the distress that he knew Mary would have to cope with when David returned.

'I have tried to tell him, but he just refuses to accept that Joe will not be coming home again,' Mary told Dickie as she poured him a glass of brandy. 'I think it would help if Joe could write to us, at least David would know that Joe has not forgotten about him.'

'He will, don't worry,' Dickie assured her. 'Joe thinks the world of your son and he'll do everything he can to let him know how much he cares.'

Dickie left the house and made his way to the Spread Eagle, where he was greeted by several regulars, who commiserated with him. Alf Spinks came in half an hour later and embraced his old friend.

'What can I say, me old mucker,' Alf said, 'what can I say?'

'Not a lot, Alf, not a lot, but thanks anyway.'

Alf told Dickie about the rumours that had been spreading about Bobby Boyce, including the known fact that Duggie Murphy was now the king of the market.

'I've heard that Duggie put a gun to Boyce's head, forced him to his knees and then pissed all over him,' Alf said with some relish.

Dickie was shocked. 'So how the fuck did my Joe got mixed up in all this?'

Alf shrugged. 'Beats the shit out of me, Dickie. I can only assume that they used Joe as extra insurance and don't forget, Micky Murphy will be banged away for a fair time as well.' Alf ordered another pint of beer for them. 'I think your Joe was in the wrong place at the wrong time and that's all there is to it.'

Dickie was reluctantly forced to accept that there had been no conspiracy by Bobby Boyce to frame his son and that the greed of human nature had been the real instigator of Joe's present plight. He had one more pint of beer and then took the train back to Dagenham.

He was greeted with a mixture of sadness and excitement when he entered the house, for Jimmy had been selected to box in the tournament on Saturday week against one of the sons of the Tate & Lyle factory workers. Part of Jimmy felt guilty at his excitement while his brother was behind bars, but he was just a boy and boys usually only think of themselves.

His father understood though, saying, 'Well done, Jimmy, go and win this one for your brother.'

Freda snorted and left the room. She had no intention of watching her youngest son being beaten up by some thug from Canning Town.

'Me and your dad will be there to cheer you on, Jimmy,' Gertie told him and Dickie nodded his encouragement.

Jimmy felt excited but also a little scared at the same time and he had asked Reggie Godber if he ever felt afraid before a contest.

'Listen, Jimmy,' Reggie had replied, 'anyone who says he's not afraid before they climb into the ring is a bloody liar. The funny thing is though, as soon as the first bell rings, you're not scared any more.

'I've had five fights now and I lost the first one by a mile, but it didn't put me off. You and me are different weights and to be honest with you, I'm glad I won't have to come up against you. Everyone who's seen you sparring knows you're a natural, so when you get into that ring on Saturday, just think of the other bloke as a sparring partner.'

This was the voice of a seasoned boxer, so Jimmy hoped that Reggie was being told the truth, but he would find out soon enough.

The next few days passed slowly and a daily telephone call to the prison produced no results, because it appeared that a place could not immediately be found for Joe in a borstal. Freda and Dickie were on tenterhooks and could hardly imagine what it must be like for their son, but after Dickie had insisted on speaking to the prison governor personally, he was told that if Joe was still being held in Wormwood Scrubs by the weekend, they would be allowed to visit him on Sunday afternoon. It was better than nothing, but the name and the reputation of the prison and the thought of their respective son, grandson and brother being incarcerated in such a place brought fear and horror to the whole of Joe's family.

Dickie had gone back to work on the Wednesday and so had Freda, while Gertie went to the over-sixties club with Ada and Jimmy carried on as usual. Apart from Jimmy, it was as though they were simply going through the motions and marking time, until they were told where Joe would spend the next year or so of his life and how often they would be able to visit him.

Chapter Nine

As it turned out, Joe only spent a few days in Wormwood Scrubs, because on the Friday, he was called into the governor's office and informed that he was to be sent to a borstal in Loughton, Essex. The governor had been impressed with the lad's maturity and dignity and after reading the court report, he believed Joe Campbell had been duped, although it was too late now to do anything about it. He invited Joe to sit and told him, 'I happen to know the governor of Loughton borstal and I've already put in a few good words for you, but before you leave here, let me give you a few words of advice.' He offered Joe a cigarette, which Joe accepted with surprise and the pair of them lit up. 'Loughton is not very far from Dagenham and the only reason they are sending you there is because I have given my opinion to the Home Office that you will not attempt to abscond. You are to be transferred this afternoon, but make no mistake about this, Joe, if you do do a runner, you will be caught and the next place they'll put you will be in the Outer Hebrides.'

Joe was grateful to the governor and responded accordingly. 'I understand, sir, but I have no intention of being a nuisance to anyone. I just want to do my time and go home to my family.'

In fact, the few days Joe had spent in Wormwood Scrubs had not been as traumatic as he had feared. The officers assigned to the young prisoners' wing were mainly elderly, or those on light duties, for the youngsters rarely gave them any trouble, unlike the hardened criminals in the main prison. The officers were happy to be assigned to the wing and usually treated their young charges benevolently, bringing in books and magazines and giving them the occasional cigarette. Even so, Joe would be glad to get out of this place; at least he would be able to be out in the fresh air once he was at the borstal.

He shuddered when he thought of the men who had been sentenced to ten years, or even life imprisonment, that had to serve their sentences in places such as this. One of the young prisoners had been sentenced to life imprisonment for murder when he was just 12 years of age and would remain in the Wormwood Scrubs young prisoners' wing until he reached the age of twenty-one, when he would be transferred to a main prison. Joe had attempted to talk with the boy, who was still only sixteen, but the boy was already morose and withdrawn and did not communicate with anybody.

One of the officers told Joe, 'Gerry Maker has not had one visitor since he was sentenced and it's as though he doesn't exist any more.'

Joe was sickened and ashamed that this so-called civilised society could treat young people in such a fashion, regardless of the crime they may have committed.

On the Ford production line, Dickie had finally managed to tighten all four nuts to the car seat, but occasionally he still missed the last one, although at least his job was safe. Dickie always packed his ears with cotton wool before entering the line area, but Tommy Smith appeared to be oblivious to the cacophony of noise that surrounded them. What impressed Dickie even more was the way Tommy leapt from the vehicle in which he was working long before it had reached the next section and actually found time to roll himself a cigarette before the next car arrived in his section. The team leader, One-eyed Wally, had drawn the foreman's attention to Tommy and although Mr Walsh considered Tommy Smith to be too big for his boots, he recognised that the man would be an invaluable member of his section and promoted Tommy to relief worker.

Dickie not only marvelled at Tommy's prowess, but he was also amazed that Tommy actually enjoyed the job. The only thing that Dickie enjoyed was picking up his pay packet at the end of each week.

Dickie hated everything about the Ford factory. He hated the infernal noise that seemed to penetrate every bone in his body, he hated the hours he was required to work and he hated the lack of human contact, for it was impossible to hold a conversation while working on the production line. Even during the rest break, most of the men were reluctant to engage in any form of interaction, they just wanted to spend their half-hour away from the line in peace and solitude. Next week, Dickie would be working the night shift from 10.00 p.m. until six o'clock the next morning and only during the war had Dickie ever worked through the night. It was something that he was not looking forward to at all.

Freda was grateful for the support she was receiving from her friends at the May and Baker factory, for none had been judgemental. Many of them knew they could easily have been in the same position, for their own sons and husbands often sailed very close to the wind. Freda had also become close to a woman around her own age, who had two children, although they were both girls, aged fourteen and fifteen. Amy Ashby lived in one of the cul-de-sacs the locals called "banjos", but the borough council preferred to refer to them as "Gardens" and Amy's house was in Eastfield Gardens, just off Heathway. Amy Ashby and her family had moved to Dagenham in similar circumstances to the Campbells, as they, too, had been the victims of German bombs, but sadly both of Amy's parents had been killed during a heavy raid in 1942, when their home had been razed to the ground. Amy and the girls had been evacuated to Somerset a year previously and Amy's husband, who was a fireman, had been miles away on duty when the bomb had destroyed their home.

Most of the women Freda worked with told tales of the war years, but the stories were almost always hilarious, for nobody wanted to relive the horrors and the tragedies that most of them had witnessed and endured, which meant Freda was not allowed to wallow in her misery over Joe and it would prove to be her salvation.

On that same Friday a letter, boldly stamped "HMPS" on the reverse, addressed to Mr R. Campbell was delivered to the house.

The postman knew "HMPS" meant that the letter had been sent from His Majesty's Prison Service. Aye, Aye, another jail bird, he said to himself as he held the letter up to the light, hoping to see its contents.

'Piss off, you nosy bugger,' said Gertie, who had watched him from the window, and she snatched the letter from the postman's hand as she rushed out of the front door.

She handed the letter to Dickie, who read it and then handed it back for her to read. It was to inform them that Joe would serve his sentence of borstal training in a place called Loughton and that he would be transferred that afternoon.

'Never heard of it, but at least it's in Essex, so it can't be all that far away,' said Dickie.

A couple of visitor's passes had been included in the letter and to Gertie's dismay, they were for the following Saturday afternoon, the day of Jimmy's first boxing contest.

'You and Freda must go to see Joe.' Gertie had almost read Dickie's mind. 'I'll go to cheer Jimmy on and with a bit of luck, you might get back in time to see him box as well.'

Dickie put on his coat to go to work. 'Thanks, Gertie, but unless Jimmy is last on the bill, I can't see us getting back in time.'

Dickie left the house and Gertie was having a cup of tea with Ada Peake from next door, when a knock was heard at the door.

'Is Dickie Campbell at home?' enquired a tidily dressed man politely.

Gertie told him that Dickie had left for work and would not be home until around ten thirty that evening.

'Would you please tell him that Jack Doyle from the council depot called and that there is a vacancy on one of our dustcarts. If he is still interested, will you ask him to come and see me in the morning?'

Gertie thanked the man and closed the door thoughtfully. 'This could put the cat among the pigeons,' she told Ada. 'I don't know how much dustmen earn, but it can't be anywhere near as much as a Ford worker.'

'Do think your Freda will try to talk him out of it?' asked Ada.

'Probably, but Dickie has always worked in the open air and that factory will be the death of him if he has to stay there for much longer.'

Ada left and Gertie prepared the evening meal for when Jimmy and Freda came home. Gertie knew that Freda had been extremely worried about Dickie, although she seemed to think that her husband was gradually becoming used to working inside the factory.

But Gertie knew otherwise. Even though her son-in-law had been a proud man when he had received the largest pay packet of his entire working life, she had a strong feeling that Freda would not be happy if Dickie's future pay packets would be almost halved.

Jimmy came home from school, grabbed a thick slice of bread and jam and then went out again to play with Reggie. Gertie made Freda a cup of tea when she came in and then told her of Jack Doyle's visit, but Freda made no comment for several minutes and Gertie did not press her.

Eventually, Freda told her mother, 'I wish to Christ that council bloke had forgotten all about Dickie. I think he would have settled in at

Ford's and if this job had come up in a few weeks time, Dickie would have turned it down.'

'No he wouldn't,' said Gertie almost angrily. 'Dickie is like a caged songbird in that place and deep down, you know it.'

'We can't afford for him to take a job on the dustcarts, not if we want to make a decent home for ourselves.' Freda was almost crying with frustration. 'I'm not going to tell him about it and neither will you.'

Gertie was shocked. 'I can't believe you're saying such a thing.'

'Don't start preaching at me, Mum. If Dickie leaves Ford's, it will be years before I can get the things I want, even with me working.' Freda's face was red and she was breathing heavily.

Gertie attempted to placate her daughter. 'I do know how you feel, Freda, but there are more important things in life than carpets and furniture.'

Freda sighed. She felt ashamed at herself, but also frustrated that her high hopes seemed likely to be dashed. 'I know you're right, Mum,' she admitted. 'I'll tell Dickie as soon as he gets in, but I wouldn't mind betting that he'll be round that depot before it's even open in the morning.'

Gertie went up to her bed before Dickie returned from work, for she had no intention of being drawn into any confrontation that she suspected would ensue. Freda was not going to sit meekly by without a struggle and let her husband give up the highest-paid job in the county.

Dickie almost dropped his mug of tea that Freda had made him when she told him of the council foreman's visit. He opened his mouth to speak and then closed it again when he saw the look upon Freda's face. Dickie had been about to tell his wife how relieved he was that he would be able to get out of that hell hole of a factory, but he knew Freda did not share his feelings. He was not sure just how much a dustman earned in a week, but he knew, without a doubt, that it would be nothing like as much as a Ford worker and Freda would know it as well.

Dickie sipped his tea and attempted to explain how he felt. 'At first, I thought it was just the noise that was unbearable, but it's more than that. It's so bloody lonely not having anyone to talk to and that conveyor belt just creeps forwards, on and on, hour after bloody hour.' He rolled himself a cigarette and then went to the sideboard to pour himself a glass of whisky. He kept his back turned away from Freda. 'I'll never get used to it, never in 100 years. Some men, like Tommy Smith, for instance, are born to it, but I'm not Tommy Smith.' He turned to face her. 'I might as well tell you now, Freda.

'I'm going down the council depot first thing in the morning and I'm going to take up Jack Doyle's offer of the dustman's job. Jack told me the binmen usually get finished early, so I might be able to find a sideline somewhere to try and make up a few extra bob.'

Freda was not surprised, although she felt hurt that Dickie had not even asked her for her opinion.

'Well, there's nothing else to be said then, is there?' she said huffily and went to bed.

Dickie did not feel guilty at all and neither did he feel selfish, for he truly believed that his sanity would be in jeopardy should he be forced to remain in that factory and he was sure he would be able find something extra to supplement his wage packet.

That night, Joe was lying awake in a dormitory, where he had been placed with seven other boys after being driven to Loughton borstal, handcuffed to another boy and accompanied by two prison officers.

On arrival, they were given their uniforms and then presented to the governor, who gave them his standard lecture. 'You scratch my back and I'll scratch yours,' and 'You can do it the hard way, or you can do it my way, it's up to you.' The governor also emphasised that any attempt to abscond would result in them being sent to another centre at least 200 miles away.

Joe had not been too keen on the boy he been handcuffed to. He had not spoken to Joe and neither had he responded to Joe's greeting when they'd first met, so Joe was quite relieved to discover they would not be sharing the same dormitory. After the governor's lecture, they were taken to their respective dormitories and told to wait there until the other boys came in from work. Each dormitory was headed by a leader and when he had been in Wormwood Scrubs, Joe had heard some scary stories about how much power a dormitory leader could hold over the other boys. He prayed that the one he would soon be meeting would not prove to be some petty tyrant.

His fears had proved to be groundless. The clatter of running feet had alerted Joe to the fact that work was over for the day and the door had burst open to allow half a dozen boys of all shapes and sizes to rush in. They stopped when they saw Joe and one of them approached him warily, as though sizing him up.

'I was told you were on your way.' The boy had made no attempt to shake hands with Joe. 'My name is Kevin Cole and I am the dormitory leader. Come and meet the others.'

He introduced them one by one, but none of them had offered to shake hands with Joe, so he assumed that they were bound to be a bit wary until they got to know him.

Lying in his bed and almost ready to drop off to sleep, Joe felt reasonably content with his situation. The dormitory leader was nothing like he had been dreading and, in fact, after their initial meeting, he had been quite friendly and helpful. Joe could feel the other boys mellowing towards him after just a few hours, although Joe did not recognise that this was because he was neither loud nor brash and because none of them felt threatened by his presence. His final comforting thought was that it would not be too long before he received his first visit.

Dickie had been aware of Freda getting up and leaving for work and knew that Gertie was also up and about. He heard Jimmy complaining that he was still tired when his gran ordered him from his bed, but Dickie stayed under the covers until he was sure that only Gertie was downstairs. Dickie had stayed up until almost 2.00 a.m. and the whisky bottle had suffered severely. Now it was his head that was suffering.

Gertie poured a mug of tea when he came into the kitchen and handed it to him without speaking.

'So are you going to give me a hard time as well, Gertie?' said Dickie.

'That's not fair, Dickie. I buggered off to bed early last night, 'cos I didn't want to get involved and I'm not getting involved now, either. It's got sod all to do with me.'

Dickie knew she was right. 'Yeah, sorry, Gertie, I didn't mean anything by it.'

Gertie accepted the apology. 'I know you didn't. Just get yourself down to that council depot and do what you think is best for all of you in the long run.'

As manager, Jack Doyle did not need to be at work as early as the binmen or the road sweepers and he had hardly taken off his jacket when Dickie walked into his office.

Jack greeted him warmly and offered him a seat. He was genuinely glad to see the man, for he prided himself on being a good judge of character and he was convinced this man would prove to be a conscientious and reliable member of his workforce.

When he told Dickie about the wages he would receive, Dickie was a little surprised, for although they were much lower than Ford's, the pay was not as low as he had thought it might have been. Even so, Dickie would still need to find a part-time job if he was to keep Freda happy. Jack told him that he would be joining a gang of five other men, including the driver and the "ganger", who was in charge.

'They are a great bunch of lads and you'll not go far wrong in their team,' Jack told Dickie. 'The ganger's name is John Townsend and he's been with us for over twenty years. His gang are always the first to leave the depot in the morning and the first to arrive back in the afternoon. I have never heard a word of complaint against them, so that's fine with me.' Jack leaned back in his chair to study Dickie.

'How do you feel about the job, Dickie? I mean, will you be able to cope with giving up your Ford's pay packet?'

Dickie smiled ruefully. 'It will be my missus who will miss it more than I will, but I want this job more than anything and I'll try to get something on the side to bring in an extra few bob and keep her off my back.'

Jack nodded. 'Have a word with John about that. He does quite a bit of building work and often needs a labourer to give him a hand. I know for a fact that he's starting a fair-sized job soon and he's looking for a mate. If you're interested, I'll tell him when he comes in, so that he'll not bother to look for anyone else.'

Dickie expressed his gratitude to the man who had gone out of his way to help him escape from the prison that Dickie now also called the Hell Hole when referring to the Ford factory. He agreed to start work on the following Monday and would report to the depot at 7.00 a.m. Jack Doyle took him to the clothing store, where he was issued with a strong pair of boots and two pairs of overalls. Dickie shook hands with Jack Doyle and then went home to get ready for his last shift, for he intended to tell his foreman that he was finishing after this shift. He knew that Freda would be furious that he was leaving before even finishing the week out, but one more shift was all Dickie felt he could manage.

Gertie was heartened to see how excited and happy her son-in-law appeared to be when he told her the news.

'And there's a good chance of earning some extra by working for the ganger as his labourer,' he told her, his eyes shining more brightly than Gertie had seen for a long time.

Dickie met Tommy Smith at the bus stop later that day, but felt somewhat disappointed at Tommy's lack of enthusiasm when he heard Dickie's news.

'If you ask me, you've not given Ford's much of a chance,' was Tommy's response. 'I reckon that in a couple of weeks, you'll be just like an old hand. Why don't you give it a bit longer?'

Dickie shook his head firmly, but did not answer.

Mr Walsh was not in the least bit surprised when Dickie told him that he intended to leave. He had privately told the team leader Wally that Dickie Campbell would not last the pace, although he admired the man's tenacity for having stuck at it for this long. Mr Walsh had known many men to crumble and desert their positions within hours of being left on the assembly line, but this man was prepared to work one last shift and that took courage.

Freda returned from work, hoping that her husband may have changed his mind about leaving his well-paid job at Ford's and she looked enquiringly at her mother when she walked through the door.

'He starts on Monday,' Gertie told her, before walking into the kitchen to make some tea.

Freda bit her lip and followed her mother, immediately spotting Dickys overalls and hobnailed boots. It was the last straw.

'Oh Christ Almighty, don't tell me, he's going to leave the house every day wearing that bloody lot, is he?' She was weeping with a mixture of frustration, anger and distress. 'Everybody will know that he's a dustman,' she sobbed. 'What will the neighbours think?'

'Sod the neighbours,' Gertie said predictably. 'It's an honest job and if you have any sense, my girl, you will say and do nothing to make Dickie believe you're ashamed of him.'

Freda reacted angrily. 'You're always taking his side against mine and it's not only me there is to think about. How do you expect Jimmy will feel when he has to tell his mates that his dad is a binman? Most of the kids in his school have dads that work at Ford's and Jimmy was proud that his dad worked there as well.'

'That's where you're wrong, love,' Gertie told her daughter. 'Jimmy knew that his dad was going after the job with the council and he told me before he went to school that he hoped he would get it.

'Jimmy told me all he wanted was to see his dad smile again, because he knew he was unhappy working inside that place. Jimmy was right and you know it. When was the last time you saw Dickie smile, I mean really smile?'

'There's not exactly been very much to smile about recently, has there?'

'No, that's true enough,' Gertie conceded, 'but even without Joe's disaster, I doubt if Norman Wisdom could have drawn a chuckle out of Dickie right now.'

Freda slumped back in her chair. She knew her mother was right – her mother usually was.

'By the way, Dickie said there was a good chance of getting some part-time work with one the blokes who does some building work on the side,' Gertie told her daughter. 'At least that may help a bit.'

'It might, I suppose.' Freda brightened a little. 'Anyway, I promise not to make a fuss about it when he comes home.'

Gertie hugged Freda. 'That's the way, good for you, girl.'

On Saturday morning, Jimmy and Reggie went to the cinema on Heathway to see the Saturday morning pictures. Jimmy sat through the whole show, including the main film that featured the cowboy Tom Mix, although he could hardly remember a thing about it afterwards. His mind was on the boxing match that lay ahead of him that evening, although he could not help but notice that Reggie's concentration was fully occupied with the adventure that was being screened. Reggie cheered at the top of his voice whenever Tom Mix appeared on his white horse and booed just as loudly when the baddy came on the screen riding the inevitable black horse. At that moment, Jimmy almost wished he had never heard of Ford's and their boxing club and he had half-hoped that now his father was no longer employed by the car company, he would not be eligible to box for them. But this was not the case, for the trainer had told Jimmy that once a boy had been accepted, he could stay on as long as he liked.

His father had promised Jimmy that he would try his best to get back in time to see him box and the trainer, who knew all about Joe, had told Dickie that he would make sure that Jimmy's bout in the ring would be put off for as long as possible. Jimmy knew that it was important for his parents to go to visit his brother, but he did so badly want his father to watch his first contest and even though his gran would be there to cheer him on, it wouldn't be the same without his dad.

The film ended and Jimmy and Reggie left the cinema and headed for the pie-and-mash shop on the other side of the hill.

Gertie had given Jimmy some money to buy them both a double helping, a rare treat for Reggie, who had five brothers and a sisters, and even as a Ford worker, his father's wage packet did not often stretch to pie and mash.

'Double pie, double mash twice and two jugs of liquor,' Jimmy announced, slapping a half-crown piece on the counter. 'And make it snappy,' he added cheekily.

'Less of your old lip, you saucy sod,' retorted the assistant, giving them both an extra dollop of mash.

They sat at a table near the door and poured the green liquid over their plates, sniffing appreciatively.

'Lovely grub,' said Jimmy with relish, to which Reggie agreed wholeheartedly.

They had only eaten a few spoonfuls, when Reggie told Jimmy, 'Make the most of this, 'cos you can't have anything else to eat until after the fight.'

Jimmy threw his spoon down with disgust. 'Thank you very much, I'm sure. Here I am, just tucking in, and you have to go and remind me that in a few hours time, I'm likely to get my head bashed in. You've just put me right off my grub.'

Jimmy was not put off for very long though, and thirty seconds later, he was matching Reggie spoonful for spoonful.

As they ate their meal, Reggie regarded Jimmy thoughtfully and tried to remember how he had felt before his first contest. He was sure he had not been as edgy as Jimmy appeared to be, but that was probably because his father had encouraged him and his three brothers to box each other in the back garden and his elder brother had punched far harder than any boy he had boxed so far.

On the way home, Reggie said to his friend, 'You don't have to go tonight, Jimmy. Boxing's not for everyone and if you don't fancy it, forget about it.'

Jimmy shook his head. 'No, I'll be there and I'll certainly give it a go. I might be shitting myself now, but I'll turn up.'

The two boys fell about laughing, for Reggie had never heard Jimmy swear before, although Reggie used that word and several other stronger ones on a regular basis.

Chapter Ten

Freda and Dickie left for Loughton before their youngest son had returned home from the cinema. They needed to take the District line from Dagenham Heathway to Mile End and then change to the Central line for Loughton. The borstal was just a ten-minute walk from the station and they realised for the first time that the family had been fortunate that Joe had been placed so close to Dagenham, for the journey took little more than an hour. Husband and wife spoke little during the journey, as they were both engrossed in their own thoughts, but there was no acrimony between them any longer, because their differences had been resolved days ago and so the silence was quite a comfortable one.

They were dismayed when they were shown into a room, where dozens of other parents were waiting to greet their sons; twelve small tables with three chairs for each one were placed in such a way that very little privacy would be afforded to any of them. Freda drew Dickie's attention to a notice on each of the four walls, which spelled out the visiting rules. Cigarettes could be smoked during the visit, but not one single one of them could be taken from the room by a trainee, alcohol was strictly forbidden, no money could change hands and confectionery and cakes must be left in a parcel or a small box, to be inspected by one of the officers before being handed over to the trainee.

'Trainee,' said Freda. 'What the bloody hell are they training Joe to be?'

Some of the parents knew each other from previous visits and chatted together while they waited for their sons to be brought in.

The door opened and a dozen boys filed in, accompanied by four men, who were wearing identification badges but were not in uniform. Each boy looked identical in their grey trousers, white shirt and red jumpers and their hair was cropped to regulation length that made Freda gasp in dismay when she saw Joe, for his once-lovely blond, flowing locks had been reduced to a half-inch of stubble.

Dickie patted his son's hair and attempted to make light of it, although he, too, had been taken aback. He could understand the boys having to wear what amounted to a uniform, but the haircut worn by Joe and the rest of the boys was the same as the one he had endured when he had first joined the army.

'Sod me, Joe, you look like a shorn sheep.'

Joe laughed. 'I think they do it like this, so that if any of us do a runner, we'd be spotted a mile away.'

Freda placed a packet of Senior Service on the table. 'Your gran sent these for you, Joe, and she sends you her love. Me and your dad have brought you a few things and Jimmy put a bar of chocolate in as well, but we had to leave them at reception.'

'Thanks, Mum, and tell me gran and Jimmy thanks as well.' Joe took a cigarette from the packet and gave one to his father and they both lit up.

'Jimmy has his first fight tonight, Dad,' said Joe, 'how's he facing up to it?'

'It's not a fight, it's a boxing contest,' protested Freda.

'It's a bleeding fight, whichever way you put it,' Dickie replied scornfully. 'I think he's a bit nervous, as you might expect,' he told Joe. 'Your gran will be there to cheer him on though, and I'm going straight to the hall after we leave here.'

'Forget about boxing,' Freda said, 'how are you getting on in this place, Joe, honestly, mind?'

Joe grinned. 'Well, for one thing, the grub in here is a lot better than what they dished up in the Scrubs and we get the chance to do different jobs every month. I didn't have a choice this time, but next month I can put my name down for any job I fancy. I'm working in the laundry at the moment, but next time I'm hoping to get out in the open air on the farm.'

'You've got a farm here as well?' said his mother.

'This is the country, Mum. We have cows and chickens that supply us with all the milk, butter, cheese and eggs that we need and there are three fields, where we grow crops.' Joe shook his head sadly. 'It's not home from home, Mum, but compared to Wormwood Scrubs, this is like a Butlins holiday camp.' Joe looked at his father. 'I reckon you've been given a sentence as well, Dad. Sentenced to years of hard labour at the hell hole they call Ford's, with no time off for good behaviour.'

When his father told Joe about his new job with the council, Joe glanced at his mother, wondering what she had said about it when his father had first told her the news, because he was sure she would not have been very happy, although she did not appear to be too upset now.

'I'm pleased for you, Dad,' he told his father. 'Do you remember telling me about our ancestors when I was a little kid? We are the Campbells, you would say, and it was the Campbells that used to climb Hadrian's Wall to raid the English villages.'

'And a Campbell needs to be wherever he can look up and see the sky,' Dickie finished for him.

'Och aye, and not the roof of a poxy factory.'

Joe laughed so loudly that those around them turned to see what could possibly be so funny. It was not really that funny at all, but it was something of a safety valve and Freda recognised it as such, although she thought to herself, nor a poxy laundry roof in a borstal.

Joe pointed out his dormitory leader Kevin Cole. 'That boy over there is the leader of our dorm and he's been good to me ever since I got here. He gives me a roll-up every now and then and has put me right on lots of things. His dad was lost at sea during the war, when the *hood* went down in the Denmark Straits, and he was the only kid. He's in here for nicking a lorry-load of ball bearings and the soppy sod didn't even know what was on the lorry when he drove off. It had been parked outside a cafe, with the keys in the ignition at the time.

'He said he just couldn't resist the temptation, but the best bit of all is, who do you think the lorry belonged to?'

Freda and Dickie did not need any clues. In unison, they both cried loudly, 'Carter Patterson.' Freda and her husband then cringed in embarrassment at the laughter from the rest of the room.

Joe had now smoked four cigarettes in quick succession and his throat was getting a little sore, but Dickie had accepted just the one.

Joe went on to explain the borstal system to his parents. 'All of us are paid a small amount of money for the work we do. It's not very much, but in here, work is considered to be a privilege and would be withdrawn for any breach of the rules. We can buy tobacco, sweets, writing paper and stamps, but we don't get paid until the first of the month.' He looked to his mother. 'Mum, will you write to Mary and David for me and tell them that I will write as soon as I can.' He reached for another cigarette and then changed his mind.

'Leave it to me, Joe,' said Freda, 'it will in the post first thing in the morning.'

It was time to go, so Joe walked back to his dormitory side by side with Kevin Cole, while Freda and Dickie left the borstal to return to Dagenham.

Jimmy was trying very hard to control the butterflies that were flying crazily around his stomach as he, his gran and Reggie entered the Ford boxing-club hall. There was a large poster at the entrance giving information as to the order of the bouts and the names of the opponents.

'That's good,' Reggie said, 'you're on second from last, so your dad should get here in time to see you. I'm on last, so he can watch me as well.'

'Doesn't your dad ever come to see you box, Reggie?' asked Gertie.

'Nah, he always goes to Romford dog racing every Saturday and that's when we have our fights.'

'It says here that I'm up against Duggie Robinson,' said Jimmy. 'Ever heard of him, Reggie?'

Reggie, like almost everybody in the hall, had heard of Duggie Robinson. The boy was considered to be one of the best boxers, pound for pound, in London.

Reggie shrugged. 'The name rings a bell.' He chortled at the poor joke and punched Jimmy's arm. 'Rings a bell, do you get it?' He saw Jimmy was not amused. 'Oh, alright. I've seen him box before and he's not bad, but he's a powder-puff puncher. He can dance around for three rounds, but he hardly ever stops anyone.'

It was a barefaced lie, for Robinson's right hook had stopped six or seven opponents during his quite short career and he had lost just one contest, but Reggie did not feel it a very good idea to inform Jimmy of that fact.

Fred Loake, the Ford boxing-club trainer, was an old-time professional boxer, who had fought in the fairground boxing booths and at venues all over the country. Fred had never topped the bill, but he had been considered a good "trial horse" for quite a few up-and-coming younger fighters, and Fred had always given his all when he'd climbed into the ring. He now trained the boys at the Ford's boxing club and prided himself that he could spot boxing talent within minutes of watching a boy in the ring. He had been watching Jimmy Campbell's progress over the past couple of weeks and he had been greatly impressed at the way the lad had quickly mastered the art of slipping punches, while at the same time administering telling blows of his own. Even some of the more experienced boys at the club were reluctant to spar with Jimmy, but Fred was a little worried that Jimmy Campbell's first real contest would be against a powerful opponent with a wealth of experience, who was quite capable of stopping Jimmy in the first round. Although Fred had every confidence in young Jimmy, he hoped that the boy would not be out of his depth.

'Be careful, Jimmy,' he advised as he laced Jimmy's gloves. 'Be careful as soon as the bell sounds, because he's likely to try and rush at you from the word go. It's one of his favourite tricks, so keep your wits about you at all times and you'll be fine.'

'Reggie says he's a powder-puff puncher, so that shouldn't bother me too much,' said Jimmy.

'Reggie Godber is talking out of his backside,' Fred told him sternly. 'Duggie Robinson can punch just as hard as you can, so you just make sure you get your one in first.'

Some of the boxers wore fancy boots and shorts, which gave them a psychological advantage over an opponent who only wore PE shorts and plimsolls, and Duggie Robinson was no exception. After making him wait for several minutes after Jimmy had climbed into the lonely ring, Duggie strode cockily down the aisle, waving his clenched gloves in the air, clad in a splendid dressing gown and boxing boots that came almost halfway up his legs. Duggie Robinson looked every inch the boxer and nobody who had ever seen him box would deny that he was a very good one, too.

'Take no notice of that flash bugger,' Fred told Jimmy. 'He can't whack you with his boots, can he?' Jimmy's throat was too dry too answer. 'Your dad's just arrived. He's over there with your gran.'

Jimmy looked over to where he knew his gran was sitting and waved his gloved fist to the pair of them.

Duggie Robinson suddenly discovered that his boot lace was too tight and his trainer spent another two or three minutes retying them. It was a deliberate ploy to unnerve the other boxer and one that Robinson had used many times before. Jimmy was left standing in his corner while the charade was enacted out before him, but, eventually, the two boxers were called into the centre of the ring by the referee. The two boxers made no eye contact at all and after being given their final instructions, they returned to their corners to await the first bell.

Reggie Godber had been right about one thing. Even before the bell had been sounded, Jimmy's butterflies had left him completely and he now felt as cold as ice. Robinson rushed towards Jimmy's corner almost before the echo of the bell had receded, intending to land the first blow. He found himself flailing at thin air, for Jimmy had anticipated the move and had slipped to one side as though he was an eel. Duggie Robinson was perplexed. He had been told that he would be fighting a novice this evening, a boy who had never been in a proper ring before, but this Campbell kid was now actually jabbing his left fist into his face and forcing him backwards towards his own corner. What's going on here? he asked himself and then fell to the canvas as a right cross, followed by a left hook, caught him high on the head. For the first time in his life, Duggie Robinson found himself on the floor, with the referee counting over him. '… five … six … seven …'

He rose just as the count reached eight and had the boxer been anyone other than Duggie Robinson, the referee might well have called a halt there and then, for Robinson looked unsteady on his feet. The referee allowed the bout to continue, only because the lad had never been stopped in any contest before and his only defeat had been narrowly lost on a points decision. This was the boxer that was being widely tipped as the next junior ABA champion of his division and the referee knew that he would be heavily criticised if it was felt that he had stopped the contest prematurely. But it was a poor and cowardly decision to allow Duggie Robinson to continue.

As soon as the referee stepped to one side and told them to box on, Jimmy struck the other boy with four vicious blows, two to the body and two to the head. Robinson crashed to the canvas again and then bravely struggled to his feet, but his legs buckled and he slumped back down again and remained motionless. The fight was all over.

The packed hall was silent as Robinson's trainer and the duty doctor rushed into the ring to attend to the stricken boxer. Nobody who was in the hall that night would ever forget the debut of Jimmy Campbell, least of all his grandmother and his father. It was as though Jimmy had been in another mode for the past few minutes and then had suddenly become Jimmy again. Duggie Robinson was still slumped on the canvas being attended to by the doctor and his trainer, when Jimmy hurried over to him. Jimmy was greatly relieved when Duggie looked up at him and said ironically, 'Where did you hide that sledgehammer, mate?'

After Duggie Robinson had been escorted from the ring, Jimmy also climbed out, to much applause, although this was tempered with some unease that an innocent-looking boy like this could suddenly turn into a savage fighting machine.

Gertie, Dickie and Reggie had also been shocked at what they had witnessed and Gertie was relieved that her daughter had not been here to see how her youngest son had performed.

'It wasn't even a contest,' she told Dickie as they waited for Reggie's bout. 'That other poor sod never even stood a chance.'

The final contest of the evening involving Reggie was something of an anticlimax, for both boxers had seen the last bout and had no wish to end up like Duggie Robinson. Reggie lost on points after a boring three rounds, in which hardly a punch had been thrown.

Although Reggie's contest had been a little disappointing, it was almost irrelevant, for every person who knew anything about boxing and who had seen Jimmy Campbell's first performance knew without doubt that this would be the first step in the career of a remarkable young boxer.

Christmas came and went and now it was almost spring again. It had been a sad affair without Joe being there with them, but this coming weekend he had been granted a forty-eight hour pass, because he was close to completing his sentence. The authorities knew that no boy would risk jeopardising his release by not returning on time and Joe had kept out of any trouble, being appointed dormitory leader when Kevin Cole had been released, and he had also been placed in charge of all the livestock of the borstal farm. Joe had been interviewed by the parole board two weeks previously and he had been told that, on the recommendation of the governor, he would be released on 1 May. Very few borstal boys were let out in less than a year of their training period, but Joe would be released on licence eleven months after he had been sentenced. Joe knew that this meant that he must live with his parents, observe a nightly curfew and report to a probation officer every two weeks and he also knew that the probation officer had the power to revoke his licence at any time and that it would be the probation officer who would decide on the type of job Joe must take.

Jimmy had written to Joe several times and told him about the market in the town of Romford, stating that apart from the cattle market on Wednesdays, it was only on a Friday and Saturday that the market came to life. Apparently, Jimmy had asked one of the stallholders where they went for the rest of the week and had been told that there were other markets in the towns of Pitsea and Walthamstow and some of them even worked in Petticoat Lane, but Joe had a feeling that his trying to find a job in a market would not meet with the approval of the probation officer.

Joe had written regularly to Mary and David and they had written back to him every week, David adding "Miss you lots, love David" at the end of every letter. Joe had promised to visit them on Sunday afternoon and his father had told him that he wanted to go to Camden as well to see his old friend Alf Spinks, although Joe knew this was all a pretence and that his father really wanted to make sure that there would be no trouble with Duggie Murphy.

Dickie needn't have worried though, for as soon as he had heard that young Joe was keeping his mouth shut, Duggie had dismissed him from his mind. Micky Murphy had been sentenced to two and a half years' imprisonment, leaving Duggie a clear field, because Bobby Boyce had sold off all of his stalls and had left Camden. Duggie was now making a lucrative living by strongly persuading the stallholders to accept stolen merchandise and those who resisted did not remain in the market for very long. Indeed, one morning, they might arrive at the market warehouse, where they had left their barrows, to find that all their goods had been destroyed by a fire or by a mysterious flood.

Joe had no thoughts of revenge; after all, he was still only just turned fifteen and was certainly no match for Duggie Murphy and his thugs. He was looking forward to the weekend and was especially looking forward to seeing his gran again, for he had only seen her twice since he had been arrested. Joe had been shocked at how frail she had appeared, although his gran had dismissed his concern, telling him she was merely suffering from indigestion. Joe had wondered at the time if his gran was being completely truthful, but believed that his parents must be aware that she was not looking too well and left it at that. Joe was also longing to see Mary and David again, even though he sometimes felt somewhat uncomfortable when he thought about Mary Davis, for his thoughts were not always as pure as he considered they should be.

Joe would leave Loughton on Saturday morning at 10.00 a.m. and did not have to return until 10.00 a.m. on Monday, leaving him plenty of time to get all his visits in.

Gertie's health had been a cause of concern to her daughter for some time now and she had insisted that her mother go and see the doctor.

'I told you it was a waste of time,' announced Gertie on her return, 'all I have to do is leave off the fried bread and eat more fresh fruit.'

What she did not tell Freda though, was that the doctor had made an urgent appointment for her to see a specialist and that he had telephoned Oldchurch Hospital in Romford, where the consultant's secretary had managed to fit her in the very next morning. Gertie was told not to have anything to eat or drink after midnight and was to present herself to the oncology clinic at 10 o'clock the following morning. Gertie neither knew nor wished to know what "oncology" meant, but, deep down, she had a good idea. Gertie told nobody about the appointment, not even Ada Peake from next door. Gertie knew her own body and her own body was telling her that something was dreadfully wrong, but she told herself that bad news travelled fast enough without hastening the process.

Dickie and Jimmy usually came home for their lunch, but Gertie told them that they would have to fend for themselves the next day, as she had volunteered to spend the morning sewing new curtains for the over-sixties club.

The next day, Gertie spent an uncomfortable three hours at the hospital being subjected to undignified tests and being prodded around by various doctors and nurses. She had what she considered to be at least a pint of blood drawn from her arm and a staggering amount of X-rays were taken and samples extracted from the most intimate of places. She was then told that the results would be completed in two weeks and was advised to make another appointment to see her doctor after that period.

Gertie felt weary as she took the bus home from the hospital, but she was not frightened – she had seen too much of death and destruction during the war to be overly concerned by her own demise. Gertie knew that her time was running out, although she had hoped it would not be this soon. She so badly wanted to see her beloved grandsons grow into manhood, but she knew this was not to be and it was with a great sadness that she turned the key in the lock of the front door. She would say nothing of this to anybody, for Joe was coming home on Saturday and nothing must spoil this weekend.

Chapter Eleven

The following two weeks passed very slowly for Gertie and as she walked into Dr Naylor's surgery, he did not look up from his file, for he was steeling himself to give the sad news to this woman. Dr Naylor was a kind and elderly man, who had been practising in Dagenham ever since it was merely a small village, although he had been forced to appoint two younger partners as the town grew much bigger over the years. Quite often these days he felt the need to retire and take things easy and today was one such day. He had received the report from the hospital of the tests conducted for Gertrude Cornwallis and the report was as bad as he had feared. Dr Naylor had a strong feeling that the news he was about to impart would not come as a great shock to this brave woman, either.

'Well, Mrs Cornwallis,' he began.

'Mrs Cornwallis,' spluttered Gertie, 'nobody calls me that any more, except them at the hospital. Just call me Gertie, like the rest of them do.'

The doctor smiled and continued. 'Well, Gertie, the results of the tests show that you have a problem with your blood. The blood should be divided into equal amounts of red cells and white cells, but your blood is producing too many white cells, which is why you have been feeling weak and run down. It's similar to anaemia, in a way.'

'But it's not anaemia, is it, doc?' Gertie looked him firmly in the eye. 'It's leukaemia, isn't it?'

'Yes, Gertie, it is leukaemia,' Dr Naylor told her gently. 'I don't think I have to tell you that there is no cure, but you will not be in any pain. You will feel weak from time to time and these bouts of weakness will increase as time goes on, but there will also be times when you will feel as fit as a fiddle.'

'How long have I got? And I want the truth,' Gertie demanded.

The doctor abandoned his stock answers of "it all depends on how determined you are", or "it's very hard to say". This woman had demanded to be told and she deserved to be told the truth as he saw it. 'I have studied your blood count, Gertie, and I have also spoken with Mr Meers at Oldchurch Hospital. Mr Meers has always been reluctant to put a timescale on one of his patients, but his best guess would be six months to a year, although I have to say that I think a year would be a bonus. I know this sounds trite and inadequate, but I am truly sorry, Gertie.'

'No, it doesn't sound trite, Dr Naylor, and thanks for being so honest with me. I'm not going to say anything to the others just yet though. I'll wait until Joe gets out of borstal.'

She stood up to leave and the doctor shook her hand. 'You may not be able to hide this for very much longer, Gertie. Soon, you will need all the love and support your family can give you.'

The next day, Gertie confided to Ada Peake, who promptly burst into tears.

'That's exactly why I don't want the rest of them to know,' Gertie told Ada. 'How can I put this on Freda's shoulders what with Joe still away? No, it will keep for another few weeks and then Joe will be back with us.' Gertie stood aggressively in front of her friend. 'And if you open your gob to anyone, I'll tell the others at the over-sixties that you've got false teeth.' Gertie knew how proud Ada was that she was one of the few members that possessed a full set of natural teeth.

Ada dried her eyes and made another pot of tea.

Freda did not believe that her mother had told her the whole truth about her health, but knew that once she had dug her heels in, hell and high water would not shift her. Freda felt that her mother was waiting for the right moment to tell the family the whole story and Freda had a dreadful feeling that it was a story they would not want to hear. Dickie agreed.

'Most of the time, she's asleep when I get home, and it's not like she's just having forty winks, either. But what really bothers me is the way that she breathes. Sometimes, it's as though it's too much trouble and she'd just as soon forget about drawing in the next one.'

Dickie looked at his wife, wondering if what he had said made any sense to her, but it did. Just lately, Gertie had not been getting up as early as she once had and often when Freda had taken a cup of tea up to her mother, she had experienced the same feeling as Dickie had just described when she had looked down at her sleeping form.

Freda told Dickie, 'I've even asked Mrs Peake, but she just said that if I was worried about my mother, then perhaps I should go and have a word with the doctor.'

'Well, we both know he wouldn't tell us anything, so there's not very much we can do about it, until your mother decides to put us in the picture. All we can do is keep an eye on her and make sure she doesn't overdo things.'

Freda reluctantly agreed, but her mother's health was almost as big a worry for her as the well-being of her two sons. Joe seemed reasonably content in Loughton and would be home on leave next weekend and then he would be released a few weeks later. She was concerned that he may find it difficult to find a suitable job in Dagenham though, for it had been made abundantly clear that he could not go back to Camden Town. Gertie and Dickie had said very little about Jimmy's first boxing contest, but Freda's workmates had shown her a copy of the local newspaper that had reported the gruesome details and Freda could not identify her angelic son with the ferocious boy depicted by the reporter from *The Dagenham Post*.

Freda did not share her friends' enthusiasm that Jimmy could be the most famous boxer ever to come out of Dagenham.

Her job at the May and Baker factory was a source of great pleasure and comfort for Freda and so, too, was the friendship that had blossomed between herself and Amy Ashby. One Saturday evening, they had attempted to make up a foursome with their husbands so they could have a drink at Amy's local pub in Oxlow Lane. But, unfortunately, it was not a success though, as David Ashby was a loud and self-opinionated man, who listened to nobody except himself, being the complete antithesis of the quiet and dignified Dickie. The exercise was never repeated.

"Flash, mouthy git" had been Dickie's opinion of David Ashby and "mealy mouthed little squirt" had been David Ashby's opinion of Dickie Campbell, but it had not affected the relationship between Freda and Amy and they continued to exchange worries, hopes and confidences at every opportunity. Quite often, they would shop together in Romford Market, spending the morning browsing around the shops and the stalls and then having a half of shandy and a pie in one of the pubs as soon as they opened.

Freda found it strange that anyone could be happy collecting other people's old rubbish for a living, but happy her husband certainly was. Since leaving the Ford factory, Dickie was like a different person. The grey pallor and the hollow eyes had disappeared from his face and Freda knew that he was much happier than he had been for a long time. Joe would be home for good soon and if it was not for the worry over her mother's health, Freda would be able to look forward to the rapidly approaching summer.

Her fears that they would find it difficult to manage on Dickie's severely reduced wages had not been realised, for almost since the first day her husband had started work at the council depot, he had been offered part-time work with his "ganger" John Townsend.

Dickie now usually worked with John three afternoons a week from around two in the afternoon until six or seven in the evening and all day on most Saturdays, and he was bringing home almost as much money as he would have earned at the Ford factory, albeit he was working much longer hours. Dickie did not care one little bit, because he was out in the open air and free from the bedlam of the assembly line and as he had rather crudely remarked to his mother-in-law, 'Gertie, I'm as happy as a pig in shit.'

Freda had refused to accompany Dickie and her mother when Jimmy had boxed for the second and third time, but she had secretly begun to paste the newspaper reports into a scrapbook. Jimmy had won all three of his contests and still had not been taken to the full three rounds.

Dickie had now been on the dustcarts for over six months and the Ford Motor Company was but a bad memory for him. His team, or "gang" as they preferred to be called, worked well together and as the depot manager Jack Doyle had told Dickie, they were, indeed, always the first to leave the depot in the morning and the first to return in the afternoon.

John Townsend had taken to Dickie almost from the moment he had laid eyes on him and at the end of the first day, had told Jack Doyle, 'We have a good 'n here, Jack. Dickie's not afraid to get his hands dirty and he can keep up with the rest of us no problem. I think he's one of us already.'

Jack Doyle had been pleased that he chosen the right man for the right gang and within two days, John Townsend had broached the subject of part-time work to Dickie when they had been having their breakfast in one of the local cafes.

'Jack Doyle told me that you might be interested in doing a bit on the side,' he had said to Dickie. 'Jack knows that I do some work now and then, but I don't let him know all of my business and I've got orders that will keep me going for at least the next six months. I work three afternoons a week and all day most Saturdays and I'm looking for a regular mate. It's hard graft, but what do you think, Dickie, are you up for it?'

Dickie had not hesitated for a second. 'Sure am, John. When do you want me to start?'

'Monday, if you can. I work Monday, Wednesday and Friday afternoons and then I quite often work a long day either on Saturday or Sunday, but sometimes my old woman likes to be taken out for the day and I suppose your one probably does as well, so I'm flexible.'

John mopped the last of his fatty fried breakfast from his plate with a piece of bread. 'I can pay you the same hourly rate as you get from the council, without having to pay tax, of course, and if there's a drink in it at the end of the job, as there usually is, I give you my word that it will be split straight down the middle.'

Dickie could not have hoped or even dreamed of anything as promising as this. 'That'll do for me, John. The only thing I have to tell you is that my eldest son is in borstal and once a month, me and the missus go to see him on a Saturday. He'll be out soon, but I think it's only fair to tell you that I may not be able to work every Saturday.'

He had then gone on to explain about Joe and the circumstances of his sentence.

'I'm sorry to hear that, Dickie, but don't worry about not being available now and then. As I said, I don't work every Saturday anyway, so

I'll fit in around you.' John had grinned before adding, 'One thing though, some of my jobs are outside and if we get rained off, it's no work no pay. After all, I'm not a bleeding charity.'

'Fair enough, Dr Barnardo,' Dickie laughed.

The two men worked well together and John was glad to have a reliable man to work alongside him. John Townsend was not an indentured craftsman the way his father had been, but he was as proficient at bricklaying, plumbing, carpentry, painting and decorating and electrics as any man who had served a five-year apprenticeship. John's father had been bitterly disappointed when his son had refused to take an apprenticeship when he had left school at fourteen, for John had preferred the much higher wages that could be earned by working as a labourer on the numerous building sites springing up all around the country. By the time he had reached twenty, John had regretted that decision, but then the war had come along and the whole world had been turned upside down. Now he was quite content, for he liked his job as a dustman and the extra money he could earn kept his wife happy, especially when he could afford to take the family to the seaside for a week every year; not in a caravan, mind, but in a proper boarding house, with all meals included.

The first job John and Dickie had completed was rewarded with a five-pound bonus, much more than John had expected, although the job had been quite intricate and it had taken all of John's expertise to ensure the end result was as near perfect as possible. John had handed Dickie an extra two pound ten shillings on top of his wages that week. It was a good partnership and Dickie quickly learned new skills, meaning that he would not just be a labourer to John.

Dickie was looking forward to the coming weekend. Joe would be home and after Sunday lunch, he and Joe would be taking the tube to Camden Town, so that Joe could visit Mary and David and he could see Alf Spinks.

John had understood that Dickie wanted the whole weekend off.

'No problem, Dickie. I think it's about time we had a bit of a break anyway and my old woman has been on at me for ages to take her away for a long weekend. She has a sister who lives in Weston-super-Mare and we can be at Paddington station by three o'clock on Friday afternoon.'

Like his wife, the one big cloud on Dickie's horizon was the poor health of his mother-in-law, who was looking increasingly tired and frail as the days went by, but Dickie knew that Gertie would tell them what was wrong in her own good time and not before.

Young Jimmy Campbell was looking forward to seeing his brother and was also looking forward to showing him around Romford Market when it was a hive of activity. Jimmy was also almost bursting with news, but was waiting until the family were all sat down together one evening before he told them; news that he had not even told his best friend Reggie Godber. Yesterday evening, after the sparring session at the Ford boxing club was over, the trainer Fred Loake had taken Jimmy to one side and told him that he had received a letter from the Amateur Boxing Association, inviting James Campbell to compete in the junior ABA Championship competition, commencing the following week. Fred handed Jimmy a form that need two signatures; one from his trainer and one from his parent or guardian. The fact that Fred had already signed his name was not wasted on him.

By this time, Jimmy had boxed eight times and had won all eight contests, with only three of them ending when the bell sounded at the end of the last round – four of his bouts had not lasted a single round and one had been over in the second round. On two occasions, he had arrived at a venue to discover that his opponent, on hearing that he was to box Jimmy Campbell, had slipped quietly away. In the junior ABA competition, sixteen boxers from each weight division would draw lots to box each other, until only two were left for the finals, which were always held in London's Royal Albert Hall and were to be transmitted live on the wireless. It was a great honour to be chosen and Jimmy Campbell was only the third boxer from Ford's to be selected in fifteen years and Jimmy would be the first contender that Fred Loake had trained. The other two boys had not managed to win a single contest, although it had been a proud moment for the parents and for their trainers when the young boxers had stepped into the ring.

Fred had already been informed that the first venue would be at York Hall in Bethnal Green in London, and if Jimmy came through that one, the next one could be anywhere in England, Scotland or Wales. All expenses were paid for by the association and Fred knew, from talking to other trainers, that the accommodation and food provided was always first class. Fred was confident that Jimmy was capable of defeating every other boy in his division, although there was just one boxer who could possibly give him a run for his money.

He hoped that they would not be drawn to box each other until at least the quarter-finals, but he was also comforted by the knowledge that the other boy's trainer would have certainly heard of Jimmy Campbell and that he probably felt the same way, too.

Fred had given the letter from the ABA to Jimmy, so that he could show his parents, and Jimmy had read and reread it dozens of times over to convince himself that this was not just a dream – he really was to become an ABA challenger!

Since becoming a boxer, Jimmy had followed the careers of all the professional fighters and knew that almost all of them, and certainly the champions, had been ABA contestants at junior or senior – and often at both – levels. Jimmy was not a very big boy and would never be a heavyweight boxer, but eventually, according to Fred Loake, he would become a lightweight or perhaps even a middleweight. The lightweight champion of Britain and the whole world had been a junior ABA champion and he had then carried on to become the senior champion at the age of eighteen. He had then turned professional six months later. Jimmy lay in bed at night dreaming the same dream for himself.

Joe was due to leave Loughton at 10.00 a.m. and he was called into the governor's office immediately after breakfast and handed his travel warrant.

'Off you go, Campbell, there's no need for you to hang around here,' the governor told him. 'Just you make sure that you give yourself plenty of time to be back at ten o'clock on Monday morning.'

Joe thanked him and then left the office, glancing up at the clock on the governor's wall. It was still only eight thirty.

He left the train at Dagenham Heathway station just over an hour after he had left the borstal in Loughton. Freda was paying the milkman as her son walked up the path to their house, so she quickly conducted her business and then rushed over to embrace him.

'We didn't expect to see you for ages yet.'

They walked into the front room, which was empty. Joe explained that the governor had let him leave early and then asked, 'Where is everyone?'

'Your dad left about half an hour ago to give one of his mates a hand to build a chicken run. He promised to be back by half ten, because we weren't expecting you much before eleven. Jimmy's still in bed, but I think I can hear him stirring.' His mother's voice was low when she then added, 'Your gran's not up yet, either.' She saw the look of surprise on Joe's face, as Joe could not remember his gran still being in bed at this time of the day, for it was now almost ten o'clock. 'She's not been too well lately, Joe, but she won't tell us anything. Perhaps she may come out with it now that you're home, but she's worrying me and your dad silly.'

'I'll talk to her the first chance I get,' promised Joe.

The sound of clumping footsteps on the stairs announced the arrival of Jimmy.

'Hello, Joe, I thought I heard your voice; how's it going?' Jimmy asked his brother.

Freda left the room to put the kettle on to make the tea, intending to take a cup up to her mother.

'Joe's home, Mum,' said Freda as she entered her mother's bedroom.

Gertie opened her weary eyes and smiled. 'Oh, that's nice; I'll be down in a little while.'

Freda left the tea on the bedside table and went back downstairs.

Gertie lay for a few minutes trying to summon up the strength to leave her bed. She felt so dreadfully tired and she knew that she could no longer keep up this pretence. This past week had been the worst, for although she had been in no pain, there had been this utter sense of weariness that threatened to overwhelm her much as Dr Naylor had promised her. Gertie knew that she must tell the family the truth before Joe went back to Loughton on Monday, because she now believed that her doctor's prediction of six months to a year had been too optimistic and that her time on this earth was running out rapidly. Gertie was crying quietly, for she was sure that this weekend was the last time she would see her beloved grandson and that she would not be here when he was finally released. Come on, you soppy cow, she chided herself, pull yourself together and get your arse downstairs.

It worked – at least for the moment. Freda was cooking breakfast when Gertie came down to greet her two grandsons. Joe would have liked to give her a big hug, but his gran looked as though she would break in two if he did, so he gently kissed her cheek, instead.

She looked much worse than the last time he had seen her and he could remember how shocked he had been then. Joe was convinced that something was being withheld from him and he was determined to get to the bottom of it before Monday morning.

After breakfast, which Gertie barely touched, Jimmy said he had arranged to meet Reggie Godber, but that he would be back by one o'clock to take Joe to Romford Market. Dickie came in soon after and opened two bottles of brown for himself and Joe, ignoring Freda's look of disapproval at their drinking this early in the day. He then poured it out into two glasses and then waited for his son to speak, because the look on Joe's face made it clear that he had something to say.

Joe's first words shocked them all. 'I've decided I'm not going back on Monday.' They all protested at the same time, forcing Joe to raise his own voice to silence them. 'Let me finish,' he said firmly. 'I know I'm only home for the weekend, but I still have a right to know what's going on here.' He looked at Gertie. 'I think you're ill, Gran, and I'm not going back until you tell me what the problem is.' He then looked at his parents. 'You're hiding something from me, but I'm serious, if you won't tell me what's going on, then I'll stay put until the coppers come to arrest me.'

'Me and your dad aren't hiding anything, Joe,' Freda told him, 'but I think your gran is hiding something from all of us and it's about time it was brought out into the open.'

'Your mum's right, Joe,' his grandmother told him wearily. 'I haven't said anything before, because I didn't want to worry you while you were still away and I thought I'd be alright until you got out for good.'

'But you're not alright, are you, Gran?'

Gertie shook her head. 'No, Joe, I'm not. There's no easy way to tell you this, so I'll just come straight out with it – I've got leukaemia and I may as well tell you the rest while I'm at it, I only have a few weeks left to live.'

Freda gasped. 'I knew it wasn't indigestion.' She began to cry. 'Oh, Mum, why couldn't you have told us sooner?'

'Because I hoped none of you would notice and until this morning, I'd intended to tell the pair of you after Joe had gone back on Monday.' Gertie bowed her head. 'I'm sorry; I thought I was doing it for the best.'

Joe went to his grandmother and stroked her head gently. 'Oh, Gran, oh, Gran,' was all he could manage to say.

Gertie patted Joe's hand. 'I wasn't going to let you go back without telling you, Joe. I made up my mind this morning that I would tell you all on Sunday night, because I can't hide it any longer.'

Dickie had not said a word he felt numb, shocked and greatly saddened that it seemed they would lose this wonderful person so very soon.

Gertie told them everything she knew about her condition, although Freda said she would take the day off on Monday and go with her mother to see Dr Naylor to hear if he had any further information. Gertie agreed willingly, for she needed her family around her now and she knew it had been a mistake to shut them out. She advised against saying anything to Jimmy until after the weekend.

'That young man is like a cat on hot bricks and he's got something to tell us before the day is out, I'd bet a pound to a pinch of sh ... snuff to it.' She grinned and winked at Joe, 'I nearly said shit then, didn't I?'

Gertie closed her eyes, the energy now all drained from her body and the weariness predicted by her doctor had overcome her yet again. Her breathing was laboured, her pallor was ashen and the three of them knew they must now come to terms with what Gertie had already accepted. Freda, Dickie and Joe left the front room, closing the door quietly behind them, and went into the kitchen, where Freda put the kettle on. Joe and his father still had their glasses of beer.

Joe began to apologise to his parents. 'I'm sorry, Mum, I'm sorry, Dad, I didn't realise that you knew nothing about it.'

Freda turned on him angrily. 'No you didn't, did you, but you just saw fit to stand there and tell us that you weren't going back, you selfish little bugger.' Freda slumped in her chair at the table and rested her head on her arms, sobbing as though her heart would break.

'She didn't mean it, son,' Dickie attempted to reassure Joe, 'it's been a big shock for all of us, even though we suspected that she was worse than she would admit to.'

Freda raised her tear-stained face to Joe. 'Your dad's right. I didn't mean it, Joe, I'm sorry.'

Mother, father and son held each other's hands, each drawing comfort from the other two.

Chapter Twelve

Gertie was still fast asleep when Jimmy returned, but he could contain himself no longer. He produced the letter from the Amateur Boxing Association and proudly showed it to his parents and Joe. Joe, who had never seen his brother box, was amazed. He was aware that only the best boxers in Britain were invited to compete in this competition and although he knew that Jimmy had won all of his eight contests, Joe had no real idea how highly regarded his brother had become.

'Well done, sunshine,' Joe enthused, 'this is great. I reckon the rest of them had better watch out, 'cos the Campbells are coming.'

It was a corny old cliché, but Jimmy was too tense to notice, because he was desperately worried that his mother would refuse to sign the consent form and he knew that his dad would not sign either, or at least not without her approval.

'If I was to win the first one at York Hall,' he told his mother earnestly, 'I could box again in Cardiff, Edinburgh or even Belfast, and Fred told me that no expenses are spared when it comes to putting us up; not just me, but you and Dad as well.' He raised his arms in a further appeal. 'Come on, Mum, it will be like having a holiday and I really need to do this.'

Freda handed the form to her husband. 'You can sign it and I suppose I'll have to as well, but I'll have nothing more to do with this. I'll not go to any hall anywhere in the country to see two boys trying to bash each other up.' Freda embraced her youngest son. 'I am proud of you, Jimmy, but I can't come and watch you. I'll read all about you in *The Dagenham Post* and you'll probably be on the front page this week, but I couldn't bear to see you in a fight.' Then she added with a grin, 'Mind you, I've never been to Edinburgh, Cardiff or Belfast, so I might come along, even if I don't watch the fights.'

'They're not fights, Mum, they're bouts,' said Jimmy.

'Same bloody thing,' said his mother.

Joe and Jimmy went off to Romford Market, where they spent several hours browsing around the numerous stalls, which were attempting to sell anything from second-hand books to moth-eaten, second-hand fur coats. Joe noticed that some of the stalls were selling quality goods and stopped to examine their wares more closely. One of the traders believed Joe was not a potential customer at all, but that he had been sent by another rival to spy on him, and he became quite aggressive when Joe fingered one of the ladies jackets. 'Sod off out of it,' he bellowed, 'and take yer bloody monkey with you.'

He meant Jimmy, of course, but Joe did not react to the insult and he sauntered casually off to the next stall to see what they had on offer. Joe was excited by the bustle and the atmosphere of the market and although it was nothing like the size of Camden Town's, this was where he wanted to work when he was released from Loughton borstal. Joe crossed his fingers behind his back. God willing, he told himself, and then uncrossed his fingers. It's got bugger all to do with God; it all depends on what the probation officer says.

Joe had never been inside a boxing ring before and was curious as to how his younger brother felt when he climbed into the ring.

'I must admit, I do feel a bit scared, Joe, but only up to the time when I climb through the ropes. Then I'm fine. I don't mean to sound cocky, or anything like that, but I feel that nobody can beat me and in a way, it's even a bit scary, but I know that I can hit harder than any of the other fighters and they know it as well.'

'I thought you were all boxers, not fighters.'

'Same bloody thing, as our mum says,' laughed Jimmy.

Joe looked at Jimmy with admiration. 'You go for it, mate. I'm only sorry I can't be there for your first one at York Hall, but you go and win it for me and I'll be there for wherever the next one happens to be.'

Gertie had perked up considerably while her two grandsons had been out and she even joined in for a game of cards for half an hour or so on their return. Dickie had been to the off-licence to bring back some brown ale, some lemonade and a bottle of whisky. Gertie accepted a generous measure and decided to take it up to bed with her for a nightcap.

'I know it's only nine o'clock,' she said, 'but I want to get up nice and early in the morning to cook us all a nice big fry-up for breakfast.'

Joe rolled his eyes in anticipation. 'I'll have some of that, Gran; all I get in Loughton is lumpy porridge.'

Gertie's final instruction to her daughter was, 'Wake me up if I'm not up and about by half seven.'

But Freda had no intention of doing anything of the kind, for she knew that her mother would sleep for at least twelve hours, if not longer.

It was a special treat for Jimmy that he was always allowed to stay up on a Saturday evening to listen to the late-night play on the wireless. *Saturday Night Theatre* was his favourite and he was now huddled around the set with the volume turned down low as Joe and his parents chatted between themselves, but his gran was not mentioned and neither would she be, or at least not until Jimmy had gone to bed after the play had finished.

After Jimmy had gone to his bed, Freda, Dickie and Joe sat around drinking and chatting together and it was Freda who broached the subject of Gertie.

'I'll be going to see the doctor with Mum on Monday,' she said as she sipped her whisky and lemonade. 'I'll be able to explain how she's been, especially this last week, because I know she won't say anything herself.'

'He's not God, you know,' Dickie said unnecessarily. 'He won't be able to tell you any more than what he's already told Gertie.'

Freda sniffed. 'Well, let's wait and see, shall we?'

Joe cleared his throat. 'The pair of you see me gran every day, but I don't think you realise what a shock it gave me when I saw her this morning. Until she opened her mouth to speak, I could hardly believe she was my gran; in fact, she reminded me of one of those waxwork models you see in Madame Tussauds.'

'I understand, Joe, and you were right to say what you did this morning,' Freda told her son. 'I think your gran was telling the truth when she said she was going to tell you about it before you went back, but at least it's all out in the open now.'

'I make you right there, but it's still bloody hard to take in,' said Dickie.

'It depends on what Dr Naylor has to say on Monday,' said Freda, 'but I don't think she can be left on her own for much longer, so I'll have to pack my job in and we'll just have to manage the best we can for the time being.'

'One good thing is that I'm getting plenty of work with John Townsend,' said Dickie. 'I'm glad we didn't get too much stuff on the never-never though, at least we can manage the repayments as they are.'

Joe added. 'And don't forget, I'll be out soon and I'll be able to chip in as soon as I get myself sorted.'

The three of them put Gertie's belief that she would not be around when that time came to the back of their minds.

Freda cooked breakfast the next morning, but waited until almost ten o'clock before she took her mother a cup of tea in bed. Gertie was still sound asleep, but, unlike yesterday morning, she awoke as soon as Freda touched her arm. Gertie did not ask what time it was, for she had completely forgotten her promise that she would cook the family breakfast that morning. Dickie and Joe were heartened when Gertie came down to the kitchen, for she looked refreshed and much better than she had the previous evening and Gertie even managed to eat a slice of toast, although she declined Freda's offer to cook her bacon and eggs.

Later, Dickie took Joe off to the Church Elm for a lunchtime pint, with strict orders from Freda to be home by two o'clock for the Sunday roast. Dickie had arranged to meet Tommy Smith and although Joe was still only fifteen and should have been too young to be served, the publican was an ex-professional boxer himself and had been following Jimmy Campbell's career with great interest. Joe looked much older than his fifteen years and the publican turned a blind eye when he walked in with his father. The publican had never been selected to compete in the ABA Championships himself, but he was proud to be associated with the family of someone who had been.

Tommy Smith was already propping up the bar and ordered a round of drinks as soon as he saw Dickie and Joe. Dickie had handed a ten-shilling note to his son before they had left home, so that Joe could also order a round of drinks himself, so as not to feel embarrassed. Dickie and Joe had three pints of brown ale each and then left the pub, leaving Tommy to have at least another two or three, for he usually had five or six pints at a Sunday "session".

'You've timed it just right,' Freda told them as they walked through the door. 'I'm just waiting for the Yorkshires to brown and then it will all be ready.'

Gertie was surprised to find that she was quite hungry and feeling much better than she had done for some time and wondered if she had been a bit premature in telling the family, but then she remembered Dr Naylor's prediction that there would be days when she would feel quite well. This seemed to be one such day and Gertie was determined to make the most of it.

Dickie and Joe left for Camden Town as soon as they had finished their dinner.

'I don't want to spend too long in Camden, Dad,' Joe told his father as they walked to the station. 'Mary will understand and so will David, when I tell them about Gran. I want to spend as much time as I can with Gran, if that's alright with you.'

'Of course it is, and I think your gran would like that as well.'

Dickie was pleased. 'Perhaps if she's feeling up to it, we could all pop over to the pub later on, it's always less crowded on Sunday nights.

'Alf brews his own beer these days,' said Dickie, changing the subject. 'He's promised to treat me to a drop or two and the pubs are all closed till seven anyway, but I'll see you at Mary's at about six, so that we can be back in plenty of time to take your gran out, if she's up to it.'

Joe got off the train at Mornington Crescent, leaving his father to carry on to Camden Town, where he would meet up with Alf Spinks.

David was waiting at the front gate for Joe and he jumped up and down with excitement when he saw him turn the corner, but when Joe went to put his arm around him, David suddenly burst into tears.

Mary opened the door and led her son gently into the house, for she could understand exactly how he was feeling.

'It's alright, David,' Joe told the boy, 'I almost did the same when I got home yesterday.'

'Honestly, Joe?' said David, raising a tear-stained face towards him. 'Oh, Joe, I've missed you lots and lots. I thought you would forget all about us and we would never see you again.'

Joe ruffled his hair. 'What, forget about my best mate? Never in a thousand years, but I won't be able to stay for very long, David. My gran is very ill and I want to spend some time with her before I have to go back in the morning.' Joe looked across to Mary. 'I'll write and tell you about it as soon as I get home and I'll post it off first thing in the morning.'

David was disappointed, although he tried very hard not to show it, for he knew that Joe was being kind to his granny in the same way that he always tried to be kind to his mummy.

'I'm sorry about your gran, Joe,' said David. 'We'll make up for it next time, shall we?'

'That's a promise and that won't be very long, either.'

Mary was also disappointed, for she had baked a fruit cake and had made a trifle, anticipating that Joe and his father would stay for tea, but, like her son, she did her best not to show it.

David and Mary had lots of questions to ask Joe, especially about his work on the farm, but the minute-hand of the clock on the wall was ticking away far too quickly and it seemed to Joe that he had been in the house for such a short space of time when his father knocked on the door.

David tried his best not to cry. 'Thank you for coming, Joe. I hope your gran gets better soon.'

'And that goes for me, too, Joe,' said Mary.

Joe hugged David one last time and left the house with his father.

Alf Spinks' first words to his old friend had been, 'So how's the arse end of the world then?'

Dickie had written to Alf several times over the past few months, so Alf knew about Dickie leaving the Ford Motor Company and taking a job as a dustman and Alf had approved wholeheartedly.

'I knew you would never last for long in a poxy factory,' he had told Dickie smugly as he poured him a glass of his brew to sample.

Dickie had almost gagged at the evil-smelling concoction that tasted almost as bad as it smelled. 'You did, indeed, Alf, that I won't deny, but at least I'm out of there now, thank Christ.'

Alf had smacked his lips as he'd savoured his home-brew. 'Now this is what I call a real drink,' he said proudly.

It's not what I'd call it, Dickie said to himself.

'So how long do you think it will be before you can get back to Camden?' had been Alf's next question.

Dickie shook his head sadly, 'I can't see it happening for years, if at all, Alf. They haven't even started to clear all the bomb sites yet, let alone started to rebuild around Camden.' Dickie took another sip of his drink and this time, it did not seem to taste quite as vile. 'Freda is happy there and so is Jimmy. Joe won't have a choice, for the time being, and if what Gertie says is true, the poor cow won't be going anywhere. I can't see any other way out, Alf, and to tell the truth, now that I'm out of that bloody factory, I don't really mind Dagenham at all.'

'Bollocks!' Alf retorted. 'Once a fucking Londoner, always a fucking Londoner, and you know it.'

Gertie was asleep in the armchair when Dickie and Joe returned, although she really looked quite peaceful. Freda made a pot of tea and her mother awoke as soon as the cup was placed beside her.

'Oh hello, you two, I didn't hear you come in,' said Gertie, yawning and stretching. To Freda, she said, 'What's for tea, dear? I'm feeling peckish again.'

'How about some cockles and whelks?' suggested Dickie. 'The seafood bloke will be round in his van soon, my treat.'

'Ooh, that'd be lovely,' said Gertie enthusiastically. 'You can't beat a few cockles and whelks smothered in pepper and vinegar.'

Joe screwed his face up in disgust. He found it difficult to understand how anybody could chew on those revolting-looking things.

Freda thought it was wonderful to see her mother looking so cheerful, but she still intended to go with her to see the doctor in the morning and her resolve was confirmed less than an hour later, when Gertie's face turned ashen and her breathing once more become laboured after having eaten only a few of the cockles. There would be no Sunday-evening visit to the pub that night.

Joe left the house at 8.00 a.m. the next morning to make sure that he would be back in Loughton before ten o'clock. He had been up since six sharing a pot of tea with his father before he'd left for work and Gertie was still in bed when he had left, but his mother and Jimmy had stood at the gate to wave goodbye to him. After seeing Jimmy off to school, Freda went up to her mother, but one look at her told her that her mother was in no condition to leave the house.

She went next door to ask Mrs Peake to sit with Gertie while she went to the doctor's surgery to request a home visit.

Ada Peake sat with her friend and knew that their friendship was about to come to an end, for Gertie was close to death and Ada had seen death too many times not to recognise that it was imminent.

When Dr Naylor was told by his receptionist that Gertie's daughter was requesting a home visit, he left his assistant to take over and drove

Freda back in his car. On the way back to her house, Freda informed the doctor that her mother had told the family what was wrong with her and she went on to tell him of her symptoms over the past week.

The doctor shook his head sadly. 'It's quicker than I thought it would be, but I'm afraid there is no cure and it can only be a matter of time.'

The doctor only needed the briefest of examinations, before announcing, 'We need to get her into hospital immediately for a blood transfusion.' Ada Peake shook her head, but the doctor continued. 'It might just buy her a little more time, Mrs Campbell, and I think she's entitled to that. I'll go to the telephone box and call for an ambulance.'

But an ambulance was not needed. After the doctor had left, Freda sat on one side of Gertie's bed, while Ada sat on the other, each holding one of her hands. There was no sudden last gasp for breath and no shudder and Gertie's eyes remained closed. She had simply just not taken her next breath.

Ada Peake kissed Gertie's hand. 'Goodbye, love. God bless.' Ada then looked across at Freda, who had not grasped what had happened. 'She's gone, Freda,' Ada told her gently. 'She's gone.'

Chapter Thirteen

It was Ada Peake who took charge for the next hour or so. After Dr Naylor had signed the death certificate and left, Ada took Freda downstairs and poured them both a stiff drink, believing that at times such as these, cups of tea are wholly inadequate. There was a dazed look upon Freda's face and Ada knew that her mother's death had not yet sunk in.

'Dr Naylor is going to phone the council depot and he said he will also ring Loughton for you,' said Ada, although she wasn't quite sure whether Freda was taking in any of what she was saying. 'We'll wait until Jimmy comes home from school before we tell him, or perhaps Dickie might prefer to go to the school himself.'

After they had finished their drinks, Ada cajoled Freda into helping her to wash her mother and lay her out, for Ada firmly believed that performing this final duty would help Freda to begin the grieving process. Together, they gently washed and dressed Gertie in her best frock, ready for when she would be placed in her coffin to remain in the house until her funeral.

Dickie and the rest of the gang were surprised to see Jack Doyle's car pull up in front of their dustcart, for he rarely left the council depot during a working day. When he opened the passenger door and beckoned for Dickie to get in, Dickie had this dreadful feeling of foreboding as he walked towards the car.

'Look at the state of me, Jack, I'd make a right old mess of your upholstery,' said Dickie, almost as though, somehow, he could avoid the news he was certain he was about to hear.

'Don't worry about that, Dickie, just get in, because I have some bad news about your mother-in-law.'

'She's dead?' Dickie knew deep down that he did not even have to ask, but went through the motions anyway.

'Yes, she died about an hour or so ago.' Jack attempted to impart a few words of comfort. 'Your doctor phoned and said that your wife and the woman next door were with her when she went and she died very peacefully in her sleep. The doctor will phone the borstal to let Joe know, but he said he will leave it to you as to when to tell Jimmy.'

Jack got out of the car. 'I'm just going to have a quick word with John and then I'll run you home.'

Jack walked over to where John was standing with the rest of the gang, leaving Dickie feeling deeply distressed. He had been orphaned at the age of three, both of his parents having succumbed to the great influenza epidemic that had cost so many lives just after the First World War. Dickie Campbell had no other relations and was raised in a Dr Barnardo's home, where he had been treated kindly but without love. Gertie had been the mother he had never known and Dickie would grieve for her as intensely as any rightful birth son would grieve for his mother.

Jack got back into the car and drove Dickie home in silence, but as he pulled up outside the Campbell residence, he put his hand on Dickie's shoulder and said quietly, 'Forget about work, Dickie, just concentrate on taking care of your family, they will need you even more now.'

Dickie knew that the depot manager was right, but at this moment, he felt as though he desperately needed somebody to take care of him.

Freda and Ada Peake were now drinking tea, although Ada suspected Dickie would need something stronger, as they had done.

She went to the sideboard to pour him a large whisky as soon as she heard his key in the door and Freda looked up at him expectantly as he entered the kitchen, as though she believed her husband could make everything alright again. She still could not take in the fact that she would never hear her mother's voice again or hear her cackling laugh when she had made a rude comment. As yet, Freda had not shed one single tear, not even when she and Ada Peake had prepared her mother for that final journey, but now the expression of despair upon Dickie's face acted as a signal of acceptance for Freda. She rose to embrace her husband, clinging to him tightly, and both weeping unashamedly as they were united in their grief.

Ada Peake let herself out of the front door and went back to her own house, feeling so very sad at having lost her good friend, although she thought to herself, no bugger will cry like that for me when I go.

At the borstal in Loughton, Mr Butler the governor sat drumming his fingers on his desk, much to the annoyance of his secretary. Mr Butler was not sure how to handle the situation that would arise as a result of the telephone call he had received from Dagenham. Joe Campbell's grandmother had just died, which was not unusual in itself, for three grandmothers and two grandfathers of trainees had passed away during the past year, but this news would be particularly hard to impart. The boys had been allowed to attend the funerals, but Home Office regulations insisted that they must be accompanied by an officer, unless the trainee had already been given home leave and a date for his release. Campbell had arrived back from home leave that very morning and now the governor must summon him to his office and tell him the sad news.

He ordered his secretary to, 'Make out a travel warrant for Campbell, Miss Lloyd, I'm giving him another forty-eight hour pass.'

Miss Lloyd had served as secretary to five previous governors spanning eighteen years and had never heard of anything like this before.

'Mr Butler, you do not have the authority to issue another pass so soon, without Home Office approval, and if you do so, it will be my duty to report it.'

'Well, well, Miss Lloyd, and here was me believing you knew your job.' The governor smiled sardonically. 'Has nobody ever informed you that governors can waive Home Office approval if he or she believes that the welfare of a trainee or prisoner is of paramount importance?' He was bluffing, but Miss Lloyd had no way of knowing that, at least not for the time being. His tone hardened. 'Now ... just ... do ... it.' He emphasised each word carefully.

Mr Butler had intended telephoning the farm where Joe was working and asking the manager to send him to his office, but then he decided to go there personally. He admired the young man and was convinced that Joe Campbell would one day make something of himself, given half the chance, but now the governor's mission was to attempt to lessen the blow he was about to deliver, at least, as much as he possibly could.

Mr Butler lit his pipe in the farm manager's office, while the manager went out to the meadow where Joe was tending the lambs.

Freda and Dickie had no way of knowing that their son had been granted another forty-eight hour pass and when Dickie opened the door to Joe, he thought Joe may have absconded upon hearing the news about his gran, but Joe soon reassured his father, by showing him the pass and the travel warrant. They walked into the front room, where Freda, who had seen Joe walking up the path, was determined not to fall apart in front of her eldest son.

Her resolve held firm as she told Joe of his gran's passing. 'Do you want to go up and see her, Joe?' she asked him. 'She looks peaceful and, well, almost happy.' She looked at Dickie. 'Wouldn't you say so, love?'

Dickie did not answer. He had seen the look on his son's face and knew that seeing his dead gran right now was the very last thing that Joe needed. 'There's time enough for that,' said Dickie. 'I was going to meet Jimmy from school, because he doesn't know yet, but there are still all the other arrangements that have to be made.'

Joe looked at the clock. 'I thought Jimmy came home for his dinner. It's gone two o'clock now.'

Freda answered, 'He knew that his gran wasn't well, so I gave him money for school dinners today.'

'I'll meet him at the school gates when they get out,' Joe told his father. 'Seeing me standing there may at least give him a clue that something's up.'

Once again, Dickie was immensely impressed at the maturity of his son. 'Thanks, Joe,' was all he could manage to say.

After Dickie had left to make the funeral arrangements, Joe once again demonstrated his caring nature by suggesting that they invite Ada Peake in for a cup of tea or a drink.

'She really liked Gran,' he said to his mother. 'Mrs Peake must be feeling lonely over there all on her own.'

Freda agreed at once. 'Yes, Joe, go over and ask her. I think it's a lovely idea, because I don't know what I would have done without her this morning.'

Joe knocked on Mrs Peake's door. He could hear the sound of shuffling feet and then a voice. 'Who is it? What do you want?'

'It's Joe from next door, Mrs Peake, will you come over and have a drop of something or a cup of tea with me and Mum?'

The door opened marginally, just enough for Joe to see Ada's red-rimmed eyes, where she had been crying.

'You've got enough on your plate without bothering about me,' she told him.

'My mum said she would like to see you. Will you come, Mrs Peake?'

A moment later, Ada Peake's door opened fully and she stepped out to follow Joe, grateful for the opportunity to share her own grief with others.

Dickie was still making the funeral arrangements when it was time for Joe to leave for school and Jimmy stopped in his tracks when he saw Joe standing outside his school, for it was only that very morning that he had waved goodbye to him, when Joe had left to return to the borstal. He walked slowly towards his brother and knew instinctively that Joe had something bad to tell him. Jimmy held his breath as he stood in front of his brother, waiting for Joe to speak. Reggie Godber usually came home with Jimmy, but he was at the dentist that afternoon, so it was just Jimmy and Joe who walked home together after Joe had broken the news to his brother.

Jimmy's first reaction was quite typical of most 11-year-olds who had not yet learned to consider anybody other than themselves.

'I hope this is not going to mean that I'm going to miss out at York Hall.'

He said it without thinking and was instantly ashamed of himself.

It wasn't that he did not care about his gran, for he loved her just as much as the rest of the family, but he so badly wanted to be a boxing champion and Jimmy virtually crossed his fingers every day, praying that nothing would prevent him from attaining his dream.

Joe read his mind. 'Don't mention York Hall for a while yet,' he advised. 'I don't want Mum to be more upset than she is now, but I'll have a word with Dad before I go back and the governor has told me I can come back again for Gran's funeral.'

Dickie had arranged Gertie's funeral and later that evening, he told the family of the undertaker's recommendations.

'The funeral will be at Eastbrook Cemetery, wherever that is, on Monday at two o'clock. They will bring the coffin tomorrow and your gran will stay in her room until the Monday morning, when they will bring her coffin downstairs and put her in the front room until the hearse arrives.' Dickie looked uncomfortable. 'They said that they could dismantle Gran's bed and dispose of it if we so wished, so that there will be enough room for the coffin and the trestles.'

Dickie looked towards Freda, who nodded. 'We don't want to keep the bed now,' she said simply.

'I'm going to Camden in the morning,' said Dickie to his sons.

'Jimmy, I would like you to come with me to invite your gran's old cronies to the funeral and Joe, you could pop in and see Mary again if you want to come with us.'

Joe and Jimmy both agreed and it was decided they would leave just as soon as the undertakers had been. Neither Joe nor Jimmy expressed any desire to view the body of their dead grandmother; in fact, Jimmy felt a little scared that on the other side of his bedroom wall lay a real body and he knew that he would not be turning his bedroom light out until after the funeral, when Joe had gone back.

'I know where Eastbrook Cemetery is,' Jimmy told them before going to bed. 'It's behind a great big fishing lake called The Chase. Me and Reggie have been there loads of times ...' he paused. 'The lake, I mean, not the cemetery.'

The journey to Camden the next morning was a sad affair and none of them felt like saying very much. Joe got off the train at Mornington Crescent and Jimmy went on to Camden Town with his father. They had agreed to stay for just two hours, but Mary was not at home and David would be at his day centre at this time of day. One of the neighbours informed Joe that Mary had volunteered to accompany David and several of his friends to the Natural History Museum in Kensington, but

Joe knew he would not have enough time to travel there and back and to try to find Mary in such a large establishment.

It had been his mother who had warned him that Mary may not be at home and she had advised him to take paper and pencil with him, so that he could at least leave a note for her. Joe scribbled a few lines, pushed it through the letter box and walked to Camden Town, where he spotted Jimmy sitting outside the Spread Eagle with a bottle of lemonade and a bag of crisps. Dickie had seen his eldest son from the window and quickly finished his beer and went out to join him, for the landlord of the Spread Eagle was not as liberal as the landlord of the Church Elm and would never allow Joe to have a pint of beer.

They were back in Dagenham an hour later.

Gertie's funeral was a lively affair and Bella and Alf Spinks had arrived from Camden Town, as had half a dozen of Gertie's old friends and neighbours from north London. Alf had hired an eight-seater minibus with a driver, so that he could have a good drink himself. 'Just to help give Gertie a good send-off,' he told his wife.

Several members from the over-sixties club and, of course, Ada were there to pay their last respects and they crowded into the front room, where Gertie was lying in her open coffin that had since been placed on trestles.

'Doesn't she look peaceful?' said one elderly woman.

'Bugger looking peaceful,' retorted Ada, 'I'd sooner be having a good old knees-up any day.'

Copious quantities of spirits, but only a few bottles of beer, had already been consumed and Dickie had made sure there would be plenty more after they had returned from the cemetery. Some of the so-called "mourners" would be drunk even before the hearse arrived, not least of all Alf Spinks, who had never been known to pass up on a free drink.

Joe had arrived at ten o'clock that morning, just as the undertakers were carrying Gertie's coffin from her bedroom down to the front room. He had now seen his gran lying in her coffin; it would have been impossible not to, for he had been helping his father to dispense the drinks in the front room, while Freda was in the kitchen making tea and coffee for those few who did not drink alcohol. Jimmy had gone to school without seeing his gran for the last time, because he was adamant that he would not attend the funeral and his mother and father did not press him, and neither did Joe, when Jimmy had told him before he'd gone back to Loughton a few days ago.

Ada Peake voiced her disapproval to Dickie as the first guests began to arrive. 'It's all part of the grieving process and it shouldn't be ignored. Look at Freda, I reckon me making her help lay Gertie out has helped her to come to terms with her mum dying right before her eyes.'

Dickie would be forever grateful to Ada, but he could not agree with her over this issue. 'I know you were a marvel with Freda, Ada, but there's a big difference between a grown woman and an 11-year-old kid.'

He poured her a large whisky and then attended to the first of the mourners as Freda opened the door to receive more of the floral tributes that were to be arranged in the front garden. The flowers had been arriving since well before nine o'clock and now there were dozens of beautiful tributes to her mother laid out all over the lawn.

She was surprised at how lovely the weather was, because when Dickie had taken her to the cinema, all the funerals she had ever seen on the screen had been conducted in the pouring rain, with thunder and lightening crashing around the actors. Freda was not sure if she was very happy that her beloved mother was to be put into the ground on such a lovely day. Behind her, she could hear the babble of voices and she could not help but feel resentful that half of those here today were here not to pay their last respects, but to have a free booze-up. She wished the undertakers would come soon and cover her mother's face away from those curious eyes and the alcohol-laden breath that some of them were breathing over her, because some of the elderly women had virtually gone from bottle to bottle, sampling the array of drinks that Dickie had provided. There was whisky, naturally gin, vodka, Pimm's, port, brandy and Babycham, the latter being strengthened with a large measure of brandy. The beer was mostly ignored, for who wanted common beer, when such a selection of spirts was available. Dickie realised that he had made a mistake within the first half-hour, although it was too late to do anything about it now, but he had been so determined to do Gertie proud on her last day on earth that none of it seemed to matter any more.

Freda stood alone by the front door, somehow feeling comfort from looking at the tributes that had now grown considerably in number and she had inspected each and every one as they had been delivered.

There was a wreath from the girls at May and Baker, a lovely bouquet from Dickie's workmates, a floral cross from the neighbours and even a wreath sent from the Ford Motor Company.

The first funeral car came into view along Heathway and Freda went into the house. 'They're here,' she announced to the gathering.

The chief funeral director asked everybody to leave the front room, so that Freda, Dickie and Joe could say their final goodbyes to their loved one in private. The director also left the room, closing the door behind him.

Joe touched his gran's cheek. 'Goodbye, Gran,' he said, and then left the room.

Dickie did exactly the same, leaving his wife alone with her mother for the very last time.

Freda looked down at her mother and then bent to kiss her forehead. 'Goodbye, my darling,' she whispered, 'sleep well.'

After the service and the committal proceedings, the funeral party returned to the Campbells' house to give Gertie the promised "good send-off".

Freda, Dickie and Joe did not join in with the wake, but even Ada Peake had imbibed far more alcohol than she was used to and was regaling the others with tales from the over-sixties club, some of them quite rude. Even when sober, Ada could tell a good story, but when she'd had a drink there was no stopping her. Loud guffaws of laughter rang around the front room that just a short time ago had been Freda's mother's final resting place, before being lowered into the ground. Freda was finding it difficult that these people could forget her mother so easily, but Ada Peake saw the look of disapproval on Freda's face and took her to one side.

'Freda, love, we don't mean any disrespect to Gertie. We all loved her in our own way and this is our way of coping with her passing – by giving thanks for the time we have known her and allowing us the opportunity to celebrate her life.'

Freda felt moved and comforted by Ada Peake's kind words and she also knew that Ada, along with all of her friends at the over-sixties club, was very much aware that their own time on this earth was drawing to a close and that any one of them could be the next person to be given a "good send-off".

Reggie Godber's mother had agreed that Jimmy could have his tea with them, but Jimmy was not hungry. The sound of merriment from his own house had horrified him and embarrassed him in front of Reggie, even though Mrs Godber attempted to ease his distress.

'When you get older, you'll learn that most adults are just children that have grown bigger, that's all. Your gran's friends are just big kids pretending they are not hurt, a bit like when you and Reggie fall over and pretend it doesn't hurt, but all the time it's as sore as h ... well, anything. It's the same with that lot next door; they're all hurting, too.'

She offered him a slice of her home-made steak-and-kidney pie.

'Go on, Jimmy,' urged Reggie, 'get that down your neck. I bet even your gran couldn't make one like this.' Reggie could have bitten his tongue off and, judging by the look that his mother gave him, she wished he had. 'Sorry, Jimmy,' Reggie told him. 'Me and my big mouth, I really am sorry.'

Jimmy nodded, accepted the pie and took a mouthful. After rolling his eyes with delight, he told Reggie, 'You were right, Reggie, this is the best steak-and-kidney pie I've ever tasted in my whole life.'

Before taking another bite, he added, 'Mind you, my dad and Joe don't like kidneys, so we never have it anyway.'

Mrs Godber ruffled Jimmy's hair. 'Cheeky monkey,' she said, with a relieved smile.

There was a knock on the door, so Reggie's mother went to answer it and brought Joe back in with her.

'Sorry if I'm interrupting your tea, Jimmy, but I have to get back to Loughton. The governor has gone out on a limb for me and I promised him I would be back by six.'

Joe had only said goodbye to his parents, none of the others, for even though his mother had tried to explain about some people's behaviour at a funeral, Joe had not been able to accept their apparent merriment, for at that particular moment, he felt as though he would never be able to laugh again.

Joe shook Jimmy's hand and wished him the best of luck at York Hall. 'Do me a favour, Jimmy, send me a couple of copies of *The Dagenham Post* the following week, so I can show the other lads what a champion I have for a brother.'

'Only if I win, Joe, only if I win.'

'He'll win, Joe,' Reggie told Joe confidently. 'Joe the bookie on Heathway has refused to take any more bets on Jimmy and he should know.'

'I expect you're right there, Reggie,' Joe laughed. 'I don't know about your bookie, but I do know that the ones in Camden can spot a sure thing a mile away.'

'Fancy a walk to the station with me?' Joe asked his brother.

Jimmy needed no second bidding and went into the hallway for his jacket. He thanked Mrs Godber, said goodbye to Reggie and then he and Joe walked up the hill to Heathway station. Jimmy bought a return-ticket to Stratford, where Joe needed to change for the Central line to Loughton, for Jimmy had no wish to hurry home, at least until it was only his mother and father that remained in the house. Joe did not protest, for he knew he would have felt exactly the same way.

Chapter Fourteen

It was Jimmy Campbell's big night. Jimmy had arrived at York Hall in London's Bethnal Green with his trainer and his father at seven o'clock, when the draw for the first round of the competition had been made. Jimmy was to box a boy called Paul Jackson from Stoke-on-Trent, which gave Fred Loake considerable satisfaction that Jimmy had not been drawn against the only boy he believed could pose his protégé a few problems.

'What do you know about this Paul Jackson, Fred?' Dickie asked the trainer.

Fred Loake had made it his business to study every boxer that Jimmy was likely to meet and he had compiled a dossier on each one of them.

'He's not a bad boxer, but he can't punch, and if he gets whacked, he goes down like a sack of spuds. He's lost all of his contests by the referee having them stopped.'

'So how many has he lost then?' asked Jimmy.

Fred had hoped he wouldn't be asked that question. 'Two,' he replied.

Jimmy refused to let his trainer off the hook. 'Out of how many?' he demanded.

'Thirty-two,' admitted Fred, 'but don't forget, he's been boxing for nearly three years and it's not how many fights he's had, it's who he's been up against and Stoke-on-Trent is not exactly noted for it's champion boxers. Anyway, he can't punch the way you can and all you have to do is to keep after him and I guarantee he'll fold. And I'll tell you both something else,' Fred said to father and son, 'none of these boys wanted to be drawn against Jimmy tonight and that goes for their trainers as well.' Fred punched Jimmy lightly on the shoulder. 'We are on third, so we have plenty of time for a cup of tea before you need to get changed. Dickie, why don't you get yourself a beer from the bar, your seat is reserved, so you can stay there if you like until they announce Jimmy will be next on.'

This sounded like a good idea to Dickie. He knew that only the trainers were allowed in the dressing rooms and Jimmy and Fred had about thirty minutes before they had to report to see the doctor and for Jimmy to be weighed. The bar was crowded and there were no seats at all, but Dickie managed to get served and found a comfortable place to stand, at least for a while. Dickie then found himself being squashed against the wall as more and more people forced their way into the bar, so he decided not to have another pint; it was far too crowded for his liking. He took his seat before the first contest had begun, just in time to hear the master of ceremonies make his announcement and introduce some local celebrities. One by one, they stepped into the ring, to be greeted by applause and cheers. The ex-British heavyweight champion received the warmest greeting, although a few of the minor film actors were afforded just polite applause. Dickie was stunned at the master of ceremonies' final introduction.

'Ladies and gentlemen, it now gives me great pleasure to introduce a young man, who is rapidly becoming one of London's most influential businessmen and who has generously sponsored tonight's event – Mr Duggie Murphy.'

Duggie Murphy rose from a ringside seat to the left of Dickie and climbed into the ring, strutting around with his two clenched fists held high above his head. None of the spectators from outside of London had heard of him, although Duggie Murphy and his brother Micky were well known and feared by the local fans. The applause was not enthusiastic, with only a few cheers, and Duggie Murphy left the ring scowling at the lack of respect he felt was due to him.

Businessman my arse, Dickie said to himself as Duggie returned to his ringside seat. He'll not fork out good money, unless there's something in it for him. I wonder what the bugger's up to, he thought.

What Duggie Murphy was "up to" was already causing some consternation among the established boxing fraternity, for he had applied for a promoter's licence. This was the third amateur event he had sponsored, believing it would meet with the approval of the officials from the British Boxing Board of Control, who were responsible for issuing all promoters, managers and trainers with their licences. Although his brother was still serving a prison sentence, Duggie Murphy still had an unblemished record, so there was no reason to refuse him his licence, but his reputation for being an exponent of strong-arm tactics was quickly becoming legendary.

Duggie was far too astute to become involved in any violence himself, but he employed plenty of men who were not too fussy about how they earned a few pounds. There were stories of stallholders who refused to deal with him being attacked, and their stalls being torched, and a market superintendent's office had been petrol-bombed while he was still inside, because the man had banned one of Murphy's vans from entering his market. The superintendent was still undergoing skin grafts for his burns by all accounts and the police were powerless to take action, without proof or a statement from one of the victims, but none was forthcoming, so it seemed almost certain that Duggie Murphy would be granted a licence to become a boxing promoter in the near future.

Dickie attempted to concentrate on the first two bouts and thought how proud Gertie would have been tonight. Gertie had written down her last wishes weeks before she had died and one of those wishes was that any money left over from her insurance policy after the funeral had been paid for should be used to rig Jimmy out with a complete boxing kit, including boots. There had been more than enough to purchase a smart dressing gown, shorts, vest and a pair of boxing boots as fine as any on display that evening.

In the dressing room, Jimmy was shadow boxing to warm up, when an official came into the room and told Fred that he should bring his boxer and wait by the entrance to the arena, until the last two boxers had left the ring. Cheers and some boos rang out around the hall as the verdict was announced for the previous bout and then the fanfare of trumpets from a gramophone signalled the entry of the next two combatants. A toss of a coin had decided that Paul Jackson would enter the ring first and Jimmy watched his opponent walk down the carpeted aisle and climb into the ring. Jimmy felt the familiar butterflies in his stomach, although he now knew that they would disappear the moment he climbed through the ropes. Jimmy was unaware of the cheers that were ringing out for him as he, too, walked that lonely path, even though he knew that he was the local favourite. Paul Jackson had only his mother and father to cheer him on, while Jimmy was being supported by dozens of fans from Dagenham, virtually all from the Ford boxing team. Many of Dickie's friends from Camden Town as well as every Londoner also packed the hall out. Jimmy did not agree with his trainer that a hometown boxer always had the advantage over an outsider, for he felt that he could box anywhere in the country, without even being aware of who was cheering for whom.

Dickie had not actually seen his son dressed for the ring before and when the third contest was announced, he could hardly believe this was his Jimmy walking down the aisle. It was not just the outfit that he was wearing; it was the look of pure concentration on his face as he looked neither one way nor the other, not even to acknowledge his father.

When the introductions were over, the bell sounded to begin the first round and the two young boxers circled each other warily. The first punch was thrown by Jimmy, who was surprised at how easily and how quickly Jackson had moved his head to one side to allow the blow to pass harmlessly over his shoulder. Jackson countered with three punches that all landed on Jimmy's chest and upper arms. They were not hard blows, but they did score points, and Jimmy was again surprised at the speed of his opponent. When the bell sounded to end the first round, Jimmy, his trainer and everyone in the hall knew that Jackson had won the first round, for Jimmy had not managed to land one telling punch in reply to the two-dozen or so thrown by Jackson.

'As soon as the bell sounds, rush him,' advised Fred. 'You know he can't hurt you, but there's no way you can win this one on points.'

Sitting in the audience, Dickie was of the same opinion and without knowing the advice Fred had given, he silently willed his son to do just that.

Jimmy was on his feet as soon as the timekeeper called "seconds out" and before the clang of the bell had faded, he was across the ring, where he landed two hard punches, one to Jackson's midriff and, as the boy's hands dropped to cover his stomach, the second blow caught him flush on the jaw. Jackson fell to the canvas and the referee began to count over him.

'One ... two ... three ...'

The referee abandoned the count, because it was obvious that Jackson would never be able to continue. The referee waved his arms to signal that the contest was over and then waved the doctor into the ring to attend to the stricken boxer. The arena fell silent as the doctor and the boy's trainer worked hard to revive Paul Jackson and there was much relief when the boy finally managed to sit up and then stand unaided. The audience had been unnerved at the savage attack by such an innocent-looking boy, but Jimmy Campbell was a name they would remember for a long time to come. They applauded when Jimmy came over to a very pale and shaken Paul Jackson's corner and escorted him back to the dressing room, with the doctor close behind them.

Duggie Murphy had been a fight fan all his life and had even boxed as a youngster, although he had soon given up when he had discovered that biting and kicking was frowned upon by the referees and the judges. Duggie had seen all the best British fighters since the early thirties and he had no doubt whatsoever that Jimmy Campbell would become one of the all-time greats when he turned professional in a few years time. That Jimmy would become a professional prize fighter was a foregone conclusion as far as Duggie was concerned and he was keen to get a piece of the action. After what had happened to his eldest son, Duggie knew that Jimmy's father would have nothing to do with a Murphy, but Duggie had plenty of time to try to bring him round. He was aware that Joe Campbell was due to be released from borstal soon and it was just possible that Duggie may be able to make his move through him.

None of the boxers or their trainers was permitted to watch the other contests, so Dickie left the arena and met Jimmy and Fred outside. Dickie was surprised to see his son looking crestfallen as he left

York Hall with Fred Loake, for he had expected Jimmy to be over the moon after such a sensational victory.

'What's up with you, Jimmy?' Dickie asked his son. 'Anyone would think it was you that had got knocked out by the look on your face.'

Fred explained, 'Jimmy thinks he was outclassed in there tonight and only won because of a lucky punch. I keep telling him that even the top professionals often feel the same way after a fight, because there's all that build up, along with the tension, and then it's an anticlimax when it's all over.'

'But he's already had eight fights,' said Dickie.

'Yes, but none as important as this one.'

Fred patted Jimmy on the shoulder. 'After you win the next one, you won't feel half as down as you do right now.' They walked towards Bethnal Green Station. 'Paul Jackson will never be able to punch as hard as you can,' Fred assured Jimmy, 'but in a few months and with a lot of hard work, you will be able to box as well as he did. I was watching you closely during that first round and you were way too slow, but it was a good lesson for me as well as for you, because on Monday we concentrate on your footwork to speed you up. We have five whole weeks to get you dancing around like Fred Astaire.'

'Or Ginger Rogers.' Jimmy shrugged off his depression. 'I felt a right prat in the first round though. I just couldn't get near him and every time I went to whack him, I found myself punching at thin air.' Fred showed the travel passes to the ticket collector and they walked down to the platform. 'You were right about him being a powder-puff puncher though,' said Jimmy. 'He didn't hurt me at all, but just think what he would be like if he could punch as well as box.'

'Like you will be, son,' Dickie said quietly. 'Just like you will be and in the not-too-distant future, either.'

'That's just what I've been trying to tell you, Jimmy.' Fred's excitement was infectious. 'In six months time, you could be the best pound-for-pound amateur boxer in the country.'

Jimmy suddenly felt depressed again. 'But I haven't got six months though, have I? You said yourself; the next one will be in five weeks.'

Dickie interrupted the conversation between his son and the trainer. 'Don't be such a misery guts,' he admonished Jimmy. 'How do you think that Jackson kid and his parents are feeling right now?

Nobody's forcing you to carry on, so if you don't fancy it, then just pack it in if you want to, but don't keep harping on about it.'

It was exactly what Jimmy needed. It was not the first time that he had felt depressed after a contest, but it had never been as severe as this.

'Yeah, you're right, Dad, sorry,' Jimmy apologised. 'Blimey, if I feel like this after winning a fight, what would I be like if I lost one?'

Dickie and Fred both laughed and Jimmy grinned rather shamefacedly.

On the way home, Fred Loake explained the next stage of the competition. 'The draw for the next round will be made at the ABA headquarters on Monday and the trainers will be notified by post by Wednesday, but from now on, we'll be told who you will be up against. We'll have plenty of time to decide what our tactics will be, but the other trainers'll know all about you, Jimmy, and will also be making their own plans. Before we left, I was told that the next round will be in Birmingham and we have to be at the arena by five o'clock on that Saturday. The train tickets will be posted out to us and the rooms have already been booked in one of the best hotels in the city.

'I was talking to one of the trainers who went there last year and he told me that the hotel chef stays on duty until well after midnight, so that even the boxers who are last on the bill will have a three-course meal waiting for them when they get back. He said they even bring out a bottle of plonk for the parents.'

Dickie was not overly impressed. 'I'm not very fond of wine; can we swap it for a pint of brown ale?'

'I don't know, I never asked, but I don't think that should be a problem. This hotel has its own swimming pool, gymnasium and a tennis court that we can use free of charge and the next morning, we're given a full English breakfast, we can use all the facilities and we're also given lunch before we leave.'

Dickie had one further question to ask the trainer. 'Do we have to decide who will be going; I mean, before they send out the tickets?'

'No, the hotel rooms are made out in the trainer's name, because they know from past experience that people change their minds about going at the last minute, especially mums. Every trainer is allocated two single rooms, one for the boxer and one for himself, plus a double room for the parents, or whoever the two guests will be.'

'So if Jimmy's mum doesn't want to go and Joe is home, he could come with us instead?'

'You can take whoever you like, as long as they share your double room.' Fred gave a dirty laugh. 'You could take one of your hairy-arsed mates if you wanted to, but I couldn't guarantee single beds.' Fred's comment had been crude in front of Jimmy and he tried to make amends. 'Dickie, it would be a shame not to make the most of the opportunity to live the life of Riley, even if it's only for twenty-four hours.'

Dickie glanced at his son to see if he could gauge his reaction, but Jimmy's face was impassive. 'Well,' Dickie concluded, 'we have plenty of time to decide who will be coming with us, so we'll leave it there for now.'

Dickie believed that Jimmy's trainer may have solved a problem that had been causing him some concern. Freda had returned to work, although she had yet to work a full week, often taking to her bed, too full of her own grief even to see Jimmy off to school, and the chip shop along Heathway provided the evening meal several times a week. Dickie would not be able to leave his wife on her own and it would be unfair to ask Joe to stay with her, for Joe would be home before Jimmy's next contest. The obvious answer was for Joe to go instead and perhaps take a friend with him. With a final handshake, Fred left them at Heathway station, as he lived in the opposite direction.

Freda looked anxiously for any sign of visible damage to her son's face as Jimmy walked into the kitchen and was relieved to find no obvious signs of wear and tear. Dickie did not go into any detail, merely telling his wife that Jimmy had won his contest. Freda was pleased, although she showed no interest in travelling to Birmingham and staying overnight in a posh hotel.

It had been a distressing day for Freda, for she had felt her mother's presence all over the house and eventually, she had known that she must take herself out, even if only for a few hours. She had gone to see her friend Amy Ashby, who had been only too happy to get out of her own house for a few hours and together, they had first taken a bus to the shopping centre in the town of Barking. However, they had not been there very long, before they decided that they preferred Romford, so, thirty minutes and one bus ride later, they were once again browsing around the familiar stalls of the market.

Amy Ashby could not understand Freda's reluctance to watch Jimmy box, while at the same time, pasting all the newspaper reports into a scrapbook that she kept hidden away in her underwear drawer.

'If he was one of mine, I'd be at the ringside shouting my head off for him,' said Amy as they had sat in one of the market cafes drinking tea.

'My Dickie took me to a boxing match when we were courting,' Freda told her friend. 'I'll never forget the sight of this old bloke – well, he seemed old to me at the time – being battered around the ring by this young fighter, who was treating him like a punchbag. It was the crowd that sickened me the most though. You should have seen the bloodthirsty look on their faces, even my Dickie, and they booed the poor sod when he went down for the umpteenth time and couldn't get up again.' Freda put another spoonful of sugar in her tea and stirred it absent-mindedly. 'I know Dickie tells me that schoolboy boxing is totally different from professional fighting, but it's what it could lead to that bothers me, 'cos I heard Dickie tell Tommy Smith that Jimmy is bound to turn professional as soon as he's sixteen.' Freda looked appealingly at Amy. '16, for Christ's sake. He'll still be only a boy and up against grown men.'

Amy's response was to remind Freda that, 'That newspaper fellow reckons Jimmy is the most exciting prospect he's seen in forty years of reporting and he predicts that Jimmy will be this year's junior ABA champion.'

Freda did not expect anyone else to understand her emotions; certainly her mother hadn't and she herself had difficulty in understanding the mixed emotions she felt with every victory achieved by her son.

Freda made Dickie and Jimmy a bedtime drink and wondered if Jimmy's contest would be reported in the national Sunday papers, as well as the local *Dagenham Post* on Wednesday. She raised the question with Dickie.

'Yes, it will be. I can remember following the results last year, although the reporters are not allowed to interview junior boxers or their trainers. Though they don't really have to, because they know which clubs the boys box for and if they have a mind to, they can soon find out all they need to know. I can remember a few years ago, when it came out that one of the senior champions had been expelled from school for bullying. It cost him the best boxer's award, because *The News of the World* decided that it was not in the sport's best interest to give an award to a boy they'd branded as a thug.'

'Best boxer award,' said Freda, 'what's that?'

'I forgot to mention it, the paper gives an award to whoever they consider had been the best boxer on the bill that night.'

'What sort of chance does Jimmy have of winning the prize for tonight?' Freda asked her husband, in spite of herself. 'And do you know what the prize will be?'

'Look out of the window, Mum, and you might see a flying pig,' scoffed Jimmy in reply. 'Blimey, Mum, I only threw two punches and the best boxer prize always goes to a fancy Dan boxer, who wins on points. Well, that's what Fred told me anyway.'

'Fred may be a bloody good trainer, but he doesn't know everything,' Dickie told his son. 'Six years ago, Don Cockell won the award twice in the senior division and neither of his fights lasted a single round and he went on to become the British champion. He went over to America after that and had a shot at the world title.'

'Yes, and I can remember how that one ended up, as well,' snorted Freda.

'So he got knocked out, but he gave it a bloody good go and we were all proud of him.' Dickie felt a little annoyed at his wife's negative attitude. 'Anyway, to answer your question about the award, it's usually a canteen of cutlery or a dinner service.'

'What happened to Cockell in the end, Dad?' asked Jimmy.

'He never fought again, he didn't have to. He made enough money on that title fight to set himself up with a hotel on the Isle of Wight and as far as I know, he's still there.'

Jimmy yawned and grinned at his parents. 'This boxing lark don't half take it out of you, I'm off to my bed. Goodnight, see you in the morning.'

Freda also felt drained and she, too, went up to bed, leaving Dickie to pour himself a large nightcap. The large nightcap became two large nightcaps as he sat in his armchair for the next hour, going through in his mind what he had witnessed that evening and wondering how Freda would react when she read tomorrow's Sunday papers, for he was positive they would have plenty to say about Jimmy Campbell.

Chapter Fifteen

Dickie was the first up the next morning and he walked to the newsagents for the morning paper, meeting Reggie Godber on the way, who was coming back with his father's newspaper tucked under his arm.

'Cor, just you wait till you read what they've written about Jimmy,' said Reggie, almost in awe. 'That must have been some fight and I only wish I could have been there to see it.'

'Jimmy thought your dad was going to take you; he was disappointed that you weren't there,' said Dickie.

'My dad said he couldn't afford it,' replied the boy. 'He could afford to go to the dog track though.'

'I'll make you a promise, Reggie.' Dickie felt sorry for Jimmy's good friend. 'If Jimmy gets to the Albert Hall, you'll be coming with us as well.'

'Do you really mean it?' Reggie's eyes were shining. 'Yeah, of course you do, and Jimmy will get to the final, I know he will. Thanks, Mr Campbell.'

Reggie skipped off home and Dickie continued on his way to buy the newspapers. He bought three different papers, *The News of the World*, *The Sunday Pictorial* and *The Observer*.

He stood outside the newsagents and read all three sports pages.

The *Observer* did not approve of junior boxing and merely listed the results without comment. But Dickie groaned when he turned to the sporting page of *The Pictorial*, for not only was there a lurid account of Jimmy's contest, but there was also a photograph that had captured the exact moment when Jackson had slumped to the floor, with a stricken look clearly visible on the lad's face. Although Jimmy was standing sideways on to the camera, he still looked menacing, for his fists were ready to strike again and his face was contorted by what appeared to be hatred for the other boy.

The reporter had written:

> Last night, at precisely two minutes past seven at the York Hall, hundreds of spectators and I witnessed the transformation of a young and innocent-looking boy of just 11 years of age into a prehistoric savage, whose ferocity shocked even the most hardened East-London crowd into a stunned silence.

Dickie read no further. Anyone seeing this picture and reading those words who did not know Jimmy would never believe how polite and well behaved he was outside the ring, but no one could deny that Jimmy was not the same boy when he climbed through the ropes.

Dickie considered throwing this particular newspaper away, but he knew somebody else would be sure to show it to Freda if he didn't.

He turned to *The News of the World* and the first words that immediately caught his attention were: Jimmy Campbell – unanimous choice as best boxer.

There was no photograph and the report was moderate, with the reason given for the award being made being that the two blows from Jimmy had been delivered with such speed, accuracy and power that the panel had considered that Jimmy Campbell had been the most outstanding boxer of the evening.

Both Freda and Jimmy were in the kitchen when Dickie returned with the newspapers and he showed the small report from the *The Observer* to Jimmy first, who then passed it to his mother. Next, his father opened the sports page of *The News of the World* and pointed to the headline.

'Mum, I've won the best boxer prize.' Jimmy was jumping up and down with excitement. 'Dad was right after all; it's not only fancy boxers who win the prize.'

Freda took the newspaper, read the report and then asked, 'What do you think the prize will be, it doesn't say anything about it here?'

'I think I can choose between a dinner service, a canteen of cutlery, or something like that, but Fred will let us know.' Jimmy was still excited by the news.

'A nice new dinner service would be lovely,' Freda smiled, 'we only have three matching plates left.'

Dickie handed *The Sunday Pictorial* to Jimmy and heard him gasp when he saw the picture that dominated one of the sports pages.

'What is it? What is it?' cried Freda, and she snatched the newspaper from Jimmy's hands.

Dickie expected a hysterical reaction, but he was amazed when Freda just handed back the paper to Jimmy.

'Prehistoric savage or not,' she told him, 'I can still give you a clip round the ear if you give me any old lip, so don't you forget it.'

'I won't, Mum, I promise,' grinned Jimmy.

After breakfast, Jimmy went off to meet Reggie Godber, promising to be back in time for the Sunday roast, while Dickie was looking forward to being the centre of attention when he went to the Church Elm for his lunchtime pint, expecting one on the house from the boxing-enthusiast publican.

With Jimmy out for the next few hours, it gave Freda the opportunity to talk to Dickie about their youngest son's boxing career before he went to the pub and so she asked him what the next step would be.

Dickie explained, 'He goes to Birmingham in five weeks' time and if he gets through that one, it will depend on who is left in, before the ABA decide where to hold the semi-finals. According to the paper, there are two Welsh boxers still in and one Scot, but the Irish lad lost on points, so you can forget about Dublin.' Dickie rolled himself a cigarette.

'I've decided not to go to Brum, Freda. John's got a big job coming up and to be honest, I don't want to leave you here on your own.' He looked at her hopefully. 'That is, unless you change your mind and want to come with us.'

Freda's emphatic shake of her head spoke louder than any words.

Dickie knew that she would not change her mind, so said, 'Joe will be out by then and I think it would be great for both of them if he went, instead. Fred Loake will make sure they'll be alright.'

This time, Freda nodded in agreement. 'They will like that, but if Jimmy gets through to the next round, I'm coming as well, no matter what it may cost and where it will be held.'

Dickie could hope for nothing more than her promise. 'I think we have to accept that Jimmy is a natural boxer and we have to go along with whatever he decides to do, but after seeing him in action last night, I reckon he will go all the way.'

There was a knock at the door and on answering it, Dickie was confronted by two men, one of whom was carrying a large and expensive-looking camera.

The other man spoke first after producing a card from his pocket, proclaiming him to be a reporter from *The Dagenham Post.*

'Hello, my name is Sidney Fullford from *The Post* and we would like to speak with Jimmy and take a photo of him for our paper.'

'You'd better come in then and have a word with my wife as well.'

The men entered and Dickie led them into the kitchen. Sidney knew that it was the mother he must convince if he was to get his story and a picture of the boy for this week's edition of his newspaper.

After Dickie had introduced him, Sidney told them in his most sincere voice, 'My editor feels that the article and picture in today's *Pictorial* has not been fair to Jimmy at all and it makes him out to be some sort of hooligan. You must be aware by now that our paper has been following his boxing career since his first contest and I have personally watched him box several times; in fact, I was at York Hall last night as well.' He produced a copy of the photograph from the Sunday newspaper. 'We want to print this, alongside another photograph of Jimmy Campbell standing in the middle of his parents, just like any other boy of his age. We were not allowed to speak to anyone last night, but the ABA is quite happy for us to interview the boxers and their families the following day.'

'I think that would be a super idea, don't you, Dickie?' said Freda.

'It's up to Joe.' Dickie was not too sure about how far to trust men from the press. 'I'll go next door and ask him how he feels about it.'

Jimmy readily agreed to pose with his parents and after half a dozen pictures had been taken, the photographer, his job having been completed, left and Sidney then took his notebook from another pocket and began to ask a few questions. On hearing that Jimmy and his family were originally from Camden Town, he told them, 'That's good; we can use that in our leader. Cannonball Campbell from Camden Town.'

'Leave it out,' spluttered Jimmy, 'Cannonball Campbell! Blimey, what do you think the kids at school would have to say about that? I'd never live it down.'

Freda was not amused. 'He's already been called a prehistoric savage and calling him a cannonball is not a lot better as far as I'm concerned.'

Sidney capitulated. 'If that's the way you feel, I'll not use the term, although if Jimmy gets through to the final, some other paper will be sure to give him a nickname, they usually do.' He folded his notebook and stood to leave. 'Oh, and there is one other thing I have to tell you, my editor will probably insist that we mention about Jimmy's brother Joe being in borstal.'

Dickie rose to his feet angrily. 'What arsehole told you about Joe?' he demanded.

'Actually, it was the sponsor at York Hall and he said to send his regards to all of you.'

'Fucking Duggie Murphy.' Dickie spat out the words.

Freda had also risen and she now placed a restraining hand on Dickie's chest as she felt he was about to attack the man.

'Dickie, Dickie, listen to me. It would have come out sooner or later and we have nothing to be ashamed of.'

The reporter had also been concerned when Jimmy's father had jumped up and he now attempted to mollify him. 'I can assure both of you that I will be as discreet as possible and these days, who cares about buying something that's fallen from the back of a lorry? We've all done it ourselves from time to time and nobody will think any the worse of Jimmy; in fact, it may even make him appear more human.' It was an unfortunate turn of phrase and Sidney quickly elaborated on his choice of words. 'What I mean is, I can make Jimmy Campbell and the whole of his family out to be one of us, a family like any other in Dagenham, except that the youngest son has the potential to be a great boxer.'

Sidney Fullford decided that the article he would write about Jimmy Campbell would portray him as being squeaky clean outside the boxing ring. He intended that the boy's parents would come to regard him as an ally, a confidant, and that they would be reluctant to talk to any reporter other than himself when the lad appeared at the Royal Albert Hall for the finals of the most famous amateur boxing tournament in the country.

Dickie showed him to the door, while Freda stayed inside muttering, 'Cannonball Campbell, the Caveman from Camden, whatever next?'

Jimmy rushed off to tell Reggie the latest news, knowing they would have a good laugh about it, for Reggie would not be at all jealous. In many ways, Jimmy was much like his older brother Joe, for neither of them quite realised that their self-effacing nature and modesty prevented all but the most spiteful or jealous people from wishing them anything other than good will. Unfortunately, there would always be the exception and on Monday morning in the school playground, Jimmy was to encounter a young boy who did not wish him well at all.

School had not yet even begun, when a boy who was in the same class as Jimmy strode over to him and, without warning, struck him a blow to the face with his clenched fist.

'How's that for a bunch of fives then?' the boy taunted Jimmy, beckoning for his friends to see what he had done to the would-be champion of the ABA.

There was a hush all over the playground as the other boys waited to see what would happen next. One of the teachers had witnessed the incident from the staffroom window, but he remained where he was, for he was also curious as to how Campbell would react. If Jimmy Campbell retaliated, the other boy would be flat on his back within seconds and even from this distance, the teacher could see the swelling appearing on Campbell's cheekbone.

Jimmy's hands remained by his side. 'What did that prove, John?' he asked the boy calmly. 'You come up to me without warning and just whack me one. Your dad works in Ford's, so if you have a problem with me, join the boxing club and we can sort it out properly in the ring and not in the school playground.'

John Mears had believed that by picking a fight with Jimmy Campbell, his reputation would be enhanced even if he lost, as he almost certainly would have. Jimmy turned and walked away and almost all of the other pupils did the same.

The teacher turned away from the window thoughtfully. He had only met Joe Campbell on one occasion, but he had been impressed by the young man's quiet dignity and his younger brother certainly showed all the signs of possessing the same quality.

The next day, John Mears was waiting at the school gate for Jimmy.

'You had one free swipe at me yesterday, but that's all you're going to get, John.' Jimmy's words left John and everybody else who was within earshot in no doubt that he meant every word.

'I want to say in front of all the others that I am sorry for what I did yesterday.' John looked around at the dozens of pupils who could hear every word he was saying. 'I was trying to be flash, but all I managed to do was to make myself look the biggest bloody prat of all time. I'm sorry, Jimmy.'

Jimmy held out his hand and John took it eagerly, his eyes suddenly becoming moist, and the other pupils broke out into a spontaneous applause.

The same teacher who had seen the incident yesterday also witnessed this morning's exchange as he came into the playground to call assembly.

'Well done, Jimmy,' he said as Jimmy walked past him and into the school.

On Wednesday, *The Dagenham Post* showed a reproduction of *The Sunday Pictorial's* photograph on the left-hand side of their front page, while on the right-hand side they had printed another photograph of equal size showing Jimmy with his parents.

Underneath the left picture was the caption, "The Cannonball Kid", with an accurate report of the contest. It was a fair and quite complimentary article that did not use expressions such as "Prehistoric Savage", although it made it clear that Jimmy Campbell was a boxer of exceptional ability and power. Underneath the delightful family photograph were quotes about Jimmy from his trainer, and quotes from Ada Peake, the headmaster of Jimmy's school and Reggie Godber, who told the reporter that he was proud to be Jimmy's best friend. The three adults spoke of Jimmy's politeness and devotion to his mother, his father and his brother Joe, who had been away for a while, but would be back home in time for the next round of the competition. Sidney Fullford the reporter had persuaded the editor not to mention anything about borstal, although the editor had insisted they would use the name "Cannonball Campbell". Sidney believed that nobody reading his article and seeing the photograph of Jimmy with his parents could ever call him a prehistoric savage, except those who had been at York Hall last Saturday.

That evening, which was not a training night, Fred Loake called round to give Jimmy the news about his next opponent and a list from which to decide the prize he would select. Jimmy did not even look at the list, but set it down to one side; he was eager to know who he would be up against in Birmingham and to discover as much as he could about his next opponent.

'It's a good draw, Jimmy,' Fred assured him. 'Probably the best we could have hoped for. His name is Billy Robson and I can tell you, he'll be no match for you, even though he can dig a bit. He relies on a clubbing right swing that you can see coming from a mile away and it can be avoided by moving to his left and keeping away from the ropes.'

'He won at Bethnal Green though, and on a knockout,' said Jimmy.

'Only because the other boy got careless. Danny Williams was so far ahead on points after two rounds that he thought it was in the bag. His trainer warned him to be careful, but he wanted to show the crowd his fancy footwork and he walked straight into Robson's right hand.' Fred accepted a beer from Dickie. 'It's not a mistake you will make, Jimmy. Robson is slow and one punch doesn't make a boxer.

'I've seen him box a few times, but he only wins against novices or those who get careless. You're no novice and I'll make damned sure you won't get careless.'

'Tell me about Ronnie Baxter, Fred.' Jimmy was curious about another boxer who had boxed at York Hall. 'One of the boxing magazine writers wrote that he would not bet a penny on either of us coming out on top if or when we meet.'

Ronnie Baxter was the one boxer that Fred wanted to avoid, although Jimmy would almost certainly have to face him sooner or later. 'Forget about Ronnie Baxter, you haven't come through the next one yet,' Fred snapped angrily. 'Robson's not going to roll over and let you tickle his tummy, you know. He's going to turn up and give it all he's got, just like the rest of them.'

Suitably admonished, Jimmy blushed as he said. 'Yeah, you're right, Fred. Sorry for jumping the gun, I'll keep my feet on the ground until after Brum.'

'Right, now you've got that sorted out,' said Freda, 'how about letting me have a look at this list of yours.'

Without looking at it himself, Jimmy handed the list to his mother.

'A canteen of cutlery.' Freda read out loud. 'A dinner service, a Christmas hamper to be delivered a week before Christmas or a cuckoo clock.'

'Sod the cuckoo clock,' Dickie said firmly. 'Alf Spinks' missus has got one of those and he said it drives him round the bend.'

'You choose, Mum,' Jimmy told her, 'it's for you anyway.'

'Thanks, son, I would like that new dinner service, so that I can keep it for special occasions.'

'I'll give them a ring in the morning,' promised Fred, 'they may even send it by Carter Patterson, you never know.'

'Fat chance,' scoffed Dickie, 'more like through the post office and it will be in fifty pieces by the time it gets to us.'

After Fred had left, Freda turned to her husband. 'We haven't had much luck since we moved here, have we, love, what with our Joe being locked up and my mum going, but who knows, perhaps we've turned the corner now. Joe will be out soon and we now have a champion on our hands.'

Dickie hugged his wife, while Jimmy sat in the armchair blushing furiously.

Three weeks later, Joe Campbell stood in the governor's office at Loughton borstal waiting for the governor to officially discharge him and for the secretary to issue him with a travel warrant. The secretary Miss Lloyd, whose dislike for Joe had not diminished, did not invite Joe to take a seat or offer him a coffee, which she would normally do on the day of a boy's discharge, just to show them that as far as she was concerned, they had now paid their debt to society and she had personally forgiven them. Joe Campbell was unlike any other boy that had passed through this establishment and it made her feel angry that he seemed to have everybody, including the governor, falling over themselves to be pleasant towards him. She was not prepared to admit to herself that she was jealous of the young man. Jealous of his popularity, jealous of his dignity and jealous because he would not bend his knee to Miss Lloyd.

Mr Butler the governor came puffing in. It was still only nine o'clock and he was running late. 'Sit down, lad, sit down.' To Miss Lloyd, he said, 'Could you get us a couple of coffees please, Miss Lloyd?'

Miss Lloyd gritted her teeth but obeyed the command.

Mr Butler was required by Home Office regulations to read out a list of conditions when a trainee was discharged. The three important rules were that Joe must not associate with any known criminals, he must reside with his parents at all times and he would have to report to a probation officer, who would liaise with the labour exchange to decide

146

on the job he would be offered. Joe would have no choice in the matter, although a caring probation officer would almost always take into account the interests and the skills of one of his charges.

With the formalities over, Mr Butler leaned back in his chair and sipped his coffee. 'Well, Joe, it's not been all bad, has it?' he asked.

Miss Lloyd sniffed at the governor's use of Campbell's first name.

'It's not been as bad as I thought it might have been, sir,' Joe replied, 'but at the end of the day, I've been inside for nearly a year and for the next two years, I have to live where I'm told and do whatever job the probation officer tells me to do.' Joe finished his coffee. 'Mr Butler, I will never forget what you did for me when our gran died and neither will my mum and dad.'

Miss Lloyd placed the warrant on the desk and then turned towards the filing cabinet, in case Campbell offered to shake her hand before he left. She had no wish to be contaminated by "scum" like him. But she needn't have worried, for Joe shook hands with the governor, but did not even bother to wish his secretary so much as a farewell.

Freda and Jimmy were waiting for him at Heathway station, but Dickie was working with John Townsend, as the job John had taken on was one that he could not complete by himself and John had promised the customer that the job would be completed by the weekend. As soon as they were indoors, Freda took out the frying pan and cooked Joe and Jimmy a huge fry-up, even though it was nearly eleven o'clock. Joe sighed with contentment as he mopped his greasy plate with the last slice of bread and butter.

'Blimey, Mum,' he told her, 'that lot will last me for the next two days at least.'

'Tell that to your brother, he'll be back in an hour demanding bread and jam.'

Freda looked critically at her eldest son. 'You've lost a lot of weight, Joe. The clothes you have on now are the same as the ones you went in with and yet your shirt collar is hanging round your neck and your trousers are at least two inches too big around the waist. But don't worry, if I have my way, I'll soon get some meat on your bones again.' Freda had no doubt that she would definitely have her way.

Jimmy had already left to meet up with Reggie Godber, having wolfed down the same quantity of breakfast as his brother, but in half the time. In fact, Jimmy intended to let his breakfast go down for at least an hour and then go for a 5-mile run with Reggie riding his bicycle in front of him as he ran all around the massive Parsloes Park. Reggie had a milometer attached to the front wheel of his bike and would call out the distance Jimmy had covered at every half mile.

Reggie Godber had proclaimed himself as an assistant trainer and took his job seriously. Jimmy had trained hard for the next contest, which was only two weeks away, working tirelessly on the speedball and his footwork, and Fred Loake had been greatly impressed with how dedicated the young boxer had become. Jimmy did love his food though, but he had the ability to burn off the calories just as quickly as he put them on.

Chapter Sixteen

Joe had written to Mary and David, telling them that he would be back in Camden to see them on Sunday morning, but first he wanted to pay a visit to Romford Market on the Saturday. Joe had an appointment to see his probation officer on Monday morning and had a plan of action that, if successful, may well impress the officer.

Joe loved the hustle and the bustle of markets, any market, and he wandered around the clothes stalls that seemed to be concentrating on selling summer wear. He waited until one of the stalls was less busy and spoke to the man who had been serving.

'Could you please tell me how I might be able to get a job in the market? I used to live in Camden and worked the market there.'

'To be honest with you, mate,' the man replied, 'I don't think you've got much chance here, at least not on a clothes stall. You could try the casuals' rank though. They queue up at six every Saturday morning, but if you're looking for a full-time job, your best bet would be with one of the fruit-and-veg boys. They're always looking for workers.'

Joe thanked him, although he felt disappointed, because he knew nothing about fruit and vegetables, and neither did he really want to.

He tried a dozen other clothes stalls and met with the same response, before realising that if he wanted a job on the market, it would not be working on a nice, clean stall that sold fine jackets or dresses. Joe knew from experience that the fruit-and-vegetable stalls were among the first to cease trading and so waited until one of them began to pack away their wares before approaching a man who appeared to be the owner.

'Excuse me,' Joe asked him politely, 'I'm looking for a job on the market and I just wondered if you might know of anything going.'

The man was glad to have a break and left his assistant to get on with the task of putting the fruit and vegetables back into boxes.

'Ever worked the markets before, son?'

Joe told him everything about himself, including the fact that he had only been released from borstal that morning.

'Well at least you're honest,' said the man after Joe had finished.

Then he grinned, before adding. 'Well, perhaps honest is not quite the right word, given the circumstances, but you know what I mean. Your problem though, will be with your probation officer, because my kid brother used to work with me on this stall, but he was also sent to borstal, although in his case he nicked a car and was done bang to rights. When he was let out on licence, they wouldn't let him come back to work the market again. They said there was too much temptation and too many known criminals around here.'

'Where is he now?' Joe asked.

'Pushing a pen in some poxy office, where he doesn't have to get his hands dirty.' The man wrote his name and telephone number on a scrap of paper. 'Give this to your probation officer and tell him I can guarantee you a full-time job starting on Tuesday. He can give me a ring anytime on Monday, because I have a day off then. I work Romford on Wednesday, Friday and Saturday and different markets on Tuesdays and Thursdays, but I could arrange to pick you up somewhere.'

Joe looked at the piece of paper and on it was written: Albert Newton DOM 637541. £2 15s per week to start.

'Thanks, Albert,' said Joe gratefully. 'I'll give you a ring myself on Monday, whichever way it goes.'

Joe left Romford thinking that at least he had made the effort on the very first day of his release and that he had actually found himself a full-time job, but now it would be up to the probation officer as to whether or not he would be allowed to accept it.

It was a lovely evening and after they'd had their tea, Dickie suggested they all go out for a drink in one of the pubs that had a beer garden, so that Jimmy would be able to sit with the rest of the family. Dickie knew that Freda did not like the idea of leaving him outside with a packet of crisps and a bottle of lemonade. Joe had told them about the offer he had received from Albert Newton, but he had also told them that the stallholder's own brother had been refused permission to work the market again when he had been released from borstal. He then told them that the governor of Loughton borstal had hinted that working in any market may not meet with the approval of a probation officer.

They took a bus to one of the country pubs that were happy to serve the ex-Londoners', who now lived a few miles away in Dagenham, even if they did not always understand everything they were saying in their strange cockney accents.

After they had settled down with their drinks in the beer garden, Dickie asked Joe, 'What will you do if this geezer says you can't work the market, Joe?'

'How do you know it will be a geezer?' asked Freda. 'There are women probation officers these days, you know, just like there are women coppers and doctors.'

Joe thought how much his mother sounded like his gran at times.

'Mum's right,' he told his father, 'I won't know who it will be until I get there on Monday, but I've been thinking about the possibility that whoever it is, they may say no. I know I will be gutted, but I don't have any choice for the next two years and then I'll have the rest of my life to work where I want to work and live where I want to live.'

In spite of his brave words, Freda was aware that her eldest son was feeling a little low. 'Come on, Joe,' she reminded him, 'just concentrate on tomorrow for now and think how much Mary and David are looking forward to seeing you again.'

Dickie nodded. 'That's right, go off and enjoy your day, but there is one thing we have to consider, not just you, but all of us.'

'And that is?' demanded Freda.

'I really hope you can get started in the market, Joe, but if you do, who will go to Birmingham with Jimmy?' Dickie believed he knew what the answer would be, but it needed to be voiced.

'I will, of course,' declared Freda. 'If Joe's not able to go, then you and me will go together. I'm not promising to go in and watch, but Jimmy's not going all that way with only that Fred to hold his hand.'

Freda looked around the table and made another decision. 'Yes, and I will watch him box as well. If I'm going all that way, I'm not going to sit on my own in a hotel room all night wondering what's going on.' Freda was amused at the looks of amazement on her husband and her two sons' faces. 'I don't know what you lot are gawping at. I said I would come to the semi-finals, didn't I? It's just that it's come a bit sooner than I expected. That's all.'

'Good for you, Mum,' said Joe, 'but I have a feeling that the governor and Albert Newton could well be right and I won't be allowed to work the market after all.' Joe shrugged his shoulders philosophically. 'At the end of the day, when this probation officer tells me to jump, I just have to ask how high.'

'There is something else you need to know, but we'll talk about it later,' Dickie told Joe.

'When I'm in bed, I suppose,' Jimmy said huffily. 'I thought we were supposed to be a family.'

'He's right, Dickie,' Freda agreed, 'what you have to tell Joe concerns Jimmy as well.'

Joe's curiosity was aroused and so was his brother's.

Dickie now had no option but to continue. 'Duggie Murphy sponsored the York Hall contest and was strutting around the ring as though he owned the place.'

The name meant little to Jimmy, but Joe was shocked and angry.

'Murphy!' he said indignantly. 'Why the bloody hell is Murphy getting mixed up with junior boxing?'

'I don't know, but there must be something in it for him somewhere. He told the reporter from *The Dagenham Post* that you were inside and then had the cheek to send us his regards. All I'm trying to say, Joe, is that the Murphys are bad news and none of us should ever forget that.'

Joe failed to see how Duggie Murphy could profit from boys under the age of twelve boxing each other, although he would heed his father's advice and keep a watchful eye on Jimmy.

When Joe had written to Mary, he had also given her the approximate time he would be arriving, so Joe was not surprised to see David waving excitedly to him as he turned the corner into Crowndale Road. David did not burst into tears as he had done the last time Joe visited, but he held on to his hand as though he was determined that his best friend would not be taken from him again, content in the knowledge that at least they could enjoy a short time together.

Mary met them at the door, 'Hello, Joe, it's so good to see you again.' Then she kissed his cheek softly and sweetly.

David continued to hold Joe's hand tightly as they entered the house, in his determination that he would not escape from them again, although his mother had told him that Joe would only be able to visit them at the weekends. David did not understand why Joe could not come back to live with them, although he had been able to grasp that something bad had happened to Joe, but held on to the hope that perhaps one day he would be able to come back and live with them again all the same. David was even happier though, when Joe told him that he would like to come to see them every Sunday, if he was not working, that is.

'That's unless your mum gets fed up with me,' Joe laughed.

'You know that will never happen, Joe.' Mary could hardly believe how much Joe had changed during the past year. She was eleven years older than Joe, but this was no longer the mere boy who had entered her life just over a year ago and the implication worried her more than a little.

Mary asked Joe if he would come with them to the Regent's Canal later after they had eaten their Sunday dinner and Joe was happy to oblige. The annual parade of colourfully painted barges was taking place that day and dozens of barges would be arriving from Little Venice, the starting point of the procession, 4 or 5 miles from Camden Lock. Joe had seen the event many times before, but he always enjoyed watching the bargees and their families get together for the annual event. The barges, some still being pulled by horses, had been the traditional homes for generations of families since the industrial revolution, although with the arrival of the petrol-driven lorries, the demand to transport commodities by canal was quickly diminishing. Even so, the parade was still a majestic sight that attracted thousands of sightseers all along the banks of the canal.

Mary had been careful in her choice of venue, for she knew that Joe would not have very much money on him and although she had more than enough to give them all a good day out, she knew that she must be careful not to hurt his male pride, stupid though it may appear to her.

So apart from perhaps an ice cream for David, the afternoon would not cost them a penny.

Joe helped Mary to prepare the vegetables for dinner and David claimed his favourite job of shelling the peas. David split open the pods, shouting, 'Here's another one,' every time he found a tiny maggot inside.

'What's the latest around the market, Mary?' Joe asked.

'Bobby's finished. I'm not sure what happened, but he's sold all of his stalls and hardly ever leaves Muswell Hill these days. I think he's looking for a place on the coast somewhere.' Mary shredded the cabbage and placed it in a saucepan. 'Duggie Murphy is the cock of the walk, without a doubt. I've heard he now owns over fifty stalls in the market, but he never goes near there himself, because he has his henchmen to make sure none of the traders try to make a little on the side for themselves. They have to sell what he decides they can sell and charge the price he tells them to. Some of the others who own their own stalls and who have worked the market for donkey's years have just packed up and moved out, the threats were so bad.'

Joe told her about Romford Market and his doubts that he would be allowed to work there. Then added, 'This is the only market for me and one day, I will be back, with or without the Murphys' approval.'

'It's not really the market that Duggie Murphy's interested in. He's applied for a boxing promoter's licence and according to this week's Camden Journal, he's almost certain to get it.'

'So that's why the crafty bugger sponsored the show at York Hall,' Joe said bitterly. 'It all makes sense now, he was using those kids to get his foot in the door.'

Mary poured the Yorkshire pudding mixture into a baking tin.

'Joe, I don't know if you realise how much money changes hands on every ABA contest through side bets and this year's competition is attracting more gamblers than ever before, mainly because of a boxer called Ronnie Baxter and your own brother Jimmy. A lot of money has already been placed on Jimmy to win this year's title and as Duggie Murphy controls all of the bookmakers around north and east London, he stands to lose a great deal of money if Jimmy becomes the champion.'

'I take it Bobby told you all of this?' said Joe, putting the kettle on.

'That and more, Joe. Bobby said to warn you that Duggie may pay you or your dad a visit before the next fight in Birmingham, but I think it's more likely to be you rather than your dad.'

Joe turned crimson with rage. 'To do what? Is he going to ask me to persuade our Jimmy to take a dive? There's not enough money in the world to make Jimmy do something like that.'

Mary placed her hand over his to calm him. 'It could be that Bobby has read this all wrong and that Murphy is concentrating on getting a promoter's licence, because then he will have another licence to virtually print his own money.'

Mary left her hand on Joe's for just a few seconds longer than was necessary, but that was quite long enough for Joe to feel a strange tingling sensation all over his body.

After their Sunday dinner, the three of them spent the afternoon on Camden Lock, watching the barges coming through the lock gates and mooring in Camden Basin to be judged, for there were handsome cash prizes awarded for the smartest horse and the best-decorated barge. It was one of the happiest days of David's life now that Joe was back and he knew that days such as this would be repeated again and again. His innocent mind did not consider the difference in the ages of his mother and Joe and he startled both of them as they walked back to Mornington Crescent, when he announced, 'Mum, you and Joe could get married, so that we could all live together for ever and ever.'

He skipped ahead of them, completely unaware of the turmoil he had caused. Mary felt devastated that her son could have frightened Joe off for good and she badly wanted him to be part of their lives, even if it was to be just as David's friend. Joe glanced at Mary from the corner of his eye, dreading the possibility that Mary may consider it better if he did not come to see them any more. His feelings for this beautiful though older woman had grown stronger and stronger during the time he had spent in borstal and he had lain awake night after night fantasising about being with her in every sense of the word. Joe knew that many boys developed crushes on older women, but the feelings he had for Mary was no passing fancy.

Mary eased the tension by adopting a true cockney accent to say, 'Cor blimey, Joe, what's that little bugger gonna come out wiv next?'

Joe laughed with her and the embarrassing moment passed, although Mary knew she must have a serious talk with David before next weekend.

The following morning at five minutes to ten, Joe walked into the probation officer's premises in Church Elm Lane, only a ten minute walk from the Campbells' house. He was informed by a friendly receptionist that Mr Wyatt was not in yet and she invited Joe to take a seat and then poured herself a cup of tea.

'I'm sorry I can't offer you a cup,' she told Joe, 'but Mr Wyatt will not allow it.'

'That's alright,' Joe said cheerfully. 'I had two cups before I came out.' Joe was encouraged by her friendliness. 'What's he like then, your Mr Wyatt?'

'He's not my Mr Wyatt, thank goodness,' she replied with feeling. 'To be honest with you, I'm leaving here just as soon as I can find another job, because the man is a pig and he talks to people as though they were something on the bottom of his shoes, me included.' She stopped, knowing that she had said too much, but with her words, Joe's slender hope of being allocated a reasonable probation officer had all but evaporated.

There was nothing to read in the office and Joe had not thought to bring a newspaper with him, so all he could do was count the roses on the faded wallpaper, while he waited for the probation officer to make his appearance. It was eleven forty-five before the door opened and a large, bald-headed man walked in without saying good morning or even acknowledging the two people in the room. He walked through to a smaller office and waited for the cup of tea the receptionist was busy making for him. It was a further thirty minutes before he bellowed, 'Campbell, in here.'

Joe went through to the outer office, little knowing that Maurice Wyatt knew all about the Campbell family, including Jimmy "Cannonball" Campbell. Wyatt motioned to a chair and Joe sat down, while the probation officer read through the borstal report. Wyatt did not smoke or drink, and neither was he a womaniser, but his great weakness was gambling and not very successfully at that. He lived in Hackney and the street bookmaker he used was under the control of Duggie Murphy. This form of gambling was illegal and any debts incurred could not be recovered by conventional means, but it was a very unwise gambler who did not pay his debts promptly. Wyatt owed his bookmaker forty-five pounds, but Duggie Murphy had sent word that there would be no pressure put on Wyatt if he cooperated in a "little matter". The little matter in question was that when Joe Campbell came for his interview, he would be given the worst job the labour exchange had to offer.

When a punter got into debt, Murphy always made inquiries to see if the man could be of any use to him, before sending his strong-arm boys to pay him a visit. A probation officer, especially one who was based in Dagenham, could be very useful, which was why Murphy had allowed Wyatt so much credit, but Duggie Murphy was now ready to collect his dues.

Maurice Wyatt did not like his job very much, but it was better than selling insurance door to door or working in a factory. He had been an army officer during the war, attaining the rank of captain in the catering corps, although he had never left England and his war had been spent on Salisbury Plain, feeding the recruits who were completing basic training before they were sent to the front line. After the war, all officers who had no job to return to were offered posts, with minimal training, as teachers, unemployment officers or probation officers. The latter had been Wyatt's choice.

He looked up from the file. 'Right then, Campbell, first things first, get yourself down to the labour exchange, get a list of the jobs they have and then bring it back to me. I'll decide which one I think is the most suitable.'

Joe explained about the job offer at Romford Market and showed Wyatt the piece of paper that Albert Newton had written on.

Wyatt glanced at it briefly and then screwed it up and threw it into his waste bin. 'You can forget about that nonsense,' he told Joe dismissively. 'Look what happened the last time you worked in a market.'

Joe stood up and walked around the probation officer's desk, having the satisfaction of seeing the fat man cringe and hold his arms up to protect himself.

'You don't have to worry about me,' said Joe, 'I just want Albert's telephone number. He's a decent bloke, who was kind enough to offer me a job, and the least I can do is to tell him myself that I can't take him up on his offer.' Joe retrieved the piece of crumpled paper and walked out of the office.

Even without pressure from Duggie Murphy, Wyatt would have taken great pleasure in taking this cocky young boy down a peg or two and he telephoned the manager of the labour exchange, another ex-army officer, with this in mind.

He was put through to the manager's office. 'Maurice Wyatt here, Mr Blake.'

'Hello, Mr Wyatt, had any good tips lately?'

George Blake was also a gambling man, although he only gambled with money he could afford to lose.

'Not at the moment, Mr Blake, but I may have a cert coming up soon. Listen, I want you to do me a big favour. There will be a cocky young git coming to you for a job and I want you to sort out the worst possible job you have on your books for him. Don't be fooled by this one, Mr Blake, he's a vicious young thug, even though he looks as though butter wouldn't melt in his mouth.'

'It shall be done, Mr Wyatt, I have just the very thing for him and I can assure you that he will not like it. Oh no, he will not like it one little bit.'

'That sounds perfect, but don't tell me what it is, Mr Blake, I want to see the look on his face when he brings the labour-exchange card back to me.'

George Blake replaced the telephone receiver, smiling at the formality the other man always observed. They had known each other since even before the war, as they were both members of the same rotary club, but never had Maurice Wyatt been known to address another member by his first name. I bet he even calls his wife Mrs Wyatt when they're on the job, George thought to himself, and then chuckled aloud as he imagined the scenario.

Chapter Seventeen

George Blake gave his instructions to the clerk who was responsible for the under-eighteens and when Joe reported for his employment card, he was told by the clerk, 'We only have one job at the moment and that's at the sewage farm in Rainham.'

The clerk was unable to look Joe in the eye when Joe answered, 'That's bollocks and you know it. Look, I'm not blaming you, because I know you have to do what you're told, but I looked at the other jobs on display when I came in and they're asking for van boys, coal shovelers on the railway and lots of other different jobs, so how can you sit there and tell me the only job you can offer me is on a shit farm?'

He snatched the card angrily from the embarrassed clerk and took it back to the probation officer, determined that he would not give that fat pig the satisfaction of showing his feelings, but Joe was in despair at the way he was being treated.

Wyatt took the card from Joe and said gleefully, 'This is just the job for you, Campbell; after all, you did work on a farm while you were in Loughton. Not this sort of farm, I grant you, but you should feel quite at home in Rainham.'

Wyatt was greatly disappointed when Joe replied, 'Yes, I'm sure I will be. I have no sense of smell and I'd much rather be there than be cooped up in some factory.'

'Well then, get yourself over to Rainham and tell them you can start first thing tomorrow morning. Then you can go home and tell your parents I will be calling on them at six thirty sharp tomorrow evening.

'I will expect them both to be at home, you included.' When Joe did not move, Wyatt barked, 'Well don't just sit there, get a move on.'

Joe refused to be intimidated. 'I will, when you reimburse me for my bus fare.'

Wyatt extracted the money from his petty-cash box and threw it across the table at Joe. 'Make sure you keep the bus tickets and bring them back to me,' he snarled.

On this particular day, Joe Campbell had brought out the very worst in Maurice Wyatt by displaying the very qualities that were so badly lacking in himself – dignity and self respect. Wyatt would dearly love to report to the Home Office that Campbell had breached the conditions of his licence, so that he could be sent back to another borstal far away from Dagenham.

Joe needed to take two buses to the Rainham sewage farm, his nose telling him he could not be very far away as the second bus approached the farm. The conductor, with a handkerchief held over his nose, pointed to a gate when the bus had stopped and Joe walked through it and along a path, until he came to a hut. Sitting outside was a wizened old man, whose age could have been from anything between sixty and eighty. He took the labour-exchange card from Joe.

'I bet you're a jailbird,' he said casually, 'only jailbirds get sent here for a job, but not many last very long, most of them would rather be back in the nick than work here.' His tone was matter-of-fact, but not unkind. 'Fancy a cup of tea then?' Joe accepted the offer and the old man introduced himself. 'My name's Errol Flynn.' He said this so seriously that Joe was not sure how to react. The man slapped his thigh and then burst out laughing. 'Nah, 'course it's not. I'm Ron Conway and I work here with my brother Jack. Jack is a dummy, 'cos he's deaf and dumb, but I won't let anyone take the piss out of him.'

At that moment, Jack walked from the hut and nodded to Joe. Joe raised his right thumb as a greeting. 'Where did you learn to do that?' Ron asked Joe.

'I didn't learn to do it anywhere; it just felt like the right thing to do.'

'You'll do for me, but will you be able to stick it here? You must have pissed your probation officer off big time for him to send you to us.'

'I don't know why, I only met him for the first time this morning, but he seemed to take an instant dislike to me.' Joe grinned when he continued, 'It didn't help when I told him how much I was looking forward to working on the sewage farm, because I had no sense of smell.' Joe shuddered. 'Gordon Bennett, I wish to Christ that was true.'

Ron chuckled. 'Yeah, it does pong a bit and that's no lie, but you do sort of get used to it after a while. The only problem is that the smell gets right into your clothes and you'll be given a wide berth when you go home on the bus after work. Me and Jack only live a ten-minute walk away and we have a change of clothes in our garden shed, so that we don't have to bring these ones into the house.'

After they had finished their tea, Ron Conway signed Joe's employment card to confirm that he would commence work the next morning at 8.00 a.m. and Joe made his way back to Mr Wyatt's office, only to be told that the probation officer had already left for the day.

'It's alright for some,' Joe remarked to the receptionist.

'Lazy, fat sod,' came her reply.

Before going home. Joe went to the telephone kiosk on Heathway and dialled Albert Newton's number. Albert was not surprised at the news, although he was pleased that Joe had taken the trouble to call him. After wishing Joe luck, he told him, 'If you ever fancy the odd Saturday, just come to the market at six and if I can't use you myself, I'll find someone who can.'

Joe thanked the generous stallholder, who had gone a long way to restore Joe's faith in human nature, even though he knew he would not dare to work the market, even on the occasional Saturday.

He walked slowly home, not looking forward to telling his mother and father where he would be spending perhaps the next two years.

Joe felt that he was being punished twice for something he hadn't done and wondered how his parents would react when Mr Wyatt paid them his visit the next evening.

'Your dad will be home soon,' Freda told him when Joe entered the house. 'Would you rather wait until he gets home before you tell us all about it?'

Joe nodded gratefully, for telling the tale once would be quite enough.

Dickie and John Townsend usually worked in their spare-time jobs no later than six o'clock on the afternoons when they worked during the week and Joe heard his father's key turning in the lock at six fifteen. Jimmy sat down with the rest of the family to hear Joe recount his day to them, trying not to sound bitter as he did so. He told them of Wyatt's proposed visit the next evening.

'When he comes here tomorrow, I think he will try to provoke you, so that he can report that this is not a suitable place for me to live.' Joe was serious. 'For some reason, this bloke has it in for me and if he reports that this is not an "appropriate environment", as they call it, my licence could be revoked and I'll find myself back inside.'

'Oh, the wicked bastard, the wicked bastard.' Freda was crying now. 'What have you ever done to him?'

'I'm young, I'm slim and I have a fine head of hair now that it's grown back. He's old, he's fat and he's as bald as a coot, so I reckon that's reason enough for someone like him.'

Dickie was distressed that anybody could treat his son in this way, while he must stand by, unable to lift a finger without jeopardising Joe's freedom and his future.

Freda turned her attention to the more practical things for the morning. 'What about your working clothes? How much money will you need for your bus fares and what will you do for your lunch?'

'I'll take a sandwich and go as far down wind as I can to eat it,' laughed Joe. He then told them of the Conway brothers' method of changing their clothes in the shed, before entering their house.

'I can do the same if you like, and I'll keep a spare dressing gown in the shed, but I'll need a bath before having my dinner.'

Dickie thought that at £3 15s a week, the wages were surprisingly good, which was at least some small consolation, for even an adult dustman only earned £6.

'I'm going to have to stay there for the next two years, because that fat git is not going to let me work anywhere else, but I'll make the best of it and Dad, if you happen to come across an old bike on your rounds, grab it for me and I'll do it up. I don't like the idea of people turning their noses up at me when I get on the bus after work and apart from that, it will save me a few bob in fares.'

Dickie's voice was husky when he replied, 'I'll be on the lookout, don't you worry about that, and there may even be one or two old bikes hanging around the yard that we could make something out of.

'It won't be forever, Joe, and I promise you, me and your mum will not say a word out of turn when this Wyatt character comes round tomorrow.'

Joe accepted a glass of brown ale from his father. 'At least I will be able to pay my way from now on and buy you a pint and get mum a port and lemon the next time we go down the pub.'

Jimmy looked up from his comic. 'And you'll be able to come to Birmingham with me, don't forget that.'

'How could I possibly forget such a thing?' Joe tried to sound indignant. 'How could I forget that The Cannonball Kid will be in action the week after next?'

Joe had checked the bus times to Rainham and knew that if the two buses were on time, he did not have to leave home until seven fifteen. Dickie woke his son at six thirty and asked him to take his mother a cup of tea before he left. Joe managed to eat a piece of toast and drink two cups of tea and then, after taking his mother her cup of tea, he left the house, steeling himself mentally for the day that lay ahead of him.

He arrived at the sewage farm about five minutes before Ron and Jack arrived. When Jack saw Joe, he gave the thumbs up sign and then drew his thumb across his chest.

'That means good morning,' explained Ron. 'The thumbs up means good, as you know, but drawing the thumb across the chest means good morning. It's like drawing the curtains when you first get up in the morning.'

Joe repeated the sign to Jack, who was delighted.

'It would mean a lot if you could learn just a few signs,' Ron told Joe earnestly. 'For instance, when he makes the tea, to say thank you, all you have to do is to put two fingers to your lips and sort of drop them in an arc down to your chest, like this.' He demonstrated the motion. 'When Jack scratches his cheek with all of his fingers, he's asking if you want sugar. Just wave your hand from side to side if you don't want any, or put one or two fingers up if you do. He will ask you if you want milk by pretending to milk a cow. To say yes, clench your fist and wag it up and down. Saying please is almost the same as saying thank you, except that after touching your lips, you only bring the hand down a few inches.' Ron looked closely at his new assistant.

'Are you sure you want to give it a try, because once you start signing, Jack will expect it all the time.'

'Yes, I would like to learn all I can, Ron; after all, I'm likely to be with the pair of you for at least a couple of years.'

Ron signed to his brother that he could use a few simple signs to Joe and Joe responded perfectly when Jack made the tea and asked Joe if he wanted milk and sugar, remembering to sign please and thank you.

Ron Conway was touched by the kindness of the young man who had been forced to take a job that most men would not touch with a barge pole, but this lad could still find it within himself to show compassion to a disabled fellow human being.

After they had drunk their tea, Ron took Joe to where he would be working for as long as he stayed with them at the sewage farm.

He explained to Joe, 'The contents of every toilet for miles around, including your own, ends up here and after we've finished with it, the water goes back into your tap to be drunk over and over again. The next time you pour yourself a glass of water, just remember that it's been through at least half a dozen different bodies.' He handed Joe a long-handled rake. 'Your job will be to clear anything that comes through that could block the filters and you can empty it into that bin over there. There will be quite a lot of debris, but a lorry will collect it twice a day and take to a landfill site in Thurrock. I will be on the next filter, which is finer than this one, and Jack takes care of the final stage. I'll be starting the pumps in a few minutes and that's when we get going.'

Joe stared down at the motionless liquid mass that did not seem to smell as bad as it had done yesterday, but two minutes later, he discovered the reason why. As soon as the pumps began to operate, the motionless mass began to churn over and so did the smell. For the first few minutes, Joe stood immobilised, overcome by the revolting smell, and then an alarm bell sounded and Ron came over to Joe's section.

'The alarm means that your filters have clogged and nothing can get through. Come on, Joe, I'll give you a hand this time.'

He took Joe's rake and unblocked the filter, scooping the obscene mess into the bin.

After Ron had left him, Joe managed to keep the filter clear by himself, until the pumps stopped at ten thirty, signalling a tea break.

It had not exactly been back-breaking work, but all Joe felt like doing was running away from that mind-numbing smell and never coming back.

In the hut, Joe managed to sign to Jack that he would like a cup of tea, with one sugar and some milk.

Jack's face lit up with pleasure and Ron was pleased. 'Now that Jack knows you can sign, he will expect it every day,' he reminded Joe. You have to remember, Joe, this is the only way a dummy can communicate and it's very important to Jack.'

Joe winced at the word "dummy", but made no comment. 'I'd like to learn a couple of new signs every day, so that I can talk to him a bit more,' Joe said sincerely.

Ron signed to his brother and Jack held up both his thumbs with a huge grin upon his face.

Jack went to a cupboard and produced a small jar of vaseline. He then scooped out a small amount and smeared it beneath Joe's nostrils.

'I should have thought of that,' said Ron. 'It may help to keep the smell out. Me and Jack don't bother any more, but we keep this jar handy for when the inspectors come round.'

Joe signed thank you to Jack and then it was time to return to the filters. The vaseline did help and the stench became bearable, but only just.

When the pumps stopped once more for their midday break, Joe took his sandwich and walked away from the sewage farm, but there was no escaping the smell of effluence that had now permeated his clothing. He tossed his sandwich to the greedy gulls that were flocking around and went back to the hut and settled for a mug of tea and a couple of hand-rolled cigarettes. Ron and Jack were impervious to their surroundings and each was tucking into a large pork pie as though they were sitting at the end of Southend Pier.

'You may not believe this now, Joe,' Ron promised him, 'but if you can stick it out for a couple of weeks, then you won't really notice it any more.'

'I'll just have to take your word for that, Ron,' but Joe was far from being convinced.

At the same time in Dagenham, Dickie was in the cafe talking with John as they were having their lunch. Dickie told John about the probation officer's visit that evening.

'This bloke is allowed to come into my house and say whatever he likes to us and we have to just sit there and fucking well take it,' Dickie said with bitterness.

'No you don't,' said John firmly. 'The probation service is divided into various sections and each section has a chief probation officer. We have the afternoon off today, so when we finish work, we'll ask Jack Doyle if we can use his telephone to find out who the head bloke is for Dagenham. I'll come round to be a witness and if he starts getting stroppy, I'll threaten to report him to Mr so-and-so, or whatever his name is.'

'Blimey, John, we used to have a name for blokes like you in the army. Barrack-room lawyers we used to call them. Thanks, John, our Joe doesn't deserve this sort of treatment from an arsehole like him.'

'Think nothing of it, mate.' John Townsend was happy to offer any assistance he could to his work partner. 'One other thing, Dickie, you can forget about trying to put a bike together for Joe. I've got one in my shed that I never use; in fact, I've even got an oilskin suit to go with it. It belonged to my younger brother, but he never came back from Burma and it's been in my shed ever since. I take it out and give it a good clean and oil the parts now and then, so it's in good condition, but I've never ridden it and I never will.' Dickie had not been aware that John had lost a brother during the war. 'Anyway, Denny would be pleased if he knew it was going to be put to good use, instead of being propped up against my shed wall. We can wheel it round with us this afternoon and give Joe a nice surprise when he comes home.'

Dickie found it difficult to express his gratitude for the support that this man was extending to his family and, 'Thanks, John, you're a diamond,' was the best he could manage, but the way it was said was enough for John.

Joe had mixed feelings when he said goodbye to Ron and Jack at four thirty that afternoon, because the work was not strenuous or boring, for he had scooped out all kinds of items that threatened to clog the filters. False teeth by the dozen, spectacles and even a glass eye, although Joe was not quite sure if it was an eye or a marble, but it would make a good story for when he got home though. Joe liked Ron and his brother, but did not feel comfortable about Ron referring to Jack as a "dummy", as he had on more than one occasion. Joe had read an article somewhere about profoundly deaf people and could not imagine how it must feel to be unable to hear any sound at all, or to utter a single word. The word Ron used to describe his brother was not meant to be unkind, Joe knew that, but he resolved to mention this the next time Ron said it.

The vaseline had helped to overcome the stench, but scrubbing his hands when they had finished did little to diminish the smell, for his work clothes had become impregnated with the sewage. Joe dreaded the return journey back to Dagenham and knew that getting a bicycle would be the only way he could cope with working in this place.

The bus conductor had worked on this particular route for many years and had taken the fares of scores of the sewage-farm workers in the past. His shift was always in the afternoon, so the morning run was divided between the other drivers and conductors, who absolutely hated the run. This conductor and his driver were well used to the smell and it did not bother them in the least, although the conductor knew it would be a different matter if the lad needed to change to another bus when they reached the terminal. The conductor and the driver of the "Shit Run", as it was called by the others at the bus station, were subjected to much ridicule when they entered the canteen for their break, with drivers and conductors scuttling away from them, holding their noses.

Joe was the only passenger for the first mile.

'First day, son?' asked the conductor.

'Yeah, but I'll be back tomorrow.' Joe looked the conductor in the eye as though daring him to doubt his word.

'Good for you, lad. Good for you.'

The conductor on the second bus was not so friendly. He would have loved to refuse to allow Joe onto his bus at all, but he was not permitted to turn away passengers, unless they were drunk. He collected Joe's fare, but made a point of sniffing loudly every time he was obliged to walk past him. Joe felt that he would rather walk the 5 miles to work than endure this humiliation every day. He estimated that it would take him somewhere in the region of one and a half hours to walk the distance and walk the distance he intended to do, at least until he could get himself a bicycle.

When Joe walked through the side entrance of his house, he could hardly believe his eyes, for propped up against the shed stood a gleaming bicycle, with a set of waterproofs neatly folded over the handlebars. The shed door burst open and out jumped John and his father.

'Surprise. Surprise,' they shouted.

'This is a sort of coming-home present from John,' Dickie told Joe. 'Look at the tyres; they're hardly worn at all.' He went to push the bicycle towards Joe and then drew back again. 'Bloody Nora, Joe, you don't half pen and ink.'

'So would you if you'd been shovelling shit all day,' Joe retorted with a beaming smile. 'This is brilliant, John, what can I say?'

'Nothing at all, Joe, nothing at all. I'll tell you something though, the last time I smelled anything as bad as you was when I was put on latrine duty during the war. I was an hour late back from a twenty-four hour pass and it cost me two days in mucking out the bogs.'

His mother had already heated the "copper", as the hot-water heater was referred to, but Joe still had to transfer it from the kitchen to the bathroom in buckets. He was at a loss as to why the gas-operated, galvanised water heater was called a copper, but he wished they could have a geyser the same as Mary had in her bathroom. All they had to do was to turn on a tap and hot water went straight into the bath. No lugging buckets around in that house.

After seven or eight trips with the buckets of hot water, Joe was able to lie back in the bath and contemplate on his first day at work.

John Townsend's gift of the bicycle would make all the difference, for he would now not have to endure the scornful looks and disparaging remarks of snotty bus conductors and other passengers, even if they did have good reason to hold their noses when Joe got onto the bus. It would be a problem about what to do with his work clothes though, because it was not practical to change every day, but his mother suggested that he leave them in the shed overnight and she would give them a good boil every weekend. Joe was glad that at least he was out in the open air for, like his father, he would have found it much more difficult to cope with being cooped up in some factory. If Mr Wyatt had realised how much Joe Campbell hated to be stuck inside, he would never have arranged for him to work on the sewage farm, the most detested job the labour exchange had to offer, at least for most people, that is.

Chapter Eighteen

Mr Wyatt was not due until six thirty, so Freda believed they had plenty of time to have their dinner before he arrived and it was now almost ready. She estimated that Joe would be in the bath for another ten minutes or so, which would give them about three quarters of an hour in which to finish their meal. John had accepted Freda's invitation to join them for dinner and minutes later, both Freda and Dickie were grateful that he had, for there was a loud knock on the door. Dickie went to answer it and was confronted by a large, bald-headed man, who could only be the probation officer.

It was, indeed, Mr Wyatt, who often used this ploy in an attempt to catch people off their guard.

'Are you Mr Wyatt?' Dickie asked him.

'Why, were you expecting anyone else?' Wyatt replied sarcastically.

'We weren't expecting you until six thirty and it's only five thirty now. We're just about to have our tea, if you don't mind.'

'Oh, don't mind me, just carry on,' Wyatt said airily. 'I'm only here to have a look round.'

He pushed past Dickie, only to be confronted by John Townsend. 'Not so fast, my friend,' said John, barring his way. 'This family is about to sit down for their evening meal and I would ask you to return at your appointed time – six thirty. In case you are wondering, I am a friend of the family, although I am not related in any way.'

Mr Wyatt's authority had never been called into question before. Nobody had ever dared to speak to him in this way, but John's next words shook him even further.

'Just in case you are considering using your bully-boy tactics, which I know for a fact completely contravenes the code of practice of the probation service, I ought to tell you that I have already spoken with your chief officer's secretary and she told me that Mr Rutherford is a fair man, who will not tolerate any of his probation officers abusing their power. She actually asked me to give her the name of the officer in question, which I did, but I told her that I would make an official complaint in the morning should it prove necessary.'

Wyatt was aware of the perspiration that was breaking out on his forehead and took a large handkerchief from his pocket to mop his brow. 'I have another meeting I must attend, which is the only reason I am early,' he said shakily. 'Tell er … er … Campbell, that I will see him another time and I will send him a postcard with an appointment.'

Dickie could not resist adding, 'Oh, by the way, Joe really enjoyed his first day at the farm, but it's a good job he has no sense of smell.'

Wyatt left the house in a great hurry. The mention of his superior's name had unnerved him, for Mr Rutherford was not an ex-forces officer like most of his team. He was a professional prison officer, who had obtained a degree in social science to qualify for his position. He had been appointed just a year ago and had called all twelve probation officers of his division into his office for a briefing. The meeting was short but straight to the point.

'Since the war ended, the Home Office has decided that it is time to reform the whole penal system, including the probation service, and I for one believe it to be long overdue. As from next Monday, flogging and birching is to be abolished and there are also plans to do away with capital punishment, although that may take a few years yet,' he'd said.

Maurice Wyatt had been outraged. 'There'll be riots in our prisons without the cat o' nine tails and our wives won't be able to sleep safely in their beds without the threat of the rope.'

Mr Rutherford had cast his eye over the large man, not wishing to antagonise him at this early stage of the reforms that were about to take place, although he knew there could be no place for such men in their soon-to-be-modernised profession.

Mr Rutherford had continued carefully. 'This country has been sickened by the carnage and the inhumanity of the war and the powers that be have decreed that we must encourage those people who have fallen foul of the law to be brought back into our society by being treated with respect and given every chance to redeem themselves.' He had addressed the whole gathering, but had looked squarely at Maurice Wyatt, when he told them, 'There will be no place on my team for bullies, make no mistake about that, but I will go out on a limb for anyone who is prepared to work side by side with me.'

Wyatt had not forgotten the words of his superior and he had already suffered the humiliation of being censured by him on several occasions for not conforming to the new guidelines. One ex-prisoner had gone as far as to make an official complaint to the Home Office, claiming victimisation, and Wyatt had been called before a tribunal headed by Mr Rutherford. Although there had been no proof of the allegation, Mr Rutherford had told Wyatt after the meeting, 'If I hear of one more incident with regards to your spitefulness, I will suspend you immediately and report your attitude to the Home Office, who, believe me, will take a very dim view of the way you think you can throw your weight around.' The chief probation officer had looked disdainfully at Wyatt's considerable bulk as he spoke.

Since the tribunal, Mr Rutherford had twice more sent for Wyatt, because of complaints from ex-prisoners, and the chief probation officer was certain that there would have been many more incidents that had gone unreported. He had told Wyatt the second time he had called him into his office, 'I have given you enough chances and now I am suspending you, until such time as I can arrange a disciplinary hearing. Harold Hardy has agreed to make a statement and will give evidence against you at the hearing.'

The only problem was that Harold Hardy had changed his mind and the charges against Wyatt were dropped. Even so, Wyatt had no wish to be reported again by the Campbells or their friend.

Joe had heard the knock on the front door while he had been in the bath and he had heard the conversation through the bathroom door. He had been unaware of his father and John's plan to contact the chief

169

probation officer's office, so was astounded when he heard the way John Townsend had spoken to Mr Wyatt. The two men were grinning like Cheshire cats when Joe emerged and they both looked extremely pleased with themselves.

'I don't think he will be giving you any more grief, Joe,' said his father.

'Did you see the look on his face when I mentioned Mr Rutherford?' said John. 'For a minute there, I thought he was going to have a stroke or something.'

'I could hear what was going on through the door, but I can tell you, I could hardly believe my ears.' Joe was still amazed. 'Who on earth thought that one up?'

Dickie pointed to John. 'That there crafty cockney. Mind you, I was standing next to him when he made the call to Barkingside and the secretary never asked for Wyatt's name and nor did John tell her he would be phoning back to make an official complaint in the morning.' Dickie looked at John. 'You're a lying sod, Townsend.'

'How dare you, Campbell,' said John indignantly, 'all I did was to be economical with the truth, that's all.'

Freda began to serve dinner. 'Well, all I can say is that this Mr Rutherford can certainly put the wind up fatso.'

After they had eaten, Dickie, Joe and John retired to the front room, leaving Freda and Jimmy to do the washing up. John produced a printed piece of paper from his pocket and showed it to Dickie.

'This is what I was telling you about yesterday. It's a football pools coupon.'

Dickie took the coupon and studied it carefully. 'So how does it work then?'

'You have to pick out eight matches that end as drawn and that counts as a first dividend,' explained John. 'One bloke won 75,000 quid a few weeks ago.'

Joe had also read the newspaper article. 'But that was because he was the only one to pick out eight draws that week,' he commented. 'Last week, so many people had first dividends that they only got £1,200 each.'

'Will you just listen to him, only £1,200,' snorted John. 'I bet you wouldn't turn your nose up at a couple of year's wages. Anyway, what I was going to suggest is that we form a syndicate between the four of us. For ten bob a week, we can pick twelve teams to get any eight from those twelve.'

Freda had now finished the washing up, but she had been listening intently from the kitchen.

'Amy Ashby's brother won £200 last year and it was only the second time he had done them. Just before Christmas it was and I'm game if the rest of you are.'

Dickie and Joe both agreed and John volunteered to make sure the postal order and the coupon was posted off every Monday.

'Now, what about picking out the numbers?' he said. 'It would be easier if we picked them out now and stayed with them for at least a few weeks, rather than have to go through it again week after week.'

'How about if we write all the numbers on pieces of paper, put them in the hat and the first twelve we draw out we stick with for say twelve weeks?' said Freda.

'Sounds fair enough to me,' John agreed.

'Shall we do it now?' asked Joe.

'Well, there's no time like the present,' said Dickie. 'I'll get some paper and a pencil.'

Jimmy had been listening in while he had been drying up and he poked his head round the door. 'One thing you may be forgetting is that it's the Cup Final on Saturday and that's the last game of the season.'

Dickie looked at John. Jimmy was right; the football season was over until the autumn.

John shook his head. 'The pools company switch over to the Australian teams at this time of the year, so we can have our little flutter all year round.'

They each took turns to pick out the twelve numbers, including Jimmy, and it was a very contented Joe who went to his bed that night.

Not only would he be able to ride to work in style the next day, but, hopefully, Wyatt would now be off his back for the duration of his probation period.

Joe spent the following Sunday with Mary and David, but this time he had insisted on taking them to the Tower of London, for he been paid on Friday. After spending over two hours in the Tower, they had a picnic lunch sitting on a bench that overlooked the impressive Tower Bridge that opened up for them twice while they were eating.

David was delighted when the great twin bridges opened fully to allow huge ships to pass through, although he was a little disappointed when Joe told him that next weekend he would be going to Birmingham to watch his brother box.

'If I get back in time, I'll come straight here, but it may not be until the evening,' said Joe. He looked at Mary. 'Will that be alright with you, Mary?'

'Of course, Joe, we'd be glad to see you, even if only for an hour or so.'

The bicycle had made all the difference to Joe's self-esteem and although he doubted whether he would ever get used to the stench of the sewage farm, he knew that he preferred even this job to being inside some factory. He had also spoken to Ron the next time Ron had referred to Jack as a "dummy", as he'd said he would.

'Ron, I know he's your brother, but it makes me cringe when you call him a dummy. I mean, what would you say if you heard anybody else call him that?'

'I'd probably do my nut, I suppose. It's a habit with me, because our dad used to call him that and I've never given it a thought until now. You're right, Joe, it's not a very nice word and I'll not use it again, even though it will make no difference to Jack.'

Saturday of Jimmy's next boxing contest soon came round and Jimmy and Joe were waiting patiently for Fred Loake to arrive, who would be travelling with them to Birmingham. Freda had already left to go to Romford with Amy Ashby and Dickie had left for work with John, before any of them had got up that morning. As there was now a spare space available, Jimmy had asked that his friend Reggie Godber be allowed to come with them and Reggie's parents had readily agreed, for it would not cost them a single penny. Reggie arrived with a small holdall, with Fred arriving soon afterwards, and then they all set off together to take the tube for Euston station, where they would make the connection to the Main Line straight through to Birmingham.

On the way, Fred told Jimmy, 'The draw for the order of the bouts was made last night, Jimmy, and this time you will be on first.'

Jimmy tried to appear nonchalant. 'That's great, it will mean we will be first back to the hotel to have a slap-up meal, without having to rush it, and then we can use the swimming pool afterwards.'

'What did you have to eat for breakfast this morning?' asked Fred.

'A couple of fried eggs, a slice of bacon, fried bread and a few mushrooms,' Jimmy told his trainer. 'My mum has made us some corn beef sandwiches in case we get hungry on the way.'

Fred looked at his wristwatch. 'When we get on the Birmingham train, you can eat two of the sandwiches and I'll get you a cup of tea, but nothing else after that. Our train is due to leave at two thirty, so if you eat at around three o'clock, it will be just about right.'

The train from Euston left exactly on time. Fred, Joe and Reggie did not feel at all hungry and settled for an insipid cup of tea in a plastic cup that only British Rail were capable of producing, but Jimmy wolfed down his ration of two sandwiches, even though he could feel the now-familiar churning in his stomach.

When Fred Loake had told them that they would not have to put a hand in their pockets, he had not been exaggerating. Even the money for the teas he had bought would be reimbursed, as long as he kept the receipt, as would the taxi fares, including a tip, from the station to their hotel. Every trainer had been advanced £3 in cash, although they were required to account for every penny they spent.

There was no delay on the journey to Birmingham and they arrived there at just after four thirty. The station was only a few minutes' taxi ride from their hotel and the arena was within walking distance. As the first boxer on the bill, Jimmy would need to be in the Bell View Centre by six thirty to be weighed and examined by the doctor.

The hotel porter took them up to their rooms and what magnificent rooms they were. Jimmy and Fred had identical single rooms next door to each other, while Joe and Reggie had been given a double room with twin beds. Fred had been told not to tip any of the hotel staff, because that would be taken care of by the ABA.

'I've only ever seen something like this at the pictures,' Reggie gasped when they entered their double room.

'Me an' all, Reggie,' Joe told him. 'So this is how the other half live.'

There was not really enough time to explore their surroundings, although Reggie managed to investigate the swimming pool and the gymnasium.

'Did you bring your swimming togs, Jimmy?' Reggie asked.

Jimmy was too preoccupied to answer and Reggie decided it was best to leave him alone to his thoughts.

Even though they could have walked the short distance to the arena, the ABA had laid on a taxi for them and it was waiting outside when they were ready to leave the hotel.

'When it's over, we have to phone the landlord of the Church Elm,' Fred told Jimmy. 'Your mum and dad are going there this evening with

Tommy Smith, so they won't have to wait until they get the morning paper before finding out the result.'

Fred and Jimmy had to go to the dressing room as soon as they arrived, but not before Joe shook his brother's hand and then hugged him. 'Go for it, Jimmy.'

Reggie felt scared for his friend, because this arena was huge and at least 200 people had already taken their seats or were standing at the bar and more were coming in all the time.

Joe had expected to see Duggie Murphy or perhaps for him to be introduced from the ring, but Murphy would take no further part in sponsoring any more events of this year's championships. Large corporations vied with each other to sponsor the quarter and semi-finals, but the BBC would fund the finals at the Royal Albert Hall. Tonight's sponsor was a company familiar to every boy and girl in the country as the makers of their favourite bedtime drink – Ovaltine.

Joe and Reggie took their seats, which, while not actually being ringside, were close enough to afford them an excellent view. Reggie tried to relax, although even Joe could feel the tension building within himself as they waited for the master of ceremonies to introduce the celebrities before the first boxers came into the ring.

Sitting opposite Joe and Reggie on the opposite side of the ring was a well-known Welsh singer with his wife and sitting next to them was another Welsh singer, who was also an actor. Joe remembered that there were two Welsh boxers in action tonight, so he assumed they were here to cheer on their fellow countrymen. The ex-British heavyweight champion, who had been at York Hall, was also present and Joe was sure that the Chancellor of the Exchequer was sitting to their left.

In the dressing room, Fred laced Jimmy's gloves after he had been weighed and examined by the doctor. Fred then gave some last-minute instructions, while Jimmy shadow boxed to warm himself up.

'Robson will go into the ring first,' Fred told him. 'You can be sure he will be watching you coming down the aisle. Look up at him and grin at him as though you're enjoying yourself, but be careful when the bell sounds, because Robson's trainer may have told him to get in first. Remember to move to his left and keep off the ropes and you'll be fine. You have put a lot of work in over the last few weeks, Jimmy, and it's paid off. You're three times as fast as you were for your last fight.'

'Contest, you mean,' Jimmy reminded him with a grin.

'Yeah, alright then,' Fred grinned back at him.

An ABA official tapped on the door and opened it marginally. 'It's time,' was all he said.

They followed him down the corridor and then suddenly, they were walking down the aisle towards the ring, where the other boxer was already waiting. Jimmy looked neither left nor right, and neither did he look up to grin at his opponent as Fred had told him to do.

The master of ceremonies introduced Robson first, which was greeted by loud applause and cheers. When Jimmy was introduced, the response was extremely modest, for the majority of the crowd were either from Birmingham or from Wales and Londoners were not the most popular of people for these regions. This had not fazed Jimmy at all, for all the butterflies had disappeared and he now stared coldly at Robson, who looked away first. The referee called the two boxers into the centre of the ring and gave them their final instructions, before they returned to their corners to await the bell.

Dickie had attempted to warn Joe about how different Jimmy would appear once he was in the boxing ring, but Joe was still amazed at the transformation, for this was surely not his kid brother, and Reggie felt exactly the same way, even though he had seen most of Jimmy's other contests.

As Fred had predicted, on the bell sounding, Robson rushed across the ring, only to be met with a still jab from Jimmy, who then circled to the boxer's left. It was a close round, with both boys managing to land telling blows upon each other, with the hardest being thrown by Jimmy just before the end of the round and he heard Robson gasp when the punch landed solidly in his solar plexus.

Jimmy sat on his stool feeling quite satisfied with the first round.

'He didn't like that last one, did he? I'll try that one again in the next round.'

'Don't get cocky,' Fred told Jimmy seriously. 'Just concentrate on what you have to do and always remember that the lad has the power to stop you in your tracks if you get careless. I think you won the round, but it was close. Now, let's see some more of the same.'

Robson rushed Jimmy again as soon as the bell rang, but this time Jimmy was not ready for him. He was assailed by a barrage of blows that landed on his head and his body and then Jimmy found himself on his hands and knees for the first time in his life. Instinctively, he stayed down, until the referee had counted to eight. The referee wiped Jimmy's gloves and looked at him closely.

'I'm fine, guv,' Jimmy assured him and the contest was allowed to continue.

Robson moved in with a confident smile upon his face, determined to finish this quickly, but all the speed work Jimmy had put in now paid dividends, as he kept moving to Robson's left to avoid the other boy's clubbing right hand. There were a few boos from some of the crowd, who felt that the Londoner should stand his ground, but Jimmy's head was now clearing and he got through the remainder of the round safely.

Joe and Reggie had been horrified to see Jimmy being battered by Robson and, like the majority of the spectators, they had not expected Jimmy to last the round. In fact, even Fred had thought his young boxer had blown his chance, but now Jimmy needed to have his confidence boosted and Fred began to do just that as soon as Jimmy sat down on the stool.

'OK. You lost that round, so it will be down to the last one. You did well, Jimmy, and I blame myself for not reminding you that he may rush in again. The thing to remember is that he caught you with at least half a dozen hefty whacks, but you're still in there; most lads would have stayed down, I can tell you. Listen to me, Jimmy. I gave you the first round, but it was close and the judges may not see it my way. I think you have to stop him to be sure of a result, especially in this neck of the woods.'

Robson had been assured by his trainer that he had won the first two rounds and that he was well ahead on points. The trainer told him that all he had to do was to coast the final round and he would be assured of the victory. Robson made no attempt to rush at his opponent when the bell sounded for the final round; a grave mistake, for Jimmy suddenly veered to the right and caught Robson with a perfect left hook to the jaw. It was Robson's turn to be on his hands and knees, shaking his head to clear his mind. Robson was on his feet far too early, the count only having reached four, and Jimmy was onto him like a terrier. Two more blows and Robson was down again. This time, he stayed down, until the count reached nine, but it would have been kinder to have stopped the contest there and then, as most referees would have. Nevertheless, this referee allowed it to continue and seconds later,

Robson was on the floor again and although he was conscious, he was fully stretched out in a gesture of surrender.

Once again, a crowded arena had been shocked into silence by Jimmy's performance and, judging by the flashing camera bulbs, once again, tomorrow morning's newspapers would feature Jimmy "Cannonball" Campbell.

Chapter Nineteen

Joe and Reggie waited outside the arena and when Jimmy and Fred appeared, they all walked back to the hotel together, but Jimmy needed time to unwind and this was felt by his brother and his friend, who held back until Jimmy was ready to talk. When they entered the hotel, Joe could contain himself no longer.

'Our dad told me you were like this after your last fight. What the bloody hell is up with you, Jimmy, we should be singing and dancing, not moping around like we were going to a bloody funeral.'

Jimmy tried to explain and began hesitantly. 'I know this is going to sound weird and I've been asking myself the same thing, but once I get into the ring, I am convinced that I can't be beaten. Even when I was on the floor tonight, I just knew I would get up and go on to win.' Jimmy glanced at his brother from the corner of his eye. 'It sort of scares me, Joe.' Jimmy attempted to make light of his words. 'See, I told you it would sound weird. Come on, let's get some grub.'

Jimmy and Reggie ran on ahead to the dining room, but Fred stopped at reception to use the telephone. He dialled the number of the Church Elm in Dagenham and the landlord informed him that his parents had not arrived yet.

'Are you going to tell me how he got on then?' asked Frank Mussett.

Fred laughed. 'No, Jimmy wants them to be the first to know, but please tell them that Jimmy is fine and is feeding his face, so I'll get him to ring back at half past eight.'

'What are you having for dinner then?' Frank had heard about these lavish ABA hotels.

'I had a look at the menu as soon as we arrived,' Fred told him.

'After the hors d'oeuvres, we are having prawn cocktail, steak with all the trimmings and Black Forest gateau for dessert. Oh, and by the way, me and Joe are having a bottle of wine between us with our meal.'

Frank had not quite grasped what Fred had told him. 'Oh well, there's no accounting for taste, I suppose.'

Fred joined the others, who were studying the menu, although the only alternative was the vegetarian dishes and that did not appeal to any of them at all. The hors d'oeuvres were already on the table and Jimmy was nibbling at tiny biscuits covered in what he thought was fish paste. In fact, it was caviar, with Black Forest gateau for dessert. Fred and Joe were to be served red wine with their meal, while Jimmy and Reggie were offered freshly squeezed orange or pineapple juice. After the first course, which was absolutely delicious and quite unlike anything any of them had ever tasted before, the waiter came to the table to take their order for the main course. As Jimmy was the star guest, the waiter came to him first.

'How would you like your steak, sir?' he asked.

Jimmy took a few seconds before answering. 'Er ... cooked, please.'

The waiter's face remained impassive as he said, 'Yes, sir. I should have asked how you would like it to be cooked. Well done, medium-rare, with just the juices escaping and slightly pink in the middle, or rare, where the meat has been only slightly cooked.'

Jimmy asked for his steak to be cooked medium-rare, as did the other three, and then after the waiter had left the table, Joe spluttered, 'How would you like your steak, sir ... Cooked, please! You wait till I tell Mum and Dad that one.'

'Well, how was I to know?' said Jimmy. 'This is the first time I've ever been in a proper restaurant, apart from the pie-and-mash shop.'

The wine waiter brought the bottle of wine over to the table and poured a sample for Fred to taste, being perfectly aware that none of his customers that evening would know the difference between a bottle of cheap plonk and one of the finest red wines that he kept in his cellar for special customers. The wine waiter hated this annual event, when he was obliged to serve the "Philistines" with even the cheapest of the wines the hotel stocked. Most of them would have preferred a pint of brown ale or a bottle of stout and he considered it to be such a waste of fine wine. Another waiter placed dishes of vegetables on the table moments before the first waiter served them with huge portions of steak that almost covered the entire platters they were served on.

Jimmy was ravenous and helped himself to the vegetables. 'These are funny-looking chips,' he said as he scooped a spoonful on top of his steak.

'They're not chips,' Fred informed him, 'they're sauté potatoes.'

'Well, they still look like round chips to me,' said Jimmy, who then turned his attention to the peas and baby carrots. The others did the same.

Joe watched in awe as his brother completely cleared his platter, for even Reggie was unable to manage all of his meal. Fred had given up before he was halfway through and Joe left perhaps a third of the steak on his. Joe and Fred refused the gateau, but Jimmy tucked into his with relish, although Reggie took much longer over his portion.

Joe had drunk two glasses of wine and was already feeling the effects, so he decided to leave Fred to finish the rest of the bottle.

After their meal, Fred signed the bill and although the association would include a tip for the staff, Fred handed the wine waiter a ten-shilling note. The wine waiter knew that there would be very little cash changing hands this evening and he had no intention of sharing this tip with any of the other waiters.

'You paid that out of your own pocket, didn't you, Fred?' Joe asked him. 'I thought the ABA took care of everything?'

'They do, but this is not the first time I've tipped a wine waiter and sometimes it pays off.'

A few minutes later, the wine waiter returned carrying a tray and he placed a large brandy in front of Fred and another in front of Joe.

'Compliments of the hotel, sir, enjoy your evening.'

Fred thanked the man and grinned at Joe triumphantly. 'See what I mean. It doesn't always work, but these two brandies would cost six bob each at the bar.'

'You crafty old sod,' Jimmy said cheekily.

'Hey you, less of the old, if you don't mind.'

'I can't drink this, Fred,' Joe shook his head, 'you'd better have mine as well.'

'I was hoping you'd say that,' Fred said gleefully as he poured Joe's brandy into his own glass.

*   *   *

Freda, Dickie and Tommy Smith walked into the Church Elm at just after eight o'clock and were immediately summoned over to the bar by the excited landlord.

'Jimmy's already had his fight and Fred told me to tell you that he's fine and they've all gone for their dinner. He wouldn't tell me whether he won or not, but Jimmy will phone here himself at half eight. I can't say I would fancy what they're having for dinner though.'

'What do you mean?' Freda demanded.

'Well, Fred told me that they're having prawns, a horse-meat steak and black pudding for afters.'

'I've heard those northerners are a funny lot,' said Tommy Smith, 'but prawns before your dinner! We only have prawns for our Sunday tea and I suppose they'll have to peel the bloody things first.'

'Horse meat!' exclaimed Freda. 'I though only those Frenchies ate horse meat.'

'And black pudding for afters,' said Dickie. 'Are you sure about this, Frank?'

Frank shrugged and began to pull them a pint. 'That's what Fred told me; anyway, your Jimmy will be phoning back soon, so you can ask him for yourself.'

They took their drinks and sat down, only to be joined a short time later by John Townsend, who was also eager to learn how Jimmy had fared. Dickie told him of the news so far.

'Jimmy must have been one of the first on the bill to be finished this early,' said John.

Freda was just relieved to know that her son was alright, regardless of whether he had won or lost. She told John about the meal they would be having in Birmingham.

'Someone's pulling your leg,' laughed John. 'My missus comes from Brum and her parents still live there. We go to see them three or four times a year and you can take it from me that they don't eat horse meat or have black pudding for afters. They have black pudding for breakfast, the same as we do.'

'Speak for yourself,' said Dickie. 'I can't stand the stuff myself.'

At exactly eight thirty, Frank indicated that there was a telephone call from Birmingham. 'Take it in the back room,' he told Dickie, but Freda declined to go with him.

A few minutes later, he emerged holding his clenched fist in the air, leaving nobody in any doubt that Jimmy had won his contest.

Freda did not ask how Jimmy had won, but she anxiously asked her husband. 'Is he alright, did you speak to him?'

'He's fine, but just you wait until I get a chance to have a word in Frank's ear.'

In fact, Frank Mussett was just about to make an announcement over the loudspeaker: 'Ladies and gentlemen, we have just received word from Birmingham that our own Jimmy Campbell, the cannonball kid, is through to the semi-finals of the ABA Championships, having knocked out his opponent in the last round of his contest. Ladies and gentlemen, let's hear it for his proud parents, who are here with us tonight – Freda and Dickie.'

Loud cheers filled the room as Freda and Dickie stood and raised their glasses.

Dickie beckoned to Frank to come over and join them. 'Thanks for the use of your phone, Frank,' said Dickie, 'but you're not all that clever at taking down messages, are you?'

Frank looked puzzled. 'What do you mean? I just passed on what Fred told me to tell you.'

Freda, John and Tommy were curious.

'Well, for a start, there was no horse meat, it was those fancy biscuit things they call hors d'oeuvres. The prawns were served in a glass bowl, with mayonnaise and pieces of salad, and with other huge, peeled prawns hanging on the outside of the rim, not out of a brown paper bag that you have to peel yourself, and your black pudding was Black Forest gateaux, with whipped cream on top.'

There was great merriment at the Campbells' table, although Freda and Dickie were also laughing with relief that Jimmy had come through his latest contest without injury.

In Birmingham, Jimmy, Joe, Reggie and Fred spent an hour wandering around the hotel soaking up the luxury of the plush establishment. The swimming pool and gymnasium were now closed, but Jimmy, Joe and Reggie resolved to be down at seven, when it reopened in the morning. The billiard room would remain open all night, so they decided to play snooker on one of the two full-sized tables. To reach the room, they needed to retrace their footsteps past the dining room and as they passed the door, they stopped and looked inside, when they heard the wine waiter remonstrating with one of the guests.

'Sir,' the waiter said, 'I really must ask you not to stand on the table.'

A very loud voice replied, 'Piss off, I've got an announcement to make and I intend to make it.' The man was standing rather unsteadily on a table and he had obviously been drinking heavily.

'Tomorrow morning, when you read the Sunday papers, you will all be able to tell your friends that you have seen the next champion of the junior ABA – my son Tommy Baxter.' He beckoned to a boy of Jimmy's age, who was sitting next to a woman, possibly his mother, and a man Fred knew to be the boy's trainer. 'Stand up and take a bow, Tommy.'

Tommy rose to his feet, but the other diners totally ignored the ill-mannered display and both father and son resumed their seats with scowls on their faces.

'Bugger the lot of you,' said the father loudly. 'What a load of snobby gits.'

Jimmy could not take his eyes off the other boy. Tommy Baxter did not appear to be embarrassed at all by the snub he and his father had received; in fact, he looked every bit as angry as his father. The only person at their table who looked as though he wanted to be miles away was the trainer.

'It's loud mouth oafs like him that give us Londoners a bad name,' Fred observed as they entered the billiard room. He ordered another large brandy for himself and three orange juices for the others, knowing that he would only be able to charge the association for the juices. Halfway through their game, Tommy Baxter came in with his father.

Mr Baxter strode over to Jimmy, ignoring Fred and Joe. 'So this is Cannonball Campbell, is it?' he sneered. 'Well, I only hope you come up against my Tommy in the next round, because a cannon needs a fuse and my boy will punch your lights out before you know what's hit you.'

'Not here and not now,' Fred stood between the man and Jimmy.

'I take it Tommy won tonight and so did Jimmy, so let's all just enjoy the rest of the evening.'

'That sounds like a good idea to me.' Joe moved to stand side by side with Fred.

Chris Baxter decided that discretion was the better part of valour on this occasion and left the room with his son, although he paused at the door and pointed at Jimmy. 'If you're drawn against Tommy in the next round, you won't even bother to turn up if you have any sense.'

They went back to their game, but the evening had been spoiled by an ignorant, loud-mouthed man, who, as Fred had stated, gave all Londoners a bad name, which they did not deserve.

It was getting late and it had been a long day, so the three youngsters went to their rooms. Fred was still angry over the exchange with Baxter and felt the need to unwind a little. It took another three large brandies before he felt ready for his bed.

Freda and Dickie returned from the Church Elm, leaving John and Tommy to have a last pint before closing time.

'Dickie, I have something on my mind that's been worrying me all week.' Freda accepted the small glass of whisky and ginger ale that Dickie had poured for her.

'About Jimmy and his boxing?' Dickie was not surprised.

'No, not Jimmy this time. It's Joe and Mary.'

'Joe and Mary?' Dickie was puzzled. 'What about Joe and Mary?'

'Of course, I'm worried that Jimmy could get himself hurt, but so could Joe.'

Dickie was not following her drift at all. 'What are you going on about?'

'I think our Joe has fallen for Mary and fallen for her in a big way.'

'Don't be so bloody soft, woman, she's old enough to be his mother.'

'She's only twenty-six and Joe will be sixteen next month. I wouldn't call that old enough to be his mother and you know that Joe acts and looks much older than his years. I've been watching him whenever he's come back from Camden on the last few Sundays and I'm telling you, it wasn't David who put that look in his eyes.'

Dickie shook his head. 'I can't see Mary Davis going in for cradle snatching. Alright, he may have a bit of a crush on her for the moment, but I bet you anything you like he'll come waltzing in here in a couple of months time with a young dolly bird on his arm.'

'Oh yeah, and where is Joe going to meet this dolly bird, down at the sewage farm?' snapped Freda.

'Give over, he's only been out a couple of weeks, give him time to make a few friends and don't forget, friends often have sisters.'

'I suppose you do know that Joe is leaving Birmingham first thing in the morning, so that he can spend the day with her and David?'

'I didn't, until Jimmy told me when he phoned,' said Dickie. 'That makes sense, anyway. The others are not leaving until after lunch and they won't arrive back in Euston until five or six.'

'What if they … you know … get carried away. Perhaps you could have a quiet word with him about taking precautions,' Freda said thoughtfully.

'No, I bloody well won't,' Dickie was aghast at the idea. 'If Joe's not clued up by now, you can bet your life she is, but I still think you're barking up the wrong tree. Apart from anything else, Joe still has two years' probation to get through and then he will have to do his National Service. I think they will always be good friends, mainly because of David, but that's all they will ever be. Just good friends.'

Freda hoped her husband would be proved right.

In Birmingham the following morning, Joe, Jimmy and Reggie had been waiting outside the swimming pool for it to open at seven o'clock. They were joined by a dozen or so other guests, including Tommy Baxter, but he and Jimmy ignored each other. Half an hour later, Jimmy's stomach warned him that it was feeding time and the three of them quickly changed and went for their breakfast. Joe knocked on Fred's door, in case he had overslept, only to be greeted by, 'Sod off.'

The last thing Fred needed after all the brandy he had consumed was a fried breakfast, but, in fact, it was not a traditional fried breakfast at all. Indeed, Jimmy was not at all impressed with what was on offer. Half a grapefruit to begin with and then either grilled kidneys or a pair of kippers.

'Give me my mum's fry-ups any day,' he grumbled.

'This is what the toffs always have for breakfast,' said Joe, 'they don't go in for all that fried food.'

The breakfast waiter had been instructed to offer an alternative if he noticed any reluctance of this morning's guests to partake of the usual fare.

'Would sirs prefer two boiled eggs with toast?' he asked haughtily.

'Yes, thank you,' Joe replied in his poshest voice, 'sirs would, indeed, prefer boiled eggs, if you please.'

'Sirs would prefer boiled eggs, if you please,' chortled Jimmy after the waiter had left. 'Where did you learn to speak like that?'

'I've seen a few Terry-Thomas films,' Joe told his brother.

A very bleary-eyed Fred Loake joined them at the table, although it was only black coffee that he needed and more than one at that.

He would have liked to leave as soon as the lads had finished breakfast, but he knew Jimmy and Reggie were looking forward to sampling all the facilities of this splendid hotel and Jimmy had certainly earned that right.

Fred asked Reggie to go to the reception desk and bring back the morning papers, which were free of charge for the guests. The hotel usually only allowed *The Sunday Times* to be placed on the reception counter, but once a year there were also other "rags" displayed as a concession to the working-class people who were staying with them.

Reggie selected *The News of the World* and *The Sunday Pictorial* and took them back to Fred, without looking at the sports pages.

Fred studied the reports in the *Pictorial* first, but this time it was a photograph of Tommy Baxter that dominated the page. It showed him standing over his fallen opponent and the newspaper reported that this had been a first round knockout. There was also a quote from his father: "Tommy Baxter is this year's ABA junior champion and if they have any sense, the others won't even bother to turn up."

'Baxter's old man talks a good fight, but its not him that has to get into the ring,' snorted Jimmy.

'*The News of the World* showed two pictures of Jimmy's contest, one when Jimmy had been on his hands and knees and another when Robson was stretched out, flat on his back. Jimmy had once again been awarded the best-boxer prize in recognition of the courage he had shown and the skill he had displayed to come back after almost being knocked down himself.

Jimmy was delighted. 'I wonder what Mum wants this time?'

'I think that if a boxer wins the prize more than once in the same competition, *The News of the World* offer a different selection. They did try to offer vouchers instead, but the association said it would compromise a boxer's amateur status.'

'I see that both of the Welsh boxers have got through,' Joe read. 'Does that mean the semi-finals will be held in Wales?'

'I should think so.' Fred was slowly beginning to feel more human.

'There is a big stadium in Cardiff, where all the professionals box, and I think the semis will be held there. They will let us know during the week and they will also tell us who you will be up against next, Jimmy.'

'And what my prize will be.'

'And that.' Fred was now on his third cup of coffee.

Joe left Birmingham a short time later and was back in Camden Town a little after one o'clock. As he expected, David was waiting at the gate for him as he walked into Crowndale Road and Mary met him at the door with a kiss on his cheek. Neither Joe nor Mary felt any awkwardness spilling over from when David had suggested they should get married, although Mary had considered whether it was wise to greet or bid Joe farewell with a kiss, but she obeyed her instincts, as it felt so natural. Joe told them of his brother's success in Birmingham and David listened solemnly.

'I'm glad you're not a boxer, Joe,' he said. 'I couldn't bear to think of anybody trying to punch you.'

'No fear of that, matey, I'm too big a coward for all that.'

Mary poured tea for all three of them. 'Will you leave the sewage farm now, Joe?' she asked him. 'I mean, would this probation officer give you any trouble if you decided to find another job?'

'Probably not, but I doubt that even this Mr Rutherford would let me work any of the markets while I'm still out on licence. I don't want to be cooped up inside and to tell the truth, now that I've got the bike, I don't mind it too much anyway. It would be different if I could find a decent job in the open air, but this will do me for the time being.' He looked at Mary and told her firmly. 'I can save some money and one day, I will be back in Camden to set up my own stall.'

'And come back to live with me and my mummy?' David clapped his hands with glee.

Mary met Joe's gaze before answering her son. 'Not for a while yet, David, perhaps not for a long while, but for the moment at least, we can have Joe with us every Sunday.'

There was a subliminal message in those few words with the message not being lost on Joe and his heart leapt at the prospect of being with this beautiful woman, even if, for the time being, it was to be only once every week.

Mary changed the subject. 'How are your mum and dad, Joe, are they still enjoying their jobs?'

'My mum's not doing quite as many hours now, but she likes to be with the other women at May and Bakers and my dad seems to have fallen on his feet at the council depot. He was telling me that John Townsend has so much work on his hands that he's considering packing in the bins and going full time.'

'Will your dad go in with him?'

'I'm not sure, it's all a bit risky and I'm not sure whether my dad will be willing to chance it at the moment.'

David tugged at Joe's arm. 'Joe, will you take me to Hampstead Heath after lunch? There's a funfair this weekend and sliding down the helter-skelter is my favourite.'

'Of course I will, matey,' Joe replied happily. 'How about you, Mary, will you come as well?'

Mary smiled. 'Of course I will, but you won't catch me going on any helter-skelter.'

Hampstead Heath was full of merrymakers, who were determined to enjoy the warm sunshine and the pleasures of the funfair rides.

David was unable to persuade his mother onto the helter-skelter, but together, he and Joe cajoled her into riding on the big wheel with them. They stayed on the heath for three hours or so, eating hotdogs and drinking tea from one of the mobile canteens, and then it was time for Joe to leave. Jimmy, Fred and Reggie would be home by now, but Joe had promised his parents that he would be home in plenty of time to give his version of last night's events. It had been a wonderful weekend for Joe and next Sunday could prove to be even better, for he, Mary and David would be spending the whole day together. They had not decided what they would do yet, but Joe promised he would take the first train to Mornington Crescent on Sunday morning and he would be with them in time for breakfast.

Mary and David walked to the station with Joe and bought a platform ticket, so that they could see him off. David hugged Joe around the waist as they stood on the platform, but Joe's eyes were locked onto Mary's.

'We'll see you again next Sunday, promise?' Mary said softly.

'You can count on that,' Joe replied huskily.

Once again, Mary kissed Joe's cheek as the train pulled into the station.

Chapter Twenty

It was still not yet ten o'clock when Joe walked into the Campbell house, so he was not very surprised to see John Townsend drinking a glass of ale with his father. Dickie went into the kitchen to fetch another glass and poured one for Joe. Jimmy had already gone to bed, but Fred Loake had told them all about the contest and the Sunday morning newspapers had given their account, so Joe merely confirmed what they already knew.

'Where's Mum?' asked Joe.

'Next door with Ada, and your mum's got the right hump,' Dickie tutted. 'Bloody women are all the same.'

'So what's Mum got the hump about then? I thought she would be pleased that Jimmy had won and she'd be getting another prize.'

'Oh, she's pleased about that alright, but John has come up with a proposal that your mother is not keen about at all.' He looked towards John. 'Tell Joe about it, John.'

John leaned forwards earnestly. 'The thing is, Joe, what with all the work that's flooding in, I think it's time we went full time. Me and your dad are going into equal partnership and we need to take on somebody else to give us a hand. A mate of mine owns a workshop in Oxlow Lane and he's looking to sell up, because he wants to retire. It would be ideal for us; we could make our own bedroom and kitchen furniture on the premises, instead of having to pay through the nose from one of the other outlets, but we need somebody to take charge, while me and your dad are out doing the fitting.'

'Somebody like you, Joe.' Dickie's voice had raised an octave. 'You could get out of that stinking shit farm and come and work with us.'

Joe stared at his father and John. 'But where will you get the money to buy this workshop?'

'From the bank, of course,' John said confidently. 'Me and your dad will put up £200 each and the bank will lend us the rest.'

'£200!' Joe laughed in spite of himself. 'Dad, you'd be hard pressed to raise twenty quid, let alone £200.'

'Your dad doesn't need to,' said John. 'I will put in his share and he can pay me back later.'

Joe was sceptical. 'So why don't you go in on your own then, why do you need my dad?'

'That's a fair question,' said John, 'and to be truthful, I feel that I need someone around me that I can rely on, which is why I would like you to come in with us as well.'

'What do I know about making kitchen units?' Joe said scornfully.

'Not a lot at the moment,' John admitted, 'but the wood machinist, who is still working there, is willing to stay on for at least a few months and work alongside of us.'

'I don't want to be a dustman forever, son,' Dickie told Joe. 'Don't get me wrong, I was bloody grateful to get the job, but this could be my big chance to really make something of myself and I mean to take it.'

'You said Mum's got the hump, so what does she have to say about it?' It was an obvious question.

'Oh, you know what women are like,' his father answered, 'all doom and gloom. Your mum thinks we will fall flat on our faces and end up with nothing, not even a job. But our minds are made up, Joe, and we have an appointment with the bank manager at three o'clock tomorrow afternoon. What about you, Joe, are you going to come in with us, it has to be better than working on a shit farm?'

Freda stood in the doorway to hear Joe's response.

'When that Wyatt bloke sent me to the sewage farm, he believed it would freak me out and I wouldn't be able to stick it. For some reason, he seemed hell bent on getting me sent back to borstal and he very nearly succeeded. Now that I've got the bike and with two great dollops of vaseline under my nose, it's not too bad and to be honest, I would feel guilty if I left right now. The two brothers have been good to me and I've, well, sort of promised to learn some more sign language, so that I can communicate with Jack a bit better.' Joe paused to take a sip of his beer. 'This job gives me a good wage and I'm saving up, because after I've done my stint in National Service, I'm moving back to Camden to get myself a stall.'

'And move back in with Mary?' Freda knew what the answer would be.
'Yes, and move back in with Mary and David.'

Freda cast a knowing look at her husband, before going back into the
kitchen. At least Joe would still have a steady job and would remain in
Dagenham for at least the next two years.

The next morning, the Campbell family went their separate ways as
usual, although this Monday, according to Freda, could prove to be a
disaster, if Dickie and John Townsend embarked upon what she
considered to be their hare-brained scheme. Joe had also left on his
bicycle for the sewage farm and Reggie Godber had been sitting in the
kitchen for at least twenty minutes before Jimmy was ready to leave for
school. Reggie was eager to get there as early as they could in order that
he could bask in Jimmy's reflected glory and boast to anybody who
would listen that he was the champion's assistant trainer.

Amy Ashby called for Freda and they walked to Dagenham Heathway
station to catch the train to Dagenham East, but Freda could hardly get
a word in edgeways, for all Amy wanted to talk about was Jimmy's latest
victory. Eventually, Freda did manage to tell Amy that Dickie was
seriously considering leaving his council job to set himself up in a
partnership with John Townsend.

Amy was horrified. 'For God's sake, talk him out of it,' she pleaded.
'You remember me telling you about my brother winning 200 quid on
the football pools; well, what I didn't tell you was that he went to the
bank with his £200 and borrowed another £1,000 to start up his own
haulage firm. Three second-hand lorries he bought and he took on
another two drivers. He had plenty of work, but the customers were not
very keen to settle their bills and one week, he wasn't able to pay his
drivers. They refused to work without pay and he went bust in less than
three months. The thing was, Freda, him and my sister-in-law had their
own house in Chadwell Heath and he had put it up as a guarantee
against the loan. When he couldn't pay, the bank repossessed his house
to get their money back and the last time I heard from him, he had split
up with Jenny and was driving a lorry for someone else up in Scotland.'
They got off the train and walked down the hill to the May and Baker
factory. 'The one good thing, I suppose, is that at least they didn't have
any kids.'

'They can't repossess our house,' said Freda, 'it belongs to the council.'

'I know that, Freda, but they can send in the bailiffs and take everything you've got. How much are Dickie and his friend going to ask for?'

'No idea, I never even asked.' The two women entered the factory and took their cards from the rack to punch into the time clock. 'By the time I get home, it will be all signed, sealed and delivered and there's bugger all I'll be able to do about it,' said Freda.

Joe cycled to the sewage farm, knowing that John and his father had expected him to jump at the chance of working with them and Joe was very much aware of how disappointed his father had been when the offer had been declined, but Joe believed he had made the right choice, at least for now. He had already told Ronnie and Jack Conway about the confrontation John and his father had had with the probation officer and this morning, before leaving their house, Jack had signed to his brother, 'Do you think Joe will be coming in today?'

Ronnie had shrugged his shoulders before signing: I hope he will, but we will just have to wait and see.

They were both delighted to see Joe sitting on his bicycle waiting for them when they entered the gate. Joe greeted Ronnie with a cheerful 'Good morning,' and then to Jack, he signed: Did you have a nice weekend?

Ronnie had shown Joe how to sign this phrase on Friday and Joe had been practising it even when he had been in Birmingham. Jack was delighted, as Ronnie had known he would be.

'That was smashing, Joe,' Ronnie told him. 'We've read all about your brother in yesterday's papers and he did wonderfully well. You and your mum and dad must be very proud of him.'

Joe smiled his agreement and applied some vaseline beneath his nostrils.

'Listen, Ronnie,' Joe said quietly, 'it's not going to make any difference about what happened with my probation officer last week. I want to stay on here until I get my call-up papers, if it's all the same to you.'

Ronnie relayed the message to Jack, who rushed over to pump Joe's hand up and down enthusiastically. Then Jack then raised both thumbs into the air, leaving Joe in no doubt about how pleased he was at the news.

*   *   *

Dickie and John Townsend finished work at midday and then went home to change, before their meeting with the bank manager.

In fact, they did not get to see the manager at all, but were shown into a small office by a young clerk, who introduced them to another equally young and smartly dressed official.

'This is Miss Platt,' said the clerk. 'Miss Platt is the head of the bank's small business services.'

'Thank you, Helen,' Miss Platt smiled at the girl. 'Please take a seat, gentlemen.'

She studied the papers that John had brought with them, including their own advanced orders, plus more orders that the present owner was willing to pass over when he sold his business. But Miss Platt was more interested in the documents that estimated the value of the workshop and the machinery that would be included.

'This estimate appears to be rather on the high side to me,' she frowned. 'We want to loan money, that's how we make a profit, but it's my job to ensure that if a small business fails, the bank does not lose its investment. The fact that you are willing to invest some of your own money is encouraging and I believe you both to be hard-working men, who will do everything you can to make this venture a success.' Miss Platt tapped her teeth with her pencil and then shook her head. 'However, hard work and enthusiasm does not always mean a successful outcome and I have to tell you that I have a few reservations over this plan of yours. If either of you owned your own home, it would be a different matter, but all you can use as collateral is a workshop and a couple of woodworking machines. I'm no expert, but even I know that it takes more than a few weeks to become skilled at using these machines.'

'We have a wood machinist, who will stay on to work for us,' said John.

'But how long for?' she replied. 'What if he decides to take his skills elsewhere? Supposing he is suddenly taken seriously ill? What would you do then?'

John stood up and motioned for Dickie to do the same.

'We will not waste any more of your time, Miss Platt,' John said with dignity. 'We understand that this bank considers us to be a poor risk.'

'Gentlemen, gentlemen,' Miss Platt said hastily. 'Please sit down. I wasn't saying that at all, I was merely pointing out the pitfalls and there are pitfalls and risks in any new business venture. On the other hand, there are wonderful opportunities for men such as yourselves, who are brave enough to grasp them.' She beamed at the two men, who had resumed their seats. 'Subject to an independent valuation of the property, I can authorise your loan application and a cheque will be paid into a joint business account as soon as we have the valuation, which I will arrange for tomorrow morning.'

She shook hands with both of them and Dickie and John left her office almost in a state of shock.

'Just like that,' Dickie said as they stood outside the bank.

'No, it bloody well wasn't just like that,' said John. 'These people have a fair idea who they will and will not lend their money to and I think Miss Platt believes she's onto a winner with us.' John punched the air, much to the amusement of an old lady, who happened to be passing by. 'And so do bloody well we.'

The bank was only just across the road from the Church Elm, so it was only natural that Dickie and John should pop in to celebrate their new partnership.

'I wonder how Jack Doyle will take it,' Dickie said as they sat down with their pints of beer. 'Both of us giving him the elbow at the same time, I mean.'

'He won't be too surprised,' answered John. 'He has a shrewd idea that me and you have more work than we can handle and I have hinted that we may soon call it a day on the bins.'

'I'll always be grateful to that man,' Dickie sounded melancholic. 'He put himself out for me and I will never forget that.'

'Oh, stop crying in your fucking beer, for Christ's sake,' John was exasperated. 'We're supposed to be celebrating, not worrying about who'll be collecting the poxy rubbish next week.'

'I suppose I'm also a bit worried about how Freda is going to react when she gets home,' said Dickie glumly.

'So let's get pissed and stay out until she's gone to bed.'

'We still have to go to work tomorrow to hand in our notice, but I must say, I could do with a few pints before I have to go home and face the music.'

Joe had received a postcard from his probation officer ordering him to report to the office after he had finished work on Monday and Joe was tempted to go straight from the sewage farm, but abandoned the idea and went home to bath and change first.

Joe chuckled to himself as he rode home from Rainham. Blimey, that would stink his office out and no mistake.

He arrived at Mr Wyatt's office at six thirty, but the perky little receptionist was nowhere to be seen and the harassed probation officer had to open the door for his callers and answer the telephone by himself. There were three other men in the waiting room and as one left his inner office, Mr Wyatt would just bellow "next". Finally, it was Joe's turn and he sat in front of the man, while the probation officer pretended to study Joe's file. In fact, Mr Wyatt was still seething at the way he had been humiliated in this boy's house, although common sense warned him that he must tread very carefully with the Campbell family and that smart-alec friend of theirs. He would do nothing to help this boy and neither would he give him a single word of encouragement, although Mr Wyatt was mindful that he dare not risk being reported again by any of his clients. He asked Joe a few perfunctory questions, without even bothering to listen to the answers, and then he dismissed Joe, saying, 'Same time again in two weeks. Do not change your job without consulting me, remain living with your parents and do not mix with anyone who has a criminal record.'

Joe had been in the probation office for over two hours and it was almost nine o'clock when he arrived home and was greeted by his worried mother.

'Joe,' she said anxiously, 'your dad hasn't come home yet and Fred Loake is here to tell us about Jimmy's next contest, but I don't even know where Jimmy is. I've tried next door but there's no answer.'

'Jimmy will be out with Reggie Godber and has probably forgotten the time, but I think my dad will be in the Church Elm. I'll go and see if I can find him.'

Joe popped his head around the front-room door, where Fred was sitting with a cup of tea in his hands. 'Sorry about this, Fred, I'll be back in a jiffy.'

'No problem,' answered the trainer, although he was not best pleased that neither his protégée nor his father appeared to be very interested as to where Jimmy would be boxing next or who his next opponent would be.

Joe arrived at the pub to be met by a relieved publican.

'Take your old man home, for fuck's sake,' said Frank. 'He's as pissed as a newt and is still asking for more, but I'm not serving him any more beer and that goes for that other drunken pillock.'

Frank pointed to the corner of the public bar, where his father and John Townsend were sprawled all over one of the tables.

Dickie looked up when Joe shook his shoulder and greeted him with the same lopsided look on his face that drunks all around the world seemed to adopt. ''allo, Joe,' he slurred. 'Me and John have gone and done it. As from next week, we are going to be gaffers.'

John suddenly pulled himself upright and to the tune of *The Red Flag* began to sing: 'The working class can kiss me arse, we've got the gaffer's job at last.'

He then collapsed back into his chair laughing idiotically, before slumping back across the table, snoring loudly. Dickie was in no better condition and the publican admitted defeat.

'Not a pretty sight, are they?' said Frank. 'Forget what I said about taking them home. There's hardly anyone in tonight, so I'll bring a couple of blankets down and cover them up and they can stay here for the night.'

It was a very irate Freda who opened the door to Joe, even before he had taken his keys from his pocket, for Freda had heard his footsteps. Joe explained the situation as tactfully as he could, but there was no escaping the fact that his father and John Townsend were too drunk and incapable of making their way to their homes under their own steam.

'They'll live to regret this day, you mark my words,' Freda told her son bitterly. 'In all the years I've known him, I've never seen him so pissed that he can't even walk and the pair of them are supposed to be at work in the morning.' She looked at Joe. 'Did they tell you that they weren't going back any more?'

Joe shook his head. 'I'm not even sure if either of them knew I was there and Frank didn't mention anything about it.'

Joe felt it would be unfair if the two men left the depot without giving proper notice, for Jack Doyle had been good to his father and indeed, a good boss to all the men who worked for him.

A subtle cough from behind the door of the front room caused Freda to spin round and rush into the room quickly.

'Christ Almighty, Fred, I'd forgotten all about you waiting in here, I'm so sorry.'

'It's not your fault, Freda,' said Fred. 'I did tell Jimmy that I would be round at half seven and it's well gone nine o'clock now. I can't wait any longer, because I haven't fed my cats yet, but would you tell Jimmy that if he wants to know where the next venue will be and who he will be up against, then he can make the effort to come to the club tomorrow evening.'

Both Freda and Joe recognised that this was a rebuke at the lack of courtesy and respect that had been shown him that evening and Freda felt mortified as she showed him to the door.

Jimmy came puffing into the house ten minutes later and looked anxiously around to see if Fred had waited for him. He was not a rude or a selfish boy, but on this occasion, he and Reggie Godber had lost all track of time as boys of his age are wont to do.

There are times, fortunately very seldom, when people can reach breaking point and feel an overwhelming urge to hit out at something or someone in retaliation for the hurt and unfairness that they feel has been heaped upon them and Freda had reached breaking point at that precise moment. The loss of her mother, the dread of losing all of their possessions, the thought of her husband lying drunk on the floor of a public house and finally the humiliation she had felt when Fred Loake had left the house was too much for her.

Joe and Jimmy were totally shocked, when both of Freda's open hands slapped each side of Jimmy's face, with the sound of the blows reverberating around the kitchen.

'You selfish little bugger,' she shouted. Freda then rushed into the front room and threw herself onto the sofa. 'Oh my God, what have I done, what am I doing?' She was crying as though her heart would break.

Jimmy had not moved and remained in the kitchen, both cheeks inflamed from the blows they had received. 'What did I do?' he appealed to Joe. 'I know I was late, but our mum has never hit any of us like that before.'

'Jimmy,' Joe was desperate for his brother to understand. 'That wasn't meant for you and when our mum realises what she's done she will be shattered, believe me.'

Jimmy's eyes filled with tears and he walked up the stairs to seek solace in his own bedroom, because Joe had now taken their gran's room.

Joe went to the sideboard and poured his mother a generous measure of whisky, adding an equal measure of dry ginger. His hands were trembling so badly that he spilt a good deal of it on the polished surface, so he poured another for himself and drank half of it, before taking the other glass in to his mother. Her heaving shoulders had lessened considerably, which told Joe that her hysteria was gradually burning itself out.

'Have a drop of this, Mum,' said Joe gently. 'It might help you to feel a bit better.' Freda took the glass but could not meet Joe's eyes.

She sat looking dejectedly at the floor as Joe struggled to find some words that would comfort her. 'Listen, Mum, Jimmy will understand and ...'

'Don't say anything, Joe, not tonight,' she whispered. 'Will you leave me on my own now, Joe? I'm alright, but I can't talk about this tonight, I just need to sit here by myself for a while.'

Joe did not reply, but took his drink to his room, for he, too, felt the need to be on his own. He felt angry that his father had been so thoughtless and was ashamed that his mother had hit out at Jimmy in a way that he would not have believed her to be capable of. Jimmy would forgive their mother, but would their mother ever forgive herself for what had happened tonight? Joe could hear her moving around downstairs in the front room and rightly assumed that she had decided to have another drink. Joe wished he had refilled his own glass before coming to bed, but he had no intention of leaving his room until he had to get up for work in the morning. Joe believed that he would get little sleep that night, but the whisky soon took effect and he was sound asleep just minutes after he had climbed into his bed.

Chapter Twenty-One

When Freda eventually went to bed, she lay staring at the ceiling for what seemed to be hour after hour, although she probably dozed off from time to time in between. When she heard the sound of a key being turned in the lock of the front door and looked at the alarm clock on the bedside table, she was amazed to discover it was 6.00 a.m.

Somehow, Dickie had managed to recover and was carefully creeping up the stairs to get changed for work, not only feeling dreadful, but also greatly ashamed that for the first time in his life, he had drunk himself totally incapable. Not even in his army days had he been in the condition he had been in yesterday and he had nobody to blame but himself, because John had certainly not held a gun to his head and forced the beer down his throat.

Freda turned her back when she heard Dickie climbing the stairs and she pretended to be asleep until he had gone.

Joe had also heard Dickie come in and was waiting in the kitchen with the kettle on to make tea for himself and strong black coffee for his father, determined not to be judgemental, although equally determined to speak his mind.

Joe told his father, 'I know you're feeling rough, Dad, but I don't think you're feeling half as bad as Mum does right now.' He went on to explain what had happened the night before. 'Jimmy will be alright,' said Joe, 'but I think our mum is going to take a long time to get over this.'

Dickie's shame was compounded when a crestfallen Jimmy came into the kitchen and poured himself a glass of milk without looking at either his father or Joe.

'I'm sorry, Jimmy,' said Dickie, 'this is all my fault.'

'Yes, it is,' Jimmy turned to look at his father. 'I'm going to take Mum up a cup of tea and tell her it's alright.'

Freda could hear the muffled voices from the kitchen but they were indistinct and when she heard footsteps coming up the stairs, she assumed it was her husband coming up to apologise. She was not ready to hear anything he had to say right now, so she turned once again to face the wall, still pretending to be asleep. There was a gentle tap on the door and she heard Jimmy's voice.

'Mum, I've brought you up a cup of tea.'

Freda could hardly bear it. After the way she had attacked him last night, Jimmy could still do this for her. Freda did not turn over, for she did not want her son to see the tears that were streaming down her cheeks. 'Thanks, Jimmy, will you leave it on the table. I'm not getting up for a while and I'm not going to work today, either.'

Freda stayed in bed until the house was empty, only getting up when she heard a knock on the front door. She put her dressing gown on and hurried down to answer it. It was Ada Peake.

'You can tell me to piss off and mind my own business if you like,' Ada came straight to the point, 'but I've just come to see if you're alright. Walls have ears as you know and my walls told me that there were ructions in this here house last night.'

Freda opened the door wider. 'Come in, Mrs Peake, I'll put the kettle on.'

Ada Peake listened carefully as Freda opened her heart to the older woman, in much the same way as she would have to her own mother. By the time Freda had finished, they were on their third cup of tea and Ada felt saddened that this lovely family seemed to have lost its way, at least for the time being.

'You have to talk to Dickie as soon as he gets home and before Jimmy and Joe get in,' Ada advised. 'From what you tell me, your husband the other bloke will be in no condition to go on to their other job this afternoon.'

'Maybe not,' said Freda, 'but they may decide to go back round the pub instead, rather than come home to face the music. I would think John's wife will have a few words to say about it as well.'

Ada put her cup down. 'I don't think he will, but, sooner or later, both of you will have to sit down and speak to Jimmy, because he may be feeling that somehow, this could be his fault.' Ada poured herself yet another cup of tea, although there was no milk left, so she had to drink it black.

'I want to tell you something, Freda,' Ada said carefully. 'Me and your mum hit it off right from the start and she was forever going on about how fond she was of your Dickie. She used to tell all of us at the over-sixties club that he was like the son she had never been blessed with, not that she wasn't blessed with you, of course. She once told us that Dickie doesn't have a bad bone in his body and neither do those two lovely boys of yours. Joe pouring you out a whisky last night and Jimmy bringing you a cup of tea this morning bears that out. I don't know much about this John Townsend, but it seems to me that if he's willing to put in Dickie's share of the deposit, he must think an awful lot of him, because he seems more than eager to have Dickie working alongside him.' Ada's face broke into a sardonic grimace. 'And I'll tell you something else, there was many a time I wished my old man had stayed in the pub all night, instead of staggering home to kick the shit out of me. Your Dickie worships the very ground you walk on and would never lift a finger to you. Tell him how you feel, Freda, as soon as he comes home; tell him how you're feeling right at this moment.'

Freda nodded. 'Thanks, Mrs Peake. I will tell him how frightened I am that we could lose everything we own and I'll tell him how bad I feel that I clouted our Jimmy for nothing.'

Ada Peake rose to leave. 'Well, I'm off. Good luck, girl, although I don't think you will need it, but one last word of advice, get your arse back to work tomorrow.'

'Yes, I intend to. Thanks again for everything.'

Dickie came home during the early afternoon carrying a huge bunch of flowers.

'I know this won't make up for last night, love,' he told Freda, 'but it's all I can think of to show you how sorry I am.'

Dickie's face was pale and drawn and Freda had never seen her husband looking more dejected. She took the flowers from him and walked into the kitchen to put them into a vase.

'Sit down, love,' she said gently, 'I'll make us a cup of tea and then we need to talk.'

With the tea made and the two of them sitting round the kitchen table, Freda took Ada Peake's advice and poured her heart out to her husband. She told him of her anguish that she had vented her anger by attacking Jimmy, her fear that they would lose all they possessed if his partnership with John Townsend failed. She told Dickie of her concern that Joe was getting in over his head with Mary Davis and also of her worry that Jimmy could end up as a punch-drunk has-been in years to come. Dickie allowed his wife to get everything off her chest and only when he was sure that she had talked herself out, did he respond.

'I'll go and meet Jimmy from school and talk to him on the way home and I'll tell him that this was the first and last time I will ever get myself in such a state, but, you know, Jimmy will bear no grudges.' He gave Freda a wry grim. 'I don't know how me and John got through our round today, but neither of us could face toast and dripping in the cafe this morning.' Dickie chose his next words carefully.

'I know that you're feeling scared about me and John starting up on our own and if I hadn't been so bloody stupid last night, I might have been able to put your mind at rest. Me and John work well together and if we can make our own kitchen and bedroom units, instead of buying them ready-made, we will be able to virtually double our profits. We already have enough work to last us at least six months working full time and most of the loan we got from the bank is covered by the workshop and the machinery, just in case.'

'In case of what?' asked Freda.

'In case of nothing, because nothing is going to go wrong. And I'm as sure about that as I've ever been sure of anything in my life. Trust me, Freda, I won't let you down.'

Freda knew that she had little choice. 'I'll go along with you,' she sighed in resignation. 'What else can I do, now that you've signed all the papers?'

Dickie felt the need for a hair of the dog and went into the front room to pour himself a glass of whisky.

When he returned, he told Freda, 'Joe will be going back to Camden one day, I think we both know that, but I still believe he will meet a girl of his own age and settle down with her. As for Jimmy, if and when he turns professional, I will ask Fred Loake to manage him and Fred will take good care of him. Jimmy will never be a punch-drunk has-been, but he could well be a true champion.'

Freda cleared the kitchen table and began the washing up. 'I'm glad you will be going to meet Jimmy. I think it might help if you talk to him before he gets home, because I don't know how I'm going to face him.'

'Leave it to me, love, it'll be alright.'

Dickie was waiting outside the school gates when Jimmy appeared with Reggie Godber. Reggie made himself scarce as soon as he saw Jimmy's father, leaving Jimmy to walk home with his dad, for Jimmy had told his friend what had happened last night. Jimmy bore no grudge against his mother, but he did feel resentful towards his father, who he felt had let all of them down.

'My mum's never hit me like that before,' he complained to Dickie, 'and Joe told me it was all down to you.'

'Joe was right, one hundred per cent, and your mum feels really bad about it.' Dickie paused before adding, 'And so do I, Jimmy, more than I can say.'

Freda did not attempt to hide her face when they walked into the house and she looked Jimmy straight in the eye. 'Jimmy, if only I could turn the clock back, but I can't. I will never forgive myself for what I did, but I hope that you might be able to forgive me.'

Freda's voice had become choked and suddenly, she was crying as though her heart would surely break.

Jimmy rushed over to his mother and put his arms around her and he, too, cried with her. 'Don't cry, Mum, don't cry,' he sobbed.

'It's alright; I know you didn't mean it.'

Dickie slipped into the back garden, for he felt that his wife and their son needed to share this precious moment together, just the two of them. He leaned against the wall and closed his eyes tightly, but still his own tears trickled down his cheeks. He was startled when he heard Ada Peake's voice though, and her head appeared over the other side of the fence.

'You're a real man, Dickie Campbell, and there's not too many of those around these days. May God bless you and all your family.'

Dickie then heard the sound of the back door closing as Ada Peake went back inside her own house.

Joe was relieved to find his brother and his parents obviously at peace with each other when he returned from work and it had not been a very good day for Joe, either, though Jack had been sensitive to his mood.

'I can tell you are sad, Joe,' Jack had signed before they left for the evening.

'Yes, I am a bit sad,' Joe had signed back to him. 'I'm sorry, Jack, I will be better in the morning.'

His mother's eyes looked red and puffy from crying, but she smiled at Joe as she poured him a cup of tea, a sure sign that all was now well in the Campbell household.

Jimmy left a short while later to meet Fred Loake at the boxing club, but was back half an hour later with Fred in tow.

'Jimmy's been like a cat on hot bricks, but I wanted to let you all know at the same time,' Fred said mysteriously.

'Well, come on, Fred,' said Dickie impatiently, 'don't keep us in suspense.'

'It's at Swansea the Saturday after next and Jimmy has been drawn against one of the Welsh boxers, a boy called Colin Jones.'

'We all know every Taff is named Jones,' Jimmy scoffed, 'but what's this one like?'

'He's won through to the semi-finals, so that should tell you he's no pushover,' Fred told him with a trace of irritability in his voice.

'He's a southpaw and he has a vicious left hook that has stopped quite a few lads in the past.'

'What's a southpaw?' inquired a puzzled Freda.

'It's a cack-handed boxer, who leads with his right hand instead of his left, and take it from me, they are awkward buggers, if you pardon my French,' explained Fred. To Jimmy, he said, 'I have already spoken to the trainer from the Tate & Lyle club and they have a southpaw at your weight, who is willing to spar with you. He's no puncher, but at least it will give you some idea of how to move when it comes to the real thing.' Fred was beaming as he pulled a leaflet from his pocket and handed it to Jimmy. 'Take your pick from that little lot,' he said, 'courtesy of the *News of the World*.'

Jimmy looked at the list briefly and then handed it to his mother.

'It's my prize from Birmingham, Mum; I want you to choose what to have.'

Freda took the list and read it aloud for all of them to hear. 'A gramophone!' Freda gasped. 'A gramophone,' she repeated. 'I've always wanted one of those.' Freda read down the list. 'A lawnmower, a radio, a petrol-driven model airplane that really flies or two tickets to watch West Ham play for their first four home games of next season.' Freda handed the list back to Jimmy. 'I had first pick the last time, now it's your turn. Wouldn't you like to take a model airplane over the park with Reggie, Jimmy?'

'Not really,' Jimmy replied, 'I'd sooner play football or cricket when I'm not running. Dad's got a lawnmower, we already have a radio and there's no way I want to watch West Ham play, unless it was to see them get stuffed by Spurs at White Hart Lane or by the Gunners at Highbury. I reckon we should go for the gramophone, so that we can all listen to George Formby and Gracie Fields.'

'Perleeeze,' Joe protested, 'not George Formby.'

'Leave it to me,' Fred laughed, 'I might even be able to dig out a few of my old records to go with it.'

'I thought you said the venue would be in Cardiff, Fred?' said Dickie.

'That's where I thought it would be, but it seems that on the same night there is a British title fight in the arena in Cardiff, so we have been moved to the town hall in Swansea. At the end of the day, it doesn't really matter where Jimmy is boxing and we still have the best of everything while we are away. We are going to be put up in the Oyster Catcher Hotel, but I have to tell you now that we have only been allocated two single rooms, one for me and one for Jimmy, plus one double room for the parents.' Fred turned his attention to Joe.

'If your mum and dad go together and you want to go as well, Joe, you will have to pay your own fare and make your own accommodation arrangements.'

'Yes, Fred,' Joe acknowledged, 'I understand. It's what I'd expected anyway and that's fine by me.'

'There's no need for you to do that,' said Dickie. 'Me and John have to get our heads down and work flat out for the next few weeks. I can't spare the time to go to Wales, because it will mean that I would lose the whole of the weekend. Joe and Jimmy can share the double room and you can take one of the singles,' he told Freda.

Freda was disappointed, although she realised that her husband's suggestion made sense, but at least Joe would be with her.

Jimmy asked his trainer, 'So what about the other Taff that Baxter is up against?'

'Actually, his name's not Jones, it's David Llewellyn, and I can't see Tommy Baxter having too much trouble with that one, so if I was a betting man, I would put my money on you and Baxter meeting in the final at the Albert Hall.'

'I suppose that would save them a few bob,' said Dickie. 'Two Londoners means they don't have to put them up in a posh hotel, I should think.'

'It doesn't mean that at all, Dickie,' answered Fred. 'All the finalists, wherever they come from, are allocated five single rooms and one double, so apart from me and Jimmy, five others will be able to go and it will be for two nights, not just one.' Fred wagged his finger at Jimmy. 'But first you have to win at Swansea.'

Fred said seriously to all of them, 'The ABA finals, junior and senior, are the biggest nights of the year for the association and they make sure that the boxers and their families are well looked after. I'm not saying you'll all be booked into the Ritz or the Savoy, but the hotel will be one of the best in London. The next day, there will be a coach laid on to take you on a sightseeing tour and then you'll have lunch as you cruise down the River Thames on a motor launch. After that, I think they take you to Madam Tussauds, the Tower of London and for a look around Tower Bridge as well.' Again, he looked at Jimmy. 'But that's only if you win the semi-final.'

'He'll get a clip round the ear from me if he doesn't,' said Freda. 'I've never had a trip down the river before and being served with a plate of pie and mash at the same time sounds like heaven to me.'

Fred saw the twinkle in her eye. 'Bugger off, you soppy mare,' he said.

The past twenty-four hours had been perhaps even worse for the Campbell family than when Gertie had died, for at least during that dreadful period they had been united in their grief. Now, they were united once again and the four members of the family would be able to sleep peacefully in their beds that night. Joe dreamed of Mary.

Jimmy dreamed of being crowned the boxing champion of the whole world. Dickie dreamed of owning a Rolls-Royce and a yacht moored somewhere in the South of France. And Freda dreamed of nothing at all, or if she did have a dream, she certainly did not remember anything about it the next morning.

Chapter Twenty-Two

The next morning, Freda met her friend Amy Ashby on the corner of Heathway and they set off to work together, but Amy had not been very sympathetic at all when Freda told her what had happened two nights previously.

'No bleeding wonder you blew it out yesterday. I can understand you and your old man being at each other's throats, but you didn't have to go and take it out on that poor little sod.'

'That's it, you go and rub it in 'n' all,' Freda retorted angrily. 'I don't bloody well need you to start on me as well.'

They got off the train and Freda stormed off ahead, with Amy hurrying after her.

'Hold on, hold on a minute.' Amy managed to catch up with Freda. 'What I meant to say was that it's a pity you didn't give your old man a smack across the chops instead of your Jimmy.'

Freda slowed her pace and grinned. 'I make you right on that one, Amy, and I might well have done if the bugger had not stayed in the pub all night.'

Freda told her friend about Jimmy's next contest that was to be held in Swansea.

'Swansea!' exclaimed Amy. 'My mum was born in Swansea and she used to take me and my two brothers there for a week's holiday every summer with my granny and grandad. When my own dad died, Mum went back to live in Swansea with her old mum, because Grandad had passed away by then. Most summers, I would take my two girls there for a holiday right up until my mum died a few years ago.'

They reached the factory and punched their cards into the time clock, although they still had several minutes before they would start work.

'My lazy sod of a husband would never come with us, he couldn't stand my mum and he spent the whole week on the piss and went and over the dog track every night. My mum's place was right on the seafront that they call The Mumbles.' Amy noticed the puzzled look on Freda's face. 'The Mumbles is the name of the road, not the name of the house, but I never did find out what it means.'

They put on their overalls and went into the production section to begin their day's work.

Jack Conway was pleased to see that his new young friend appeared to be in a much better mood when Joe rode through the gates. They signed to each other and then Joe took the vaseline jar to apply his usual liberal dollops underneath both nostrils and then, on the spur of the moment, he also daubed a blob on the end of Jack's nose. Jack pretended he did not know what it was and tried to focus his eyes on it, which only resulted in him staggering around with his eyes crossed. It was silly, it was childish, but it was far better than the depression they had all experienced the day before.

Joe was looking forward to spending the day with Mary and David on Sunday, for David loved animals and the three of them planned to spend the whole day wandering around London Zoo, and Mary insisted that she treat them all to lunch in the cafeteria. After the distressing incident of two days ago, Joe felt as though a great weight had now been lifted from his shoulders and he was sure that the rest of the family would feel the same.

This was certainly true for Dickie, who was now working out his notice, Friday being his and John's final day at the depot. When Joe had refused the offer to work with them, the two men had approached Jack Doyle the foreman and invited him to work with them. Jack had reluctantly turned the offer down, because he had three children and a mortgage to take care of and he dare not risk taking the chance. On that last Friday though, Jack made sure that every team of dustmen finished work at midday and they all went to the pub, staying there until they were more or less thrown out at half past three. The only members of the depot who remained sober that afternoon were Jack Doyle, Dickie and John.

Joe left early on Sunday morning after consuming one of his mother's substantial cooked breakfasts, but as he left Mornington Crescent tube station, he was startled when a huge hand gripped his shoulder.

A gravelly voice hissed at him, 'Not so fast, Campbell, someone wants to have a word with you.'

Joe turned to look at the man and that one look was enough to warn him not to argue. Although no more than perhaps 5 feet 10 in height, this man was built like a tank, had a broken nose, a cauliflower ear and a livid scar that ran from his left ear right down to his chin.

'My name's Shirley Temple,' said the man, guffawing at his own sense of humour. 'Duggie Murphy wants a quick word; he's sitting in his car just over there.'

He led Joe to a smart Bentley that was parked on the other side of the road. Duggie Murphy was sitting in the back with an open cocktail cabinet that had been cleverly installed between the passenger seats.

Murphy's minder opened the car door and Joe was left in no doubt that he had no choice but to get in and sit next to Duggie Murphy. Murphy was already drinking and pointed to an impressive array of liquor.

'What's your poison, Joe, Scotch, brandy, vodka, or a Martini, perhaps,' said Murphy.

Joe shook his head. 'What do you want with me? You and your brother have given me enough bleeding grief already and you know I didn't grass on him. I don't owe you a thing and I want nothing from you, either.'

'Joe, Joe,' Murphy admonished the young man. 'Don't be like that. You only did what all Londoners do, you kept it buttoned. That's only to be expected, but you did well and I am now in a position to do us both a bit of good.'

'I want nothing to do with either you or your brother and how did you know I'd be coming here today?'

'It's no secret that you've been giving Boyce's sister a good seeing to and my little birds tell me you've been coming to see her every Sunday since you got out.'

Joe managed to keep his temper. 'I'm not giving anyone anything, not that it's any of your bloody business.'

'That's right, Joe, it is none of my business and I didn't invite you over to discuss your love life.' Murphy took a huge cigar from his cigar case and lit one. 'This is the bottom line, Joe, and I'll not beat around the bush. You may have heard that I have now been granted my promoter's licence and I am promoting my first bill in three weeks' time. Now, the point I am trying to make is that if I take a dislike to a fighter, he doesn't get on my bill and I would make sure that no other promoter would touch him, either. Are you getting my drift?'

'I don't see what that has to do with Jimmy, he's still only eleven.'

'He is now, but we both know that he will turn professional as soon as he's seventeen and a friendly promoter will be able to do him the power of good.' Murphy poured himself another brandy. 'A lot of money changes hands on the result of the ABAs and this year, I stand to lose a bundle if your kid brother even gets to the finals, let alone wins it.

'I control all of the bookmakers in south and east London and it seems that most of the punters in the capital have been putting their money on Jimmy. Many of them have placed a two-way bet, so that even if Jimmy gets beaten in the final, they will still pick up a fair slice of my money. If your brother was to win, I stand to lose a bloody fortune, although I can't see him beating Baxter anyway. Now, if Jimmy was to lose in Wales next week ... need I say more, except that there will be fifty quid in it for him: £25 before the fight and another £25 afterwards.'

Joe went to open the car door, but the minder, who had been standing close by, anticipated the move and blocked the exit.

'I haven't quite finished yet, Joe,' Murphy told him. 'Before you go running off to your old man, think about your brother's future and at least give him the chance to make up his own mind. If he says no, there will be no threats, no recriminations or any rough stuff.

'After all, Joe, I am now a respectable boxing promoter and I have my reputation to consider. Just remind him that there will be other years when he can win an ABA title and next time, you can be sure I'll lay off all the bets, but if he doesn't play ball, this will be the last ABA competition he will be invited to and he can forget all about turning pro when the time comes.' He nodded to the minder, who stood to one side, allowing Joe to leave the vehicle. 'Oh, and by the way,' said Murphy, 'give my regards to Mr Wyatt the next time you see him and tell him I was asking after him.'

Joe then continued on his way to Mary's house, now believing that Murphy must have some sort of hold over Wyatt, which would account for the way he had been treated by the probation officer. But Joe was far more disturbed about the implications for Jimmy and felt unsure of how he should handle this bizarre situation, because even though most people had heard rumours about professional fighters throwing fights, Duggie Murphy was offering a bribe to a boy, who would not be twelve for another month. The dilemma for Joe was whether or not he should tell his father as soon as he returned home that evening or, as Murphy had put it, give Jimmy the opportunity to decide for himself. His father's reaction would be unquestionable, for there was no way he would condone Jimmy taking a dive for money or for any other reason, for that matter. But Joe was not so sure about his brother, not that Jimmy would throw a fight just for the money, but would he be tempted by Murphy's hint that he could further Jimmy's career? There may even be the possibility that Jimmy would be worried that his whole boxing future may be at risk if he refused to cooperate on just this one occasion. In the meantime, Joe decided he would say nothing to Mary and he put the problem on hold until later.

David was waiting at the gate for him when he turned the corner and Joe was determined that the three of them would still have a great day out at the zoo. They did, indeed, have a wonderful day, with Mary promising that as Joe would be in Wales next weekend, she would make them a special dinner the following Sunday and they could stay at home and listen to the radio and play David's favourite games for a change.

David had clapped his hands together with excitement. 'Just like a real family,' he said, forgetting what his mother had told him about not embarrassing Joe.

Jimmy was in bed when Joe arrived home and although Joe needed to speak with his brother before making a decision as to whether to tell their father, it was not until Monday evening that Joe found the opportunity to talk to Jimmy. Their father was hard at work with John and their mother was next door having a cup of tea with Mrs Peake when Joe related his conversation with Duggie Murphy as accurately as he could, leaving Jimmy in no doubt as to what would be expected of him.

'He must be having a laugh,' said Jimmy in amazement. 'It sounds like something out of a Jimmy Cagney film.'

'This is no laugh,' Joe told his brother sharply, 'this is bloody serious and I think we should talk to Dad about it as soon as he gets in.'

'No, give me a bit of time to think about it first.'

Joe was becoming angry. 'You don't mean to tell me that you'd even consider taking a dive for a toerag like Murphy, and what about all those people who have put their money on you? You'd be robbing them as well as yourself.'

Jimmy was pacing up and down the room. 'I didn't ask them to bet on me and I didn't even know they could bet on us kids until you just told me. I want to be a proper boxer, Joe, and I don't think you know just how badly I want to be up there with the all-time greats. I'll do whatever it takes to get there.'

'Even selling out to a shitbag like Murphy?'

The kitchen door opened and their father walked in. Neither of them had heard him enter the house.

'I heard Murphy's name being mentioned, so I stood outside for a while to hear what was going on.' He pointed his finger at Joe accusingly. 'You should have told me as soon as you got home last night, not lay it on a young boy's shoulders.'

'Jimmy may only be a young boy, Dad, but it's his future at stake, not mine, and not yours, either. I think I was right to tell him about it first. Anyway, what would you have done if I'd told you last night?'

'I don't know,' Dickie conceded, 'I've not had time to think about it yet.'

'Does it really matter who Joe told first?' said Jimmy. 'In the end, it would be up to me if I decided not to try very hard in Swansea, but I'm going there to win, even if this Duggie Murphy does reckon he can stop me from boxing again.'

'I think we're giving Murphy too much credit,' Dickie told Jimmy. 'If you reach the finals, you will automatically be invited back next year and Murphy has no influence with the association. Granted, he might try to make things awkward if you decided to turn professional, but that won't be for years yet.'

'Dad's right,' Joe agreed, 'and you still have another five years as a junior before you have to decide whether you want to turn pro or box on as a senior.'

'Well, that's it then,' said Jimmy firmly. 'How will you let them know I'm not going along with it, Joe?'

'I'll tell Shirley Temple on Saturday. Murphy said he would send him to meet the underground at Paddington and all I needed to do was to nod or shake my head to him.'

Joe went on to describe Murphy's muscleman, slightly exaggerating the man's awesome appearance.

'He sounds just like Mighty Joe Young to me, you know, that great big gorilla in the film me and your mum saw at the pictures,' laughed Dickie.

'I thought that was King Kong,' said Jimmy.

'Him as well,' Joe ruffled his brother's hair. 'The three of them all look the same in the dark.'

They were still laughing when Freda came in to find out what it was they had all found so amusing.

'It was nothing.' Dickie had decided not to tell his wife about Duggie Murphy's approach to Joe, as he was sure that she would only get herself in a state.

'I bet it was something smutty,' said Freda as she began to prepare the evening meal.

Joe had not mentioned the fact that Duggie Murphy knew Mr Wyatt, for he felt only contempt for the fat man, who could do nothing to cause him any more distress and he did not want his father to worry any more than necessary, either.

The next few days flew by and it was Saturday morning before they knew it. Freda, Jimmy and Joe were waiting in the kitchen for Fred Loake, with their suitcases packed and all ready to go.

When Fred arrived, the first thing he asked Jimmy was, 'Have you had a good breakfast?'

'Of course he has,' Freda answered indignantly. 'Do you think I'd let him go all that way on an empty stomach? He's had the whole works, including a good portion of bubble and squeak to go with it.'

'Of course, Freda, of course,' said Fred hurriedly. 'Sorry, no offence meant.'

Suitably mollified, Freda accepted the apology. 'And none taken, Fred.'

After an hour or so journey on the underground from Heathway, they arrived at Paddington Main-line Station to catch the train to Swansea in south Wales, when Joe spotted Murphy's minder, who was waiting close to the ticket collector's office. But when Joe shook his head, the man turned and walked away. None of the others had witnessed the exchange, not even Jimmy, who had forgotten all about it in his excitement. There was a notice at the entrance to the platform, where the Swansea train should have been standing, informing passengers that there would be an hour's delay, due to a signal failure.

'We can get ourselves a cup of tea while we're waiting,' said Fred.

'I want Jimmy to have a light meal at about two o'clock, but there is a buffet car on the train and we can all have a bite to eat once we get under way.'

The one-hour delay turned into almost three hours and it was gone five o'clock when they arrived in Swansea. The first contest was scheduled to begin at seven, so Jimmy and his trainer would have to drop Joe and Freda off at the hotel and then go straight to the town hall for Jimmy to be weighed and examined by the doctor. There were several taxis outside the station and they all piled into the first one on the rank, Fred giving the driver the address of the hotel, with a request that he and Jimmy be taken on to the town hall afterwards.

Of course, there was no mistaking the London accent and the driver wound his window down to call, in Welsh, to a porter who was standing close by. 'Another load of cocky knees.'

'You just make sure you fumigate your cab afterwards, boyo, you don't want to pass on their fleas to the other passengers, look you now.'

Fred Loake had not understood a word of what had been said, but he recognised when a rise was being taken and so did Freda.

'I think those pair of monkeys were taking the piss out of us,' she told Fred.

'And so do I, but he'll be laughing on the other side of his face when he doesn't get a tip.'

The taxi dropped Joe and Freda off and then went on to the town hall, where they were met by a harassed-looking official. Fred paid the driver and, as he had vowed to Freda, did not include a tip.

The driver stared at the exact fare that Fred had placed in his hand. He had been driving his taxi for over twenty years and this was the first time he had not been given a tip, however small. He smiled at Fred ruefully. 'You're not as green as you're cabbage looking, as my da used to say.'

Fred had not heard the expression before, but somehow he understood that this was the driver's way of apologising. Fred put his hand back into his pocket and pulled out a shilling to give to the driver, who grinned, touched his cap and drove off.

'Thank goodness you managed to get here,' said the official, ushering them into the town hall. 'Your opponent is already here, Jimmy. The other lad from down south, Tommy Baxter, came down yesterday and he will be on first, you will be on second.' The official mopped his brow. 'We've put another six bouts on tonight to make a full bill but, at the moment, we have just four boxers out of sixteen.'

'Ten', came a voice from behind a desk. 'The station master has just telephoned to say that the Manchester train has arrived and six more boxers are on their way right now and the Liverpool train is only ten minutes away. We are expecting another four on that one.'

'Thank God for that,' the official put his handkerchief away, 'at least we can still go ahead, even if the rest can't get here.'

He took Jimmy and Fred to the weighing area and then Jimmy presented himself to the doctor, when butterflies began their crazy dance in Jimmy's stomach once more.

In the Oyster Catcher, Joe and Freda were greeted warmly by the landlady.

'There's pleased to see you, so I am,' she said, in her delightful, lilting accent. 'Dai bach,' she called to her husband, 'put the kettle on and I'll make us a nice cup of tea, while you take the suitcases upstairs.'

Dai obeyed his wife, who showed her guests into a large sitting room that had a splendid view of the sea. The landlady made the tea and also brought in a tray of buttered scones and small pots of assorted jams.

'Now, my name is Maeve Reece and my husband's name is Dai. It would be nice if we could all call us by our first names while you are staying with us.'

Freda warmed to the woman and told Maeve their own names, before helping herself to one of the delicious-looking scones and Joe did the same.

Maeve poured the tea and told them, 'I have no idea what time you will be back after the boxing match, but whatever the time is, there will be a hot meal prepared for you. If any of you like fish, I have some fresh mullet caught this very morning and it's lovely, so they are, or I have some tender sirloin steaks that are sitting in my freezer just begging to be grilled.'

'Fish and chips sounds good to me,' said Joe.

Maeve was horrified. 'Chips!' she cried. 'I would never serve chips in this hotel. Sauté potatoes, perhaps, but not chips. No, I prefer to offer my guests new potatoes flown in from Jersey.'

Joe thought this was a bit snobbish, but Freda understood. 'Of course, Maeve, new potatoes will be fine and to make things simple, we'll all have the steak.' Freda glared at her son. 'Won't we, Joe?'

'Yes, Mum,' Joe replied obediently.

Freda and Joe left the hotel at six thirty and walked the short distance to the town hall, even though Fred had told them that they could take a taxi, but Freda did not believe in wasting money, even if somebody else was footing the bill. They were shown to their seats, which were on the second row from the ringside, and Joe immediately recognised the very loud and very drunken man sitting opposite them on the other side of the ring.

'That bloke opposite, the one with the big mouth, is Tommy Baxter's old man,' said Joe to his mother. 'He's just as pissed as he was the last time I saw him.'

The elder Baxter was shouting insults to the Welsh fans and he then began to sing, 'Maybe it's because I'm a Londoner, that I love London town.' He was so drunk that he could only remember the first line and his awful voice was mercifully drowned out by a Welsh choir that had travelled all the way from Aberystwyth to support the two Welsh boys. They sang *Men of Harlech* and *Land of My Fathers,* which seemed to be accompanied by every Welsh voice in the audience, and as Chris Baxter had no chance against the powerful Welsh voices, he wisely sat down and kept quiet.

Joe heard his mother gasp and as he looked to where she was staring, he knew the reason why, before he had even looked.

'Duggie bloody Murphy,' said Freda. 'What's that sod doing here?'

It was a rhetorical question and Joe merely answered, 'Perhaps he's come here to see how he should promote his first bill.'

Joe wondered if Murphy had got to Fred Loake and offered him a bribe, but then he felt ashamed that he could even think such a thing. Murphy might be capable of anything, but Fred was as straight as a die.

After the master of ceremonies had introduced two ex-Welsh champion boxers, a Welsh world-famous singer and an equally famous rugby player to the crowd, the choir once again began to sing *Men of Harlech* as the first Welsh boxer walked down that lonely aisle to the ring. Joe thought the boy looked sick with fear and he was not wrong. Young David Llewellyn was beaten before he had even climbed into the ring. He had convinced himself that there was no way that he could beat this boy Baxter and even though his father and his trainer had done their best to convince him otherwise, he had simply not believed them.

In contrast, Tommy Baxter swaggered down the aisle, jigging up and down and punching the air. Chris Baxter was on his feet once again and shouting, 'Go get him, Tommy, take his bloody head off.'

Almost everybody in the hall hissed and booed at this odious man, but Baxter was too drunk to care.

It was all over within one minute. It was as though Llewellyn just wanted to be out of the ring as soon as possible and he succumbed to a barrage of left hooks, upper cuts and right crosses, leaving the referee with no alternative but to call a halt.

Naturally, Chris Baxter was on his feet jeering and gesticulating at the crowd, ensuring that for a long time to come, very few Londoners would receive a welcome in these particular hillsides. Jimmy Campbell was another Londoner and he would almost certainly be given the most hostile reception that he had ever received, thanks to Tommy Baxter's father.

Chapter Twenty-Three

J immy came into the ring first and although the Welsh contingent did not go as far as to boo him, neither did they afford him a warm reception. When their own boy entered the arena, the choir again went into action, with another rendition of *Men of Harlech*, but Jimmy hardly heard them, because all of his concentration was focused on what lay ahead of him.

Colin Jones had heard of Jimmy Campbell, although the other boy's reputation did not faze him at all, for Jones was a confident boxer and felt sure that his powerful left hook would put paid to the Londoner sooner or later. Indeed, his left hook landed on Jimmy Campbell's forehead in less than thirty seconds of the first bell sounding and Jones was dismayed when his opponent did not falter, but kept coming forwards. Another crashing left hook from Jones stopped Jimmy in his tracks, but still Jimmy stayed on his feet, although Jimmy was unable to land any telling blows of his own on the Welsh boxer and the first round would certainly be awarded to Colin Jones. The second round was very close, but Fred Loake believed Jimmy had just shaded it.

'It's all down to this last one, Jimmy,' Fred told him at the end of the second round. 'You can outbox him and keep your left jab going in, but for Christ's sake keep away from that left hook of his.'

Jimmy did exactly as his trainer had told him and when the final result was announced, Jimmy Campbell was declared the unanimous winner.

Jimmy went over to the other boy's corner to embrace him. It had been a hard-fought contest, with both boys having given it their all, but only one of them could be declared the victor. The sporting Welsh supporters acknowledged that the better boxer had won on the night, but all of them were proud that their own boy had put up such a brave fight, although they were generous in their applause to Jimmy as he left the ring.

While Jimmy was getting changed, Freda and Joe went to the telephone kiosk to give the news to Dickie, who would be waiting back in the Church Elm. Like her husband and Joe, Freda had hardly recognised her youngest son when he had walked down the aisle and climbed into the ring, but she now knew beyond doubt that like it or not, Jimmy would be a boxer. All she could hope for was that he would be a very good one.

After they had made the call to Dagenham and passed on the good news, they left the hall and waited outside for Jimmy and Fred.

'Are you leaving the first thing in the morning to see Mary and David?' Freda asked Joe.

'Not this time,' answered Joe. 'I told them I would see them again next Sunday, so I'll be spending the morning here with you. I don't think our train is until three o'clock, so we have plenty of time to have a paddle and take a stroll along the beach.'

'That will be nice, and Maeve said she would make sure we all had a good lunch inside us before we leave.'

'What did you think of it, Mum?' Joe was curious, for his mother had said nothing so far.

'What did I think of it?' Freda struggled to voice her feelings. 'I don't like boxing and I never will. The way that Baxter boy humiliated the other Welsh boy in the first contest reminded me of the one and only time I went to see a boxing match, when your dad took me all those years ago. It made me feel quite sick way back then and I felt the same way tonight, but in a way, Jimmy's contest seemed, well, different somehow. The Jones boy fought his little heart out and so did Jimmy and after it was all over, it was almost as though they loved each other like brothers.'

'I don't think Jimmy would put it quite like that, Mum, but they were brothers in there tonight, not brothers in arms, but brothers in gloves.'

Freda dug her son in the ribs as Joe almost doubled up with laughter.

'I'll give you brothers in gloves in a minute, you saucy bugger.'

Jimmy and Fred came through the door and they went back to the hotel together, where the news of Jimmy's victory had already been relayed by another guest at the Oyster Catcher, who had come across from north Wales to cheer on his only nephew, Colin Jones. Mervyn Jones had left the hall immediately after his nephew's bout and was now sitting on a bar stool when the Campbell party walked in. Maeve had shown them into the lounge while she prepared their meal, but both Fred and Freda felt the need for a stiff drink first. Mervyn Jones held his hand out as Fred went to pay Dai Reece.

'This one is on me,' he insisted. Then he pointed to Jimmy. 'I was in the hall tonight when yon boyo took on my nephew and beat him fair and square. It was a clean fight and I was proud of our Colin for losing to a sportsman who happened to be better on the night. Mind you, he did manage to catch your lad with a couple of cracking left hooks that most others would have gone down from.'

'You can say that again, especially in the first round,' agreed Jimmy. 'I had to hang onto him while my head cleared.'

Dai served the drinks: two large whiskies for Fred and Freda, a pint of best bitter for Joe and an orange juice for Jimmy.

'I can't say I cared very much for the father of your other boxer though,' Mervyn could not resist the jibe. 'His lad is a good boxer, but his da was lucky not to get himself thrown out of there tonight.'

'He'll get thrown out of the Albert Hall for sure, if he behaves like that on finals night, what with the BBC broadcasting the whole evening,' Fred told the Welshman. 'I make no apologies for the man, we can't stand him, either.'

Fred ordered another round of drinks, which Freda insisted on paying for, because she knew the association, generous as they may be, did not extend that generosity to large measures of whisky and pints of beer. Half an hour later, Maeve showed them into the dining room, where a bottle of champagne was nestling in the ice bucket, with Dai standing in attendance waiting to pop the cork. He presented the cork to Jimmy.

'A cork for a corker,' Dai said with a straight face.

Jimmy's face was far from straight as he accepted the offering. It was a delicious meal and as it was still light outside, the four of them decided to go for a walk to the end of the Mumbles, where there were several pubs and amusement arcades. Jimmy loved to play on the penny-in-the-slot machines and Freda considered he had done more than enough to deserve a treat. Within seconds of entering the arcade, they knew it had not been a wise move, for Chris Baxter had already antagonised some of the locals from the pub opposite.

'Sheep shaggers!' yelled the elder Baxter. 'Sheep shaggers, that's what you lot are.'

Neither Tommy Baxter nor his mother was with him and it appeared that Baxter senior had been thrown out of the pub, because two men now stood by the pub door to bar his entry should he attempt to get back in.

'I'd rather shag a sheep than shag you, boyo,' said the bigger of the two men. 'Why don't you get your arse back to London where you belong?'

Baxter was very drunk, but he still had enough sense not to take on the two young men. The Campbell family and Fred Loake, who had left the arcade and were now walking on the other side of the road, intending to go into a different pub further on, so to be as far away as possible from Baxter. But, unfortunately for the Campbells, he had spotted them and decided to have some fun with them instead.

'Well, well, look who we have here,' he sneered, 'if it's not the Cannonball Kid. Cannonball my arse, more like a tennis ball from what I saw tonight.'

'We are out for a nice, quiet walk,' Freda told him, 'so just disappear and find someone else to annoy.'

'I'll go where I bloody well like, you saucy cow,' snarled Baxter, standing with his hands on his hips. His whole body language was menacing, but Joe stepped forwards before any of the others could react.

'Don't you ever speak to my mother like that again.' He said it quietly, but there was something about the way it was said that made Chris Baxter back off.

Baxter turned to walk in the opposite direction, but not before pointing his finger at Jimmy and warning him. 'If you've got any sense, you'll not turn up at the Albert Hall, 'cos my Tommy will give you what for, I'll make sure of that.'

Jimmy suddenly turned pale and Fred Loake put an arm around his shoulder. 'Don't let that loud-mouthed git get to you, Jimmy,' said Fred.

'It's not that, Fred,' Jimmy mumbled, 'I've got this really bad headache. It started just after the fight, but it's getting worse now.'

'Let's get you back to the hotel and I'll give you a couple of aspirins.' Freda did not like his colour at all.

Jimmy could only walk slowly. He was having trouble focusing his eyes and he was so very relieved when they eventually reached the Oyster Catcher. He sank into one of the armchairs, though by this time he was looking deathly pale and was barely conscious.

'It's not aspirin he needs,' Fred told Freda. 'Jimmy needs a doctor. I'll go and ask Maeve and Dai if they can phone one for us.'

Fred left the room leaving Joe and his mother looking down at Jimmy, whose breathing had become so shallow that Freda was desperately afraid that it would suddenly stop altogether, just the way her mother's had.

'This is what I've always been afraid of, Joe,' she said, her voice shaking with anxiety. 'That's why I was against it right from the beginning.'

This was neither the time nor the place for Joe to remind his mother that she had been quite happy to select from the prizes Jimmy had won, because Joe was also deeply concerned for his brother.

Fred came back into the room. 'The doctor is on his way and will be here in five minutes. It's the same doctor who was in attendance at the hall tonight, so he knows Jimmy and would have seen him boxing.'

'And he would have examined both boxers after the match, wouldn't he, Fred?' Joe asked.

'Yes, he did, and he found nothing wrong with either of them.'

The doctor arrived a few minutes later and examined Jimmy, while the others looked on anxiously. Jimmy responded when the doctor pinched his arm, although he did not respond coherently to any of the questions he was asked. The doctor remembered this boy's contest very well and he had already been told that for the third time in succession, Jimmy Campbell would be awarded the best-boxer prize by the Sunday newspaper. The doctor had spent more time than usual with Jimmy after the contest, because he had seen two heavy blows land on his head during the first round. The doctor had been surprised that Jimmy had still been standing after the first punch and he was quite sure the second blow had been even harder.

He now believed it would have been better if the lad had gone down after the first blow and stayed there. It was almost certain it was the second blow that had caused this head injury, but without further tests, it was not possible to ascertain just how severe the injury might be.

'We need to get him to hospital, Mrs Campbell,' he told Freda. 'I will give Swansea General a ring to arrange an ambulance. It could be concussion, but they will keep him in overnight as a precaution.

He may be as right as rain in the morning, but I must tell you that I have to report this to the Amateur Boxing Association and I think it will be most unlikely that they will ever allow Jimmy to box again.'

'Do you really think I'd allow him to carry on after this?' Freda said bitterly.

Fred said nothing, for he felt Freda would turn on him if he dared to open his mouth.

Jimmy was taken straight to the emergency room as soon as the ambulance arrived at the hospital. Freda, Joe and Fred were shown into the waiting room, where they were joined a few minutes later by a man, who introduced himself as George Burke. He told them that he was the senior official of the ABA and that he had been at the town hall that evening. George would be available for as long as was necessary to fend off the reporters, who were already milling around outside, and to attempt to alleviate at least some of the stress being suffered by the boy's family.

A young doctor came into the waiting room accompanied by a nurse. The doctor did not introduce himself, but told Freda bluntly, 'Your son has now lapsed into a coma, but I have managed to get hold of Mr Thomas, who is the foremost neurologist in the whole of Britain, and he will be here in about two hours.' The doctor nodded towards George Burke. 'Mr Thomas has been engaged in a private capacity and Mr Burke here has guaranteed his fee.'

The doctor left the waiting room and George Burke then took charge. 'I think we should try to get Mr Campbell here as soon as possible. Is there any way you can contact him by phone? Otherwise I can arrange for the local police to get a message to him.'

Freda was still in a state of shock, but managed to say, 'He will still be in the Church Elm pub long after chucking-out time tonight. The publican is a big boxing fan and will let Dickie and the others stay on to celebrate.'

George Burke looked towards Joe. 'Perhaps Joe could give the pub a ring and let him know what's happening. If you could tell your father that I will pay for a taxi at this end and that I will arrange for his driver to stay overnight.'

'That's very kind of you,' Joe said gratefully, 'I'll go and make the call right away.'

Joe was allowed to use the telephone at the reception desk and was put through to Frank Mussett's pub almost immediately. Frank handed the telephone to Dickie as soon as he knew Joe was on the other end of the line and Frank, John Townsend and Tommy Smith watched Dickie's face turn pale, his hands shaking as he listened to what Joe was telling him. There was no doubt in the other men's minds that something was terribly wrong in Swansea.

'Ring me back in ten minutes, Joe,' they heard Dickie say. 'I'll sort something out and I will be with you as soon as I can. I don't know where the hospital in Swansea is but we'll soon find it.'

Dickie replaced the receiver and told his friends what had happened. None of them offered the usual platitudes that everything would be alright, because they could see that Dickie just wanted to be in Wales with his family.

John Townsend shook his head in despair. 'Isn't it always the fucking same? Just when we need it most, my van's in the garage for a gearbox change, so I told the mechanic we wouldn't need it until Monday morning and that we'd take the bus this weekend.'

Frank Mussett picked up the telephone and dialled a number.

'Bert? It's Frank here. Listen, Bert, I need you to take Dickie Campbell to Swansea right away.' There was a pause before Frank continued. 'Where's Swansea? It's in bloody Wales, you pillock.

'Dickie will tell you what it's all about on the way, but you will be put up for the night in a hotel the other end.' There was another short pause. 'Good on yer, Bert, see you in five minutes.' He then turned to Dickie and said, 'You know Bert Mullins? Well, he might appear to be a bit dim at times, but he'll get you there safe and sound. You can stop off at your house and throw a few bits and pieces in a bag and tell your next-door neighbour what's happening.'

'Thanks, Frank. I'll go and wait for him outside. Will you tell Joe that I'm on my way when he rings back?'

In less than fifteen minutes, Dickie had told Ada Peake as much as he knew, put a few toiletries and a change of underwear in a bag and was on his way to Swansea.

Back in Swansea General Hospital, the consultant Mr Thomas had briefly introduced himself before going to see Jimmy, who had been transferred to the high-care ward.

A nurse came into the waiting room. 'There are two boys outside,' she told Freda. 'One of them is called Colin Jones and the other is Tommy Baxter. It seems as though they are both boxers and they have come to find out how Jimmy is.'

'Are there any adults with them?' Joe asked.

'Yes, both of their mothers have come with them.'

'You go and talk to them, will you, Fred?' said Freda. 'I can't face anyone right now.'

Fred went outside, where a tearful Colin Jones and a sorry-looking Tommy Baxter were waiting for news of their fellow boxer. Fred was surprised to discover that the younger Baxter was nothing like his father and that he genuinely seemed concerned about the boy who would have been his next opponent in the finals of the championships. Both Colin Jones and his mother were distraught that this catastrophe was the result of two 11-year-old boys participating in a sport that was hundreds of years old.

'Is Jimmy going to die?' Colin asked Fred.

'All we can do is pray for him, son.'

'I will, Mr Loake,' Colin promised earnestly. 'I'll pray for Jimmy as soon as I get home.'

'And so will I,' said Tommy. 'I'll pray for Jimmy harder than I've ever prayed for anything in my life. My dad doesn't know that I'm here, 'cos he's still out on the booze and he probably won't let me come back tomorrow before we leave, but I'll write to Jimmy and send it to your club.'

Fred was touched at the young man's sincerity and ashamed that he had been so quick to judge him, just because of his crass, drunken father.

'Thanks for coming, Tommy,' said Fred, 'and you, too, Colin. This was a freak accident, so don't go blaming yourself. Just remember, you did nothing to Jimmy that Jimmy wasn't trying to do to you.'

Fred went back to the waiting room, but it was another hour before Mr Thomas could bring them any further news about Jimmy.

'There is some good news,' Mr Thomas told Freda, 'but there is also some not-so-good news. The good news is that Jimmy does not appear to have suffered a blood clot or a cerebral haemorrhage, because any of those conditions could have proved to be very serious, even fatal.' He was aware of the relief that his words had given to the family, so he hastened to add, 'However, we still have a grave situation here, which cannot be resolved at this hospital. I do not believe Jimmy's life is in danger, but he is in a coma and until he regains consciousness, there is no way of knowing if he has suffered any permanent brain damage. The internal bleeding to the brain has stopped, which is a relief to all of us, but you have to understand that he could remain in a coma for hours, days or even weeks.' The neurologist paused, looking round to see if anybody wished to ask him a question. Freda, Joe and Fred remained silent, so Mr Thomas continued.

'I have arranged for Jimmy to be transferred to the University College Hospital in north London, the hospital you probably refer to as the UCH. I trained there with the consultant neurosurgeon, who is the head of the department, and he is a first-class specialist. Jimmy will be taken there by ambulance in the morning, but there is nothing more that can be done before then.

You are welcome to stay in this waiting room all night if you wish, but I would strongly recommend that you return to your hotel and try to get some rest.'

'My husband is on his way to the hospital, so we have to stay until he arrives,' Freda told him.

'As you wish, Mrs Campbell. I am going home now, but I will be back at eight tomorrow morning to check on your son before he leaves.'

Freda nodded and Joe said respectfully, 'Thank you for coming to see Jimmy, Mr Thomas, we all appreciate it.'

After the doctor had left, George Burke told Freda, 'There is another single room available at the Oyster Catcher for your husband's taxi driver, if he wishes to stay overnight, and perhaps Joe could move into the single room, so that you and your husband can have the double.' George stood up. 'I'm going to my own hotel now, but I'll be back in a couple of hours, so that I can take you back to your hotel when you're ready.' George motioned to Fred, who followed him outside. George handed Fred an envelope. 'This is for the taxi driver,' said George. 'There's enough in there to cover the fare and quite a good tip, plus another few pounds for his bed and breakfast at the hotel. I think he will be quite happy with what's in the envelope.'

Bert Mullins drove his taxi into the hospital car park just a few minutes before 1.00 a.m. and Dickie was allowed to spend the next fifteen minutes with Jimmy, Freda and Joe at Jimmy's bedside.

Fred went into the car park to give the driver the envelope, watching the man's face light up with delight when he counted the contents.

'Are you going to spend the night in the hotel, Bert?' Fred knew what the answer would be.

'Not bloody likely,' came the reply. 'I spotted an all-night cafe a couple of miles down the road and after I get myself something to eat, I'll have a few hours' kip in a lay-by. Sod wasting all this money on some flea-ridden hotel bed.'

Freda, Dickie and Joe left the ward after kissing Jimmy gently on the cheek and joined Fred in the car park. Apart from a swollen eye, which was already showing signs of discoloration, Jimmy looked perfectly normal, just as though he was sleeping. George drove them all to the hotel as promised, where Maeve and Dai Reece were waiting up for them. George Burke had telephoned them from his hotel room and told them that there would be an extra £10 bonus if they waited up for the Campbells to make sure they were well looked after. Dai was behind the bar as soon as he heard the car pull up outside, for there were no restrictions on when he could serve alcohol to his guests and every drink he served meant a little more profit for their establishment. Like all seaside hotels and guest houses, the Oyster Catcher must make the very most of the summer months, because after September, the only rooms that would be taken were those by travelling salesmen or the odd courting couple, who invariably signed in as Mr and Mrs Smith.

George led them into the lounge and said, 'I don't know about you, but I'm having a large brandy, will you join me?'

Fred and Freda accepted the offer, but Joe said he would rather have a beer. Maeve came into the lounge carrying a very large tray piled high with some roast beef and some ham sandwiches and a dozen of her home-made scones.

'We were so sorry when Mr Burke told us about Jimmy,' she said to Freda. 'Such a lovely boy he is.'

Freda thanked Maeve and Dai, who were now ready for their bed.

'Help yourselves to another drink,' Dai told them, 'Mr Burke will settle up with us in the morning.'

After the Welsh couple had left, Fred and George took their brandy into a smaller lounge to give the family some privacy.

'I know the Association is quite generous,' Fred said to George, 'but I'm pretty sure it doesn't run to rounds of double brandies and paying over the odds to persuade a landlady to stay up until two in the morning to serve sandwiches.'

George knew he would not be able to bluff this old-timer. 'OK. Fred,' he confessed, 'they will foot the bill for the taxi fare to bring Jimmy's dad to Swansea, but they will not pay for the driver's accommodation. I also offered the hotel owners a little inducement to stay up until we came back, which I will not be reimbursed for, and it goes without saying that the ABA will never pay for any alcoholic drinks.'

'So it's all coming out of your own pocket then, even the doctor's fee?'

George smiled. 'Have you ever heard of a London store called Harris and Burke, Fred?'

'Who hasn't?' said Fred, and then he sat with his mouth wide open. 'Are you trying to tell me that you're that Burke?'

'Not exactly, but my father is and one day it will all be mine. My grandfather, who founded the store with Jacob Harris, left me enough money to indulge my passion for amateur boxing, so I can assure you that the money I have spent tonight is not important at all.'

'Gordon Bennett!' Fred was astounded. 'I've been past that store dozens of times, but I've never been able to afford to buy anything there.'

George handed Fred his business card, 'Fred, I'll keep in touch when we get back to London, but if you feel that the Campbell family need any help, will you let me know?'

Fred took the card then said candidly, 'George, I've never met a real toff before, but as I see it, you're not much different from the rest of us.'

George laughed and slapped Fred on the shoulder. 'Come on, Fred, let's go and get ourselves another double brandy.'

Chapter Twenty-Four

Mr Ronald Randall the neurosurgeon at the University College Hospital in London studied the X-rays of the young patient, who had just been brought in by ambulance from Swansea General. He then studied the notes written by Mr Thomas, whom he remembered well from their student days, and contemplated the other man's findings and his prognosis.

Mr Randall felt anger that this young boy should have suffered such an injury in the name of sport. It would have been tragic if his condition had been caused by falling from his bicycle or being hit by a car, or even by a branch falling from a tree, but for him to be lying in a coma for such a barbaric reason was beyond his comprehension.

Mr Randall had written many papers on the subject of head injuries and had regularly lobbied his Member of Parliament to outlaw boxing completely, along with heading the ball in a football match, urging for the compulsory wearing of safety helmets, not only for motorcycle riders and their passengers, but for ordinary bicycle riders as well. Many of his associates considered Mr Randall to be somewhat eccentric, but the neurosurgeon had seen too many young lives cut short by reckless activities in his time and he could only hope that Jimmy Campbell would not be yet another statistic.

Mr Randall did not relish talking to the relatives of his patients, a task he usually left to his houseman Dr Young, and it was Dr Young who had spoken to Freda and Dickie after they had been driven back to London by George Burke. Fred and Joe had also travelled back to London with them, but instead of going to the University College Hospital, Fred had promised to go and see Ada Peake before he went home and Joe wanted to go to Mornington Crescent to see Mary and David, after he had telephoned Frank Mussett at the Church Elm, where the regulars would be waiting anxiously for news of Jimmy.

The sporting pages of all the Sunday newspapers told of the young boxer, who was lying in a coma, fighting for his life, which perhaps was true, but it was not something the boy's family needed to be reminded about. Not one of them bought a newspaper and Maeve had actually put the ones that had been delivered to the hotel under the counter until they had left, but Joe had seen the front page of one of them at the station.

Dr Young introduced himself to Freda and Dickie. 'Mr Randall is the senior consultant and you will probably meet him later this afternoon. We have looked at the X-rays and have studied Dr Thomas' report, but it is too soon to come to any conclusions at this time. We have arranged for your son to have a electroencephalograph, or an EEG as it's better known, which we expect will give us a clearer picture of his brain activity; in fact, he is having it done at this very moment, but it will be some time before we have the results.'

'Has he shown any signs of coming round?' asked Freda.

'I'm afraid not, and to be perfectly frank, neither Mr Randall nor myself would expect him to for a little while yet. Anybody suffering from a head injury that renders them unconscious for more than an hour or so rarely regains consciousness in less than twenty-four hours and sometimes, it can be even longer than that.' If at all, he thought to himself. Dr Young looked at his watch. 'I suggest you go to the canteen and have a cup of tea and perhaps a bite to eat. Come back in a couple of hours or so, when we should at least be able to tell you a little more.'

Neither Freda nor Dickie felt hungry, but as they could do nothing except wait, they took Dr Young's advice and went to have a cup of tea, giving Dickie the chance to have a cigarette while he was at it.

* * *

David had not known Joe would be coming, but Joe could hear the boy sobbing as he rang the doorbell. Mary opened the door and it was obvious that she had also been crying.

'Oh, Joe, I'm so sorry about Jimmy,' said Mary. 'How is he this morning? Is he still in Wales?'

'No, they took him to the UCH earlier this morning. My folks are with him and I'll be going back there later. They can't tell us anything until they've done more tests, but he's still in a coma. How did you and David find out about it, did you buy a newspaper?'

'No, it was on the radio this morning. The announcer said that Jimmy was fighting for his life in Swansea General Hospital. David heard it, too, and he's not stopped crying ever since.' Mary took Joe's hand. 'Come and talk to David, Joe, but please don't give him any false hopes.'

She led Joe into the front room and David rushed into his arms as soon as he saw him. 'Oh, Joe. Oh, Joe,' he cried though his tears, but could say no more.

'Come on, big fella,' Joe stroked the boy's hair, 'we all have to be strong now for Jimmy, including you.'

David wiped his eyes and looked up at Joe. 'Is your brother going to live in heaven like my daddy, Joe?'

Joe gulped before he answered, remembering what Mary had said about not giving David any false hope. 'We don't know, David. Jimmy has been badly hurt and the doctors have not been able to wake him up yet. He's now in one of the top London hospitals and they will do all they can for him. There are a lot of people saying prayers for him, David, and it may help if you could say one for him as well.'

'He already has, Joe,' Mary told him. 'We both prayed for Jimmy as soon as we heard what had happened.'

'David,' Joe said to the boy, 'my dad has asked me to go and see his friend Alf Spinks to tell him what is happening. Do you want to come for a walk with me?' David nodded eagerly and rushed off to put his jacket on. 'My Dad's already phoned John Townsend and I've spoken to the guv'nor of the Church Elm. Fred Loake will call in on Ada Peake, so that should take care of everybody in Dagenham,' Joe explained. 'I'll not be too long with Alf and then I'll come back here for a while before going back to the hospital.'

Mary stroked his cheek tenderly. 'Will you tell your mother and father that David and I will be thinking of you all?'

Joe barely had time to return the gesture, before David came rushing back with his jacket and shoes on, but it was time enough for both Mary and Joe to accept that nothing would ever be the same again between them.

Joe and David did not spend very long with Alf Spinks, for Joe desperately felt the need to spend a little time with Mary before he returned to the hospital.

Mary felt the same way and turned to David on their return, saying, 'David, will you have your bath now, so that you can stay up a little later and say goodbye to Joe?'

David readily agreed and took himself off into the bathroom, where Mary had already run the bath for him. Mary and Joe sat together on the sofa, but it was Mary who took the lead. She kissed him full on the lips, gently at first and then with increasing ardour as her breath escaped in small gasps. It was an incredible experience for Joe, who had never even kissed a girl before, let alone a mature woman, but neither of them felt that this was the right time to take things any further. One day, it would be inevitable, they were both acutely aware of that fact, but not now.

Freda and Dickie were at Jimmy's bedside by the time Joe hurried back to the hospital and Joe thought Jimmy looked much the same as when he had last seen him in Swansea. Joe had only been back for a few minutes, when Dr Young came into the room with another man, whom he introduced as Mr Randall.

'Thanks to the latest equipment we have these days,' Mr Randall began, 'we are in a much better position to judge the extent of damage to the brain after a head injury. I must advise you, however, that until your son regains consciousness, we will not know for sure whether he has suffered any permanent damage.'

'But he will come round, doctor?' Freda pleaded.

'Oh yes, Mrs Campbell. Let me show you the graph of the EEG.'

Dr Young handed his superior a roll of paper that looked similar to a toilet roll. Mr Randall unrolled it on Jimmy's bed and pointed to the lines that went from side to side, some only moving an inch either way, while others almost reached the outer sides of the paper.

'The large, squiggly ones were when I asked Jimmy a question,' Mr Randall pointed out, 'and even though he was unconscious, his brain was still receiving messages. Judging by these results, I would expect that your son will be back with us in perhaps twenty-four hours or so.' There were huge sighs of relief from Joe and his parents, but Mr Randall quickly reiterated what he had told them previously. 'I only said he will be back with us; I have already told you that we cannot tell at the moment exactly how much permanent damage has been done.'

'Will Jimmy definitely have some brain damage then?' asked Dickie.

'Almost certainly,' answered the surgeon. 'In ninety-nine cases out of a hundred, a patient who has been unconscious for this length time will have suffered some form of irreparable damage to the brain.'

'Could you please give us at least some idea of how bad it could be?' whispered Freda.

Mr Randall frowned. This was one of the reasons that he did his best to avoid meeting the relatives of any of his patients. 'I really do not like to play guessing-games about my patients, Mrs Campbell.'

Joe spoke for the first time. 'My mother did not ask you to play at guessing-games, doctor,' he said, with a quiet dignity. 'All we would like is your professional opinion about Jimmy.'

Mr Randall and Dr Young turned their attention to the young man, who they assumed must be the elder brother. Dr Young was intrigued as to how Mr Randall would respond, for Mr Randall, while being one of the foremost neurosurgeons in the country, was not used to having a decision questioned, least of all by a relative, but Dr Young was pleasantly surprised when the surgeon nodded.

'Very well,' said Mr Randall, 'but the only thing that I am able to tell you for certain at this moment is that his mobility will not be affected, although I am not so positive about his hand movements.

Jimmy will probably suffer from epilepsy for the rest of his life, but this could range from a petit mal fit, which is quite mild and, in fact, can sometimes be hardly noticeable, although he could also be subject to what is known as grand mal seizures, which are much more severe.'

'Is that when you have to put a spoon in their mouth to stop them swallowing their tongue?' said a horrified Freda.

'Not these days, thank goodness.' Mr Randall was aware of the distress his words were causing, but the younger Campbell had insisted on being told as much information as possible. 'There could be some loss of speech, possibly some hearing loss and, occasionally, sight can be affected, but we will know nothing for certain until the boy comes round. Now, please excuse me, I have other patients I must see, but I will be back a little later.'

Mr Randall left the room, leaving Dr Young to explain the other details that the family would need to know. Dr Young was a sympathetic man and he felt ashamed that he was unable to offer the families of patients any of the basic comforts that he knew were now being offered by so many hospitals throughout the world.

'I am sorry, but we do not have any facilities here for relatives. By the early fifties, every hospital will provide restrooms with beds, washing and shower rooms and tea-making facilities, so that a relative can remain at the hospital overnight if they wish. All I can offer you now though, are two armchairs, because only two people are allowed to be at a patient's bedside at any one time.'

'We understand, doctor,' said Freda, 'and thank you for your kindness.'

After he had left, Freda said to her husband, 'You and Joe go home and then you can come back again in the morning, there's no point in both of us being here all night.'

'It would make more sense if I came back in the morning,' Joe suggested. 'You can't really afford to take time off work, Dad, and John will not be able to work on his own, will he?'

Freda nodded. 'Joe's right, Dickie, but what about your own job, Joe?'

'Ron and Jack will have read the papers, so they probably won't be expecting me anyway, but I'll give the farm a ring in the morning.'

'Thanks, Joe,' said his father, 'I'll tell John I need to pack up early tomorrow, so that I can get back here as soon as I can.'

A couple of porters brought two comfortable-looking armchairs into the room and Freda sank into one of them gratefully.

'Ah, that's better,' she sighed. 'Right, you two, get yourselves off and leave me in peace. I'll get myself some pie and chips later from the chippy on the corner.'

When they reached Dagenham, Joe suggested that they go and see Mrs Peake and let her know what was happening. Mrs Peake was relieved when Dickie informed her that although Jimmy was still very poorly, they had been assured that he would pull through.

'I'm so glad to hear that, Dickie, and so will those three mates of yours, who are sitting in your front room. Four times they've come banging on my door this afternoon, so I let them in with the spare key Freda asked me to keep and they're in there now, waiting for you to come home; I hope you don't mind.'

'No, that's fine, Mrs Peake,' said Dickie, 'and I'm sorry they've given you so much trouble.'

Father and son went into their house to find John Townsend, Jack Doyle and Tommy Smith sitting in the front room, each with a quart bottle of brown ale by the side of them, which they had bought from the off-licence. The three men were relieved when Dickie was able to tell them that Jimmy's condition was at least not quite as serious as the newspapers and the radio had reported.

'There was a right stroppy cow who answered the phone at the hospital and she refused to tell me anything at all, even though I told her that you were my business partner,' complained John. 'All she would say was that information could only be given to close relatives and that Jimmy Campbell's close relatives were already with him.'

'I'm going to have a drop of Scotch.' Dickie went towards the sideboard. 'Does anyone else fancy one, or are you sticking with your beer?'

There were nods of acceptance from the three men as Dickie held up the bottle, but Joe shook his head and went into the kitchen to grab himself a beer. He saw a large saucepan on top of the cooker that he did not recognise, so he lifted off the lid to see what was inside. 'Rabbit stew,' he said out loud and his stomach began to rumble, for he had not eaten since earlier that morning and he knew his father hadn't had anything, either.

Dickie heard what his son had said and came into the kitchen.

'What's this about rabbit stew?' he asked.

Joe showed him the saucepan. 'Mrs Peake must have cooked it for us.'

'That woman is an angel, make no mistake,' said Dickie, sniffing the now-cold concoction. 'We'll reheat it after those three have buggered off.'

'Oi, we heard that,' called John from the front room, 'and we were about to depart from this humble abode anyway, thank you very much,' he said sarcastically.

The men finished their drinks and went off, leaving Dickie and Joe to make short work of the now piping-hot, delicious stew.

*   *   *

Freda was quite surprised when one of the nurses brought her a tray of lamb cutlet, with mixed vegetables, a peach Melba for dessert and a small pot of tea.

'Mr Randall left instructions that you and your husband should be provided with an evening meal and a breakfast for as long as you intend to stay overnight.'

Freda had already decided that she would not leave Jimmy's bedside, because she did not feel very hungry anyway, but she was surprised to find just how hungry she really was after she had taken her first mouthful. Freda drained the last drop of tea from her cup and then almost dropped it when she glanced at Jimmy, whose eyes were wide open. He was looking very puzzled.

'Jimmy, Jimmy, can you hear me, son?'

Jimmy smiled and said, 'Of course I can, am I late for school, Mum?'

Freda pulled the alarm cord and a staff nurse appeared within seconds, closely followed by Dr Young, who had been about to go off duty. The doctor examined Jimmy and then motioned for Freda to follow him from the room.

'It's very promising, Mrs Campbell, but I must warn you that he could relapse at any time within the next hour or so. Mr Randall has asked me to keep him informed and I will telephone him right away.

'In the meantime, I will arrange for a nurse to be with him at all times and she will be making notes of any changes she may feel that Mr Randall and I should know about.'

Freda went back into Jimmy's room, where Jimmy was looking round with the same bemused look upon his face. Another nurse had taken the place of the staff nurse and was sitting by the other side of the bed, with a notebook and pencil at the ready.

'How are you feeling, Jimmy?' said Freda. 'Can you remember anything about what happened in Swansea?'

'Swansea!' Jimmy shook his head. 'I know it's somewhere in Wales, but I've never been there.'

It was as though the motion of him shaking his head had caused some sort of a reaction within his brain, for Jimmy's eyes slowly closed and he was unconscious once again. The junior nurse pulled the cord and this time, it was Dr Young who got there first. The nurse told him what had happened and the doctor was moderately pleased.

'I'm not too worried that he remembers nothing about what happened in Swansea,' he informed Freda. 'That's quite usual in head-injury cases, but it's encouraging that he recognised who you were and he knew that he goes to school. Mr Randall told me that he suspected that this might happen, but he still believes that your son will be fully conscious before very long.'

Freda fell asleep from sheer and utter exhaustion in the early hours of the morning, while different nurses spent two hours each by Jimmy's bedside, notebook in hand, although not one word had been written until exactly eight o'clock, when the chimes of the nearby church clock seemed to rouse Jimmy. It was the nurse who happened to be by his bedside that roused Freda and pulled the cord. Freda moved quickly to her son, but was dismayed when she saw that his mouth had drooped to one side and that saliva was dribbling down his chin. Freda gave a sob of relief when Mr Randall hurried into the room with one of the senior nurses. He asked Freda to wait outside until he'd made his examination, which took no longer than ten minutes, and then he invited Freda to accompany him to his office.

'Mrs Campbell,' he said to Freda, 'your son has all the symptoms of somebody who has suffered from a stroke. The left side of his face and his left arm are partially paralysed, and his left eye is not responding very well, although he has not lost the use of it completely, and I fear his left ear may also be impaired.' Mr Randall wished his houseman was here, because James Young was much better at this sort of thing than he was. 'It will take time and a lot of effort from your family, the speech therapist, the physiotherapy teams and, of course, Jimmy himself, but I would expect him to make a good recovery in time. I'm afraid the whole family are facing a difficult time ahead of you, although I have a very strong feeling that you will be able to cope.'

'Will he be able to speak properly with his face all twisted up like that?'

'Perhaps not for some considerable time, Mrs Campbell, but yes, I believe his speech will eventually return to normal. Time and a lot of hard work will be required though and you must all be prepared to be patient.'

Joe arrived a few minutes later and was met by the ward sister as soon as he arrived and she told him what had been happening. She escorted him into Mr Randall's office and indicated to the surgeon that Jimmy's brother was aware of the situation.

'Your mother was asking me about the effect this will have on Jimmy's speech,' Mr Randall addressed Joe. 'I have arranged for a speech therapist to work alongside the physiotherapist and they will begin work this afternoon. It will be their job to make an initial assessment and then to decide between them how and when the sessions will continue. I do not believe in keeping anything from my patients, so I have told Jimmy about the physio and speech therapists and he knows that he has been injured due to a boxing match, although he just shakes his head whenever Swansea is mentioned. I am quite sure he remembers nothing at all about last Saturday and that is upsetting him a little as you might expect. The most important thing, and this will be reiterated time and time again by the speech therapist, is that if Jimmy tries to speak to you and you can't understand what he is saying, you must make him say it again and again until you do. Don't pretend you know what he's talking about if you don't.' Mr Randall looked at his watch. 'I have to go now, but I have told Jimmy that I will see him again later this afternoon.'

Joe left the surgeon's office and went to Jimmy's room. A nurse brought in a bowl of what looked to Joe like some sort of porridge and began to spoon-feed Jimmy. Joe was devastated when he saw his brother, because the last time he had seen Jimmy, his brother had merely looked as though he was only asleep. Joe knew that his mother could barely bring herself to watch him eat.

'I can do that, nurse,' Joe said firmly and he took the bowl from the nurse, who did not protest. Jimmy managed to finish three quarters of the bowl, before shaking his head to indicate that he did not want any more. He did not answer when his mother asked him if he was feeling any better.

'Listen, Jimmy,' Joe said earnestly, 'we know that you are not able to talk very well at the moment, but the more you try to speak, the sooner you will be back to talking the hind legs off a donkey. Mum's going home now to get some rest and Dad will be here a bit later. Will you try and say goodbye to Mum, Jimmy?'

Jimmy looked at his mother, his eyes filling with tears as he struggled pitifully to force from his mouth the words that were formed in his head. He attempted to say, 'Goodbye, Mum, I love you.'

But all Freda and Joe could barely distinguish was the word, "Mum".

Joe spent the day with his brother, only leaving his side when the speech therapist and the physiotherapists arrived to begin their assessments. He knew that Jimmy had pretended to be asleep several times, when he had wearied of Joe's attempts to persuade him to speak, and Jimmy felt even wearier after two hours with the therapists. The speech therapist asked Joe to step outside and explained to him that Jimmy must be encouraged to pronounced words that began with the letter "W".

'This is one of the best ways to stretch and strengthen the face muscles,' she explained to Joe. 'I'm sure you will appreciate that we are unable to be with Jimmy every waking hour and that's why we need the help and support of the family and any of his friends that may come to see him. The other thing you must all remember is that what Mr Randall has already told you about not accepting anything Jimmy says unless you completely understand him is absolutely vital to his recovery.'

'How long do you think it will be before he can talk properly again?'

The therapist shook her head. 'I think we could be looking at months rather than weeks and there may always be a slight speech impediment, but I can give you my word that it will only be slight.'

She held her hand out to Joe who shook it gratefully. 'I believe you must be Joe,' she said. 'My name is May and the physio in there with Jimmy is Jill.'

They went back to Jimmy's room, where May said goodbye to Jimmy, who attempted to answer, but it sounded nothing at all like goodbye to Joe, although May seemed to be satisfied with her patient's response.

Chapter Twenty-Five

Joe needed to leave the hospital before his father arrived, as he had an appointment with his probation officer at six o'clock that evening.

He said goodbye to his brother, promising that he would be back in the morning, but Jimmy made no attempt to answer, merely waving his hand feebly, for he felt completely exhausted by the relentless regime he had been put through that afternoon. Dickie arrived not long after Joe had left and after a brave attempt at saying 'Hello, Dad', Jimmy went back to sleep.

Mr Randall opened the door and asked Dickie if he could talk to him in his office. He led him into the office, offered him a cigarette, that Dickie gratefully accepted, and then took a bottle of gin and a bottle of tonic from a filing cabinet.

'Terrible habits for a doctor, but will you join me, Mr Campbell?'

Dickie was too surprised to answer, although he nodded his head eagerly.

The surgeon poured generous measures into two glasses and they sat down.

Dickie chuckled. 'My wife will think I'm having her on when I tell her I've been having a fag and a G and T with a professor.'

'Well, I'm not a professor, but we won't split hairs,' Mr Randall said with a laugh. 'Incidentally, I am now off duty, which is why I can have a drink, but I wanted to talk about the progress that has been made this afternoon with the therapists. Jimmy can actually say quite a lot, but only highly trained staff will be able to understand him. I am quite relieved that he has sensation in all of his extremities, which is a good sign, because I initially felt a little concerned about his left arm and fingers.'

'I'm not quite sure what extremities means, doctor.'

'Extremities are the tips of all fingers and toes,' explained Mr Randall. 'Jimmy is also able to make a fist with each hand, which I suppose should not surprise us too much; after all, he is a boxer. All things considered, we at this hospital, and Mr Thomas from Swansea General, whom I spoke with this afternoon, believe your son has had a narrow escape, even though you and your family will find that difficult to believe right now.' The surgeon sipped his drink. 'I want to keep Jimmy with us for the next two weeks and we will conduct an EEG scan every day, which should tell us if there is still a possibility of Jimmy being vulnerable to epilepsy. Naturally, the physiotherapist will continue to work with him twice daily, but after that, we have to decide where your son will be placed. There is a head-injuries unit not too far from where you live and they have a vacancy at the moment. It's in a place called Brentwood and it's in Essex, do you know where that is?'

Dickie shook his head. 'I've never heard of it, but while Jimmy is in this hospital, can one of us stay with him all the time?'

'No, I'm afraid not, and that is the main reason I needed to speak to you this evening. After tonight, I have to ask you and your family to observe the normal visiting hours. Jimmy is no longer in any danger and apart from the strain on yourselves, I would ask you to take my word that it would actually impede Jimmy's progress if there was a visitor constantly at his bedside.'

Dickie had finished his drink and Mr Randall stood with his hand outstretched, to indicate that the meeting was over. Dickie thanked the surgeon, shook hands with him and then went back into the room to see his son. Jimmy was fast asleep.

Joe sat in the probation office, waiting until Mr Wyatt bellowed, 'Campbell.' The receptionist was a new girl and seemed to Joe to be very nervous as she fumbled in a filing cabinet looking for Joe's file.

'Come on, come on,' Wyatt said irritably, 'if you can't even find a simple file, then you're no bloody use to me.'

The poor girl was almost in tears by the time she found the file and handed it to the probation officer, who snatched it from her hands. Joe gave her a sympathetic smile and a shake of the head as he followed Wyatt into his office.

Maurice Wyatt was fully aware of the misfortune that had befallen the Campbell family, for every Sunday newspaper had covered the story. His bookmaker had informed him that although Duggie Murphy had saved a considerable sum of money now that Jimmy Campbell would no longer be competing in the final, he had lost a great deal already, because Joe Campbell had refused to persuade his brother to lose in the semi-finals. Duggie Murphy had made it clear that he would consider it to be a personal favour if the probation officer could somehow revoke Joe's licence and have him returned to borstal. Murphy wanted everybody in Camden to know that nobody could cross him and get away with it. A year ago, before the reform bill had been passed through Parliament, any ex-prisoner who took a day off work must present his probation officer with a certificate from his doctor stating the reason why, but this was no longer the policy and Wyatt's hands were tied. One of the great joys of being a probation officer for Wyatt had been the feeling of absolute power that he wielded over the boys and men in his charge and in the past, he had taken great delight in sending one of them back to prison or borstal. But now his power had been reduced considerably, although he still wielded enough to make things difficult for any of his probationers that he disliked and Joe Campbell was one such probationer that Wyatt detested intensely.

Joe attempted to explain why he had been absent from work that day.

But Wyatt was not interested. 'No excuses,' he barked, 'you get yourself to work tomorrow or I will apply to the magistrate to have you sent back to where you belong. Let your parents take care of your brother, it's their responsibility, not yours.'

'It's a family responsibility, Mr Wyatt, but perhaps you wouldn't know anything about that.'

The barb struck home where it hurt most, because Wyatt's wife had walked out on him after barely three months of marriage and he had not seen her since. Wyatt had ignored the fact that he was still legally married and had enrolled in several of the marriage bureaus that had sprung up since the war. None of the women he had been introduced to had been able to bear his company for more than one occasion and he had been refused further introductions by all but the most disreputable agencies, whose female clients expected to be paid for their services.

'Don't answer back, boy,' he roared at Joe. 'You will report back to work in the morning or by God, you'll be back in that borstal by teatime.'

'No, Mr Wyatt,' Joe said calmly and politely. 'Tomorrow morning I will be with Jimmy at the hospital and my father's friend is going to ring your area officer Mr Rutherford to explain the situation,' Joe added innocently. 'You do remember my father's friend John Townsend, I take it? He was the man at our house when you came to visit us not so long ago.'

Wyatt's face took on such a violent shade of purple that Joe was convinced the man's blood vessels were about to burst.

'Get out! Get out!' Wyatt was almost screaming now as he leapt to his feet, but then he collapsed back into his chair as Joe left his office.

Wyatt could take no more, at least not for this evening, so he ordered the receptionist to tell the three men who were waiting to see him to go away and come back next week. 'And you can fuck off as well, you useless cow,' he told her nastily and loud enough for everyone to hear.

She gave no reply to the verbal abuse and went back to the main office to relay his message to the men, who were embarrassed for the girl. Maurice Wyatt took a half-bottle of whisky from his briefcase and gulped it neat, straight from the bottle. Suddenly, his door was opened and the receptionist stood looking at him with contempt.

'How dare you burst into my office without knocking,' he spluttered indignantly. 'You're sacked, do you hear me, you're fired.'

'Oh yes, Mr Wyatt, I hear you, and so did all of those probationers when you called me a useless cow and used the F-word to me. I intend to make a complaint to area office and I'll be giving them the names of Joe Campbell and the other three men, who I am quite sure will be only too willing to testify as to how you have spoken to me.' The girl had courage, although she knew that she was now out of a job.

'You are a dinosaur, Mr Wyatt, and the sooner the likes of you become extinct, the better it will be for all concerned.'

She took her coat from the hook and left the office for the last time, although she fully intended to report Wyatt to area office the next day.

Wyatt remained in his office drinking steadily, until he had finished the half-bottle of whisky, and then he went to the off-licence to buy a full bottle, which he took back to his office. Before he began drinking again, he took a printed form from the filing cabinet and completed it while his hands were still relatively steady. It was an application form to apply for early retirement. Wyatt continued drinking for a further two hours and then left his office, posting his resignation letter along with the office keys to area office in the nearest postbox.

Jimmy was awake when his mother returned later that evening and he listened carefully when his father told them what Mr Randall had said a few hours previously. Jimmy was relieved when he heard his father say that after tonight, they would have to observe the same visiting rules as any of the other visitors. Jimmy was beginning to find it very irritating to find somebody sitting by his bedside every time he opened his eyes, asking him stupid questions and bullying him into giving them an answer. Jimmy's memory was gradually returning to him and he could now remember boarding the train at Paddington station, although he still had no recollection of arriving in Swansea.

He knew that the hotel they had stayed at was called The Oyster Catcher and he could clearly picture the faces of the two owners, although their names escaped him and neither did he remember leaving the hotel to go to the hall for the boxing contest. What he did know though was that he had been hurt during his fight, for Mr Randall had told him so. Mr Randall had also told him that he had not become ill until several hours after the contest and not only had he won his bout, but he had been awarded the best-boxer prize by *The News of the World*. However, Mr Randall had not told Jimmy that he would never box again – Jimmy knew that for himself.

Freda was upset at Mr Randall's decision not to allow her to stay overnight after today, but she knew that she had no choice other than to accept his appraisal.

'Mr Randall wants to arrange what he calls a case conference at the end of the two weeks,' said Dickie. 'We are invited, of course, and so is Joe. The two therapists will be there and a welfare officer will also be in attendance as well.'

'Jimmy doesn't need any welfare officer when he has us to look after him,' said Freda angrily.

She was actually angrier that they were being denied what she considered to be their right to be with Jimmy, regardless of the opinion of Mr "God-Almighty" Randall, as she'd dubbed him.

Compared to some hospitals, the visiting times at the UCH were not too stringent at all – two hours every evening – whereas many hospitals only allowed one hour, with an extra hour on Wednesday, Saturday and Sunday afternoons. Dickie believed Mr Randall had made the correct decision, although he did not tell his wife that and in time, he believed Freda would also reach the same conclusion, especially if Jimmy needed to be transferred to the rehabilitation unit in Brentwood, wherever that was.

Jimmy sighed with relief when his mother left the next morning, knowing he could look forward to the evening visiting time; he would try to guess who it was that would be coming to see him throughout the day.

He knew who would be coming to see him at ten o'clock that morning though, and he was not looking forward to his next session with the two physios he had already mentally nicknamed Gert and Daisy.

Mr Randall's decision meant that both Freda and Joe could return to work. Joe would go back to work on Wednesday, but Freda decided not to return until Thursday, so that that she could take advantage of the Wednesday afternoon hospital visit. Joe telephoned Ronnie at the sewage farm and told him that he would be back the following morning and then he made the most of his extra day off, by taking the train to visit Mary, knowing that David would be at his day centre.

His father had left for work and his mother had gone to bed for a few hours rest when Joe left the house. Mary was delighted to see him and relieved that Jimmy appeared to be making good progress. They sat together on the sofa holding hands and they kissed tenderly but without passion, for they both felt that once again, this was not the right time.

It was Joe who grasped the nettle, so to speak. 'Mary, will you let me stay with you on Saturday night?' He said the words so quietly that Mary wondered if she had heard them correctly.

'How do you mean, Joe?'

'I mean really stay with you and be with you all night long.'

'David sometimes has bad dreams and comes into my room and most mornings, he is up before me and comes into my bed for a cuddle. If he sees you in my bed, he will know about us. Is that what you really want?'

Joe nodded. 'I want him to know that I will be in the lives of both of you for ever, Mary. If I stay, there will be no nonsense of me jumping out of bed before he wakes up the next morning and pretending that I've been sleeping in my old room.'

'If you stay out all night, your mother and father will want to know where you are, because you can't just say nothing.'

'Then I'll tell them the truth. My mum and dad will find out sooner or later and I have no intention of hiding anything from them.'

Mary stood up. 'It's too soon, Joe,' she told him. 'It's too soon after what has happened to your brother. I want this as much as you do, but not until Jimmy is at least out of the hospital.'

Joe was disappointed, but he knew that Mary was only thinking of his parents and he felt that he had been selfish and inconsiderate by not thinking the same way. He was not to know that when a young man's hormones are on overdrive, all young men are naturally selfish and inconsiderate.

David was always collected from home and dropped off again by the bus from the day centre and he was ecstatic upon seeing Joe, for he had not expected to see him again until Sunday. After Mary had cooked dinner, Joe played games of snakes and ladders, ludo and dominoes with David, who clapped his hands with delight every time he won a game.

Mary watched them from the other side of the room and it troubled her that Joe was only six years older than her son. It brought it home to her that she was eleven years his senior and she was sure that some people were already gossiping about her being a "cradle snatcher". Mary was as sure as she could possibly be that this was no adolescent crush that Joe felt for her and she truly believed him when he had said that he wanted to be with her and David for ever. Joe was not the kind of man who would trifle with people's affections and seeing how he interacted with her son brought a lump to her throat, because Joe was both a brother and a father to him. The word "man" came naturally to her when she thought of Joe, for even though he was only sixteen, he was more of a man right now than many men twice his age would ever be. It would not be long before Joe would be spending the night with her, of that she had little doubt, and she wondered how David would react when he saw Joe in her bed. Mary also dreaded to think how Joe's parents would react when they found out.

Freda was warmly welcomed back to the May and Baker factory by her workmates and her friend Amy Ashby had organised a collection among the workers to raise a very respectable amount of money for Jimmy.

'The trouble is, Freda,' said Amy, 'we're not sure what to get him. One of the girls suggested sending a bouquet of flowers to the hospital, but somehow, I can't see your Jimmy as being a flower person.'

Freda laughed loudly. 'I can just imagine the look on his face if you had. It would be nice if you kept hold of the money for now and then when he's back on his feet again, we can put it towards a nice day out to somewhere like Brighton. Thanks, Amy.'

'Think nothing of it,' Amy said, with a dismissive wave of her hand. 'Are you back working full time now?'

'Personnel have agreed that I can have Wednesday off next week, so that I can visit Jimmy in the afternoon. Then there is the case conference at the hospital on the following Monday. After that, I'm not sure what I'll be doing, because the doctor was talking about sending Jimmy to some rehabilitation unit in Brentwood.'

'Brentwood!' Amy said with concern. 'That's a bloody awkward place to get to from where we live. You would have to catch the bus to Romford station and then get the train to Brentwood, and you can bet your life the place will be nowhere near the station.'

Freda and Amy went for their usual short walk for a little fresh air during their break and it gave them time to talk in private.

'How are you planning to work around the visiting times, Freda, and what about shopping and cooking?' asked Amy. 'I'd be glad to help out, whenever I can, if you like.'

'Thanks, Amy, but Mrs Peake said she would come in every day and cook something for us that we can reheat when we need it. Me and Joe usually get in before Dickie and he'll come over to the hospital later. Joe and me will do the weekly shopping on Saturday, while Dickie visits Jimmy in the afternoon.'

They sat down on a bench to rest for a while before returning to their positions on the conveyor belt.

'Your Mrs Peake is turning out to be a real diamond,' said Amy.

'What about Joe, is he still going back to Camden to see that woman?'

Freda frowned. 'He had the day off on Tuesday and never came home until gone ten. I didn't ask where he'd been, but I'm sure it was with her and the boy.'

'How will you and your old man feel if they … well, you know, get it together?'

'To tell you the truth, I don't really know.' Freda felt somewhat reluctant to discuss the matter even with Amy. 'I think we'll just have to wait and see if anything comes of it.'

Deep down, Freda knew that Joe's relationship with Mary would grow stronger with time and even if she so desired, there was nothing she could do to prevent it. Freda was not sure that she would even want to, for she could no longer imagine her eldest son being with a girl of his own age.

When Joe returned to the sewage farm, he was greeted with concern, but with genuine pleasure, by Ronnie and Jack Conway.

Jack signed, how is your brother, Joe?

Joe understood and managed to sign back that Jimmy was still in hospital, but that he would be better soon. All three men worked in different areas to clear out the filters, so they only met up before work, during their breaks and when it was time to go home, unless there was some sort of an emergency with one of the filters. This meant that Joe had time to himself to think things through and consider what the future would hold for him. His future would be with Mary and David, of that he had no doubt. For, as young and inexperienced as he may be, Joe knew instinctively that Mary's feelings for him were as deep and lasting as were his feelings for her.

He knew that very soon, they would make love to each other and he tried not to allow his thoughts to dwell on that too much, for he knew he would be very nervous the first time, although he also knew that Mary would be gentle and understanding.

Joe dreaded being conscripted into one of the branches of the armed forces for his mandatory eighteen months' National Service, not because he was worried that he may be called upon to defend his country, but because it would mean months of separation from Mary and David. It would also mean months of separation from his mother, his father and his brother, but Joe knew that it would be Mary he would miss the most.

Dickie and John had spent the first weeks of their partnership being taught how to use the machinery in the workshop by Stanley Stone the machinist, who had agreed to stay on with them for at least three months. Of course, it was impossible for them to acquire in a couple of weeks the expertise that had taken Stan years to attain, but they had at least managed to grasp the basic rudiments of wood machinery. John Townsend was a skilled craftsman, with Dickie becoming more and more confident with each job they took on.

They no longer took on any jobs outside, because of the often fickle weather, but, instead, they concentrated on fitting new kitchens and bedroom furniture in the homes of people who owned their own property in the surrounding private neighbourhoods. This meant that they were able to work as many hours as they wished, without the fear of being "rained off".

Dickie and John took the afternoon off to meet with their accountant Peter Gathercole, as they had now been in business for a whole month, and the news was very promising. Peter had put aside money for their income tax and had done some calculations for the wage they paid to Stan Stone, an estimate for electricity and some rough figures for the materials they would need to purchase for their forthcoming orders, and allowed some to cover the repayment to the bank. Peter was able to quote them a figure to be divided between the two men that was way beyond their original expectations.

Peter was cautious as he told them, 'Even though you may have had an exceptionally good month and these are not your final figures, you still have not been paid for the Gants Hill job and you are already three days into the one at Newbury Park. So far, every single one of your customers has paid on the nail and in cash, except for the one in Gants hill, but it won't always be like that. There are bound to be times when you will have to chase after customers for weeks before they pay up and you may even have to take one or two of them to court. My advice to you is that you both agree to draw a set salary, at least until the end of the financial year in April. The money left over will be earning interest and it will cover you if you have a lean month.'

Dickie and John knew that it made sense and they duly agreed a weekly wage for themselves and John told Dickie that he was quite happy to wait until the end of the financial year before discussing any repayment of the £200 he had advanced him. Their agreed weekly wages were more than they had been able to earn with their combined jobs as dustmen and odd-job builders and were more than Dickie had earned even in the Ford Factory.

They shook hands with excitement after the accountant had left.

'We're on our way, Dickie,' said John, 'we're bloody well on our way.'

Chapter Twenty-Six

Now that Jimmy had more time to himself, he actually looked forward to visiting times, never knowing who would be likely to enter his room when the bell rang at six thirty every evening, and at two o'clock for the afternoon visits on the allotted days. His mother came every evening and his father and Joe came as often as they could.

Fred Loake came to see him several times, each time bringing Reggie Godber with him, and everybody knew that it would be Fred that paid the boy's train fare, for his father certainly wouldn't.

Tommy Baxter had been in twice and the Welsh boxer Colin Jones, who felt responsible for Jimmy's condition, had come all the way from Wales with his father to see him. They had brought with them a present of a musical box that played *Men of Harlech* from Maeve and Dai Reece of The Oyster Catcher.

Alf Spinks, John Townsend, Tommy Smith, Jack Doyle and the landlord of The Church Elm, Frank, Mussett had all paid Jimmy a visit.

Gradually, Jimmy was overcoming his embarrassment at not being able to speak clearly and by the middle of the second week, he was making a concerted effort to communicate with his visitors, even though they could hardy make out a word he said to them. Jimmy took great delight in swearing at them, knowing that they could not understand him, and he used every naughty word he could think of, especially when Reggie Godber came to see him, for it was Reggie who had taught him these words in the first place. His twice-daily sessions with "Gert and Daisy", while being boring and often uncomfortable, were beginning to pay dividends and that much became apparent when Freda brought Ada Peake to see him on the second Wednesday afternoon.

'Hello, Jimmy,' said Ada, leaning over his bed to give him a big sloppy kiss. 'I thought you would have been up and about by now.'

'He will be once we've gone,' said Freda, 'but the hospital rules say that all patients must be in bed at visiting times.'

'Bloody stupid rule, if you ask me,' Ada retorted. 'Anyway, forget about silly rules, what's the food like in here, Jimmy?'

'Like … shit,' Jimmy replied, and then realised with horror that the words had come out perfectly clearly. He attempted to apologise, but Ada Peake would have none of it.

'Good on you, son,' she told him. 'I never thought I would be so glad to hear you talk just like a navvy.'

Although Jimmy had struggled to form the words, once they were out they were perfectly clear and his speech and physiotherapists were delighted when they were informed of his progress before they began the afternoon session. From that moment on, Jimmy was able to communicate verbally, albeit very slowly and with a great deal of effort, but never again would he be able to swear at May, Jill or any of his visitors, for that matter.

Joe received a postcard asking him to visit the probation office on the Friday evening before Jimmy's case conference. He was met by the same very chirpy receptionist that had been there on Joe's first visit.

'Hello, Joyce,' said Joe, 'I thought you had left.'

'I did, Joe, but Mr Rutherford actually came to my house and asked me to come back, so here I am.' Joyce could hardly contain herself. 'Just wait until you see what's waiting for you behind that door.' She jerked her thumb at what used to be Maurice Wyatt's office.

Joe had no idea what Joyce was talking about, but before he could enquire any further, the office door opened and a feminine voice called, 'Mr Campbell, please.'

A very startled Joe found himself face-to-face with a rather large but friendly looking woman, whose age could have been anything between thirty and fifty.

'Hello, Joe,' she greeted him with her hand outstretched, 'my name is Mrs Durkin and I will be your new probation officer. Mr Wyatt has decided to take early retirement.'

Joe shook hands with the woman and then sat down while she studied his file. Although Mrs Durkin had been a probation officer for over ten years, it was not until Mr Rutherford had been appointed as their area officer that she had felt the service could move with the times. She had been captivated by the man's enthusiasm when he had addressed them at the first meeting, but she was well aware that at least half a dozen other officers would find it impossible to comply not only with Mr Rutherford's ideals, but with the new guidelines that were being laid down by the Home Office. Maurice Wyatt was now the third probation officer to resign during the past twelve months and Mrs Durkin knew of at least another two, who should leave but could not afford to give up their well-paid jobs. They could be reasonably certain that they would not be dismissed, unless less they committed an act of gross misconduct, but Mrs Durkin was appalled at the bullying and spiteful tactics adopted by some of the officers, especially this one that she had taken over from.

Joyce had told her about Wyatt's treatment towards the young man sitting in her office and although Joe Campbell seemed a pleasant enough lad, she did not need to wonder at what on earth he could have done to bring Wyatt's wrath down upon his head.

The common denominator in Joe's and in two other cases that Wyatt seemed to have singled out for his sadistic treatment was that they were all under the age of twenty-one. Even though Mrs Durkin had not met the other two yet, she would have put money on it that all of them would be slimly built, with a fine head of hair, and that they would all have come from a close-knit family. She put the file down.

'You can leave the sewage farm whenever you like, Joe,' she told him. 'I can telephone the labour exchange first thing on Monday morning and make an appointment for you to see the manager.'

'It was the manager, who told the clerk to inform me that the sewage farm was the only job available in the first place,' Joe told her.

'Not this time he won't, Joe, you have my word on that.'

Joe felt that he could trust this woman, but he then went on to explain about the promise he had made to the Conway brothers, feeling as though a great weight had been lifted from his shoulders with the departure of Wyatt. Like most people upon meeting Joe Campbell for the first time, Mrs Durkin quickly recognised the fine qualities of the young man sitting in her office.

She stood up and shook hands again. 'I hope everything goes well with your brother on Monday, Joe.'

Joe left the office wondering how she knew about the case conference, because he had not said anything to Joyce. Then he remembered that he had told Mr Wyatt and realised that he had probably made a note of it on his file.

Freda, Dickie and Joe all took the Monday off for the case conference, which was scheduled to begin at ten o'clock that morning. Jimmy was wearing his best suit that looked a little small on him and Freda made a mental note to buy him a new one as soon as he came home. They all believed that Jimmy's speech had greatly improved over the past couple of weeks, although the physiotherapist Jill Reynolds thought otherwise. She believed that the family were becoming so used to the way he was speaking that they now considered Jimmy's impediment to be normal. Though the speech therapist May Peabody considered that Jimmy's progress, while not startling, was quite satisfactory and she expected even better results over the coming months.

Mr Randall chaired the meeting and after opening the proceedings, he asked the speech therapist to report on Jimmy's progress.

May Peabody told them, 'Jimmy still has a long way to go, but he has made good progress so far. He will need not only speech therapy, but also physiotherapy, for some time to come, possibly as long as six months. In my opinion, this could be achieved as an outpatient for perhaps three sessions per week.'

'I asked for your report, not an opinion,' Mr Randall said testily.

'You may give us your professional opinion later, but not before we have heard from Miss Reynolds, the family and, of course, Jimmy himself.'

Suitably mollified, May flushed as Mr Randall called upon Jill Reynolds to make her report.

'Jimmy has not made the progress I had hoped for and the main reason for this is that he has simply not worked hard enough and I'm sorry to have to say this, but neither have his visitors.'

'What do you mean, neither have his visitors?' Freda demanded.

Mr Randall raised his hand to silence Freda. 'Yes, Miss Reynolds, I think you had better elaborate on that remark for all of our benefits.'

'Very well, Mr Randall,' she nodded confidently. 'Jimmy's family were asked specifically to persuade him to repeat any word that they could not understand, but three days after we began the therapy, I found a notebook on the top of his bedside cabinet, which Jimmy had been using to communicate, instead of attempting to speak. Of course, I confiscated it, but that gave me quite enough reason to eavesdrop outside the door whenever his visitors came in to see him.

'Time and time again, Jimmy was not asked to repeat a word, even though it was obvious that he had not been understood.' Jill looked at the hostile faces of Jimmy and his family. 'It was not only the visitors, Mr Randall,' she added, 'but many of the junior nursing staff also ignored our instructions, they are just not trained to deal with somebody with Jimmy's type of injury. Above all, Jimmy will only do the exercises when under supervision, which has impaired his progress.'

Jimmy was crestfallen, but he had to admit that Jill Reynolds' report was not unfair and he now bitterly regretted the hours he had wasted by reading his comics, instead of exercising his facial muscles.

Freda and Dickie were also forced to admit to their lack of commitment to the programme, although Joe had at least made the effort whenever he visited Jimmy.

'Thank you, Miss Reynolds,' said Mr Randall, without further comment. He introduced a prim-looking, middle-aged woman to them all.

'This is Miss Thompson, who is the welfare officer for this hospital.' He nodded to the woman. 'What have you to say on the matter, Miss Thompson?'

Miss Thompson looked at them over the top of her glasses. 'I am able to tell you that I have provisionally booked a place for Jimmy in a

12-room rehabilitation unit that is situated in Brentwood. Every patient they accept has suffered from a head injury of varying degrees of seriousness and Jimmy's injury would be considered as perhaps fairly routine. All patients stay in the unit for a minimum of six months and receive far more therapy than even this hospital can provide. I know that they have achieved some quite remarkable results in the past, especially with those stupid boys who crash their motorcycles.'

Mr Randall thanked the welfare officer and adjourned the meeting for a thirty-minute coffee break.

The atmosphere in the hospital canteen was considerably sombre as the Campbell family sat around a table drinking their tea.

'I ... don't ... want ... to go to ... Brent ... wood.' Jimmy was almost in tears.

'None of us want you to go there, Jimmy,' Dickie told his son, 'but we have to consider what will be best for you in the long run.'

'Do you want to stay the same way as you are now?' Joe said bluntly. 'You can hardly string two words together, let alone a sentence, and you need all the help that's on offer.'

Jimmy was shocked at his brother's seeming lack of compassion, although Freda knew that her eldest son was hurting inside just the same as herself and her husband. Sometimes, we have to be cruel to be kind, she quoted the old homily to herself.

After their coffee break, Mr Randall addressed the meeting.

'Before we proceed any further, I would like to tell Jimmy and his family a little about the Brentwood Centre. Frankly, I am grateful that Miss Thompson has managed to secure a place there, for it is one of the most progressive units in the country and the demand for a place there is extremely high. I have visited the unit several times before and believe me, it is just like a luxury hotel. There is a swimming pool, a gymnasium and a billiard room and they even have one of those things they call a television, which I am told will be sitting in the front room of every house in the country within ten years.' Mr Randall shook his head in disbelief. 'I must say that that seems a bit far-fetched to me, but who am I to argue?'

He returned to his enthusiastic description of the unit, for he was genuinely impressed with the work that was carried out there. 'Jimmy would have a private tutor for two hours each day on a one-to-one basis, so his education would not be neglected while he was there.

'Another big plus is that they have a minibus that takes the patients out several times a week to museums, castles or just for a fun day out at the seaside. Believe it or not, they even have an archery range and a bowling green. All the patients are encouraged to help each other wherever possible, because they all know how frustrated the others may be feeling from time to time.'

Mr Randall had been watching Jimmy closely whilst he had been speaking, but he knew that the boy had not been overly impressed with the rosy picture he had attempted to paint, although there had been just a faint glimmer of interest when the television had been mentioned.

'Jimmy, I will ask you how you feel about it in a few moments, but first I would like to hear from a member of your family.' Mr Randall looked at Dickie. 'Mr Campbell, would you like to tell us how you feel? It doesn't have to be the same as the rest of your family see this situation and if they disagree with you, they will have ample opportunity to say so.'

Dickie glanced around the room, aware that all eyes were fixed firmly upon him.

'We all want Jimmy to come home with us, Mr Randall, and we hope you and the others will agree. Joe has told us that he is willing to leave his job to stay with Jimmy until he is ready to go back to school again.'

Mr Randall thanked Dickie and then spoke gently to Jimmy. 'I want you to think very carefully about this before you make any decision, Jimmy, because I'm not sure if you realise the burden that this could place upon your family.'

Joe rose to his feet. 'Jimmy's no burden, sir; he is a son to my parents and a brother to me.'

'Quite so, quite so, young man, and I stand corrected,' Mr Randall acknowledged Joe's indignation. 'Well, Jimmy, will you tell us what you would prefer to happen in the months to come?'

Jimmy took a deep breath and then began to speak. 'I ... want ... to ... go ... home.' The words, although relatively simple, were easily understood by the people in the room. Jimmy wished that he did not have to elaborate, but he knew Mr Randall would not allow him to stop there. Jimmy continued slowly. 'The ... unit ... sounds ... nice ... for a ... holi ... day ... but ... I ... want ... to ... be ... at ... home ... with ... my ... mum ... and ... dad ... and ... Joe.'

'Thank you, Jimmy,' said Mr Randall. 'That would not have been easy for you, well done. Miss Peabody, your opinion now, if you please.'

'I feel even more confident that Jimmy should continue his rehabilitation at home, now that I know his brother will be with him. I could spend this afternoon with Joe and Jimmy to make sure Joe is familiar with all the exercises and I see no reason why they shouldn't go home today. Joe can bring Jimmy back here twice a week for more intensive therapy.'

'Thank you, Miss Peabody. Miss Reynolds, we await your valued opinion.'

Jill Reynolds could never be too certain when Mr Randall was being sarcastic, for the man could be extremely derisive at times. She decided to direct her remarks to Jimmy personally.

'Jimmy,' she said sternly, 'I strongly recommend that you accept the wonderful opportunity to continue your treatment at the Brentwood Unit. If your speech is not corrected very soon, you will have a speech impediment for the rest of your life, simply because you will no longer be aware of it. I firmly believe that you need daily treatment by professional therapists, who will not allow even the slightest indistinct word to go unchecked.'

Jimmy had not once met Jill Reynolds' steely gaze while she had been speaking and he now shook his head, not in defiance but with sadness, for he believed that after her speech, he would surely spend the next six months away from his family.

'Dr Young?' Mr Randall nodded in the direction of the doctor, who had listened carefully but had made no contribution to the case conference as yet.

'I agree entirely with Miss Reynolds,' he said, avoiding eye contact with any of the Campbells. 'I believe six months of intensive therapy with little or no input from the family is imperative. Like Miss Reynolds, I, too, have witnessed them ignoring incoherent sentences and even single words over the past two weeks. One other thing that has not been mentioned is that there is weekend-only visiting, because apart from the intensive therapy, the patients help each other, without any influence from the outside, and I believe this to be the key to their success.'

Dr Young knew that he had sounded abrupt, but he felt that the well-being of his patient was more important than hurting the feelings of a colleague or upsetting the family.

Mr Randall could identify with the passion of the young doctor – had not he himself been just as zealous in his younger days?

I suppose I must have been, he thought to himself, but I'm buggered if I can remember when.

After years of working in various London hospitals, Mr Ronald Randall often slipped into the lax mode of speech he heard every day. His wife had often been acutely embarrassed when, during a dinner party, cocktail party or some other function, he would crudely inform another guest who was making a statement that he disagreed with, with something along the lines of, "You're talking out of yer arse", or "What a load of old cobblers". Mr Randall often thought in cockney these days, although he was careful not to use it in his professional capacity.

Mr Randall thanked his subordinate and then rendered his decision.

'There is no doubt that Jimmy will need months of therapy, but I do not feel that sending him miles away from his family and where visiting hours are greatly reduced will benefit a lad of his age, quite the reverse in fact. I will go along with Miss Peabody and discharge Jimmy today into the care of his family.' He turned his attention to Jimmy. 'Jimmy, I may see you again from time to time, but Dr Young will be in charge of your case and he will need a lot of convincing that you are working hard at home and not just when you come back as an outpatient. You are aware that I have disregarded the advice of two of my team, so don't let me down.'

'He won't let you down, Mr Randall,' Joe answered for the whole family, 'and neither will we.'

'Good, good,' smiled the surgeon. 'Now, Miss Peabody, Miss Reynolds, I would like you to arrange a two-hour session with Jimmy and his brother as soon as possible. It would be better if this could be together, but it can be done separately, although I wish this to be completed within the next two days.'

May Peabody happily agreed. 'I have a few non-urgent appointments this afternoon that I can cancel, so I can see Joe and Jimmy after lunch.'

'Impossible.' Miss Reynolds was extremely peeved that her advice had been ignored. 'I have already cancelled two appointments this morning and I am fully booked for the whole of this week and Monday and Tuesday of next week. I will not be able to fit him in until Wednesday week at the earliest.'

This was a battle of wills and it was a battle that Mr Randall had no intention of losing.

'These good people have already taken the day off work to come here, not to mention the cost of the train fare and the countless visits they have made to be at Jimmy's bedside. I would like this to be completed today, but if you insist that it is not possible, I would ask that you come in on Saturday morning, because I think it is important for Jimmy's parents to also be aware of what the therapy involves. This way, they will not need to take any more time off work.'

Mr Randall knew perfectly well that Jill Reynolds left London every Friday evening and drove up to Leeds in Yorkshire, where she spent the weekend with her lesbian lover. Jill would not willingly sacrifice one second of her precious time with Gloria and Gloria could be very fickle. On the rare occasions that Jill had been delayed, her lover would sulk and not allow Jill into the bedroom that evening. Indeed, if Jill did not arrive until Saturday afternoon, Gloria would probably not even allow her into the house at all, let alone the bedroom, from what he had heard.

Mr Randall offered the physiotherapist a way out, where she would not lose too much face. 'Miss Reynolds, I would take it as a personal favour if you could delegate your other appointments to one of your assistants and team up with Miss Peabody this afternoon.'

Miss Reynolds seized the lifeline she had been offered. 'Yes, Mr Randall. Now I come to think of it, one of my assistants is in her third year of training and she should be able to take over for a couple of hours for me.'

'Well that's settled then,' Mr Randall beamed at them. 'We'll break for some lunch and meet back here at two o'clock.'

Mr Randall decided to take lunch with Dr Young, knowing that Dr Young would sulk through most of the starter and the main course, but he was quite sure that he would have mellowed by the time the dessert trolley was wheeled in. It was his way of mollifying the man.

Before they left the room, Mr Randall said to Dickie, 'I think Jimmy's probably had enough of hospital food to last him a lifetime, but there's a great pie-and-mash shop just up the road. I eat there at least a couple of times a week. It's called Peter Piemans and if you tell Peter that I sent you, he will give you all an extra dollop of mash.'

The Campbells took his advice and Jimmy could hardly wait to sample the delicious pies that were baked on the premises.

'That Mr Randall 'ain't half a card,' the proprietor told them as he scooped the promised extra portion of mashed potatoes onto their plates. 'He sometimes brings visiting consultants in here and some of them are from all around the world. You should see the look on their faces when I pour on the liquor.'

Double pies, double mash with the extra helping and the green speckled sauce that they called "liquor" poured liberally all over was Jimmy's idea of a gourmet meal and the others also tucked in with relish.

'I don't know about you, Dickie, but I can't say I was over struck on that Miss Reynolds very much,' Freda said to her husband.

'Her … name … is … Les,' Jimmy informed them.

'That's a funny name for a girl,' replied his mother. 'Anyway, how do you know what her name is? I bet she hasn't said to you, "Please call me Les, Jimmy," has she?'

'No … but … I … heard … one … of … the … porters … tell … his … mate … that … she … was … a … Les.'

Dickie almost choked on the forkful of pie he had just put into his mouth, while Joe pretended he had not heard and poor Freda hardly knew where to put herself.

'Well, you just make sure you only call her Miss Reynolds,' she warned Jimmy. To herself, she thought, talk about out of the mouth of babes.

Jimmy was completely oblivious to the reaction his words had created.

'Not … much … fear … of … that … Mum … she's … a … miserable … old … cow.'

Freda was aware that a few of the other customers were staring at Jimmy, for he was dribbling from the left corner of his mouth when he ate. She wiped his chin from time to time with a table napkin and glared at the rude, ignorant people, who appeared to find some morbid fascination in watching a young boy, who had an obvious disability, attempting to enjoy his meal. Her ferocious glare soon made the offenders turn their attention elsewhere, but it brought home to her more than ever the need for all the family to work hard to get Jimmy back to anything like normal.

Joe was also upset by the attention Jimmy had been attracting, although in some way it did not surprise him. Joe had witnessed Mary's son suffering the same indignity when he had taken David out and then there was Ronnie Conway, who had told Joe that Jack was often subjected to ridicule from strangers who did not know him.

Dickie, however, had not noticed anything at all, for he was too busy conjuring up a mental scenario as to how he would relate to John Townsend the tale of Jimmy and "Les" Reynolds.

Chapter Twenty-Seven

It was a gruelling afternoon that the Campbell family were subjected to with the two therapists after they had finished lunch, and as they travelled back to Dagenham on the train, Freda, Dickie and Joe felt exhausted but happy that Jimmy was with them once more. Jimmy was fast asleep within seconds of taking his seat and needed to be woken each time they changed trains, but he was soon asleep again once they had boarded the next train. Freda said that she would not be going back to work the next day, giving Joe the ideal opportunity to work one final day at the sewage farm and to say his goodbyes to Ronnie and Jack Conway. Joe had no intention of making any rash promises that he would be back working at the farm as soon as Jimmy was well again, but he would be forever grateful to the brothers for making such a revolting job bearable for him. Although Joe knew that he must obtain permission from his probation officer before leaving his job, he believed that Mrs Durkin would raise no objection when he went to see her that evening. Had Mr Wyatt still been in post, then it would have been out of the question, but that odious man was now spending most of his time drinking himself into an early grave with bottles of whisky, in his tiny, one-room flat.

Joe would be seeing Mary and David on Sunday and this week, he intended to ask Mary if he could stay overnight the following weekend. Joe was almost certain that his mother and father would be upset and may even decide to confront Mary, but the love they felt for one another knew no boundaries and nothing they did together could ever be wrong. Joe ached to hold her in his arms, not just to make love to her, but to stroke her hair, tenderly kiss her sweet lips and to be completely at peace with one another.

Freda sat opposite Joe on the final leg of the journey home and she could see that her son had entered a world all of his own. At that precise moment, his dreamworld did not have room for the rest of the Campbell family, but Freda was as certain as she could be that she knew who or what it was that had bewitched Joe. She had mentally used the word "bewitched", because that was exactly how she felt about Joe falling for the older woman. There was no doubt in her mind that Joe was head over heels in love with Mary and Freda felt guilty that she was actually looking forward to when Joe was called up for his National Service, because she was convinced that after a few months away from Camden Town, he would forget all about Mary Davis. But Freda was as wrong as wrong can be, although she had no way of knowing that as the train pulled into Dagenham Heathway station. Reggie Godber had bought a penny platform ticket and had been on the station platform since midday, scanning train after train in the hope that his friend would be coming home with his family on one of them. When he was finally rewarded with the sight of Jimmy being helped from the train by his brother, Reggie rushed forwards to greet him and then suddenly burst into tears. Joe put his arm around one of Reggie's shoulders and Jimmy put his arm around the other.

'Come on, fella,' said Joe softly, for he was only barely able to control his own voice. 'It's plain sailing from now on.'

Freda wiped her eyes and Dickie blew hard into his handkerchief.

Dickie went with Joe to see the probation officer later that evening. Mrs Durkin had no objection to Joe giving up his job at the sewage farm, but she did have a duty to ensure that he was gainfully employed and not claiming any "dole" money.

'It will be almost like a proper job,' Dickie assured her. 'Between us, Mrs Campbell and I will make sure that Joe gets as much money each week as he would have got from working on the farm.'

'Joe may receive as much as he would have done if he was employed, Mr Campbell, but the government won't, will they? No tax will be paid by Joe and no national insurance contributions, either.'

Mrs Durkin put down the pencil that she had been fiddling with.

'I would not be able to justify Joe leaving the farm unless he takes another job or unless he declares himself as a self-employed worker.'

Dickie understood immediately. 'That means he has to pay his national insurance stamp and he must declare his earnings at the end of the year to pay his taxes, the same as me and my partner have to.'

'Exactly, but I will need to see the monthly receipts for the insurance stamps to record in Joe's file.' Mrs Durkin smiled at Joe. 'I still have to comply with Home Office regulations, Joe, it's all part of my job.'

Joe smiled back at her. 'I understand, Mrs Durkin, and as soon as Jimmy is back to school, I'll find myself a proper job until I get my call-up papers.'

On their way home, Dickie said to his son, 'When Jimmy is better, I would like you to come and work with me and John. We have put in a tender for fitting all the units in the bedrooms and kitchens of twenty-four houses that are being built in Chadwell Heath, but it will be about six to nine months before we can make a start. We will need to take on three extra men to meet our deadline, so why not be one of them? You could take your pick of either working in the machine shop with Stan Stone or working on site with me, John and whoever else we take on.'

'How do you know your tender will be accepted?' Joe asked.

'Because we've well and truly greased the palm of the site agent,' said his father ruefully. 'That's the way things are done in this business, you grease my palm and I'll grease yours and the more grease, the bigger the contracts.'

'Sounds good to me,' said Joe. 'After being away from the shit-farm for six months, I can't imagine that I'll be in too much of a hurry to go back there again.' Joe glanced sideways at his father.

'Dad, is it working out with you and John?'

'Better than either of us could have imagined,' Dickie said earnestly. 'Stan Stone has now promised to stay with us for at least another year and we have already taken on a young lad, who has been deferred from his National Service, because of a perforated eardrum.

'Stan is showing him how to operate the machinery, but we will still need another operator to cope with this contract.' Dickie took a deep breath. 'This is only the beginning, Joe. If we can do a good job in Chadwell Heath, the contracts will come flooding in thick and fast and already, the site agent is hinting at an even bigger job that's being planned in Barkingside. Mind you, I think it will have to be more than his palm that we'll need to grease to get the contract for that one, more like grease his arse, I should imagine.'

Joe laughed with his father, but then told him, 'You know that I'll be moving back to Camden to try to find myself a job in the market as soon as I finish my National Service?'

'Moving back to Camden, or moving back to Mary?' Dickie asked his son.

'Both,' answered Joe. 'Have you talked to Mum about it?'

'Not really, but she has a fair idea, anyway. Are you sure that Mary feels the same way, Joe?'

Joe nodded his head firmly. 'Absolutely. I may as well tell you now that I intend to spend the weekend with her and David the week after next and I think it may be better if you could tell Mum, instead of me.'

Joe was taken aback at his father's reaction. 'Not bloody likely, if you want to piss off for a mucky weekend, then don't expect me to tell your mum that I feel fine about it, because I don't feel fine at all.

'I expected something might happen in a few years' time, unless you found someone nearer your own age, but for fuck's sake, Joe, you're not even seventeen yet.'

Dickie strode off ahead, leaving Joe in no doubt that he would not be able to count on the support of his father, at least not at this stage.

Freda sensed the atmosphere between her husband and her eldest son as soon as they walked through the door, although she chose to ignore it. Her priority at the moment was that Joe would be allowed to remain at home to look after Jimmy, while she and Dickie went out to work. Freda knew that people would wonder why she could not be the one to stay at home, instead of Joe, but both she and Dickie believed that Joe would be able to stretch Jimmy far better than either of them were capable of.

The environmental health officer had been informed by Mrs Durkin that Joe Campbell would not be working at the sewage farm after tomorrow and he, in turn, had relayed the news to Ronnie Conway. Ronnie told his brother Jack the news through signing and he shook his head sadly, for not only were they losing a good worker, but they were also losing a young man that they had both come to regard as a friend. When Joe arrived for work the next morning, he was presented with a tiny package and a leaving card.

'You can open the card now, but wait until you get home before you open our little present,' Ronnie told him.

'It's not a dollop of shit, is it?' Joe laughed and signed the same sentence to Jack; well, more or less, but Jack knew what Joe meant.

Does it feel like a dollop of shit, Joe? Jack signed back to Joe.

Joe had to admit that it felt far too hard for that and he looked forward to unwrapping it at home after he had finished work. Joe promised to write to both of them, for he knew that Ronnie would translate his letters for Jack, who had never been taught how to read and write. It was a sad and touching moment for all three men, when Joe rode away from the sewage farm for the last time later that afternoon.

After he had bathed and changed his clothes, which he had then stuffed into the dustbin, Joe opened the package that Ronnie and Jack had given to him. It was a tiny silver shovel encased inside a velvet box and inscribed on the blade were the words: For Joe – A fine shit-shoveler. From Jack and Ronnie.

'They only knew I was leaving yesterday,' Joe said to his mother, 'so how could they have had this made up so quickly?'

'They knew two weeks ago,' said Freda, 'or at least they would have had a fair idea that this would be the outcome after Jimmy was hurt.'

Freda was right. Ronnie and Jack had both known that they would lose Joe and they accepted this as being only natural. Ronnie had been to a silversmith to have the shovel made and engraved ten days prior and they had both hoped that Joe Campbell would remember them whenever he opened the velvet box to look at his "Shit Shovel".

Jimmy's memory had still not completely returned, although he could now remember everything about their journey to Wales. Then there was Maeve and Dai Reece at the Oyster Catcher and the first round of his contest with Colin Jones. After that, his next recollection was of waking up in the University College Hospital of London.

Common sense had told him that his dream of becoming a professional boxer was over, but it still came as a blow when Fred Loake brought him a letter that he had received from the Amateur Boxing Association. The letter stated that, after consulting the medical team, it had been decided that James Campbell could no longer box for any club affiliated to the ABA. It was all the more ironic that Fred had received the letter on the Friday, when the finals of all the divisions of the competition were to be held at the Royal Albert Hall the following evening. Jimmy, Joe and their father sat together in the front room and tuned in their radio to listen to the broadcast. Freda went next door to have a chat with Ada Peake, for she wanted nothing to do with boxing ever again.

Before the first contestants were called into the ring, the commentator and master of ceremonies Eamonn Andrews presented Tommy Baxter with his championship medal and reminded the audience that there was one boxer who could not be with them that evening and that boxer was Jimmy Campbell, who had been seriously injured during his semi-finals victory in Swansea.

'Ladies and gentlemen,' Eamonn's voice boomed out all around the hall. 'Those of us who were privileged enough to see Jimmy in action will never forget his skill and courage, but sadly, he will never climb through these ropes again. Please join me in wishing Jimmy a speedy recovery.'

The cheers and applause lasted for a full minute and it was all too much for Jimmy. He left the room and went into his own bedroom, knowing that his hopes and his dreams were now a thing of the past.

Dickie turned off the radio, guessing the medal would go to last year's winner. 'Do you think one of us should go in to him?' he asked Joe.

'Not right now, Dad. He'll be fine in a day or so, but I think we should leave him by himself for the time being. Deep down, Jimmy has known all along that this was the end of the line as far as boxing was concerned and now it's been well and truly confirmed.'

Dickie poured them both a glass of brown ale. 'How do you think this speech therapy is coming along, Joe?'

'It's going quite well as far as I can judge, but we'll have to wait and see what Dr Young has to say when we see him next week. Miss Peabody seems to be pleased with Jimmy's progress, but having said that, the other one's not giving much away.'

'I take it you mean Les,' Dickie chortled and Joe spluttered into his beer.

'I bet you've told that one a few times down the pub,' said Joe. 'Seriously though, if Miss Reynolds and Dr Young report to Mr Randall that our Jimmy is not making the progress that they expect of him, Randall could still ask us to send him to Brentwood. Jimmy is working hard and I don't let him get away with a thing. I make him go over and over with the words that I know he finds difficult and he never gets the hump or sulks the way he used to.' Joe downed his glass of beer. 'Jimmy will come through this, Dad; after all, when all is said and done, he's a Campbell through and through.'

'You're not wrong there, lad,' said Dickie as he poured them both another drink. 'Och aye the noo, the blood of our forefathers is still flowing through these veins of ours.'

'You daft old sod,' Joe laughed affectionately.

'Not so much of the old, if you don't mind,' replied his father.

*   *   *

Joe left Dagenham early on Sunday morning and arrived at Mary's house at a little after eight thirty, and David was at the gate to greet him as usual.

'My mum said we should wait until you get here before we have breakfast, so that we could all eat together,' he announced even before Joe had pushed open the gate.

'That will be nice, David. Eggs and bacon will go down a treat, especially on top of a slice of fried bread,' said Joe as he ruffled David's hair as they went into the house.

'Hello, Joe,' Mary kissed his cheek.

'Hello, Mary.'

Joe hugged her while David looked on, not being quite sure how he felt about Joe holding his mother in a way that he had never seen her being held before, not even by his Uncle Bobby. David smiled to himself. His mummy seemed to enjoy it, so that must mean it was good for Joe to hug her the same way as Joe often hugged him, because when Joe hugged him it always felt warm and safe inside and he instinctively knew that Joe was a warm and safe man.

After breakfast, Joe helped Mary with the washing up and then they took the bus to the West End to join the hundreds of visitors from all around the world, who were now flocking to England. With the war over, more and more people were able to find the time and the money to broaden their horizons and London was top of the list for many of them, especially the Americans. Joe, Mary and David joined the queues to enter the Tate Gallery and Madam Taussauds waxworks. Then they fed the pigeons in Trafalgar Square and walked along the south side of the embankment, where preparations were in progress for the "Festival of Britain" celebrations that were being planned for the new decade. The festival would not only herald in the 1950s, but it would also commemorate the thousands of people who had lost their lives during the struggle to overcome an enemy that had fully intended to grind this island under their heels.

They walked back across Blackfriars Bridge, had tea and cakes in a Lyons Corner House and then made their way back to Mornington Crescent, stopping off to buy portions of fish and chips to take home with them for their evening meal. David was exhausted and went to his bed much earlier than usual, leaving Joe and Mary with time to be alone together for the next few hours. Mary was still not sure how she would respond to what she was sure Joe would be putting to her very soon. But she did not have long to wait.

'I want to stay with you all night next week,' Joe whispered as they snuggled up together on the sofa. 'I could be here on Saturday afternoon. You said we should wait until Jimmy is better and now he is.'

Mary sat up and lit a cigarette. 'I think David will understand, but what about your parents, Joe? How are they going to react to a scarlet woman, who they will probably feel is leading their son astray?'

'My dad already knows,' said Joe. 'At least he knows that I intend to be with you for more than just Sunday day next weekend.'

Mary sat up quickly and Joe could see she was not at all pleased.

'Thanks for letting me in on your plans. I should have been the first to know, not your father. So what was his reaction?'

Joe had no option but to tell her honestly, word for word, what his father had told him.

'Mucky weekend. Well, it's hardly surprising, springing it on him like that,' said Mary. 'Honestly, Joe, I gave you more credit than to just blurt it out on the spur of the moment.'

'I know and I'm sorry. Does this mean you would rather I didn't come next week?'

'I didn't say that, and you know it, Joe. What I am saying though, is if that was your dad's reaction, I dread to think what your mother will have to say about it.'

'I'm going to tell her tomorrow, so that she will have the rest of the week to get used to the idea, but somehow I don't think she will be all that surprised.'

'Just as long as she doesn't come after me with her rolling pin,' Mary managed to laugh, although she was troubled as to how Freda would take the news.

In fact, Freda took the news far more philosophically than her husband had, although this did not lead to her urging her son to take the usual precautions. Halfway through the twentieth century as may be, there were still certain things that mothers did not discuss with their sons and birth control was one of them. Freda was more than a little surprised at her husband's narrow-minded attitude, for she had always been led to believe that fathers approved of their sons sowing their so-called "wild oats" while they were young. But she still believed that Joe was merely infatuated with the older woman and held on to the fact that it would not be too long now before he was called up and possibly sent to the other side of the world.

The week began much the same as any other week, but it was the week that would change the lives of the Campbells for ever. Dickie and John Townsend had not only been awarded the contract for the houses in Chadwell Heath, but they had also been promised a far larger contract for 150 premises that were to be built in the nearby town of Barkingside.

Joe had joined in the celebrations at the Church Elm the night before, but had already left for Mornington Crescent on Saturday afternoon, when John came rushing into the house waving a copy of *The Evening Standard* in the air.

'Well fuck my old boots,' he shouted as soon as Dickie opened the door. 'We've only cracked it, Dickie; we've only gone and won the fucking pools.'

Under normal circumstances, Dickie would have objected to such language being used within earshot of his wife, but normal circumstances these were not.

'Do you know how much?' was Dickie's first response.

'No, of course not,' John replied. 'We have to send a telegram to get our claim in and then wait for the pools people to contact us.'

'The post office is closed on a Saturday afternoon and won't be open again until Monday morning,' Freda advised them.

'I bloody well know that.' In his excitement, John was forgetting his manners. 'We can send a telegram over the phone though, and the operator will tell us how much it will cost. The Church Elm has a phone we could use.'

'We can't phone from the Church Elm, otherwise the whole pub will know about it in seconds,' said Dickie. 'We'll use the call box on the hill.'

Freda picked up her purse and emptied its contents into Dickie's hands. 'You'll need plenty of change if you're going to send a telegram.'

Dickie and John walked up the hill to the telephone kiosk. 'Can you Adam and Eve it?' John was almost in a state of shock. 'I thought when we got that contract that things couldn't get much better than that, but now this. Pinch me, Dickie, just to make sure I'm not dreaming.'

Dickie laughed. 'Come on, John; let's not get too carried away. If every other bugger picked those same draws, we could end up with twenty quid between the four of us.'

'Miserable old git,' John retorted. 'Trust you to go and spoil a bloody good dream.'

The pools coupon was in the name of John Townsend, so it was John who sent the telegram to the company that was based in Liverpool. On the way back to the house, Dickie called at the off-licence for a bottle of whisky, for they both knew that neither of them would manage much sleep that night without several large measures. John would sleep on the sofa and in the morning, they intended to buy all the Sunday newspapers, because each one of them attempted to predict how much that week's lucky winners would receive.

Joe had brought a half-bottle of brandy with him to Mornington Crescent, because he felt certain he would need a little "Dutch courage" later on. The brandy was never even opened though, for after playing several games of snakes and ladders, David's eyelids began to droop and Mary led him unprotestingly to his bed. Mary then took Joe's hand and led him to her own room.

'I've never ...' Joe whispered huskily.

'I know, my love,' Mary said softly, 'but we have all the time in the world.'

That night, the whole world seemed to stand still for Joe Campbell.

Chapter Twenty-Eight

Joe was awake the instant that David opened the bedroom door the next morning, but Mary did not stir. David looked at Joe and then went back to his own room without saying a word, although Joe could tell that the boy was confused. He slipped out of bed without waking Mary, dressed quickly and went into David's room, where David was sitting up in his bed. David did not greet Joe as he would normally have greeted him, for he had never seen Joe in his mummy's bed before and he was not sure that he liked the idea one bit.

Joe sat on David's bed. 'David, your mummy and I love each other very much and we both love you more than we can say. If I could stay with you both all the time I would, but at the moment, I can only be with you at weekends. I hope you can understand that, because we love each other so very much and we need to share everything that we can together.'

David looked at Joe. 'Do you mean just like a real mummy and daddy?'

'Yes, David, just like a real mummy and daddy.'

'Does this mean that you are going to be like my new daddy, Joe?'

'If you'll let me, David, but first I have to go into the army for a while, but when I come back home, I will be staying with you and your mummy for ever.'

'My real daddy joined the army, Joe, and he never came home again. Will you promise to come back to us?'

Joe took the boy into his arms. 'I promise you that I will come home, David. Nothing will stop us all from being together where we belong.'

Joe was aware that Mary had entered the room and she joined them on David's bed. The three of them cuddled each other, but from that moment onwards, David would never again enter his mother's room without first knocking when Joe stayed overnight.

After breakfast, they went off to London Zoo, for David never tired of watching the antics of the monkeys and the majesty of the elephants, the rhinos and the giraffes.

'Do you think David will tell his friends about us and maybe even Bobby?' Joe asked Mary.

'I think he probably will,' Mary replied. 'But I'm not going to tell him that this must be kept a secret, because he's accepted us as being together and that's how it should be. If anybody has a problem with that, then that's how it has to be – their problem and not ours.'

Mary and Joe sat in the sunshine, while David fed the monkeys with monkey nuts. Joe still felt a wonderful glow that seemed to warm the whole of his being and he could not help but wonder if other people would be able to tell that he was not the same person as he had been yesterday. He dismissed the notion as nonsense, but he was nonetheless reluctant to let go of Mary's hand and they took it in turns to squeeze each other's fingers.

'How long do you think it will be before you're called up, Joe?'

'Well, Jack Atkins went in when he was seventeen and a half, but Danny Williams didn't get his call-up until he was well past eighteen. My name begins with a "C", so that should mean I'll be called up fairly soon after I turn seventeen and a half, which is the minimum age.'

They both lit a cigarette and David returned for some money to buy more monkey nuts. After David had rushed off again, Joe carried on where he had left off.

'Apparently, they take in batches of recruits every twelve weeks, because that's how long basic training lasts. There's a good chance that I could be in and out before I'm nineteen and then I'll be able to work where I want and live where I want.'

Mary squeezed his hand again. 'I'm a bit worried about what is going on in the Middle East. You know; this Palestine situation between the Arabs and the Jews over Israel. Some of our boys have already been sent out there to try and keep the peace and this morning's *Observer* says that we will need to keep our troops out there for years to come.'

'You won't have to worry about me,' Joe told her earnestly. 'I'm going to apply to go into the stores, where I can dish out all the uniforms.'

Mary dug her elbow into his ribs and they both lapsed into peals of laughter, but then she told him seriously, 'Joe, I'll not hold you to anything if you wake up one morning and find that this has all been a big mistake.'

'I love you, Mary,' Joe told her tenderly. 'I love you more than life itself and if that sounds like something out of a Hollywood film, then so be it.'

'No, Joe,' she told him. 'It sounds like something straight from your heart.'

He kissed her hand and with his free hand, he brushed away the tears from her eyes.

Joe left Mornington Crescent just in time to catch the last train back to Dagenham and he was shocked and more than a little frightened to find not only his parents but John Townsend all in the front room, for it was now almost midnight.

'What's happened?' said Joe. 'Where's Jimmy?'

'Jimmy's in bed and nothing's happened,' Dickie was grinning broadly. 'Well, that's not exactly true, because you won't believe it when we tell you.'

'Oh, for Pete's sake, tell the lad and get it over with,' Freda said impatiently.

'You tell him, John,' Dickie bowed to his partner. 'After all, you are the brains behind our syndicate.'

John poured a generous measure of whisky into a tumbler and handed it to Joe.

'I know you're not overkeen on the amber nectar, but you might need it when you hear the news.'

'News. What news?' said Joe.

John was enjoying himself immensely. 'We have come up with a first dividend on the pools and tomorrow morning at around ten o'clock, a man from Littlewoods will be bringing round our cheque to present to us.'

John had been right about Joe needing a drink. He took a swallow and felt the effect almost immediately. 'Do we know how much?' he asked John.

'No, not exactly, but me and your dad were up and waiting outside the newsagent's to buy every paper that they sold and the *Sunday Pictorial*, the *Observer* and the *News of the World* are all predicting that anyone who has twenty-four points this week can expect …' John waved his hand at Dickie. 'You tell him, mate.'

'They know that there have been eight telegrams sent in so far, but that doesn't mean a thing. Not everyone checks their coupons on a Saturday evening and even now, there could be another dozen claims, so we just have to sit tight and wait until tomorrow,' Dickie added.

'Are you going to tell me how much the papers predict or do I have to go and buy one and look for myself?' Joe suddenly felt both tense and excited at the same time.

'Between ten and fifteen thousand.' It was Freda who answered. '£15,000. That's over £3,000 for each of us and that's more money than I could earn in about six years.'

'Don't count your chickens, Freda,' warned Dickie, 'we haven't got a penny until the pools bloke turns up in the morning.'

Joe took another swallow of whisky, his head swimming not only from the whisky but from the almost unbelievable news he had just received.

'I take it that nobody will be going to work in the morning then?'

'You take it right, son,' said Dickie. 'How can we concentrate on the job in hand until we know for sure how much we are worth?'

'Three grand is an awful lot of money, but it's not enough to retire on.' Joe knew he was stating the obvious. 'My share will be more than enough to buy myself a stall in Camden Market though.'

'Did you not listen to what I told your mother about not counting the chickens before they were hatched?'

Dickie was desperately attempting to keep all their feet on the ground until the morning.

'If there were hundreds of winners, then the pools people would not be sending round one of their representatives now, would they?' Joe argued. 'They would just send out cheques or even postal orders.'

'Joe's right, Dickie,' said Freda. 'I think we must have won a lot of money, just like the papers say we have.'

'Whatever we've won, it would have been divided between five of us, not four,' Joe reminded them.

This was perfectly true, for when Gertie had died, the rest of them had paid her share between them, rather than begin a new plan all over again.

'Trust you to put a damper on everything,' his mother said, although she was not really angry at Joe. She was angrier at herself, because she had not even considered that had she still been alive, her mother could have treated herself to many of the luxuries that she had only dreamt of.

Joe understood and so did the other two men and nothing more was said for the time being. None of them went to bed that night and they just dozed on and off in armchairs and on the sofa, until Jimmy came into the room to tell them that it was gone eight o'clock. Joe made the tea and Freda prepared breakfast for Jimmy, although none of the rest of them could face anything to eat. Jimmy was told that they had won some money, but even though no figures had been mentioned, he knew it must be quite a lot to have kept them up all night and from going to work this morning.

At five minutes to ten, Freda peered out of the front-room window as a car pulled up outside the house. 'It must be them,' she announced and went to the front door.

There were two men, one of them holding a camera, and they reminded Freda so much of the reporters from *The Dagenham Post*.

'My name is James Maxwell,' the first man said, handing Freda his card. 'This is my colleague Daniel Varley and I'm quite sure you know why we are here this morning.'

Freda led them into the front room and as soon as Dickie spotted the camera, he told them, 'We put a cross on our coupon for no publicity, so you can forget about taking any pictures.'

James Maxwell reassured them all. 'No photographs will be taken without your permission, but almost everybody puts a cross on their coupon, it's almost a tradition. Can I just ask who is who before we go any further? I get the feeling that perhaps you all have a share in this win.'

John made the introductions and James now knew the person whose name would be written on the cheque.

'Mr Townsend,' said James, 'you and your little syndicate have won a great deal of money, but before I tell you how much, can I first put a proposal to you?' James did not wait for an answer. 'Publicity is the lifeblood of our industry and we are prepared to spend a considerable sum of money to achieve our fair share of it. You may have seen the picture a few weeks ago, when a winner was presented with his cheque by Gracie Fields, and I can assure you that Miss Fields is just one of the many film stars and sports personalities who are more than happy to do this little service for us. Incidentally, that winner also put a cross on his coupon, and he and his family spent two nights of pure luxury being wined and dined at the Savoy Hotel, all at our expense.'

John was tempted. 'When you say sports personalities, who exactly do you mean?'

'From cricket we have Len Hutton and Fred Truman, and there is Bombardier Billy Wells and Marcel Cedan the boxers. We also have Stanley Matthews and Walter Winterbottom from the world of football and the jockey Gordon Richards.'

'Stanley Matthews,' Dickie was also tempted. 'Do you mean to say that he would be prepared to present our cheque to us?'

'All it would take is one telephone call,' James assured Dickie.

'I don't care if you could persuade the king himself to come along,' Freda told them forcibly. 'We agreed that we didn't want any publicity and as far as I'm concerned, that's the way it will be.'

'With respect, Mrs Campbell,' said James, 'the person whose name is on the coupon is Mr Townsend and he must have the last word.' He looked at John. 'Can't you just imagine how it would feel to shake the hand of one of your heroes?'

'The last word has already been said and Freda was the one who said it,' John told the man. 'Now, will you tell us how much we have won, please?'

James knew when he was beaten. 'There were ten other winners, who selected eight of the ten draws, but your coupon also had two away results, which means that you have won a little more than most of the other winners.'

'Will you stop fart-arsing around and tell us how much we've got coming to us,' demanded Freda.

'As I said, there were ten winners altogether and your share is a little over £17,000,' James told the stunned group.

Nobody uttered a word. The expression "words failed them" was entirely appropriate for the enormity of the sum that James had almost casually presented them with, as it had temporarily robbed them of speech.

'You must surely realise that a win as large as this will be almost impossible to keep a secret?' James warned them. 'My company have the right to announce that the winner comes from Dagenham and one of the local newspapers will probably offer a reward to anybody who can identify the lucky person or people. In my experience, it's far better to get it all over and done with from the beginning and so far, six of the other winners have agreed to have their picture taken with a celebrity. The comedian Tommy Trinder is one of them, as a matter of fact, and Stanley Matthews is another.'

John Townsend shook his head. 'That's up to them, but we'll take our chance on that. Can we have our cheque now, Mr Maxwell?'

'I never did like Tommy Trinder much anyway,' sniffed Freda.

James Maxwell handed over the cheque and the two men left the house.

The four members of the pools syndicate each took turns to hold the cheque and to reflect on what this huge sum of money would mean to them. Freda would do everything in her power to persuade her husband that they should move, but never back to north London. Freda had seen some of the lovely houses in the rural towns and villages of Upminster, Hornchurch and Elm Park and it was in those areas where she would most like to spend the rest of her days.

John would take his share and invest it for his retirement, for he planned to buy himself a little house on the seafront of either Westcliffe or Southend-on-Sea in a few years time. Joe knew that his share would be put to one side for when he came out of the army and he intended to buy himself a stall in Camden Market, where he believed his true destiny lay. Dickie had still not recovered from the shock and had no clear idea of what he would do in the future, other than he would carry on working with John.

John studied the cheque once more. '£17,350,' he said, as though any of them needed to be reminded. 'I think we should take £4,000 each and put the rest into a trust fund for Jimmy.'

'You would be willing to do that for our son, John?' said Freda quietly.

'We could dedicate it in Gertie's name,' replied John.

'I think that would be wonderful,' said Joe. 'Thanks, John.'

Jimmy had been sitting almost unnoticed in the corner of the room, but now it was his turn to speak.

'My ... gran ... used ... to ... tell ... me ... that ... what ... goes ... around ... comes ... around ... and ... now ... perhaps ... it ... has ... come ... around ... for ... us ... Campbells ... and ... you ... Mr Townsend.'

'I make you right there, Jimmy,' said his father.

Freda took the cheque from John. 'It's in your name, John, so how are you going to share it out?'

'It's not a problem,' John answered. 'I have my own bank account, so I will take the cheque there this afternoon and get the manager to make out three cheques of £4,000 for each of you and then I will open a trust fund for Jimmy with the rest. You won't be able to draw on the cash for a week, but you will all need to open up a bank account, although Jimmy is too young at the moment. Why don't we all go together?'

'We could use the same bank as you.' said Freda. 'The manager might be able to give us some advice about setting up a trust for Jimmy and give us a few tips at the same time.'

'That makes sense to me,' said Joe.

'Right then,' Freda busied herself tidying the room. 'Dickie, you and John get yourselves along to the phone box on Heathway and give the bank manager a call to make an appointment for this afternoon and then you can bring us all in some fish and chips on the way back. Jimmy, you can help me with the washing up and Joe ...'

She could think of nothing for him to do. 'Oh, go with John and your dad, but if you call in at the Church Elm, make sure you only have the one pint.'

Dickie winked at John. What on earth is the point of going into a pub for just one pint of beer? he thought.

*   *   *

It was not every day that a customer walked into Mr Dixon's bank with a cheque for £17,000 and not only that, but one that also brought in four new customers at the same time. In fact, that was the understatement of all time, because in over twenty-five years in banking, Mr Dixon had never experienced a day such as this one was bringing to him. John Townsend had held a personal account with the bank for several years and not long ago, Mr Dixon's assistant Miss Platt had approved a small business loan for Townsend and his new business partner Richard Campbell. Now it appeared that they had won a great deal of money on the football pools and it was to be his bank that would profit from their good fortune. Mr Dixon would give them sound advice, for he was a professional financial adviser, but he always kept one eye on the commission he would be entitled to and £17,000 would mean a nice tidy sum of money for himself.

Mr Dixon knew that the money would be divided between four people, each receiving £4,000, with £1,350 to be held in trust for a minor. £4,000 represented four years of his own salary, for he was a well-paid, middle-class bank manager, but this amount of money would mean perhaps eight years of toil for the average wage earner of the working classes. He believed that Mr Townsend and the elder Mr Campbell would pay off their small business loan and possibly reinvest into their business, which was already looking very healthy, indeed. And Mr Dixon was hoping to persuade the younger Mr Campbell and his mother to invest in the property market. It was true that he would receive a very generous commission from the estate agent, but he truly believed that a house available for £400 or £500 today would double in value within the next ten years. So Mr Dixon was a little disappointed when the Campbell family and Mr Townsend left his office without agreeing to any of his suggestions having spent over two hours with him.

As expected, Mr Campbell senior and Mr Townsend were only interested in paying off their loan and plunging the remainder of their windfall into their business, and the trust fund for Jimmy would only yield a modest commission for Mr Dixon. Mrs Campbell, however, showed some interest in buying not only a home for themselves in a more upmarket area of Essex, but also seemed quite amenable to his suggestion that she might consider buying one or even two other properties that she could rent out until such time as it became prudent to sell.

The younger Joe Campbell did not seem at all interested in making his money work for him and was quite content to leave the whole sum in a deposit account, where it would earn a mere pittance in interest. Mr Dixon could not comprehend how someone, who seemed to be quite intelligent, could have the sole ambition in life to stand out in all kinds of weather and sell shoddy goods from an even shoddier market stall, but each to their own.

Once back at home, Freda put the kettle on while Dickie, Joe and John took out the inevitable bottles of brown ale from the cupboard.

'I reckon we all deserve a bloody good holiday,' Freda announced.

'And we could ask Ada and Reggie to come with us as well; it will give us all a treat.' She wagged her finger at Dickie and John, 'And don't give me a load of old codswallop about your business not being able to do without you, because that contract of yours doesn't start for another three months yet.'

'What do you have in mind, Mum?' Joe asked.

'A whole week in a nice boarding house in Blackpool, so that we can see the lights and go to the top of the Tower.'

'And have a dance in the ballroom, I suppose,' said Dickie with a grin, for he quite liked the idea.

'And that as well,' answered his wife. She could tell that Dickie would not need too much persuading. 'I've always fancied being twirled around the floor while that Wurlitzer organ thing plays a tango.'

'Bugger dancing to a tango or a fandango,' said Dickie, 'I might be able to manage a waltz though.'

'What about you, Joe?' Freda asked her son. 'Will you come with us?'

Joe was aware that unless he was prepared to go with the rest of the family, his mother would probably veto the whole idea. It was emotional blackmail, but he also felt that he owed this time to his family.

'I'm up for it,' Joe told them, 'except that you're forgetting something.'

'What's that, Joe,' asked his father.

'We don't need to stay in some poxy boarding house. We can stay in the best hotel in Blackpool. Have you forgotten? We're bloody well rich!'

'And ... can ... Reggie ... really ... come ... with ... us?' Jimmy could hardly believe what had happened that weekend.

'Of course he can,' said Dickie, 'although we may get a rollicking from the headmaster for him bunking off school.'

'Do you think Ada will come with us as well?' Joe was a little doubtful. 'I can't help feeling that she may be a little set in her ways and don't forget, she has all those animals to take care of.'

'I hadn't thought of that,' admitted Freda. 'Anyway, I'm sure we can sort something out if she wants to come.'

Ada did, indeed, want to come with them and Reggie Godber needed no second bidding. That decided, John Townsend arranged for the whole entourage, including his own wife, to occupy two double rooms and four single rooms on the third floor of a Blackpool hotel that was used for the annual conference of the Labour Party.

Joe knew that Mary would understand and he fully intended that only one weekend would be spoiled for them. As soon as the coach reached London on the Saturday after the holiday, Joe would make his way to Mornington Crescent and into the arms of his beloved Mary.

Chapter Twenty-Nine

The holiday in Blackpool was memorable, especially for Ada Peake and Reggie Godber, for neither had ever been on a real holiday before and the hotel was just like something they had only ever seen at the cinema. Blackpool was fast becoming a major tourist attraction and this year, the organisers had surpassed themselves and made the mile-long promenade a gigantic display of flashing lights, illuminated models of cartoon characters and nightly firework displays. There was a pier at each end of the promenade, with a theatre at the end of each one, where they saw Gracie Fields at the north theatre and Max Miller at the south end.

'I heard that Max Miller on the radio once,' Ada said after the Max Miller show. 'I thought he was smutty then, but he's even worse on stage.'

'Get off with you,' said Freda, 'I thought you was going to wet your drawers the way you were laughing.'

'I know,' admitted Ada. 'He was so funny though.'

Joe missed Mary and David and told himself that he would bring them back here for at least a long weekend at some point, because he knew that David would love to see Donald Duck and Mickey Mouse all lit up and he was sure that Mary would love this hotel that they were staying in. The meals were absolutely delicious and they sampled the delights of northern cuisine on many occasions, if they could find enough room inside their tummies, that is. Jimmy and Reggie could always find space and Ada had surprised them all at how much food could be tucked away into her quite tiny frame.

It was a lovely week and the weather was kind to them, but then it was time to board the coach and return to the real world.

The remainder of the year passed uneventfully, with Jimmy making good progress, mainly thanks to Joe's diligence, although Jimmy had made a tremendous effort on his part. His speech was not quite back to normal and his face still had a slight droop on one side, but in the few months since he had left the hospital, Jimmy's improvement had been so great that he had returned to school just four months after being discharged, enabling Joe to work full time with his father and John. Joe was a quick and eager learner and he soon became part of the team that had grown from three men to seven and the firm of Townsend & Campbell was certainly booming.

True to his promise, Joe booked himself, Mary and David into the same hotel in Blackpool and they had spent three whole days and nights in that fairy-tale resort. They had also been to see Gracie Fields, but had decided that Max Miller would be a little too much for David, even if he would not be able to understand most of what the comedian was alluding to.

Three days before Christmas, Joe received a buff-coloured envelope from the war ministry ordering him to report for a medical examination that would determine whether or not he was fit for active service. Joe was 17 years and 7 months of age. Naturally, Joe was not drafted into a nice, safe little unit like the stores, but after his medical, where he was classified as A1, he was assigned to the 4th Battalion of the Essex Regiment and would complete his basic training in the army barracks at Colchester in Essex. Joe had applied, unsuccessfully, to enlist in the Royal Fusiliers, for he knew that the recruits from that regiment completed their basic training at the Tower of London, hardly more that a stone's throw away from Camden. Colchester was perhaps the second best option though, because Joe knew that some of his ex-school friends had been sent all the way to Edinburgh. Even a twenty-four hour pass would mean that he could spend a few hours with David and Mary and when he was fortunate enough to be granted a forty-eight hour pass, he could also spend some time with his family.

Joe was a very resilient young man and did not find the army discipline too much of a hardship, unlike some of the other conscripts, who deserted after only a few days and were ultimately dismissed by the service as being lacking in moral fibre or LMF, as it was contemptuously abbreviated. On the final week of their basic training, Joe's platoon was informed that they were to be sent to Palestine and they were given a ninety-six hour embarkation leave.

Joe knew that he could be overseas for many months and almost every day, the newspapers reported casualties among the British troops that had been sent there to keep the peace. No soldier was allowed to leave the barracks in civilian clothing and neither were they allowed to report back for duty out of uniform, so, as he had done on his first and only forty-eight hour pass, Joe went to Dagenham first to change, for he did not wish David to see him dressed as a soldier. The last time David had seen his own father was in uniform, when he had gone off to war and had never returned.

Dickie was proud of his son and found it difficult to understand why Joe was so reluctant to come to the pub with him in his uniform.

Dickie wanted to show off his soldier son to the other regulars, many of whom had been in the services themselves. But Joe finally relented on this occasion and was highly embarrassed as loud cheers greeted him when he went into the Church Elm with his father and Tommy Smith. Joe spent the night in Dagenham and then left the next morning for Mornington Crescent, leaving his uniform behind in the now spare bedroom, intending to change back into it before returning to Colchester after his leave. Neither his mother nor his father had made any reference to his overnight stays with Mary, but Joe knew that he must tell them very soon that he would definitely be moving back to Camden after he had finished his National Service stint. He did not believe it would come as too much of a surprise to them, but it might be a different story when he told them that he intended to marry her. In fact, it would come as somewhat of a surprise to Mary as well, for he had not even asked her yet.

David, as usual, was waiting for him at the gate and was well wrapped up, for it was a chilly March morning and the sun was too low to give very much warmth. Mary had told David that Joe would be going away for a while, but that they would have three whole days together first, and she had plans of her own as to how they would spend the rest of his leave.

'Hello, Joe,' Mary greeted him with a kiss and poured them both a drink. 'Listen, Joe, I wanted to do something special for us, because it could be months before we see each other again and I think it's important for all of us to remember these next few days while we are apart.'

Joe was puzzled. 'What have you got up your sleeve for us this time?'

'I want us to go to Paris for the next couple of days. I want us to go up to the very top of the Eiffel Tower, and then go on to see the Mona Lisa and Notre Dame Cathedral and then cruise along the River Seine.'

Joe shook his head in disbelief and looked at his wristwatch.

'Mary. It's gone ten o'clock. By the time we get down to Dover, catch the ferry and then travel all the way to Paris from Calais, it will be well gone midnight, and then we'd have to do it all over again on the way back.'

Mary took an envelope from her handbag. 'We won't be going over on the ferry; we'll be flying from London Airport. A car will be picking us up at eleven, another will be waiting to take us to our hotel from the airport in Paris and we will be in our rooms by three o'clock at the latest. Everything has been arranged for the return journey as well and we will be back in time for lunch, giving us plenty of time before you have to leave.'

Joe stood staring at the airline tickets. 'Fly,' he was amazed. 'I've never been in a plane before, have you?'

'No, but there's a first time for everything.'

In fact, it was Mary who appeared to be the most nervous of the three of them as their plane began to taxi down the runway, with Joe and David each holding one of her hands tightly as they soared into the air. Joe could not help wondering if Mary was actually as frightened as she made out to be, for she soon recovered and accepted a large gin and tonic from the hostess when she brought round her trolley.

They made their way to the Eiffel Tower soon after they arrived at their hotel in Paris and the mechanical lift took them all the way to the top. The view was magnificent, for it was a clear day, and David was enthralled at how high they were from the ground, for compared to Blackpool Tower, this structure was colossal.

Joe took a small box from his pocket and opened it to show Mary an exquisite diamond ring. 'Will you marry me, Mary?'

Mary was taken completely by surprise. 'Oh, Joe, I can't take your ring, not right now, but if you ask me again when you come back from Palestine, I would be proud to wear it.'

Joe was bitterly disappointed. 'I love you, Mary, and I thought you loved me.'

'Don't ever doubt my love for you, Joe, but things could change for you once you get out into the big wide world and I will never hold you to anything, at least until we are both sure that this is what we truly want.'

Joe put the ring back in his pocket. 'This is what I truly want, but as soon as I get back to England after my National Service, I'm going to bring you back to Paris and up to the top of this tower to ask you again.'

'You don't need to do that, Joe; the middle of Camden Market will do for me.'

Paris, like London, was gradually getting back to normal after the ravages of war and could there possibly be a more romantic place than Paris in the springtime, even if it was not quite spring yet? Joe certainly did not think so as they cruised down the River Seine at twilight drinking champagne and he was positive that Mary would say yes the next time he asked her to marry him, whether it was at the top of the Eiffel Tower or in the middle of Camden Market.

The following day, they went to the Louvre to see The Mona Lisa and then on to Notre Dame Cathedral, where David was captivated by the story of the hunchback bell-ringer and the beautiful Esmeralda. The next stop was the Arc de Triomphe where, after an hour or so's exploring, they sat outside a street cafe along the Champs-Élysées for their lunch. That evening, they dined in the hotel restaurant and then took a bottle of brandy to their room, for poor David was exhausted, but Mary and Joe found a new lease of life after David had fallen fast asleep in his adjoining bedroom.

They arrived back at Mornington Crescent in the early afternoon of the next day and Joe would be able to stay for one more night, although he would need to leave quite early on his final day's leave.

'Are you going to tell your mum and dad that you have asked me to marry you, Joe?'

'I think it's only fair to tell them that I will not be coming back to live in Dagenham, at least not for very long,' Joe told her. 'Even if you turn me down or find another bloke, I know that Camden is the only place I want to be.'

'Oh yes, there are dozens of other blokes outside the door right now begging to take me out, I don't think.' Mary had not intended to put Joe under any pressure, but she could not help whispering, 'Come back to us, Joe. Please come back to us.'

'Just try and stop me,' said Joe, meaning every word.

They had both heard the news reports on the radio that a British presence would be needed in the Middle East for many months and possibly even for years to come, so both Joe and Mary were resigned to the fact that they probably would not see each other again for quite some considerable time. David's concept of a long time was measured in a few days, but even he seemed to grasp that Joe would be away for a very long time. They said their goodbyes in the house, as Joe believed a tearful farewell on the railway platform would be too upsetting for David and he was not too sure that he would be able to handle it very well either.

Before leaving Dagenham to return to his barracks in Colchester, Joe told his parents of his plans for when he left the army, indicating that he had already asked Mary to marry him. Freda and Dickie were not surprised, although neither of them was overjoyed at their son marrying a woman who was so much older than himself. His mother kissed him goodbye and Joe shook hands with his father and his brother as they stood on the platform of Heathway station and watched his train approach.

'Come back safely, Joe,' said Freda.

'Bring me back a nice present,' said the mercenary Jimmy, with hardly a trace of hesitation in his voice.

'Good luck, son,' said his father.

They stood on the platform and watched the train take Joe further and further away from them.

'Did you see the front page of this morning's *Daily Mirror*?' Dickie asked Freda.

'Fat chance I've had of reading the paper while I'm running around after you lot,' Freda retorted, and then asked, 'Why, what was on it?'

'A picture of 300 young nurses, who are being sent out with our troops on the same ship as Joe is on. It will take them six weeks to get to Palestine and who knows what could happen before they get there.'

'Nothing,' Freda was adamant. 'Nothing will happen as far as Joe is concerned, because he will be coming home to Mary.'

'I suppose you call that a woman's intuition,' said Dickie.

'No, I call that a mother's intuition,' she replied.

Freda would be proved right, even if her husband did not believe that his red-blooded son would be able to resist the temptations of all those lovely-looking girls for a year or more. As it so happened, quite a few of those lovely-looking girls took a shine to Joe Campbell, who appeared to be so much more mature than the other young soldiers on the ship, but word quickly spread that Joe was spoken for back in England. Joe was not the only recruit who had a girlfriend back home; in fact, two of the young men were actually married, with babies on the way. The army did not consider their carelessness to be an excuse to wriggle out of their National Service and they received no concessions at all when they had been posted overseas. Purely chosen at random, some recruits never left Britain at all, although many did not consider this to be much of an advantage, having just spent a freezing winter in Edinburgh Castle or on the mountains of Wales.

Joe had only done what was expected of him, no more and no less, heeding his father's advice not to volunteer for anything. He was a competent soldier, without drawing attention to himself, and was popular with the other men, who knew he could be relied upon.

There were quite a few trouble areas in Palestine, where Joe's platoon had been sent in order to monitor them and where several British soldiers had already lost their lives through hostilities from both sides of the bitter dispute. But the casualties were mainly from the elite forces of the Royal Marines and the Paratroopers and Joe was never actually called upon to fire his rifle, other than on the practice range.

Joe was aware that British troops had been in Palestine since the Second World War had ended and the European Jews who had suffered so much at the hands of the Nazis had been promised a land of their own in the Middle East. The British had attempted to stem the tide of the Jews, who came flooding in their thousands from all over Europe, but those determined survivors of the Holocaust refused to be denied and this had caused much anguish on both sides. The British soldiers had no wish to fight the Jews, but the Jews would fight anybody who tried to stop them from creating their own country. The British had finally withdrawn and in May 1948, much of Palestine was declared to be the State of Israel, but the Arab States that surrounded Israel subsequently declared war on that tiny state, which was why a peace-keeping force from Britain, America and Australia had been transferred back there in an attempt to keep the peace.

Joe had been told all this by a corporal he had met on the troop ship coming over and this would be the corporal's second tour of duty.

'What's it like there, Corp, I mean, do we get a chance to have a bit of leave and visit other places?'

'You get two chances, young Joe. Slim chance and no chance. During the first three months of my last tour, we lost four of our lot and nobody knew whether it was the Arabs or the Jews who slit their throats. A few months after that, two British sergeants and a Yank lieutenant were found hanging from a tree, so when you're not on patrol, keep your arse safe and sound inside the barracks.'

'Sounds like good advice to me but what about the sending and receiving of letters, and can we phone home?'

'The only telephones are at Headquarters and certainly not for the likes of you and me, but we can send two letters each week through the Red Cross – the plane flies in from Malta every week. Mind you, half of what you write will be pencilled out by one of the censors.'

Joe had written his first two letters even before his ship had anchored, but it was another three days before they were actually sent. One was to Mary and David, and the other to his mum, dad and Jimmy. It was just one week later that he received a reply from Mary, but not one from his parents. Joe told himself it was sure to arrive with the following week's delivery but it was two whole days before the censors had read through every single letter sent to the soldiers, except the officers, of course. Mary's letter was the first 'Real' love letter Joe had ever received and he bitterly resented that it had been read by somebody else first, as had the letters he had sent home. His own letters had both been approved by the censor, without having had anything crossed out.

Mary's letter was also unmarked by the censor's pen, probably because she had been aware that all letters would be censored, so she had been careful not to make any references to the conflict, although she did not hold anything back with regard to her feelings for Joe.

David had added a row of kisses at the end and Joe's heart was heavy at the thought of not seeing David and his beloved Mary for what could be a very long time.

The letter from Joe's mum, dad and Jimmy arrived the following week and it did not escape the censor's pen. Both his dad and Jimmy, who was learning how to write again after his injury, had written to tell Joe that some of the newspapers were reporting that Egypt and Syria would be attacking Israel at any moment and so one of the censors sent for Joe before handing the letter over.

'Private Campbell, did you not inform your friends and relatives that they could not write anything about what the papers or the news broadcasters believe is or is not going on out here?'

'Well I did tell them, sir, but they must have forgotten.'

'Tell them again in your next letter home; otherwise, all your letters will be destroyed before they even leave Britain.'

Joe knew this was no idle threat and did as he had been ordered, desperately afraid that all links to Mary and his family were in danger of being severed, but his father and Jimmy, whose writing was becoming more legible with each letter, made no further reference to what the newspapers or the wireless portrayed ever again.

And so the weeks dragged on and Mary's loving letters were like a lifeline for Joe, but this was certainly not the case for many of the soldiers who regarded Palestine as something of a soft option, even though they were confined to their barracks unless going out on patrol. Both the married men and those who had children confided in Joe that they were glad to be away from a nagging wife or a screaming nipper and one even said that he intended to sign up as a regular soldier after he had finished his National Service.

Joe asked him, 'What does your wife have to say about that?'

'I dunno, I haven't told her yet. Anyway, I only married her 'cos she was up the duff, so if she don't like it, she can bloody well lump it.'

Joe knew that his life with Mary would never sink to such depths and he felt sad that one so young could be so cynical about married life.

It was a great surprise when the news was broken to them one morning while on parade that the Essex Regiment was to be sent back to England after serving just over six months in Palestine. Joe immediately wrote to his parents and to Mary, asking them if they would all meet him together at Southampton when his ship docked.

He knew that Mary and David would be there, but he was not so sure if his parents would agree.

Both of the letters arrived in England a week after HMS *Vanguard* had left the Middle East with Joe on board.

Freda showed the letter to Dickie, 'So nothing has changed and now it's up to us.'

'How do you mean?'

'I think we should go and see Mary and talk this through with her. We have to accept the fact that Joe is going to marry her, whether we like it or not.'

Dickie agreed and they decided they would go to Mornington Crescent on Saturday morning.

Mary was not sure what to do about Joe's letter, for she did not believe she had the option of going to see his parents in Dagenham, so it was with some relief that she answered the door to Freda and Dickie on the Saturday morning after receiving his letter, because at least everything would now be out in the open.

'Hello, Mary,' said Freda. 'We thought it was time we had a little chat.'

Mary asked David to play in his room and then made some tea and took it into the front room.

Freda came straight to the point. 'Joe told us he has asked you to marry him and that he will ask you again when he gets home. What will you tell him, Mary?'

'I will tell him yes. I thought he may change his mind, but he hasn't and I don't think he even thinks about our age difference.'

'You can't expect me and his mum not to worry about it though,' said Dickie.

'Of course. I knew you would be concerned, but I had hoped that you would give us your blessing, because now I know he still wants me, I can't give him up.'

Freda looked at Dickie before answering and then said, 'We thought you would say that, but we wanted to meet you face-to-face and tell you that Joe's happiness comes before anything else. Perhaps we could all travel down to Southampton together.'

Mary went over to her future in-laws and hugged them both.

'That would be lovely,' she said. 'You'll never know how happy this makes me and I know that Joe will feel the same way.'

'We can send a message to him by ship to shore radio,' said Dickie.

'Jimmy will be coming with us to meet his ship and I expect David will want to come as well.'

'Just try to stop him,' laughed Mary.

*   *   *

Joe was stood by the rails on the deck of HMS *Vanguard* five weeks later as the mighty ship was towed to its mooring. There were thousands of cheering people, waiting to greet their loved ones, and Joe thought that it would be impossible to pick anyone out in the sea of faces.

But Joe was picked out – by David – whose shrill voice soared above all the others.

'Joe! ... Joe! ... Joe!'

And there they all were: his mother, his father, his brother, David and his lovely Mary.

It was probably a trick of the light but, for a moment, Joe was sure he could see his gran standing next to his mother and waving to him as frantically as the rest of them.

A trick of the light! Perhaps it could have been, but who knows.